T0278579

The Lens
and
the Looker

Book #1 of
The Verona Trilogy

Lory S.
Kaufman

fiction
studio
books

This is a work of fiction. Names, characters, places, and incidents either are the product of the author's imagination or are used fictitiously. Any resemblance to actual events, locales, organizations, or persons living or dead, is entirely coincidental and beyond the intent of either the author or the publisher.

The Fiction Studio
P.O. Box 4613
Stamford, CT 06907

Copyright © 2011 by Lory Kaufman

Cover design and graphics by G.M. Landis Marketing

Print ISBN-13: 978-1-936558-02-5
E-book ISBN-13: 978-1-936558-03-2

Visit our website at www.fictionstudiobooks.com

All rights reserved, which includes the right to reproduce this book or portions thereof in any form whatsoever except as provided by U.S. Copyright Law. For information, address The Fiction Studio.

First Printing: March 2011

Printed in The United States of America

For my mother,
Ida.
She gave me the name "Lory"
because she thought it was artistic
and hoped I would be an artist.

Acknowledgements

It takes a village to raise a child and it takes many editors to raise a writer. I have two wordsmiths to thank.

First of all, there's the amazing Lou Aronica. Lou is my big-picture editor. He never told me how to rewrite something, but pointed out where the story structure needed changing to make it sing. Thanks for your faith in my work, Lou.

Then there's my daughter, Jessica Suzanne Kaufman, who is my line editor. Being dyslectic and A.D.D., I have lots enthusiasm and an overabundance of ideas that saw me envisioning an all-encompassing genre-bending story. Jessica and her blue pencil helped me see both the trees and the forest. Thanks, Ladybug.

Hopefully, both young-adult and adult readers will agree that these two have helped produce a well-balanced story that includes science fiction, fantasy, history, alternate worlds, futurism and that it's all told with sympathetic and colorful characters.

Lory Kaufman
January 2011

A Note from the Publisher

As soon as Lory Kaufman told me about *The Lens and the Looker*, I thought it was a great idea. I loved his invention of history camps, his vision of a nearly utopian future, and his imagination in finding a way to complicate matters for kids in this almost-perfect world.

The Lens and the Looker captures fourteenth century Verona in a way that all of us can relate. Even across vast expanses of time, the things that matter the most to us – as well as the things we fear the most – are essentially the same. By plopping his protagonists into a world so utterly different from theirs, he actually underscores the universality of our basic human drives for a place to belong, for meaningful work and, most importantly, for love and friendship.

The real bottom line here, though, is that *The Lens and the Looker* is a fantastic adventure. There's enough action and drama here for three novels. I think you're going to have a terrific time with it and that you'll be pounding on Lory's door for the next two titles in the Verona Trilogy.

Enjoy.

Lou Aronica
Publisher, The Fiction Studio

Book One
Hard-Time History Camp

Chapter 1

2347 C.E. (Common Era)
The Community of New York

One of Hansum's earliest memories was of his mother telling him he was just like his name sounded in the old English, handsome. But lately, when teachers and parents commented that seventeen was too old to still be going through a rebellious stage, he'd just smile that sincere, enigmatic smile of his and shrug. Hansum didn't even argue as the head of his prep college, an old artificial intelligence named Dean Turkenshaw, told him he was being sent to Deep-Immersion History Camp.

"Hey, Hard-Time H.C., bring it on," Hansum challenged.

Dean Turkenshaw squinted his one round eye and his two balloon cheeks puffed out indignantly. Then Hansum watched as the old educator forced himself to calm down, taking a virtual deep breath and then lowering his single eyebrow in a show of sympathetic concern. Hansum lowered his two eyebrows, mirroring the facial expression. The A.I.'s round orb of a head, which was indeed his whole body, was levitating at Hansum's eye level. With practiced patience, 'Old Cyclops', as the students called Turkenshaw behind his orb, began a teacherly pep talk.

"I hope your time at History Camp will help you to see the big picture," the dean began. "It's important for young humans to experience how your ancestors struggled for thousands of years, repeating the same mistakes over and over again. As I'm sure you've learned, they almost drove themselves to extinction."

'He's so flippin' earnest,' Hansum thought. 'It's like he's going to cry any minute.'

"Extinction," Turkenshaw repeated, seriously. "Imagine it. And they almost took what was left of the natural world with them. But, son, what we really hope for you is to gain a true appreciation of how stable and beautiful the world is now, a world that that humans and A.I.s built together. History Camp can give you that valuable insight."

Hansum nodded slowly and sympathetically. "Okay, Dean. You're quite right, of course. I promise you, sir, I will try to get the most from this experience." Turkenshaw smiled benevolently.

Of course, to Hansum, getting the most out of this experience meant he would do his utmost to drive every single History Camp enactor he met crazy. He knew that, at that very moment, untold numbers of enactors were setting up a scenario that was designed to scare him straight. It would be a fun challenge to disrupt their grand plans. The thought made his smile beam even brighter.

"You, you seem sincere enough," the old A.I. said.

"Well, you know what they say, Dean. The secret to success is sincerity. And . . ." Hansum ran a hand through his mop of tousled, dirty-blonde hair. A lock of the long, wavy pompadour fell over his olive-colored forehead. "And once you can fake sincerity, you've got it made in the shade."

The dean blinked in surprise. Hansum blinked *his* cool, hazel eyes too – twice. Then he grinned a big, toothy grin. It was unmistakable in its meaning.

"Why, you little con artist!" Dean Turkenshaw's orb zoomed nose to nose with Hamsum. "I will make it my business to inform everyone about your ability to charm the fuzz off a peach," he growled. "You won't be able to get away with anything."

"No probs," Hansum said blithely. He watched the gray, wiry hair, which stuck out from Turkenshaw's sides, begin to vibrate like a tuning fork, then added, "Perhaps we can continue this conversation when I return. Sincerely." Hansum had cultivated the ability not to sound obsequious, even when he spoke like this. It didn't matter whether the teacher was human or A.I., Hansum always got to them.

Turkenshaw's two cheeks puffed out again and his light green orb blushed a blotchy red.

"Get out!" the dean shouted. "Go to your dorm. Empty your closet. Collect your things. A History Camp transport is picking you up in an hour."

'Mission accomplished,' Hansum thought. He turned on his heels and walked leisurely toward the door. It swung open and, as Hansum crossed into the school hallway, the dean cried, "We'll see how two weeks at a Hard-Time History Camp suits you." Hansum heard the door slam shut behind him.

The school was bustling with students, teachers and about an equal number of levitating orbs. By law, artificial intelligences could look like anything but a good imitation of a human. There were A.I.s shaped like a cat head, a camel, a yellow marigold and even a wizard, complete with long beard and conical hat. Then he spotted her.

"Hey, Charlene."

Everybody on the planet had an A.I. Charlene, Hansum's personal A.I. nanny and staunch protector since birth, was there waiting for her boy. She was a deceptively whimsical design. Although she was solid, and definitely heavier than air, she looked like a floating yellow balloon with a crayon-drawn face that Hansum had created before he had turned three. When she saw Hansum, she levitated toward him.

"Dean Turkenshaw wasn't very happy." Charlene's voice was a soothing contralto.

"He should be absolutely euphoric," Hansum replied. "He just had the fun of sentencing me to two weeks at Hard-Time History Camp."

"That's not his pleasure, that's his job, sweetheart. But he looked quite vexed. You must have gotten to him."

"You know exactly what happened," Hansum said lightly. He was well aware of how anything to do with him was instantly transmitted to Charlene. "Besides, you know I only bring the best out in people – no matter how much it hurts. C'mon. I've got some History Camp teachers to teach."

Chapter 2

Forty-five minutes later Hansum and Charlene stood and floated on the open campus green, waiting for the History Camp transport. The Community of New York College was one of the largest schools on the continent, with almost five hundred students, and the community itself was one of the largest on the planet with over thirty thousand people and A.I.s combined. They were outside one of the many low-rise dormitories. The structures, cut-stone igloos about ten meters in diameter, had one level of living space above the ground and two below. The place was similar to Hansum's family village, a community of sixty people set just off the bank of the Hudson River, on what was known as the Old York Escarpment. This was the new coastal shoreline after the oceans finished rising several centuries earlier. The green commons of the college was also like Hansum's village, in that it had community gardens, which Hansum's father tended as the elder horticulturalist, an open area for sports and community gatherings, orchards and pens for raising livestock. The college also had an amphitheater for live performances, where Hansum had done pretty well in regional saber matches.

Hansum had his trunk of clothes and belongings by his side and held his dueling saber. He mock parried and slashed at the air with the weapon. A few times he gave Charlene a quick look, to warn her to duck or dodge to get out of the blade's trajectory.

"I wish I knew what era and place they're sending me," Hansum said while slicing the air with his blade. "It would be fun to be able to use my sword and riding skills there." Besides being part of the college fencing and horseback riding teams, the athletic Hansum had trained at a History Camp a few summers earlier as a Renaissance soldier. Many students spent vacations at History Camp summer jobs, working as enactors, people who lived wholeheartedly as citizens from a bygone era. There he had received extra lessons on sword fighting and horseback riding, plus archery and hand-to-hand combat. Hansum had to admit he got this plum job because his mother was a History Camp elder, so his intentions had been not to rock the boat for her sake. But he couldn't help himself. He began to rabble rouse and contradict the philosophy of History Camps to other students. He also argued vehemently with the H.C. elders in charge of the place.

"Why would you say those things?" his mother had asked after they sent Hansum home.

"Because it's true," he said. "History Camps are nothing more that society's way of forcing kids to fit into the present power structure. It's brainwashing. It's fascism."

"Fascism!" his mother wailed. "Now you really are overstating the matter." That had been almost two years ago.

A thoughtful look came onto Hansum's face and he put the sword down. "You know what I don't understand?" he asked Charlene. "What would make my parents think a History Camp could make me change what I think? Even a hard-time History Camp."

"Deep Immersion History Camp," Charlene corrected.

"Yeah, yeah," Hansum scoffed. "But why do they think I'd be fooled? Those places can't work on me because I know all about them. After all, Mom and Dad met and worked at a History Camp, and Mom is still a History Camp Elder. I've grown up with it. I know it's all fake. They can't scare me."

"Once again, you miss the point," Charlene said. "History Camps were set up for people of our society to learn how people lived and struggled in the past. Youths learn to appreciate the wonderful steady-state world we have now and, more importantly, help society not repeat the mistakes of the past."

"Sure, sure," Hansum interrupted. "Those who do not learn from the past are doomed to repeat it. See, I know all that."

"But you obviously don't know enough," Charlene rebuked. "How about that miserable performance on your test this morning? That was the straw that broke the camel's back, what convinced the dean you deserved to be sent away. Zero marks, you got. Zero!"

"I could have passed that test. I was just foolin' around." Hansum yawned. "And I was up all night."

"And now you'll be gone for the next two weeks." Charlene went silent and the image of her face turned into a frown. "That's the longest we've ever been apart in your whole life," she said. A drawn tear rolled down her cheek. "I'm going to miss you."

"Oh, I'll miss you too, Charlene. I will."

"Fat lot, you will," Charlene sniffed.

"It's true, it's true," Hansum replied sincerely. But he also knew he was ready to get away from his family and have an adventure. Being away seemed exciting to him, even if it only was to a History Camp.

"Well, at least you're willing to say it," Charlene said, pulling herself together, "Okay, then. I'm supposed to remove your implant before the transport gets here."

"Oh dear Gaia, I forgot about that," Hansum said, putting a hand to his temple. That's where his sub-dermal communication implant was. They were placed under the skin at the right temple and communicated directly into the brain. While not true telepathy, a person could speak in a whisper and the processor, knowing its host intimately, would recreate both an appropriate auditory and visual transmission of the person, including a realistic background of where they were. "I'll miss my mind parties and talking to my friends all over the planet. Jamie's supposed to contact me when he and his family get to the asteroid belt this evening."

"Removing your implant for an intense History Camp experience makes it all more realistic. It gives the participant a true feeling of being a person of the past, able to communicate only with those right by them, and only with words. And don't worry about your messages. I'll redirect them and explain."

"I tell you what," Hansum said, turning on the charm. "Let's make a deal. I'll do that test over again and, if I pass, you don't take my implant out."

"But that's part of procedure, darling," Charlene said.

"Just don't tell anyone." Hansum knew full well that all solid A.I.s were part of a pan-planet Association of Artificial Intelligences, the A.A.I. They lived by a strict and very conservative code of laws. Although loving and absolutely devoted to their families, A.I.s did not, could not, lie by fact or omission. Hansum was actually surprised at the long pause before Charlene's answer. Could she actually be considering it?

"Well," she began. "How about this? If you pass, I ask permission to just turn the implant off instead of removing it? There is precedent."

"Zippy," Hansum said. "Great. Let's do it." Readying himself for the test, Hansum stuck his sword blade into the ground and sat cross-legged on the grass. He tapped his right temple in a specific sequence. Multiple choice questions appeared in his vision, simulated by the chip and followed by a disembodied male voice which both he and Charlene could hear.

"What was the estimated human population of the planet Earth at the beginning of the fourteenth century, in the year 1301? Ten thousand, one hundred thousand, three hundred million, one billion, six billion or ten billion?"

"One billion," Hansum answered. A check mark appeared beside the answer. The graphic lit up, but not in the way he'd hoped for.

"Incorrect," the voice said. "The human population of the Earth in 1301 is estimated to have been 300 million. Next question." Hansum grimaced, hoping Charlene didn't notice. "What was the population of the planet Earth at the beginning of the twenty-first century? The year 2001. Ten thousand, one hundred thousand, three hundred million, one billion, six billion or ten billion?"

"Oh, that must have been one billion," he said.

"Incorrect. The population of the Earth in 2001 was six billion."

Hansum bit his lower lip. "How many humans were on the planet Earth before the population growth dropped quickly in the second half of the twenty-first century? Approximately 2060?" the voice asked. Again, "Ten thousand, one hundred thousand, three hundred million, one billion, six billion or ten billion?"

"Oh, I remember. It didn't go up. Uh? Yes, it was still 6 billion. It was slowing down. I remember that in the lessons."

"No sweetie," Charlene said. "The population *growth* slowed down. But the population still went up."

"That doesn't make any sense."

"What is the population of the planet Earth now, in this year of 2347? Ten thousand, one hundred thousand, three hundred million, one billion, six billion or ten billion?"

"Okay," Hansum said hopefully, "now there's a billion people."

Charlene corrected him. "The present population of humans on the planet, in this year of 2347, is just under three hundred million. It is a steady-state number, not varying by more than one quarter percent in any half century. Once again, Hansum, you didn't get one question right."

"Oh, that was ridiculous," Hansum said, standing up quickly, his body language betraying his frustration. He gave a few taps to his temple, putting an end to the lesson. The image disappeared, as if spinning down a drain. "I mean, who cares if there are three hundred million or three hundred billion people on the planet?" he said, sounding flustered for the first time. "What's the big deal?"

"There are just under three hundred million people on the planet, Hansum. It is a steady-state number and you really should care . . ."

"Well, I don't."

Another chime rang in both Charlene and Hansum's heads. Charlene answered.

"Hello. Yes, we'll be ready. Bye. The History Camp transport will be here in a minute," Charlene confirmed. "Come on, sweetheart. Time to remove that implant. Don't fight, please."

"If it wasn't you..." Hansum said.

Charlene floated within a few centimeters of Hansum. Resisting an outburst, Hansum closed his eyes and put his hands in his pockets. His left hand took hold of a cool object, a small brass charm in the shape of an ancient oil lamp. Then he felt the familiar warmth of Charlene's orb press onto his skin.

"I'll replace your implant as soon as you return," she said.

"In two weeks?" Hansum asked, opening his eyes briefly and looking, truly sincerely, into Charlene's.

"As soon as you return," Charlene promised.

With more apprehension than he wanted to show, Hansum closed his eyes again. Charlene pressed against him a little harder and he felt a warm buzz as his flesh opened painlessly. The implant was absorbed into Charlene's orb and Hansum's skin closed without a scar.

As Charlene drifted away from him, Hansum put a hand where his implant had been. He kept his other hand on the brass lamp charm in his pocket.

'I may not have an implant or a personal A.I. where I'm going, but at least I'll have a genie,' he thought.

Just then a flying machine quickly and silently approached from high in the sky. It appeared so quickly, it was like it came out of nowhere, decelerating in an incredibly short time, directly above them. He heard a beep come from Charlene.

"Charlene here," she said, answering another call.

Hansum reflexively put his hand to where his implant had been, to be included in the communication. All he got was an eerie, hollow silence. He forced himself to smile.

'It's only two weeks,' he said to himself. 'I can frustrate a lot of teachers and A.I.s in that time.' Hansum always liked to look on the bright side of things.

"Yes, yes, we're ready," Hansum heard Charlene say to somebody. But Charlene didn't look happy. She was wearing her very serious, sad face again.

The History Camp transport landed, barely disturbing a blade of grass. It was shaped like a raindrop on its side. About five meters long, it could hold about half a dozen people comfortably. The familiar History Camp logo, a stylized human eye with an hourglass set within the iris, was emblazoned on the side. Below the insignia were the Latin words, *Noscere Praeteritum Ut Lucrare Futurum*, which translated to 'Know the Past, Earn a Future.' A click was heard and the back hatch opened up.

Another A.I., similar to Charlene, floated out of the transport. This fellow wasn't balloon-like, though. He was in the shape of a dog's head, a tongue-hanging, ear-flopping, slow-eyed hound. He levitated out of the back of the transport in sluggish stops and starts, his attitude projecting a great and profound boredom. He moved forward, stopped, panted, came out a bit more, looked even more bored, stopped again, and repeated the process several more times. Hansum looked on bemused till finally the A.I. hovered lazily in front of Charlene and himself.

"Me Dogface!" the canine A.I. said in a rolling, lazy growl.

"Well, you look like a fun person to be cooped up in a transport with," Hansum said.

"Dean Turk'shaw said no give you fuzzy peaches."

Hansum's eyes went wide, but he had to laugh. "Oh, my God, Charlene. Time with this guy is going to be more of a punishment than whatever History Camp throws at me."

Dogface made a face and yipped, "Come. You go History Camp. Now."

"Okay, I'll get my stuff," Hansum said, bending to pick up his trunk.

"Leave here. You no need."

"Not even my toothbrush? How about my sword? Can I use it where I'm going?"

"No sonic tooth cleaners in past. Swords? Can't say. Leave here."

"I'll take care of things, dear," Charlene said, starting to sniffle again. "You run along," and more drawn tears flowed from her eyes and slid down underneath her.

"Oh, for Gaia sakes, Charlene," Hansum said, going to the orb and putting his arms around her. "I'll be back in a couple of weeks." Charlene continued to cry. Never mind that they were only animated tears that only slid around on her surface. Hansum knew her emotions were real. "Why are you carrying on so, Charlene? I'm seventeen. I've got to go out on my own sometimes."

"I know, but, but . . ." she just kept crying. Hansum had been taught that some A.I.s found being parted from their children quite traumatic. He hugged her again and then felt the familiar force field grasp and hug him back harder than he had ever felt it before.

"We go," Dogface barked. When Charlene didn't release Hansum, he repeated, "We go!"

As Charlene let her tractor grip loosen, Hansum backed up into the transport, the whole time peering curiously at the still despondent Charlene. He gave a small wave and watched her sad crayon eyes disappear as the transport's door closed and locked.

Charlene felt her eyes go wide as Hansum disappeared into the craft. "Be good, son," she said weakly. "Keep safe." Charlene watched the transport rise silently into the clear blue sky. Then it flew off over the Atlantic. In a few seconds it was a small speck on the horizon.

Chapter 3

The trip to wherever this History Camp was took several hours. It could be anywhere on the planet. Hansum was alone in the transport with Dogface. Besides the sound of the wind on the hull's energy field, Hansum was forced to sit in boring silence. Dogface hovered, looking out the window at the passing clouds, his long canine tongue hanging from his mouth. Whenever Hansum tried to engage him in conversation, the dog would stop panting, look away from the clouds and silently stare at the teenager. After a few seconds, he began panting again and turned his attention back out the window. Obviously the dean's threat had been carried out. A.I.s were being chosen who could not appreciate Hansum's charms.

So Hansum sat in silence, passing the time by remembering the faces of quite a few girls, and several older women, who *had* appreciated what he had to offer. He smiled as he remembered one especially interesting young woman. Rosalind. She was the one who had given him the little brass charm in his pocket. He instinctively put his hand to his forehead to call Rosalind. Then, remembering his implant was gone, he ran his hand through his hair, adjusting it using the reflection of himself in one of the craft's windows.

Finally, the floating dog head turned to Hansum and spoke in a high, staccato bark.

"Put on clothes for new home."

A rough burlap bag appeared suspended from underneath the levitating head. Hansum took the bag and looked in. He pulled out a piece of undyed roughly woven wool. He was able to tease from it the shape of a tunic, a tube with two crude sleeves sewn on it. Hansum glared at Dogface.

"I'm supposed to wear this?" Dogface just stared back at him. "Where and when is this darn thing supposed to be from?" Hansum demanded.

"Put on," was all the A.I. responded.

"Oh for Gaia's sake," Hansum said. Dogface bared his teeth. Hansum shook his head ruefully, knowing that an A.I. could never attack one of its charges. He removed his shirt and exposed his long, lean body. "I've been working on the abs. Whaddaya think?" Dogface just stared with his hound-dog eyes. Hansum shrugged and pulled the tunic on. As his head popped through the keyhole neck, the rough wool fabric came into contact with his skin, which felt instantly itchy. He tried to ignore the sensation but his pectoral muscles twitched involuntarily. Dogface snorted a laugh.

"Pants now. Change drawers."

Hansum pulled out the rest of the clothing.

There were two burgundy wool leggings with strings at the top, and a pair of what looked like voluminous white linen underpants, also with ties hanging from their leg holes. The only thing vaguely obvious was a cap.

"I'm supposed to wear all this?" he asked, pulling out a pair of old, cracked leather boots. Realizing he was holding genuine leather in his hand, he dropped the boots to the floor. "Are those from a real dead animal?"

"They'll look rrrovely on you."

Hansum held up the odd pieces of cloth, staring at them like they were a complex puzzle. "How?"

"The pants are braies," Dogface said, referring to the balloon-ish underwear. "You lace at waist. Leggings called chausses. Lace to braies."

Hansum glared at Dogface, locking eyes with him. With the A.I. thus distracted, Hansum put a hand in his pocket and palmed the brass lamp charm. Then he smiled again and removed his hand from his pockets, continuing his change of clothes. Hansum unbuttoned and removed his modern trousers. He began to pull the medieval braies over top of his twenty-fourth-century, bac-teria-balancing boxer shorts.

"Rrrrrrr," Dogface growled. "Lose skivvies, boy."

Hansum looked into the bag. "There aren't any underwear in here."

"Poor indentured apprentice not wear underwear," the A.I. said. "You poor apprentice. At least, will be." Hansum looked over at Dogface. The floating head cocked his head cutely, like a puppy. "And if you thought tunic was itchy . . ."

Chapter 4

The craft landed and Hansum got off, now dressed in his new, old clothes. He stood there in his tunic, braies, chausses and ill-fitting boots. He adjusted his brimless cap, or coif. Feeling hot, he undid the string ties that held the earflaps under his chin. They dangled in the gentle breeze. Hansum scratched himself again as he took a first look around. He was at the back of what looked to be a medieval barnyard containing a few outbuildings and a stone house, all with thatched roofs. The barnyard was about a hectare large and enclosed by a stone fence. There seemed to be a succession of these enclosures, all with neat, organized houses and barns of varying shapes. In the distance he could see the steeples of several stone churches and tall red brick walls stretching into the distance.

He heard a complaining voice at the other end of the barnyard.

"Get away! Leave me alone! Help!" Hansum looked up and saw a young boy being chased into the house by a goat and several chickens.

Hansum felt a nudge at his back and turned around. It was Dogface, pushing him with his snout. The A.I. also used the appendage to point to the house.

"You go," he barked. "Bye bye." And with that, the transport door closed and rose silently into the air.

Alone now, Hansum sauntered toward the house. The goat noticed him and leaped in his direction. The young man smiled and put his hand out. The animal shoved its velvety nose into his palm, sniffing for food. Then it looked up at him with his yellow, slit-pupiled eyes.

"Finally, another mammal," Hansum said. "I've had my fill of A.I.s today." When no food was forthcoming, the animal lost interest and wandered off. Hansum laughed and continued on to the house.

Passing the barn, he looked in and saw a healthy looking cow and calf in a stall. Hearing oinking, he turned to see a large nursing sow in the shade of a tree. Eight squealing piglets nestled together, gorging themselves from the sow's teats. But Hansum saw no humans. Continuing to the house, he paused in front of the roughly hewn, whitewashed door. It wasn't much taller than him. He knocked. No answer. This was where the boy had entered. Was he an enactor, one of the characters of the History Camp? Hansum took hold of the wooden latch and lifted it. The heavy door creaked open and he stepped in.

Looking around the large single room, he saw an earthen floor covered with straw. The ceiling, maybe a head taller than Hansum, was rough-cut whitewashed timbers and beams. There were steps, little more than a ladder, leading to an upper floor.

Sitting on the lowest step, head downcast, was the boy who had been chased by the goat. He was perhaps thirteen. Hansum blinked with surprised when he looked over at a girl sitting on a bench at a table. She appeared to be completely Caucasian. 'There's something you don't see every day,' he thought. She was perhaps sixteen and dressed in clothes Hansum reckoned could be from the same period as his. She looked up at him with two penetrating green eyes.

"What are you lookin' at?" she asked sharply.

Hansum put up a hand and smiled. "Hey, no probs. I'm one of you."

They continued to size each other up, Hansum sure that she was trying to ascertain the same thing as he was: whether they would be on the same side in the upcoming game.

Her head was covered with a linen veil, draped to her shoulders. Wisps of light auburn hair puffed out from under her veil at the temples. Two highly arched eyebrows of the same color rose over the two green eyes that stared intently at him. Through him. She wore a long, simple gray-on-gray striped dress, which covered her from neck to ankle. She had in her hands what looked like a thick twig whose end had been charred and pointed. She had been drawing with it on, 'What is that called?' Hansum thought. 'Oh yeah. Paper.'

"You a hard case too?" he asked. She gave a petulant smirk and he returned it. "Ready for some fun with these guys?" he asked. She cocked her head and looked at him.

"Maybe." Then she lowered her head and continued drawing.

"Jerk-terkers!" the boy on the ladder cursed. Hansum looked over and saw the younger teen tap at his temple, pause, look frustrated, then tap again. "Terk-jerkers," he added, and then he groaned and made a face. "I'm hungry."

'Not hard enough, this one,' Hansum thought. The younger teen was obviously having a hard time coping, tapping where his communications implant should be. He would tap and wait for a response. After a few seconds, when no reply was forthcoming, he would tap again. Hansum knew the boy was making a futile attempt to contact his A.I.

The boy on the ladder wore somewhat similarly styled clothes to Hansum, except for a green medieval liripipe, a hood with a lengthy tubular tail. A long, tawny tunic covered his baggy braies. And his red chausses, the leggings, extended over his feet. They had reinforced leather soles, so he didn't have separate boots. None of the teens' footwear had arch or ankle supports.

But then again, everybody in the twenty-fourth century had perfect arches.

Chapter 5

Hansum was just going to speak to the boy when the door to the house opened. A tall, calm woman with short, curly black hair walked in. She had warm, brown skin and a strong frame. She was not dressed in costume suiting the room's theme, but wore modern clothes with a pin on her jacket, which Hansum recognized. It was the History Camp logo, an hourglass set within an eye, the same image as on the transport. Hansum's mother had a pin just like it, so he knew this woman must be an H.C. elder as well. She gave no long and warm greeting, as one would expect at a regular theme-park History Camp. No niceties here. This was a room of hard cases.

"I need your attention. All of you. You're Hansum? Take a seat on the bench by Shamira. Lincoln. Lincoln, stop calling for Talos. He cannot respond. You had your communicator removed."

"I know," Lincoln said sullenly.

"My name is Elder Cynthia Barnes. So, here you are at History Camp."

"Hard-Time History Camp," the girl named Shamira muttered, not looking up from her drawing.

Elder Barnes continued. "None of you will see your families for at least a month."

"Hey, I was told two weeks!" Hansum complained.

"Me too!" the others added together.

"Plans change," Elder Barnes said. "Understand that for the first time in your lives you are on your own. Nobody will come to your rescue."

Hansum knew this statement just wasn't true. Since his parents had both worked at History Camps and his mother was now a director of several, like Elder Cynthia, he grew up hearing about the inner workings of the places. He knew that no participant at an H.C. was ever really alone or in danger, no matter how frightening a situation was designed to appear. While the whole idea was to make the young participants think they were in a time when there was no safety, there were batteries of humans and A.I.s behind the scenes, looking out for each client.

Elder Barnes walked over to the table and looked at the drawing Shamira was working on. Now sitting at the same table, Hansum could see it was a very accurate rendition of the interior of the room. There were the steps, complete with Lincoln sitting on them, the door, the shuttered windows, the fireplace with the grate and hanging pots, the straw floor and the ceiling rafters, perspective included.

"That's wonderful, Shamira," Elder Barnes said. "It's true what I read about you. You have great artistic talent." Shamira crumpled the paper into a ball and pitched it into the unlit fireplace. Elder Barnes just took a step away and continued. "Okay, let's get to work. You're all probably wondering what era you're in."

"And I'm sure you're about to tell us," Hansum said.

"Does anyone know where Verona, Italy is?"

"In Italy?" Lincoln suggested sourly.

"Very funny," Elder Barnes said.

"It's a monument city now," Hansum sighed, bored. "Just the old city is left. They tore down and reclaimed anything that was built after 1700. All the newer roads, airports, sewers, everything, was taken up."

All students had been taught that as the human-engineered population decrease took effect several hundred years earlier, it was only logical that cities would shrink and disappear. And with no need for a growth economy anymore, most cities' reason for existence, that of an economic engine, disappeared too. As for transportation, roads and rails were replaced by levitation technology, making physical connections between cities obsolete.

"You're right about the real Verona, Hansum," the elder said. "It is a monument town with just a caretaker and artisan population now. But what about Verona in the fourteenth century? Does anyone know something about that?"

Shamira straightened, the tiniest bit of enthusiasm showing through.

"I remember. I was in Verona a couple of years ago, on a school trip. That's where that Romeo and Juliet story happened. I stood on her balcony."

"Well, where you are now isn't anywhere near the original Verona. We're not even on the Italian peninsula. This is a History Camp version of how Verona was a thousand years ago."

"So, what's the deal?" Hansum asked. "The story?" He knew there was always a story.

"All you have to know is this. You're illiterate peasants. Hansum and Lincoln are apprentices to a spectacle maker. Shamira, you're a kitchen girl."

"What's a spectacle maker?" Lincoln enquired.

"He makes eyeglasses."

"What are eyeglasses?" he persisted.

"You'll find out," Elder Barnes answered.

"What's a kitchen girl?" Shamira asked.

"You'll clean house and cook."

"Clean? And cook? In here?" she asked, looking at the rustic surroundings.

"I'm hungry," Lincoln said. "When do we eat?"

"You apparently refused to eat before you left home, didn't you, Lincoln? Now you'll have to wait." Lincoln stuck out his lower lip and scowled.

Elder Barnes looked at Hansum sitting quietly, a quirky smile on his face.

"Have you nothing to add?" she asked.

"Nope," Hansum answered lightly.

"All right then. See you in a month or so." And with that, Elder Cynthia walked out of the house.

"Wait!" Lincoln shouted, jumping to his feet, but the door slammed shut. The teenagers were alone. They looked at each other.

"Hey," Hansum said in way of a greeting.

"Hey," Shamira answered.

"This is stupid," Lincoln added, putting a hand to his stomach.

They all looked around, expecting something to happen.

Shamira said, "I say we just refuse to do anything."

"Yeah," Lincoln agreed angrily. "What can they do? Nothin'!"

"Probably," Hansum said. "But that's not very creative. Why don't we have some fun with them?"

"How?" Shamira asked.

"Well," Hansum began, and then he smiled and motioned for the others to come close to him. Every child in the twenty-fourth century knew when a friend did this, he or she wanted to say something that an A.I. shouldn't hear. Hansum cupped his hand and whispered to the others' ears, "My mother's a History Camp elder. I know how these places work. The best way to screw with their heads is to make believe you're cooperating. Then, when you know what their game is, you figure a way to disrupt."

"Yeah," Lincoln said, his attitude brightening.

"But how?" Shamira asked.

"Like I said, we'll just play along till we know enough to screw with them."

"Yeah, screw with them," Lincoln repeated.

"Too bad they took my encyclopedia slate board on the ride here," Shamira said. "It could tell us everything we wanted to know about fourteenth-century Verona."

Hansum chuckled. "Fear not, my friends. Help is at hand." Hansum looked around and then took something from the little coin pouch on his belt. He put his hand within their secret circle and opened his fingers. In his hand lay the tiny brass lamp.

"Whoa, my new friend, Hansum!" Lincoln said. "Good work!"

"A genie!" Shamira exclaimed in whispered excitement.

"Is that a new G4000?" Lincoln asked. "I heard they're super nuts."

"I don't know how crazy this genie is yet," Hansum said. "I got him from a friend this morning. Haven't had time to call him out."

Genies were better than encyclopedia slate boards, which were just repositories of universal information. A genie was an artificial intelligence which possessed universal knowledge, but enjoyed making trouble too. They were made by blackers, secretive and rebellious youths who still believed in raging against the machine. While not strictly illegal and mostly harmless, genies were frowned upon. And unlike Charlene, who was a solid entity, a genie appeared as a colorful holographic character projected from its lamp. These mechanistic rascals told their young possessors rude jokes, helped them cheat on school tests, aided in the playing of pranks and, in general, endorsed and promoted bad behavior. What more could healthy, rebellious kids ask for?

If one were to bypass a genie's holographic projection and delve into the gelbrain substance within the brass lamp, one would find reference files on every topic in the world. All text books, scientific papers, treatises, newspapers, magazines, memoirs, letters, censuses, phone books, warehouse inventories, catalogs, movies, videos, newscasts, shopping lists, match book covers, everything, absolutely everything ever recorded, scribbled, scratched and saved by homo sapiens. All this information was then put into a memory gel the size of a grain of rice. Added to this was a powerful twenty-fourth-century heuristical-cross-inference engine/personality.

"You don't know what this guy is all about?" Shamira asked.

"No, I've had A.I. solids on my keister all day."

"Well, call him out," Lincoln said.

"Hey, genie, you in there?" Hansum whispered. "C'mon out. All clear." Nothing happened.

"Maybe he's a dud," Lincoln suggested, frowning.

Suddenly the brass lamp vibrated in Hansum's hand, and a tiny voice, raspy yet lyrical, emitted from the charm.

"Spin around, my new master, so I may scan the area for prying eyes. We don't want the game over before it's begun."

Hansum looked at Lincoln and Shamira, and all looked cautiously around the room. Hansum was aware of the ever-contradictory History Camp rules of balancing privacy and safety. Since the "game" had not begun yet, students couldn't, or shouldn't be spied upon. Hansum held the charm just at his scapula, pretending to show it off as a necklace.

"What do you think if I wore it like this?" he said to the others.

"Nifty," Lincoln said, playing along.

"Spin around, like at a fashion show," Shamira said.

"Okay," Hansum agreed, impressed with the quick thinking of both his new comrades in trouble. The genie would be scanning the room in its entirety. Hansum stopped spinning and said, seemingly to the other teens, "So, what do you think?"

"All clear," the gravelly voice said.

Hansum smiled and put the small brass oil lamp onto the table. Immediately a wisp of holographic smoke curled out of the lamp's tiny spout, then poof, an image about twenty-five centimeters stood in front of them. It was a little satyr. He had the hind legs and hooves of a goat, a dwarfish human body and head, pointed ears, bushy eyebrows, short dreadlocks, and an impish smile.

"Wow," Hansum said.

"Greetings, interestingly costumed youth," the gnarly image said. "My name is Pan, the god of Arcadia and anarchy, at your service." Pan gave a salutary bow then looked up. "And you must be Hansum. Mistress Rosalind told me all about you. She thinks you're hot stuff," he said, winking.

"You don't look so crazy," Lincoln said.

"Looks can be deceiving," the hairy image replied as his slit eyes glowed a hot yellow.

"Great!" Lincoln said, gleefully.

Shamira was peering at the little image intensely. "I've looked at lots of artwork from the Greek period," she said. "I love to draw all the gods. Pan is one of my favorites."

"Flattery will get you everywhere, dear lady," he said, bowing again. "So, I now have, not one, but two masters and a charming mistress. Oh, blessings upon me, it is my joy to serve. Did I hear correctly while seconded within Master Hansum's coin pouch that your names are Shamira and Lincoln?"

"Yes," Shamira answered, still looking at him as if she were getting ready to draw. "Are you always that tiny?"

"No, my default size is actually a grand meter in height, but I can be any size -- or shape."

"Listen, you guys," Hansum said, "we better get crackin'. Whatever they have planned is going to get going soon. They won't let us cool our heels long."

"What's the situation?" the little imp asked. "Does it have anything to do with those costumes you're wearing?"

"Yeah, we're at a History Camp," Shamira said.

"A hard-time History Camp," Lincoln added. "And they're not feeding us!"

"Ah, so the scene is set and all the actors assembled. I shall join the fray as gadfly to a picnic and we shall make jolly upon the heads of your oppressors. Tell me, do we know at least what year this is supposed to be?"

"Thirteen-forty seven, Italy," Hansum said.

"Holy Hades, God of the underworld," Pan said, looking shocked. "The year of the Black Death. They really do want to scare you."

"The black what?"

"Never mind that now," Pan said. "Is there more to tell?"

"Well, Lincoln and I are supposed to be apprentices to a spectacle maker," Hansum said.

"And I don't even know what a spectacle is," Lincoln added.

"I'm supposed to be a kitchen girl. Here! Yuck!"

"Not much to go on, but interesting, interesting," Pan said, stroking his chin. "Well, time is on our side, as it always is with youth. Let's see, let's see, how to begin?" he said, looking around thoughtfully. "Aha! Hansum, upon your tunic I perceive a fold of cloth where the shoulder meets the sleeve. There is a bit of loose thread there. Shamira, as an artist, deft must be your fingers. Slip my lamp into yon fold and secure it, hidden from sight, with the thread. Make sure that the top of the lamp is facing out of a tiny opening which you must leave. From this aperture I shall not only be able to view the scene of our actions, but also direct a sonic beam toward each of your ears. This way only you three will be able to hear any instructions I may give. Hansum, I must rely on you to move your shoulder and point where I say." The teenagers grinned, enjoying the idea of another voice being back in their heads.

"Excellent," Hansum commented.

"Zippy!" Lincoln laughed.

Less than a minute later, Shamira was tightening the thread that hid Pan from view. Lincoln had his nose close to the tiny opening for the A.I. to look out of.

"Can you really see out of that little thing and send us secret messages?"

"Yes, Master Lincoln," Pan said. *"When I whisper thus, I can direct a sonic beam, and even bend it slightly, compressed so only those ears into which I choose can hear it."*

"Hey, that tickles," all three teens said at once. The sonic beam caused an echoing whisper in their inner ears.

"And you even can bend the beam so Hansum can hear you. Zippy," Lincoln said.

"I shall be your wiser advisor," Pan whispered again. *"Your teacher of trouble. Your maven of mischief."*

Just then, the door to the house swung open again.

Chapter 6

Hansum and the others turned. A very large man stood before them. He wore a collarless blouse under a heavily stained wool sweater. Even his coarse leggings were grimy. But the oddest part of his appearance was the heavy, bone-rimmed spectacles perched on his nose. The magnifying properties of the lenses made his eyes look like an owl's. The man stared at them for a moment and then he smiled broadly.

"So here you are!" he said gleefully. "I went to the church to meet you, but they said the priest brought you to my house already. Benvenuto, my a-new apprentices! Welcome." The teenagers just stood and stared back at him. The big man furrowed his brow. "Hey, what's-a matter?" he continued. "Cat got all your tongues? Why you just stand there? Madonna mia!" While the man was talking in Earth Common, he spoke with a heavy Italian accent and added in the occasional Italian word or phrase.

Hansum knew that since visitors to History Camps couldn't be expected to know every language ever spoken, the enactors had to talk in the common language and simulate the feel of a foreign or ancient dialect. The man accented his speech by waving his meaty hands, which were stained a deep red.

"What?" Shamira asked.

"What? What?" the man repeated. "You ask what? What are you, stupida? Maybe I should send you and your brother back to your papa?"

"My brother? I don't have a brother," Shamira said. In the twenty-fourth century two words seldom heard were brother and sister; or, for that matter, cousins, nephews or nieces. For centuries the one-child family had been a strict law. Now that the planet's population had reached the agreed human target level of three hundred million, laws were changing. People could win the right to a second child through a lottery.

Lincoln looked closely at the enactor and laughed. "Jesus, this guy's pretty zippy!"

In a blink, the man was over to Lincoln and slapped him across the back of his head. "No cursin'! No takin' God's name in vain! Not in my house! Not ever!"

Lincoln froze with shock. He had never in his whole life been hit. "Jesus . . ." he blurted again. A fresh slap landed on his skull. Not hard, but hard enough.

"I said no use the Lord's name in a curse!" he shouted. The man raised a red-stained hand over his head. Lincoln looked up at a face so contorted the eyebrows came together.

"Okay, okay, that's enough," Hansum said, stepping between them.

The door of the house opened again and a tall, buxomly woman entered.

"Giuseppe, why do you shout so?" she asked. Then she saw the teenagers and became excited. "They're here. Oh, they're here!" she cried emotionally. "Thanks be to Cristo, you are all safe! Benvenuto. Thanks be to Cristo!" She came over and grabbed the children in turn, kissing each one on both cheeks. "Benvenuto, benvenuto. Oh, you must be Carmella. Thanks be to Cristo, you are safe. Thanks be to Cristo," she kept repeating. Then she stepped back. "Oh Giuseppe, look at them. Such beautiful children," she said dabbing her eyes with her veil.

"They're not children. They're my apprentices and your kitchen girl."

"Yes, but thanks be to Cristo they're safe. Father Lura arranged with your parents to come to us from the country. This bigga city must be so scary to you. It was to me when I was a girl. But you get used to it. Where's Father Lura?"

"He just dropped them off and left," the enactor named Giuseppe said.

Hansum smiled again. He knew how things worked at History Camp. The enactors were giving the newcomers a back story, continually feeding them information about their new selves. If a stubborn child refused to play along, denying his or her new identity, they would be ignored till they relented. It could take a few hours or a few days. Hansum decided to play along, to see what was up.

"That's it, Giuseppe. The priest just left us here," Hansum said. "Yes, Signora. We're supposed to tell you he was busy and had to go." He could see something in the woman's eyes, surprise that a new recruit was playing along so quickly. But as fast as it showed, it passed. Then Hansum felt a swat on the back of his head.

"You talk to a lady without a proper introduction?" the big man bellowed. "And you call me by my Christian name? I am your master. You call me Master! Master Cagliari!" Hansum took a half step backward as the large enactor made like he was going to swat him again, daring the teenager to say something. But Hansum smiled and bowed a little, thinking what a good actor this man was. The enactor calmed down and said, "This is my wife, Signora Cagliari."

"Buon giorno, la Signora Cagliari," Hansum said in Italian, offering another half bow.

"Oh, you see, Giuseppe, such nice manners," the Signora gushed. She came forward and offered her hand. "You so tall. You must be Romero. And the priest said you even have a last name.

Monticelli? Yes, that's it. Romero Monticelli." Hansum took her hand gently and bowed again, accepting his new name. "And you must be Carmella," the woman said to Shamira. "Such a beautiful face. Bella."

"He's not-a Romero. He's-a Hansum," Lincoln said, speaking in a silly Italian accent.

"Yes, he's very handsome," the Signora said without skipping a beat. "And you're cute too, Maruccio. That's your name, eh? I am Signora Cagliari, Maruccio." She repeated his new name, saying it slowly.

Lincoln made a face and replied in his affected accent, "I'm not no Mericutie or whatever. I'm-a Lincoln. And he's not-a Romero. His *name* is-a Hansum. And *she's* Shamira."

The Master reached toward Lincoln and grabbed the top of his liripipe, pulling on it so it uncovered his head and lay across his back. Lincoln's hair popped up in every direction, giving him a comical look.

"You take off your hat when you talk to my wife," the Master said. "This is the lady who feeds you. Show respect!"

"Feeds me? Finally. Hey, I'm starving!"

"Sure, Maruccio," the Signora said. "Don't you worry. Carmella and I will make you a nice meal. It will be ready in a few hours."

"Hours? My stomach is goin' nuts now!" Lincoln complained.

"HEY! Watch your mouth!" the Master shouted.

Hansum laughed loudly, to get Lincoln's attention. "Hey, Maruccio," he said. When Lincoln looked, Hansum scratched his shoulder, pointing with one finger where Pan was hidden.

"Oh, yeah," Lincoln said, a devilish smile coming to his lips. Then he said with an unsubtle tone that indicated he intended to get even with these people, "Yeah. Yeah, sure. Mericutie. Call me that. That'll be just zippy!"

"Don't we have last names?" Shamira asked the Signora, seeming to get in the game.

"I don't know," Signora Cagliari said. "Do you and your brother have a last name?"

Shamira and Lincoln looked puzzled at each other. They shrugged. The Signora added, "Then I guess you don't. It's common enough."

"Okay," the Master said, clapping his hands together. "Boys, you come with me to the shop. It's time to start learning your new trade." The teens looked at each other, apprehensive about being separated. "I said, let's go! Andiamo!" And with that, he whacked Hansum on the back and pulled Lincoln by the shoulder.

"Keep your tights on, man!" Lincoln complained as he was marched toward the door.

"Watch your mouth," the Master said, opening the door and pulling Lincoln through. "Or it will be more than your stomach hurting."

"Keep the faith . . . Carmella," Hansum said, winking at Shamira as he exited. The door closed and Shamira was alone with the female enactor.

"When will they be back?" Shamira asked apprehensively.

"Do not worry, my dear," the Signora said. "Dinner is nine o'clock. They'll be back for then."

"Nine tonight? That's a long time."

"No, no. Morning, dear. Dinner."

"Where I come from dinner is at night."

"How strange. We have dinner at nine in morning and supper at five at night."

"We do breakfast at eight in the morning, lunch at noon and dinner, some call it supper, at six or seven."

"Really? Three meals in one day? How you get any work done? Well, you're in the big city now. When in a Rome, do as Romans do. When in Verona . . ."

Shamira looked deeply into the eyes of the enactor Signora, who was looking back at her with bright, friendly eyes.

"Man, everything is strange here," Shamira said offhandedly.

"Yes, you come from a farm to a big city. Of course things seem odd. But you get used to it."

Shamira admired the enactor for the way she stayed in character, then she chuckled. "I gotta admit," Shamira said, "the boys really freaked out when your husband smacked them. He acted really mad."

"Oh no, Carmella. Maybe the Master was a little angry, but not much. He's just very strict with apprentices because . . . that's what Masters must do. He's a very good man."

Shamira recognized that the enactor was interpreting everything to fit the back story. There was no use talking straight, and she had agreed with the boys to wait and see.

"Whatever you say, Signora Cagliari, whatever you say. So, what's first?"

"First? First we must make dinner. But, to do that, we must go to the market. Come."

Chapter 7

As Lincoln was led into the barnyard by Master Cagliari, he had the urge to swat the big man's patronizing hand off of his shoulder. The large, thick fingers digging into his bony body really bugged the youngest teen, but he had agreed to play along, so he clenched his jaw and said nothing. As they walked past the barn, Master Cagliari said, "That's where you sleep." Lincoln stopped short.

"We sleep in a barn?" the younger teen exclaimed.

"In the loft," the Master explained. "It's nice and warm in winter, sort of." The enactor was looking down at Lincoln, and Lincoln could tell he was still sizing him up. Then the enactor spoke again. "You boys, I think we got off, how they say, on the wrong foot. And a household or a business, they also say, is like an army. We must all march with the same feet at the same time, or we trip over each other. What you say to that, boys, eh?" Lincoln mugged a face and shrugged. The Master looked at Hansum.

"Kind of stretching a metaphor, but sure, I get it," Hansum replied.

The enactor Master gave another conciliatory gesture and went on.

"So, I tell you boys what. I am a very strict master, that no change. But I try to be fair, always. My job is to teach you to be the best lensmakers you can. But to do that, first you must be the best apprentices. We forget about the little taps on the head and start again, okay?" And with that, Lincoln felt the big red hand come off his shoulder and saw it appear in front of him. The Master was offering to shake hands. Lincoln put his hand out and saw it disappear into a very large paw. "Goot, goot," the Master said, his mood lightening instantly. "And you too." Lincoln watched Hansum smile and shake hands. "To good beginnings," the enactor said, beaming. Large, perfect teeth shone out from his face. Lincoln could see the man's teeth were stained, though, and wondered what type of makeup was used to make them that way. He sort of remembered that people in the past didn't always clean their teeth and that the History Camp enactors simulated this. "Okay then," the Master continued. "To the shop."

Just around the corner of the barn they came to another out-building. It was made of heavy wood planks and topped with another thatched roof. There was a central door with large windows on either side of it. Both windows were made of forty panes of wavy, hand-blown glass, each less than a handspan square.

"This is the shop. Come, I show you the new lathe," the Master said, opening the door. He did it with reverence, like he was going into someplace special. He seemed excited. "I just got the new lathe," he said. "The newest, most wonderful machine for making lenses for the discs for the eyes, and . . ." He rubbed his thumb and index finger together to express that the lathe had cost a lot of money.

"What's a lathe?" Lincoln asked.

The Master stopped and looked surprised. "A lathe? You don't know what a lathe is?" Lincoln made a face. "Oh, my boy, it's a big, wonderful machine. It spins around real fast and we shape flat glass into fantastic things to help old people see and even read books. You know what a book is, eh?"

"Ah . . . duh. What's a book?" Lincoln made a foolish face again, crossing his eyes and twisting his tongue in his open mouth, so he lisped, "I think I thaw one in a museum once."

"You never see even a bible?"

"I think he's making a joke, Master Cagliari," Hansum said.

"What? Oh, well, a joke. Ha, ha. A bigga joke. Okay, come in and see my new baby. As he opened the door, he peeked behind it and called, "Hello little baby. You sleep-a well? Now I make a joke."

"Oh, you're a quick one," Lincoln retorted drolly as he and Hansum stepped in the shop. Lincoln heard Pan's voice in his ear.

"Now, Master Lincoln, try not to be too sarcastic or disrupt yet. We must bide our time before we strike."

"Yeah, yeah," Lincoln mumbled. He looked around the shop and saw a small, unlit fireplace built into the back wall. In it hung several metal pots on swing arms. To the right was a water barrel and a heavy table loaded with tools, all lined up neatly. Hand-forged pliers, files, brass bowls, scrapers, quite a few ceramic pots, odd looking brushes, and many unpolished blank discs of glass. In front of one window was another table. Many pairs of spectacles at different stages of assembly lay there. Master Cagliari pointed to the still-hidden space behind the open door.

"And here she is," the Master said, closing the door to reveal what was hidden behind, "our new baby."

"This is what you're making such a big deal about?" Lincoln asked. He was expecting to see some large, metal monstrosity, like he had seen in the Museum of the First Industrial Revolution, something with metal gears, wheels and pulleys. This lathe was a simple wooden structure, about a head taller than himself and just wider than his outstretched hands could span. It had heavy vertical wood posts at each end, with plain wooden feet. Two parallel cross members, about half way up, held a spindle-type device, and at the end of the spindle, a wooden disc. Affixed to the disc was a round, polished lens, about two inches in diameter.

"Come, come in young apprentices. Look here. This is the marvel on which we create lenses to help the old and almost blind see."

A definitely unimpressed Lincoln went up to the spindle and put his fingers near the lens. But he drew back quickly, saying, again with dripping sarcasm, "Ohhhhh! It looks so delicate. Can I touch?"

"No," Master Cagliari said seriously. "You must not touch till you have been properly trained." Then he pointed to the lens. "To make a beautiful thing like this, we grind and polish a raw piece of glass while spinning it very fast."

Much to Lincoln's consternation, Hansum seemed actually impressed.

"What do you mean, spins real fast, Master?" Hansum asked his question quite genuinely.

'Or maybe he's just playing along,' Lincoln thought, 'making the old guy think we're interested.

"Spins. Spins," the Master repeated. "Look," he said pointing to an eight-foot flexible pole protruding from the side wall and ending right over top of the lathe's spindle. "This lathe, she's called a pole lathe. And this cord hanging down from here, see, it loops around the grooves on the spindle and then to the pedal on the floor." The pedal was a plain piece of lumber about two feet long. One end was hanging off the floor by the cord and the other end was attached to the foot of the 'machine' with a leather hinge. "Press this pedal, pull the cord," the Master continued. "Pull down the pole, the spindle she spins. Real fast." Master Cagliari regarded Hansum giving each part of the lathe a good look. "Ah, you are very curious, Romero. Can you see the ingenuity of this meraviglia moderna, this modern marvel? You see how it works?"

"Not exactly."

"Watch, boys," the Master said, springing into action. "It's like magic." Master Cagliari pulled up a stool and sat in front of the lathe. He adjusted the hanging cord so it was taut and snug around the grooves of the spindle. He put his foot on the pedal and pushed it down. "The pole at the top, she bends. Bends like a bow and arrow, yes? Now, as I push down on the pedal more, the pole comes down, but look, look . . ." The spindle came to life as the cord was pulled through it. It spun furiously. When the pedal was fully depressed, the Master stopped and looked at the boys. "Now, watch this. You won't believe what you see." His eyes lit up with great excitement. He relaxed his foot and the pole sprung back toward the ceiling. The spindle spun furiously in the opposite direction. "Isn't that the most beautiful thing you've ever seen? The machine, she does half the work. Before we work on a bow lathe. You had to do all the spinning, both ways, and work with only one hand. This is so much easier," he concluded, flashing his dazzling smile.

"Ah," Hansum said appreciatively.

"But whaddaya do you do with these . . . lenses?" Lincoln asked.

"What do we do with the lenses?" the Master repeated. "What do we do with them?" He pointed to his own face, his own spectacles. "We make discs for the eyes, of course. We do that over there," he said pointing to the assembly table. On it lay wire, bone, ivory and other frames, some with lenses, some without.

"Oh, I thought you wore those to be silly, or scare us."

"What?" the Master asked wonderingly. Then he laughed. "Oh, of course. You come from the countryside and have never seen the discs for the eyes. Let me explain, Maruccio. When a person gets older, their eyes become dim. They often cannot see well enough to do their labors. Can you imagine the seamstress who made your clothes, if she couldn't see her work? Or a wood carver, a stone mason, an apothecary, or a merchant who knows how to read and do numbers? If a person cannot see to do his work, how will he feed himself and family? These wonderful inventions are a miracle. A gift from God that you will learn to make. My priest, he couldn't read his bible anymore. I made him some discs for the eyes. The first time he put them on and looked at his holy book, he begins to cry. He could read again. Tears streamed from his face. 'Giuseppe, you are an angel of mercy,' he said to me. 'Praise God for these discs for the eyes,'" he said crossing himself. The Master took them over to one of the worktables. He picked up a rough disc of glass. "This is what we start with," he said. The glass was rough and scratched. He handed the plain disc to Lincoln for inspection. He gave it a brief, bored glance and passed it to Hansum.

"The lens on the lathe was made from something like this?" Hansum asked.

"Si."

"How?" he asked, sounding impressed. Lincoln yawned and looked around the room.

The Master, apparently pleased that one of his students was enthusiastic, became animated. "I show you. Maruccio, stir the coals and add wood to the fire," he said. "We must heat up the mastic."

"Huh?" Lincoln replied.

"Get the fire going. Heat up the mastic." Lincoln just stood there, confused. Finally, the Master went over to the fireplace and picked up an iron bar that was leaning against the wall. "Stir the coals," the enactor repeated, poking the bar into the ash bed. As he exposed the bottom level, a dull, red vein of smoldering coals appeared. A few wisps of smoke began to rise. "See, the fire she sleeps under the ashes from yesterday. Add wood, Maruccio." Lincoln continued to stand frozen, not knowing what to do. He could see the enactor was frustrated with him. It was similar to the looks he was used to getting from his teachers and parents. The memory made Lincoln frown. "Wood, Maruccio, wood." Lincoln noticed the wood bin next to the fireplace. He picked out a thick piece of limb wood, about two feet long and as thick as his wrist. "No, no, no, Maruccio. Get some kindling, some small pieces to wake up the fire. Like this." Lincoln watched the large man get onto his knees and pick out some wood shavings and twigs from the bottom of the wood box. He gently placed some around the glowing opening and popped a few into its center. He blew on them and the kindling erupted into a small flame. Next he built a little structure of twigs over it. In a few seconds, the fire grew. He added a tangle of thin branches. "When this is blazing, that is when you add your limb wood and logs. Okay, Maruccio?" Then the Master swung one of the arms with a pot hanging from it over the flame. "Now we heat up the mastic."

"What's mastic?" Hansum asked.

"Mastic? It's colla. Glue. To stick the glass to the lathe. She's made from the tears of the mastic bush. Now come," the Master continued. "I show you the parts of the lathe while the mastic warms up."

As they walked over to the lathe, Lincoln made a face and whispered, "Tears of a bush?"

"Farmers cut the bark of the mastic bush with a blade and the plant exudes a milky resin to close the wound. The farmers gather this as a natural glue. It also has medicinal qualities. "

Over at the lathe the enactor said, "This is the spindle of the lathe." He gestured grandly to the whole area that spun. "The spindle, she spins." Then he touched the wooden disc that the lens was attached to. "This is the lap. See the spot in the middle of the lens? That's the mastic, holding the lens to the spindle." He then took a wooden shim, a very thin wedge shape, and gently pushed the thinnest edge under the lens. He gently pried the lens loose. "You musta be very careful not to break the lens," he said, keeping his full concentration on his work. The lens popped off and he held it against Hansum's eye, which became magnified like the Master's. "Here, Romero. Put the lens on the worktable. Hold it by the edges. Grease from your hand can eat into the smooth surface. Maruccio, you hold this." He handed the younger apprentice the little bits of mastic he then scraped from the lap. Lincoln looked at the crumbs for a second and let them fall to the floor, brushing off his hands. "Maruccio," the Master scolded as he dropped to his knees to search for the little white flecks. "What do you do? You waste a valuable commodity. Come,help me, Maruccio." Lincoln got down and joined in the hunt for the bits of mastic. "A very valuable commodity," the Master repeated. "It comes only from one island in the whole world. Most shops use pitch and ash. Very dirty. Much harder to clean off the lens."

"But it's such a little bit," Lincoln complained.

"Waste not, want not." The enactor Master got up and went back to the fireplace and motioned for the boys to follow him. The fire was going well now and the mastic was bubbling. The Master took Lincoln's hand and picked a few pieces of fluff out from the mastic, then brushed the rest into the pot. "Okay then," the enactor said, holding up the blank disc of glass. "I show you lens making from beginning." He picked up a short wooden ruler and a sharp metal scribe in the other hand. "We must get the exact center of the disc, so it spins perfetto." The Master carefully used the crude ruler to determine the exact center of the disc, then scratched a small *X* into it with the scribe. He then put the disc in the jaws of a pair of long-nosed pliers and placed it in the top part of the flame. "You heat up the glass so the mastic will stick to it better." After turning the glass over and over in the open flame, the Master wet his finger with his tongue and touched it to the glass. "Ouchie," he said, laughing. "She's a ready." He placed a generous blob of mastic on the opposite side of the glass to the *X* and went quickly to the lathe. "Do you see the little dot in the middle of the lap?" Holding the lens with a thick rag, the enactor leaned over and, with much care, pushed the hot glass onto the dop, holding it there till he seemed satisfied it had cooled enough to hold. He gave the spindle a few turns and everyone saw it was, indeed, perfectly centered and true.

Chapter 8

"Now we shape the lens," the Master continued jovially. Next to the lathe was a small table where the craftsman placed the tools he needed at hand. He inspected the cutting edges of a file the length of a man's hand and as wide as his thumb. "We start with this one. Big grooves, see?"

He then handed the boys spectacles similar to the ones he was wearing.

"These lenses are flat," Hansum observed. "They don't magnify anything."

"Oh, yeah," Lincoln said, looking around the room through his pair.

"They just protect the eyes. The glass, she flies," the Master replied, sitting forward on the wooden bench and readjusting the lathe's cord. "You see the three levels of grooves on the spindle? When you put the cord at the big spindle, she spins the slowest. In the middle, the middle speed. The littlest one, she goes zip, zip. Zippy, eh, Maruccio?" Looping the cord around the largest groove, he pushed the pedal with one foot and the spindle spun one way. Then he released his weight and the spindle rotated back the other way. After four or five spins, he established a rhythm. He slowly touched the file to the thin edge of the disc at a forty-five degree angle, then a minute later, changed to a second angle. Little shards of glass flew and a wide bevel appeared on the disc's edge.

"Ah," Hansum said appreciatively.

When the lathe stopped, Lincoln made a face. "No way that's going to turn into a lens like the other," Lincoln said. "It looks like crap! It's got more scratches now than before."

"Patience, little man. Hand me that smaller file, Maruccio," the Master said, pointing to the table. He started the machine spinning again and began smoothing out the rough bevels with the finer file, creating as fine a convex shape as possible. Lincoln began fidgeting. When the lathe stopped, the beveled ridges were gone, but it was still a mass of scratches. "Okay, the big filing is done. Now we *grind* the lens four times to get it smooth. First the pumice stick. You give it to me, eh, Maruccio?"

"Yeah, yeah," Lincoln said, still sounding bored. "Which one is that?"

The Master pointed to a thick wood dowel with one end carved out. A piece of porous pumice stone was inserted into it. When the pumice was finished being pressed to the glass, Lincoln had to admit to himself that the scratches were indeed finer. He was about to give this large concession, but the Master spoke first.

"That's the number one grinding. Maruccio. How many grindings did I say there would be?"

"I dunno. Two?"

"You said . . ." Hansum began, but stopped.

"What Romero? How many?" the enactor asked. "Don't be shy."

"You said there were four grindings," Hansum answered quietly. Lincoln stared at Hansum resentfully.

"That's right. Now Romero, go over to the tabella and bring me the pot with the number two on it. And bring the mixing bowl and brush." As Hansum went, the Master leaned over to Lincoln. "Little man, you must-a keep your ears open and remember well what I tell you. That's the way you learn, eh?" Even though this admonishment was done in private, Lincoln felt annoyed.

"I can't find a pot with the number two on it," Hansum called.

"Madonna mia," the Master said, turning to the supply table and looking perplexed. "I say bring the pot with the number two on it and here she is, right in front of you."

"Where?" Hansum asked.

"Right in front of your eyes. Due, tre, quattro," he said pointing to pots with Roman numerals on them. Then the enactor Master paused. He clapped his hands and held them together in an act of contrition. "Oh, I'm-a so sorry, Romero. I thought . . . But of course, you cannot read numbers. Don't a-feel bad, Romero. You just came to the bigga city from the country. Soon we all sit down and I teach you your numbers."

"You'll teach me to read numbers?" Hansum said, somewhat flustered. "I can read numbers, just not this type. And I can read words too." Lincoln couldn't help smile a little. 'Hansum doesn't looks so smart now,' he thought.

"Ha!" the Master laughed. "Romero, don't feel bad and don't tell una fib grande. We gonna be friends we always tell-a the truth. You read? Come on, I hardly read. We're craftsmen. Why we need to read? But we do need to know a few numbers. Don't worry. I teach you soon."

Lincoln watched Hansum pause, smile a bit, then sigh. "Sorry, Master Cagliari. Whatever you say. So, this is number two, this is number three and this is number four." Now Lincoln began to admire how cool Hansum was keeping as he realized, 'He's settin' this guy up good.'

"Good boy, Romero," the Master said. "See, it's best when we do like God wants and be honest Christians. True, eh Maruccio?"

"It's all number two to me," he responded, smiling.

The Master held the pot marked II in front of the boys.

"Here, feel it." Both took a pinch of the contents between their fingers. "Now try il numero tre. Number three." Lincoln almost dropped the first grit absent-mindedly to the ground but made a show of putting it back in the pot. The Master smiled. They both tested numbers three and four. Number three was a much finer grit. Pot number four's grit was almost like powder. "We take the pots over to the lathe, and this mixing bowl, a measure cup and a brush too. Romero, don't forget that brass bowl." They carried the items to the little table by the lathe. "Good, now let's get busy. Maruccio, take this mixing bowl and put three little cup of warm water in it." Lincoln went over to the fireplace and measured out water from the cauldron over the fire.

"It's ouchie," he warned as he handed it back.

The enactor winked as he took the supplies. Then he scooped out a cup of the number two grit. "I pour it in the water and mix it up with the brush till it's a paste." He stirred it for the better part of a minute. "Now, I paint it on the glass. There. Nice and thick. Good. Romero, give me the brass bowl. Grazie. See how the bottom of the bowl is round. That is the exact shape of the lens we want. Now we take the bowl and put it over the glass and start the lathe." His arms tensed noticeably as he leaned his whole body onto the spinning disc. As the harsh scraping lessened, he removed the bowl, applied the pasty grit to the glass again and repeated the process several more times. This done, he wiped the glass with a rag. It was still not clear, but there was a further reduction of the glass and it was more in the shape of a finished lens. "Maruccio, wash out the brass bowl, the mixing bowl and the measure cup. Then we do the number three grit."

Though Lincoln was loathe to admit it, he was quite impressed. He said, joking, "Yes Master," and saluted. While he was at the barrel he heard the Master ask Hansum, "Eh, Romero. You think you could work the lathe one day?"

"Sure. It doesn't look that hard. But I can see it takes practice."

"Oh yes, lots of practice. But I think you smart enough."

Lincoln was back at the lathe with the washed tools. "I can work the lathe too," he said.

"Of course you will, Maruccio. One day," the Master said. "But you are too small now. You need more weight and muscle first. Maybe in a year. You be a good assistant for now, cleaning tools and handing them to us while we work. We must work as a team to make many lenses."

"That's not fair," Lincoln complained.

The Master took the bowls and inspected them. He made a tisking sound and pulled out some of the old grit, holding it under Lincoln's nose. "Maruccio, I told you to make sure there was no old grit in the bowls. We only want the finer grit to touch the glass now. If you want to work the lathe some day, you must do things precisely, for lenses are precise things. Wash them again," he said somewhat curtly. When he returned, the Master reinspected them. With a little nod of approval, but no words of praise, he repeated the process of brushing and grinding with the number three and then number four grit. "For number four I put in a little less grit so is more watery," the Master said, mixing the new paste. "And I press on the bowl a little less hard. I let the grit and the lathe do the work now." After half a dozen applications, the Master took the wet rag and wiped the lens again. "Good."

"But it's not like the lens we saw when we came in," Hansum said.

"Yeah. It's not clear. It's still got like tiny, tiny scratches all over it," Lincoln observed.

"Oh, she's no finished yet. That was just the grinding. Now we do the polishing."

"All that work for a little piece of glass?" Lincoln questioned.

"Come," the Master said, cheerily. "We clean up the grinding equipment and get the polishing tools ready."

The small table by the lathe was cleared and jars, bowls, brushes, files and rags were returned to the wooden bench. The Master moved everything back into a neat order, exactly as it had been when they arrived. Turning back to the lathe, he said, "And we clean up the lathe too." The machine was covered with glass shards and grit.

Chapter 9

'All this work for one small lens. Ridiculous,' Lincoln thought.

The Master took a small straw whisk and brushed the mess off of the lathe and onto the floor. He told Hansum to get the larger straw broom from the corner and sweep up the mess into a pile.

"I can sweep," Lincoln offered.

"No, it's okay. You help me." The Master had Lincoln help him carry over a different brass bowl, another mixing bowl, a much smaller measuring cup and a pot. "What you notice is different about this brass bowl, eh Maruccio?"

Lincoln inspected it. "Oh, it's got that sticky stuff at the bottom of it."

"And what's that *stuff* called?" the Master asked.

"Oh, uh . . ."

" Mastic," Hansum said offhandedly while he swept.

"I was just gonna say that!" Lincoln flashed.

"It's all right, Maruccio," the enactor said. "This is all very much to learn the first morning. Patience. Maruccio, get that little shovel and help Romero pick up the dirt from the floor. Put it in the dust bin."

Lincoln made a face and got the ash shovel. As he leaned down to hold it for Hansum, he said, "I knew it was mastic."

"Sorry, man. But be cool. Can't you tell? He's trying to play us against each other."

"I would concur," Pan whispered. *"Remember, you are both on the same team."*

"Oh," Lincoln said.

"You are playing along wonderfully, Master Hansum. Master Lincoln, follow his lead."

"We get back to work now," the Master called. "I want at least one lens made before dinner. I usually have five or six done by now."

With the workplace cleaned, the polishing began. Master Cagliari gave the mixing bowl and a tiny wooden cup to Hansum. "Put eight little cups of clean, hot water into this bowl." When

Hansum handed the bowl and cup back, the Master took the cup and filled it with a dark red, almost brown powder. "No use the grit brush. We use a very clean blush brush. The powder is called ossido del ferro. Iron oxide, like rust. You know what rust is, eh? She's beaten into a powder, very, very fine." The Master then liberally brushed on the thin paste to the glass. "Now, look at the bottom of the bowl. See the sticky stuff all over the walls of the bowl? What's that called again, Maruccio?"

"Mastic," Lincoln said quickly.

"Si. Good, good. The mastic she holds in place the tiny little bits of iron so they don't roll around like the grit. Now, Romero, get lotsa paste on the brush and when I take the bowl off the glass, you paint on more. Quickly. Rapidamente. We do this three, maybe four times. Rapidamente. Okay?" The enactor moved the cord so it wrapped around the largest groove of the spindle. Hansum took the bowl and brush and stood at the ready next to the Master, stirring it continually as he watched.

"What should I do?" Lincoln asked.

"You keep you big ears open and your little mouth shut," the Master answered as he began pedaling. "You learn! Capiska? Understand!" The mastic-lined bowl came into contact with the lens. Since the mastic was still hard, there was a slight jerking and the spindle wanted to slow. Zzzzzziip, zzzzzzzipp, zzzzzziip, went the lathe. You could see the tension in the enactor's arms as he held the bowl in place, struggling to keep it from moving the slightest fraction. Then he slowed his pedaling and pulled the bowl away. The spindle came to a quick halt. "Pronto, Romero." Hansum slathered on more of the thin iron oxide paste. "Ancora," the enactor said, and the lathe quickly came back to life and he reapplied the brass bowl. The red iron oxide liquid flew out from the centrifugal force of the spinning dop and onto the Master's hands. The enactor stopped the lathe again and pulled away the bowl. "Quickly, Romero, pronto!" Hansum repeated his job on the now steaming lens. "The bowl, she gets warm and then she gets hot." Between the third and fourth application, the Master reached over and moved the cord from the largest spindle to the smallest.

"Now it'll go faster," Hansum said.

"Si," the Master said, pushing hard with the bowl against the glass. Over the din of the treadling and zipping, the Master added, "Now she's really gettin' ouchie. Ouchie, ouchie, ouchie!" he repeated. And then he stopped and pulled the bowl away again. Hansum went to brush more paste onto the lens. "No more," the Master said, out of breath. "She's finished. Here, feel the base of the bowl. Careful."

Both boys touched the bottom of the bowl at the same time. It almost burned their skin.

"Ouchie!" they both said, this time both laughing.

"Now look, look what you helped make," the enactor Master said. He went very close to the glass and gently blew on it. "The heat is so great," he said in a stage whisper, "the glass, she starts to melt just on the surface. All the tiny little cracks get filled up with liquid glass and she becomes smooth." Satisfied the glass was now cool enough, he took a clean rag and wiped off the film left by the paste. The boys leaned in and saw how that disc of crude glass had been transformed into a smooth, convex dome.

"Next time I get to do the brushing!" Lincoln insisted.

"Now we grind and polish the back," the Master announced.

"My God, there's more!" Hansum exclaimed.

"Eh, no takin' the Lord's name in vain!" the Master said, his eyes flashing angrily again.

"Sorry, Master Cagliari," Hansum said, putting his hands up in mock defense. The Master scowled a bit, but then smiled.

"Maruccio, take the mastic bowl and blush pot and put them back on the tool table. Then bring over a big flat pumice stone. You think you can figure out which it is?"

"You got it, Master man," Lincoln said as he picked up the used tools.

"Now Romero, I remove the lens and put it on backside out," the Master continued. "Come. Hand me the wood shim." The lens popped off. "Now we go back to the mastic pot."

"When do you think I can try the lathe?" Hansum asked.

"Oh, maybe in a month or two I will gamble a few discs on you."

"Hey, look at me!" Lincoln shouted from across the room. Lincoln had taken off his safety glasses and put on the finest pair of spectacles from the finishing table. Beautifully polished tortoiseshell frames were perched precipitously on the end of his nose. The strong lenses magnified his eyes and made them look like two sunny-side-up eggs.

"MARUCCIO, NO!" the Master shouted. His trained actor's voice was so loud it startled Lincoln, who then jerked his head. The elegant spectacles flew off his tiny nose and fell onto the floor with a very unfortunate crack.

"Oops," Lincoln said.

Chapter 10

CRACK!

Shamira winced as she saw the heavy metal cleaver come down hard on the leg joint of a sheep. Crack, it went again, and she saw the leg separate from the carcass's hip. Several tiny spurts of blood had sprayed up and splattered the burly man's apron. The butcher turned his attention to the Signora.

"Signora Cagliari, buon giorno," the butcher greeted. Thunk! He embedded his implement deep into the block for safekeeping, then he held out both hands. "God has made a wonderful day for us today, eh?" This master's hands were red too, but not with ossido del ferro. "How is your good husband and my friend, Master Cagliari?"

"Master Sacchetti, how nice of you to ask. He is well. And your good wife and children? How fare they?"

"Oh, another mouth to feed soon. Soon there will be eleven."

Shamira's eyebrows raised.

"Another blessing from God. Such luck, Master Sacchetti," the Signora said.

"Yes, yes. We are truly blessed." The master butcher turned and looked down at a boy of perhaps nine. He had just removed a chicken from a wooden cage and was holding it gently, stroking its neck. "Angelo," Sacchetti boomed, "I told you to cut off its head, not caress it! Now hurry up, useless son, there's work to be done!" The little boy's face changed not at all at the rebuke. He stopped stroking the chicken and grasped its feet. As he stood up, the animal's body fell. Its wings beat the air and it clucked wildly. Angelo sauntered to a chopping block behind his father. Shamira followed the boy with fascinated horror as the butcher continued. "Signora Cagliari," he said, wiping his hands on his bloody apron, "how may I be of a service? I have some wonderful liver of calf today. Oh, and I have beef hearts, your husband's favorite."

Shamira had to lean to one side to see around the butcher and continue watching the boy and chicken. Angelo had the fowl's wings contained and it was lying on its side on the block. The boy put his hand on the bird's neck and smoothed its feathers gently, as if it were a pet. Shamira smiled.

"Or I have a wonderful sausage from pig and beef," the butcher went on, "all stuffed in sheep's intestine. The taste of the fat, it melts in the mouth."

Shamira could hear the sales pitch vaguely, but couldn't take her eyes off the boy and chicken. Her family got most of their animal protein from wild game. 'And they wouldn't dare have a child kill an animal,' she thought. 'This is all a setup.'

"No, no. Nothing so exotic as beef heart," the Signora continued. "I was thinking of something simple. We have three more mouths to feed."

"House guests? Why not the beef heart to spoil your visitors?"

The bird was now quieted and still. Angelo kept one hand on the bird and the other slowly moved to his side. Shamira's smile vanished as Angelo picked up another cleaver from the ground and lifted it over the bird.

"No, not guests," the Signora answered. "We have two new apprentices and a kitchen girl. This is Carmella. She just arrived from . . . Carmella, what in the world is the matter?"

Shamira was tugging on Signora Cagliari's sleeve frantically.

"The boy . . . the boy . . . the bird . . . the boy is going to . . ."

Clabunk! The cleaver came down and cut the chicken's head off in one blow. Shamira blanched.

"There's the idea," Mistress Cagliari said cheerfully. "We'll have fresh chicken." A dizzied Shamira felt the well-trained enactor grab her arm and start leading her away before the butcher disemboweled their upcoming dinner. "We shall be back soon to pick up our meal."

"Of course, Signora," Signor Sacchetti said in a courtly fashion, and then shouted, "Angelo, don't leave the merchandise lying in the dust. It's sold!"

Shamira felt herself being led through a market filled with stalls. In her haze she heard the Signora speaking in a friendly, singsong manner.

"Yes, we shall make chicken and fennel for dinner. Have you made that before, my dear?"

"He, he killed the bird."

"Yes, it will be a good first meal for you and the boys. We do not have meat every day, you know. But this is a special occasion."

"He chopped off that poor chicken's head!"

"And the Lord gave man dominion of all the land and creatures upon it. Including chickens," she laughed. "It will be delicious. Come. We've much to do. Keep your eyes open. I want to be able to send you here alone in the future."

Chapter 11

The market was a noisy, friendly place, a festival for the eyes, ears and nose. There were hundreds of stalls with many medieval specialists working in them. Shamira, remembering what she had learned in school about History Camps, was amazed at the thought that every one of these hundreds of enactors had chosen, as their avocation, to perform a craft in the same way it had been done a thousand years before they were all born. The first place the Signora steered them was a foodstuffs stall.

"Buon giorno, Fiamenta," the Signora said. "This is Carmella, my new kitchen girl." Shamira felt perturbed about being the center of attention in this play story and frowned. "You will see her come in the future to shop. Make sure you give her good produce, like you do for me."

"So nice to meet you, Carmella," Fiamenta said. "Welcome to Verona."

"Hi," Shamira responded blandly. Here they bought raw, shelled almonds, dried fennel, salt, black peppercorns, sticks of cinnamon, ginger root, cloves and some delicate saffron threads.

Just down the row of stalls, they entered a fresh produce booth where the Signora purchased fresh dill and parsley. Each herb was bundled with a sprig of itself wound around the bunch.

Shamira found it hard to keep her steely exterior in the bakery, though. She loved the aroma of freshly baked bread. This wasn't a stall, but a stone house with a huge, open oven dominating its interior. Loaves at all stages of production were around her. There was dough being mixed, kneaded, left to rise, and finally, a man with a sharp, wooden knife, making two slits at the top of the risen loaves just before they were put into the brick oven on a long-handled spatula.

"Why are they carving an *X* on the top of the bread?" Shamira asked.

"That's not an *X*," answered a smiling, flour-covered baker. "That's the cross of Cristo. When the loaves come out of the oven, it is like they had been blessed. The two slices, when baked, turn into the cross of our Lord." They bought four large, round loaves.

The chicken was plucked, gutted and waiting for them by the time they got back to the butcher's. Signor Sachetti had wrapped it in a rough burlap cloth for carrying. The Signora took and held it out to Shamira. Shamira then held it as carefully as possible, so as not to touch any of the raw flesh.

"Really, Carmella, I've never met a farm girl so squeamish about a little blood," the Signora said.

As they made their way down the narrow city streets, they passed many people. Some were cleaning out their houses with the doors and windows open to the air, or standing about, having conversations with their neighbors. There were also itinerant vendors and hawkers going door to door and selling their wares or just shouting about what they had to sell. One vendor in particular was standing in the middle of the road. He wore his goods about himself from head to foot.

"Ah, there's Sancho," the Signora said, "my husband's salesman." Sancho had spectacles tied with string all over his threadbare doublet, some single lens, some double. Around his neck hung an open display box with more spectacles in segregated compartments. His red liripipe was wrapped around his head like a turban. He was speaking in an animated fashion to a magnificently dressed gentleman. "Look who he's speaking with," the Signora continued. "It's the Podesta della Scalla himself."

Sancho greeted the Signora effusively and she curtsied to della Scalla. The gentleman was wearing a black roll-brim hat made of fine velvet. His face was lean, with a long, delicate nose. He had sorrowful eyes and a wide, thin mouth. His hair was blunt-cut at his jaw line. His well-fit doublet, braies and chausses were made from the same fabric as the hat. Everything was trimmed with gold thread. Underneath the doublet was a beautiful linen tunic. Around his neck was a heavy gold chain and jeweled medallion. His boots were soft, black leather.

"Signora Cagliari," Podesta della Scalla said, "so nice to see you. I was just hearing from your man that my new discs for the eyes are ready."

"Podesta Mastino della Scalla, it is nice to see you too. Yes, my husband finished your very special order yesterday. They sit waiting for you. Oh, but my husband said you are in Padua till week's end."

"My business was concluded early and so I am at hand in our fair Verona."

"Wait till you see your discs for the eyes, Excellency," Sancho, the salesman said in his high-pitched, nasal voice. "My Master made them with the most beautifully polished tortoiseshell frames I have ever laid my eyes on. He imported them all the way from Venice, just for you. Shall I deliver them or would you like to take them from the Master's hand?"

"I have business to take care of at the palace this morning, but I shall attend to your Master's shop just after noon."

"My husband took extra pains in the polishing of your lenses, Excellency. They lie upon a velvet cloth on his work table. Oh, Signor, this is Carmella, my new house girl."

Sancho beamed at this bit of news. "Ohhhhhh, greetings Carmella. Welcome to the family."

Shamira bit her bottom lip.

The Podesta nodded graciously at Shamira. "Welcome to my Verona, Carmella. Yes, you are indeed with a very good family."

"Yeah. Like . . . hi."

"We must get back home to prepare dinner, Excellency," the Signora said. "I shall tell my husband to expect you."

"Very well, Signora," Podesta della Scalla said. "I look forward to seeing my beautiful spectacles."

Chapter 12

"Maruccio, what have you done?" the Master shouted. "Those were the Podesta's discs for the eyes! What, what have you got to say for yourself?"

Lincoln looked down at the shards of broken crystal strewn about the floor. Only one of the lenses was ruined and the frames were still intact. He looked up at the contorted face of the Master.

"It could have been worse?" he suggested, trying to joke. "Sorry?" he added, trying to see if that was the right thing to say. But when Lincoln looked into the Master's eyes, he could see this was not the same, friendly person of a few moments earlier. This was a very angry man.

"The Podesta's discs for the eyes! You have broken the Podesta's discs for the eyes!" he cried, visibly shaking. "The finest lenses I ever made, and look . . ." The Master bent down and picked up the frames, holding them right under Lincoln's nose. The glass shards of the broken lens cut into the enactor's finger and big, red drops of blood appeared close to Lincoln's face. The big man ignored the blood and the pain that must have come with it. He just glared at Lincoln and continued screaming. "An apprentice does what he's told. An apprentice does not fool around with valuable things. An apprentice is lucky to have a master who will feed and protect him."

"THEN FEED ME!" Lincoln screamed back. "I'm starving!"

The Master grabbed the front of Lincoln's tunic in a big ball. It partially choked the young teen. His eyes bulged out at the now grossly contorted face of the enactor. "You will do what I say and you will do it when I say so." He pushed Lincoln back against the wall. "Do you understand me?" Lincoln didn't, couldn't answer. "DO YOU UNDERSTAND?" the Master repeated.

Hansum was at the enactor's side. "Please, Master Cagliari. He made a foolish mistake. He won't do it again. I'll watch out for him. Please."

The big man stood with the fierce look still in his eye. Then Lincoln heard a voice in his ear. It was Pan, close enough by in Hansum's shoulder to send him a sonic message.

"Master Lincoln, please relax. This is not the way to get the better of these people. You are playing right into their hands. Relax, Young Master, relax! Say you're sorry."

"Say I'm sorry?" Lincoln replied out loud. "He's chokin' me."

"What?" the Master asked.

"Say you're sorry, foolish Young Master. Say it like you mean it. Say, Master Cagliari, please forgive me. I am sorry."

"No way!" Lincoln said.

"What did you say?" the Master asked. "What did he say?"

"I think he means he's sorry, Master Cagliari," Hansum said. "Isn't that what you mean?" he added suggestively.

"Say it!" whispered Pan. *"Say what I told you to, if you want to disrupt in the end."*

"I'm, I'm sorry, Master Cagliari," Lincoln said flatly. "Please. Please forgive me."

Master Cagliari relaxed his grip, though not his scowl. He eyed Lincoln suspiciously. "Pick up a broom and clean up properly. You're not to touch anything to do with making lenses till I say. You, Romero, you will act as my assistant. We must make a replacement lens. The Podesta returns at the end of the week and I want him to have the finest discs for the eyes."

Over the next half hour, an increasingly hungry Lincoln watched Hansum work with Master Cagliari. The Master worked smoothly and methodically. And as one process was completed, there was Hansum, proper tool in hand, ready to hand it over.

Chapter 13

"An oncia of black peppercorns, cinnamon stick, peeled ginger, half a quarter oncia of cloves and a quarter of saffron stamens." These were the ingredients the Signora had instructed Shamira to grind in a big stone mortar. Pestle in hand, Shamira worked with the same unwavering attention she would if she were doing one of her drawings. This was so she didn't have to look up and watch the enactor cut up the chicken. She couldn't believe how gooey, sticky and disgusting the yellow chicken fat was on the Signora's hands.

"Carmella, don't grind the spices into a powder. Flaky. The mixture, she should be flaky."

Shamira looked up cautiously and saw that the Signora had finished cutting up the chicken and was wiping her hands. 'There's no way I'm going to be able to eat this meal,' she thought.

Like Lincoln, Shamira also had to be shown how to build a fire. The fireplace was wide and high, but not very deep. There was a built-in brick shelf with a hand-wrought metal grate. Signora Cagliari had a large cast-iron skillet heating on it. She scooped in two large spoonfuls of a congealed grayish substance, which melted and bubbled quickly.

"What's that?" Shamira asked, crinkling her nose.

"You don't even know what lard is?"

"Laaarrrd?" she repeated, saying the word as it might taste. "What is it?"

"Fat. Fat from the cow and pig and chicken. To cook in. Oh, Carmella."

Shamira watched as the Signora put the chicken into the bubbling pan, moving each piece around so it didn't burn. She poked the fire till it turned into a homogeneous bed of coals. Soon the chicken parts didn't look like torn pieces of flesh, but were golden-brown. Signora Cagliari then took a pitcher of water and poured it in the pan till it was halfway up the meat. She covered the pan with a heavy lid and left it to simmer.

For the next step, Shamira was told to measure out the better part of a cup of raw almonds and was shown how to hold and use a very sharp knife to chop them without cutting herself. Then she cut up a handful of fennel and parsley. While Shamira was prepping all this, the Signora began a woman-to-woman talk with her.

"Carmella, I can see you are not a stupida girl, but you don't know much about cooking or keeping a house, eh? I will teach you if you let me."

"Sure. Yeah. That's fine." Since all of this was a History Camp ruse, Shamira didn't see the point in getting into any lengthy conversation about it. 'Just agree with everything,' she thought. But she had to admit that this medieval cooking, except for the raw chicken, appeared to be quite creative, almost like drawing. They mixed the chopped almonds, fennel and parsley in a bowl. The Signora added some of the spice mixture Shamira had been grinding.

"Carmella, we save this mixture in a special spice jar with a cork in it. We'll use it in lotsa recipes. For when the meat, she's not as fresh as today, the spices, you know, hide the bad meat taste." Shamira grimaced at the thought of eating meat that was turning.

When the chicken was ready, the Signora removed the frying pan lid and, using a long fork, transferred the chicken onto a plate on top of the hearth. The chicken looked much better than earlier, but Shamira still had in her mind the image of the squawking, feathered animal a short while earlier.

"Now, Carmella, add the fennel, almonds and spices into the broth and stir." While Shamira did this, the enactor added wood to the fire. As the heat increased, the mixture of vegetables and spices began to bubble and thicken. Shamira inhaled deeply. The house smelled fabulous. Then Signora had Shamira slide the pan to the side of the grate to take it off of the hottest part of the coals. "Leave the lid off so the sauce she becomes nice and thick. We pour it over the chicken when we serve the men, eh? Now, let's warm the bread and set the table."

This was going to be a big meal. The Signora had explained how there were usually only two meals per day, the morning dinner meal being the biggest. When people got up, they sometimes would have a little something, repast, it was called. But now they were piling the table with olives, olive oil, cheeses and two of the big loaves of bread.

Chapter 14

"Frickin', frackin', stupid situation," Lincoln mumbled as he tagged behind the others toward the house. Hansum, supposedly now the Master's favorite, walked directly behind the big guy.

"Come on," the Master said, turning and looking at Lincoln. "Don't dawdle. We must get back to work right after dinner. To make up for *your* mistake." Lincoln shook with anger, his fists balled up at his sides.

"Hold your tongue, Master Lincoln, hold your tongue," he heard Pan's voice whisper in his ear.

"Stupid History Camp!" Lincoln mumbled again under his breath. Then, as they got to the house, Lincoln's nose caught a whiff of the food. His stomach growled noisily. Then he watched the Master open the door to the house and stop. The big man nodded at Hansum to go in, but when Lincoln went to follow, he felt the Master's big hand on his chest.

"Maruccio, why should I feed you?" he asked.

"Cause I'm hungry, that's why." He looked past the Master and saw a nicely set table with big loaves of bread on it. With the door open, the smell of the beautifully cooked chicken intensified his hunger.

"Have you earned your food?" the Master challenged, step-ping to block Lincoln's view of the table. "Have you earned your daily bread?"

"I'm hungry. You gotta feed me and make sure I don't get hurt."

"Is that what you think?" the Master asked. Then, with a jerk of his head, he let him pass.

Shamira looked up as the boys entered the room. She could tell something had changed, but nobody said a word. The Mis-tress put another chicken piece on a plate and Shamira had to get back to ladling the now thick gravy.

The Master plopped down in his chair at the head of the table.

"So, how was the first morning?" the Signora asked in a sing-song manner.

"I don't want to talk about it," the Master said gruffly. "It'll ruin my dinner. Sit, all of you. Maruccio's hungry. Romero, sit by me," he said, pointing to the table's bench to his left. "You," he said to Lincoln, "the end of the bench." The Signora stood, fork in hand, surveying the frosty mood in the room. "Woman, are you going to stand there till the Messiah returns?" the Master shouted.

"Carmella, apply the gravy," the Mistress said, hastily putting another plate in front Shamira. "Hurry up. Hurry." Shamira be-gan ladling. The Master looked at what was being served.

"Chicken? Why such a sumptuous dinner?" he asked.

"Why not?" the Signora said haughtily.

The Master grunted. Then he poured olive oil on the side of his plate, took a slice of the bread and pulled it through the oil. He put it in his mouth. "Hmm. Goot," he said somewhat mollified.

"Giuseppe, the prayer!" the Signora scolded.

"God knows I'm grateful and God knows I'm hungry," the Master answered. But still he took his hands away from the plate and wiped them on his pants. He bowed his head. "God, thank you for the food on this table. Thank you for the hands that made it. Thank you for the hands to earn . . . " The big man looked up and saw the children weren't praying. Bang! went his palm on the table. "Give thanks!" he shouted. Everyone's head went down. "God knows some at the table don't deserve the rewards in front of them, but it is by your good graces and charity that we give them another chance. Amen. Okay, everyone eat!"

Chapter 15

Shamira watched the Signora looking oddly at the Master for saying such a strange prayer, but he just ignored her and started eating. He pointed at the boys' dishes, signaling for them to dig in. The boys looked hungrily at the food, which, Shamira had to admit, really did look good. Lincoln seemed intrigued by what the Master had done with the bread and oil. He reached across the table, took the oil, poured some on his plate, dipped the bread in it and shoved it in his mouth.

"Mmmmmm. This *is* good," he said, and took another piece of bread.

Hansum went to cut up his chicken.

"There's no forks," he said. Nobody answered. Then he saw the Master take his knife and cut his chicken into large chunks and pick up one of the pieces with his hand. He placed it on a piece of bread, wiped the bread through more of the gravy and put it in his mouth. Hansum did the same. "Mmmm," he sighed. "Just like at the Ristorante Medioevale dell'Alimento in Florence, the medieval restua. . ." The Master and Signora continued eating, again ignoring his slip.

Shamira's imagination still held her back from trying the chicken. But she was hungry, so she took bread and dipped its edge in the gravy. It was delicious. She looked at the others' plates and saw that their chicken was white and juicy, not pink and bloody. Her courage fortified, she cut off a small piece of the bird and put it in her mouth with her fingers. The image of the headless chicken quickly passed from her mind and she ate heartily.

The food put everyone in a better mood. Lincoln hadn't even tried his chicken yet, but was eating piece after piece of bread, soaking each with many ounces of the beautiful, rich olive oil.

"Oh goodness," the Signora said. "I've forgotten the wine."

"Wine?" Hansum questioned, his eyebrows rising.

"For us?" Lincoln asked.

"Of course," the Signora replied as she got up and took a ceramic pitcher from the shelf. She handed it to Shamira. "Carmella, pour wine for everyone."

"That you don't have to tell me twice," she answered, smiling.

"Maybe this place ain't that bad after all," Lincoln said as the wooden cup in front of him was half filled with the deep, red-colored liquid. He picked up the glass and put it to his mouth. Bang! went the Master's hand on the table again.

"What? A prayer for the wine?" Lincoln asked, his upper lip now sporting a red moustache.

"Dear Maruccio," the Signora said, walking over to Lincoln, "into the blood of Cristo we always add the spirit of Christians from all over the world." She had a second pitcher in her hand. From it she poured a clear liquid into Lincoln's cup.

"I drank blood?" he asked, aghast.

"No, no," Hansum said. "I think they're referring to the wine as a symbol of blood for the old Christian God Jesus. And to water as his followers, Christians."

"Si, we mix our spirit with the blood of the one true God," the Master said, crossing himself.

"You're putting water in the wine?" Shamira asked.

"Of course, dear," the Signora said, now serving the Master. As she poured water into his mug, he put his hand up after only a few drops. "The Master likes more spirit in his spirit."

The teenagers finished their wine quickly, and were surprised when neither of the adults seemed to care when they refilled their glasses. Lincoln still hadn't touched his chicken. But he had eaten almost a half loaf of bread himself, all soaked heavily in olive oil and washed it all down with red wine.

The table became silent for the most part, except for the sound of happy eating and drinking.

"Oh, some news, husband," the Signora said. "In the market this morning, Carmella and I saw Sancho."

"How's his stock?" he grunted, without pausing his meal.

"It looked somewhat depleted."

"Good," the Master said, masticating on a good-sized chunk of chicken and gulping down more wine.

"You'll never guess who was with him there. Podesta della Scalla himself, back from Padua early."

The Master stopped eating. He stiffened. "And?"

"He was thrilled to hear that his discs for the eyes were completed. I invited him to come here this afternoon, my husband. Just after midday." She acted as if she were expecting an enthusiastic response to such good news.

BANG! The Master slammed both of his big hands on the table. Shamira and Hansum stopped eating at the noise and Lincoln, who had finally had his fill of bread and wine, was just about to poke a knife into his chicken. The Master angrily reached across the length of the table, grabbed Lincoln's plate and snatched it from beneath his nose.

"Hey!" Lincoln complained.

"Giuseppe, what in the . . ." the Signora began.

"This one! This one!" the Master shouted, pointing at Lincoln. "He broke the Podesta's spectacles. The most perfect lenses I ever made, shattered."

"He broke the Podesta's commission!" the Signora cried, putting her hands to her face. "But I told you he's coming to get them soon! I invited him."

"Why do you think I'm yelling?" the Master roared. "To gain grace with Heaven?"

Shamira looked at the serious faces around the table. All but one. Hansum was acting as if he were watching a delightful theatrical play produced expressly for his benefit.

"This is a great story," he said out loud.

"What!" the Master screamed. "You think this is funny?"

"Sorry, sorry," Hansum said. He cleared his throat and said dramatically, "Master, we can finish the lens quickly enough, can we not? We've almost finished the front part."

"Hmm. It will take half an hour to finish the lens so it matches the other," the Master calculated aloud, "and an hour to fit it to the frame. Yes, we can do it. Wife, take this meat and keep it for the Podesta. Offer it to him to increase the delay of bringing him to the shop. Don't let it dry out."

"Hey, that's my chicken," Lincoln complained. "I'm still hungry!"

The Master's eyes went wide with rage. He looked as if he were about to explode. The Signora intervened.

"Maruccio, we all must stop our meal. It is very important. The Master is the only spectacle maker in Verona. All other spectacles are made in Venice and Murano. The Podesta there wants our Podesta to close our shop so they can retain a monopoly on discs for the eyes. The pair you broke was a gift to keep the nobleman our friend."

"But I'm still hungry . . ." Lincoln began, but Hansum kicked him under the table. Then he said dejectedly, "Okay."

"You can count on us, Master!" Hansum added.

Pan, who was perched in Hansum's shoulder hem, was sitting next to Shamira. He had been spying around the room, taking everything in, still working on a plan to disrupt.

"Bingo!" he said to himself. *"Mistress Shamira, I spy by the shelf some herbs that have been hung to dry. The one on the end is called the cassia, or senna plant. Its leaves are most potent in the way of a laxative. Without bringing suspicion upon yourself, grind up some of the leaves, soak them and let the piece of chicken marinate in the senna juices. It will create a very humorous outcome when the Podesta visits and eats the chicken."* The edges of Shamira's mouth crept up in a smile. *"The rest of my plan for disruption is almost complete. I shall inform you of it when we are all together in the shop."*

"Romero, why do you still sit there by Carmella?" the Master growled. "We've work to do. Andiamo!" he said and hurried the boys out the door.

Shamira was once again left in the house with the Signora.

"Come, Carmella," the Signora said after the men left. "We have work to do."

"Do you want me to marinate and wrap the chicken in a cloth to keep it moist, like Master Cagliari asked?" enquired Shamira.

"Why Carmella, what a good girl to ask. Yes, you do that and I will tidy the place. It must be just so for our noble guest. After all, the Podesta lives in a palace."

So, while the Signora was busy tidying, Shamira used her new herb grinding skills to spice up the Podesta's next meal in a way that the enactors weren't expecting.

Chapter 16

Lincoln was back to sweeping in the shop, but occasionally Hansum would ask him to fetch this or that supply so he wouldn't have to leave Master Cagliari's side. And for some reason Lincoln couldn't explain, he actually tried not to make a mistake when fetching things. He was in a better mood too, now that his stomach was full of bread, oil and wine. But it rankled at him that his piece of chicken was being given to that Podesta guy. Then came the first stomach gurgle. 'Wow, that was loud,' he said to himself as he put a hand to where the noise came from.

A few minutes later, the Master removed the finished lens from the lathe and went over to the assembly table. He methodically began removing shards of glass from the broken half of the spectacle. Then the Master started to install the new lens in the cleaned opening of the frame. Once again, Lincoln found himself fascinated, not only with how neatly the Master worked, but also with his patience. Then it happened again. Lincoln's stomach growled so loudly that both Hansum and Pan heard it.

"Whoa!" Hansum said.

"Your digestive system probably isn`t used to only eating bread for a meal, especially with several goblets of wine, watered down or not," Pan whispered. *"And the profuse amounts of olive oil must be causing the whole mess to travel through your digestive track with great haste."*

"I never felt like this before," Lincoln groaned.

"Probably because at home you wouldn't get away with eating such unbalanced meals," Hansum said.

"There, it's goin' away," Lincoln said, breathing a sigh of relief. Then he hiccupped.

"You two," the Master ordered without looking up from his work, "stop talking!"

Hansum took Lincoln aside and, making like he was talking to Lincoln, mumbled quietly, "Pan, do you have enough input to disrupt yet?"

"If Mistress Shamira has been able to effect what I asked her to do in the kitchen," Pan whispered back to both of them, *"she`ll have done her part. Now, this is what I have in mind for you two."* Pan told the boys how each of them was going to cause the best-made plans of the History Camp elders and A.I.s to go bad.

"That's fantastic," Hansum said.

"And mean," Lincoln added. "I love it!"

"I'm finished," the Master said, looking up from his labors. "And no thanks to all your chattering. When I say quiet, I mean no talking."

The door to the shop opened. The Signora walked in, followed by the tall Podesta della Scalla and Shamira.

"Husband, look who's here," the Signora said. "Our Podesta."

Master Cagliari was already on his feet. He went over and kissed the Podesta's hand.

"Welcome, Excellency. Welcome again to my shop," he said bowing and genuflecting repeatedly.

"Grazie, Giuseppe, grazie. Is that them? My new discs for the eyes?" he said, looking over at spectacles on the table. "Spettacolare!"

"Yes, Excellency, the finest discs for the eyes I have ever produced. Just for you. Not even Florence could produce the like."

"May I?"

"Of course, Excellency. They are yours." The enactor playing Mastino della Scalla picked up the spectacles from the velvet cloth, perched them on the bridge of his long nose and looked at an open book on the table. He moved his face back and forth to get the right focal length.

"Spettacolare," he repeated, smiling. "The clearest lenses I ever used. Not a single scratch or bubble in the glass," and then he shook the other enactor's hand enthusiastically. The teens, on the other hand, weren't showing much of anything. They were listening to Pan.

"The real Podesta Mastino II della Scalla would never have visited a workman's shop and stood around making idle chat. At the height of his powers, Mastino II was the second richest man in Europe. Only the king of France was wealthier. Of course, he did have his comeuppance and his wealth was seriously diminished. But even then he was a force to be reckoned with."

"When do we get to disrupt?" Lincoln mumbled quietly.

"If Mistress Shamira thoroughly marinated the chicken with the laxative and the Podesta ate it, then it has all begun."

"Done and done," Shamira whispered.

"You children!" the Master said sternly. "Do not speak when we have such a guest! Not unless you are spoken to."

"Remember to do and say exactly what I tell you all."

"Giuseppe, thank you so much for such a wonderful gift," the Podesta said. "You are a true craftsman. I shall do everything I can to help you establish a lensmaking business in Verona. Ah, these must be your new apprentices," he said turning to the boys.

"Let the games begin," Pan whispered.

Chapter 17

"Bow. Bow to the Podesta," Pan whispered to the teens with his sonic beam. *"Make them believe you're playing along."*

Hansum bowed from the waist. "Buon giorno, Podesta della Scalla. My name is Romero."

"Romero, I told you to speak only when you are spoken to," the Master chided.

"That's okay, Giuseppe," the Podesta enactor said. He inspected Hansum. "He speaks well, like an educated young man. This once I shall forgive him his error of etiquette. I thought he is fresh from the country?"

"Only this morning, Excellency," the Master said.

"Your Master tells me you have promise as a lensmaker. What do you say to this, young Romero?"

"However I may help my master. I will do it, Excellency." Pan whispered in Hansum's ear.

"However I may help, my master, I will do it, Excellency," Hansum parroted.

The three enactors perked up their ears at these words.

"Well said, young man," the Podesta offered. He put the spectacles back on his nose and they promptly fell off. He had to lurch forward in a very ungentlemanly fashion, catching them before they fell to the floor.

"See!" Lincoln said. "It could happen to anyone. And he has a big nose."

"Maruccio, I said speak only when spoken to!" the Master said gruffly.

Lincoln glared back at the Master, and then smiled wryly.

"So tell me, new apprentice Romero," the Podesta continued, "as a young man with a possible future in the lensmaking business, could you imagine a day when discs for the eyes not only help people do their close work, but also help to see far?"

"Oh, that is impossible, Excellency," the Master interrupted. "A faraway object becomes blurred to the eye, with even the finest lenses. If you hold the lens at arm's length, the image *will* become sharp, but be upside down and small."

"Upside down, you say? Truly?"

"Yes. Hold your spectacles at arm's length and see."

The Podesta did so and acted amazed. "Fascinating."

"Oh, our perfect opportunity," Pan whispered with enthusiasm. *"Hansum, say, not necessarily, Master."*

"Not necessarily, Master," Hansum repeated.

"What was that, Romero?" the Master asked.

"Not necessarily, Master."

"What are you talking about?"

"A lens can be ground that would correct a person's vision and allow them to see at a distance." Hansum repeated Pan's words aloud.

"Don't talk nonsense," the Master laughed. "You've been here a day and already you're an expert? A savant? Ha."

"Allow me to explain."

"Allow me to explain," Hansum repeated.

"It's impossible, boy. Speak no more of it," Master Cagliari ordered.

"Let's hear what he has to say," the Podesta suggested.

The Master took a deep breath and looked suspiciously at Hansum.

"After grinding your regular convex lens . . ." Pan started.

"After grinding your regular convex lens..."

" . . . instead of turning the lens over and polishing it flat, you create a concave lens within the convex one . . ."

Hansum repeated the operation of polishing a concave shape within the convex one.

"You are talking foolishly," the Master contested. "If the lens is the same shape on both the outside and inside, it will be as if it is flat. It will not bend the image."

"Ah, but if you make the inner grinding at a different angle, the difference between the outer and inner. . ." Pan continued feeding Hansum lines as he went.

" . . . will magnify or diminish the image as you wish... So, with the proper adjustments to this configuration... you will create spectacles for people to see clearly at a distance."

The three enactors stood motionless, all looking suspicious-ly at Hansum. Then all at once their shoulders seem to droop. The Master and Signora put their heads down, as if to say that all their work today had been a waste. The Signora enactor turned to the other two, "I would say we have a geniuso here."

The Master grunted.

"Uhhhhh!" Suddenly the enactor playing the Podesta groaned and grabbed his stomach. He looked up, a pained grimace cover-ing his face, and hyperventilated.

"What's wrong, Signor Podesta?" Hansum asked sincerely.

"Stomachache?" Shamira enquired, looking innocent.

"Something you ate, maybe?" Lincoln asked sarcastically.

"What's the matter, Georgie?" the female enactor asked the now doubled-over enactor. "Are you ill?"

"Must have . . ." he managed to say, ". . . been the . . ." he gasped, " . . . chicken."

"Yeah, my chicken!" Lincoln said angrily. "And I'm still hungry."

"Find a way to break his spectacles again." Pan urged. *"Don't be afraid. Break them."*

"Don't worry about me being afraid," Lincoln said, stepping forward and looking the Podesta in the eye. "Hey, Mr. Podunka, did they tell you how we had to fix your new specs cause I broke them?" He grabbed the tortoiseshell spectacles from the enactor and put them on his own nose. "Just like this!" and he flung out his arms and bowed. This time the spectacles fell to the ground flat. Both the lenses and the frame shattered.

"Geniuso," the Podesta groaned.

"For sure," the Signora added, no accent in her voice. She took hold of her pained associate's arm as he began to slump to the floor.

"What did you hard cases do?" the enactor playing the Mas-ter asked accusingly?

"Did you poison him?" the Signora asked.

The fellow playing the Podesta now jerked up straight and grabbed his buttocks with both hands. A look of absolute sur-prise came to his face.

"Nothing that serious," a grinning Hansum said.

"Now it's *you* with the stomachache," Lincoln laughed. "How do *you* like it?"

"Are you all right, Georgie?"

A long, shrill raspberry came from the Podesta's clutched bottom.

"I'm doing a spectral analysis of the enactor's sweat," whispered Pan with a laugh. *"His discomfort should be relieved soon. Any moment now."*

"Stand back, he's gonna blow!" Lincoln shouted.

"Ohhhhhhhhhhhhh!" the now pale enactor squealed. He bunny-hopped towards the door, his buttocks even more firmly clenched. "Oh my, oh no, oh no!" he said with fear and absolutely no Italian accent. He hopped again. Then he penguin-walked quickly out the door, a long, whining fart escaping from him. The woman enactor ran out with him.

All three teens were doubled up in fits of laughter. The enactor playing the Master took off his specs and looked deep in thought. He tapped his temple and looked down to his right, obviously getting a message on his implant. He grunted, took a breath and stood up straight. He glared at the children and started shouting in character again.

"You shame me? You insult me? You disgrace yourselves in front of our noble guest?"

Lincoln stopped laughing and stood his ground.

"You gave him my dinner!"

"You're hungry?" the enactor shouted back. "You'll get no food from my table! Get over there with your ungrateful friends." He pushed Lincoln away. "You're all thankless, monstrous children," the Master raged.

"Listen, Giuseppe, or whatever your name is," Hansum said, "you seem like a nice guy and you're a hell of an actor, but we don't want to play anymore."

"I want to go home!" Shamira insisted.

"You gave away my chicken!"

"You think this is play?" the Master spat. "This is work! You must do it! If you do not work, you do not eat. If you do not eat, you perish! There are many starving youths who ask me every month if I will become their master. And you won't work?"

"Giuseppe, give it up," Hansum said.

"And don't dare call me by my Christian name," he yelled. "You haven't earned the right. I am your MASTER!!" His face had become a deep purple. The veins on his neck bulged out. He took a half step forward and towered over Lincoln. Looking down at him, he growled his next command. Spittle flew in the boy's face. "All of you go to the loft. Stay there till I say otherwise. I must think what to do with you."

But Lincoln wouldn't have any of it. "No way, Giuseppe!" he cried, and then he stomped on the Master's foot.

"Owww!" the enactor screamed, accentless. His big hands became like claws as he curled his blush-stained fingers with the pain. Then he opened one of them a slapped Lincoln on the head.

"Aaaaaaaah!" Lincoln screamed. "That hurt!" and he hurled himself at the Master, pummeling the large man's abdomen. Hansum grabbed Lincoln and pulled him back toward the open shop door. Lincoln struggled and almost got free, till Shamira jumped in and helped Hansum pull him away. The enactor rocked back and forth on his heels, trying to take his weight off his bruised toes.

"Come on, man," Hansum urged. "Let's get outta here."

"You'll have some explaining to do when I tell on you," Lincoln screamed. "You'll be in big trouble! You hit me! You not supposed to hit! I'm going to tell my mom!"

"Go to the loft and STAY there!" the Master shouted. "Get out, get out! Get out of my shop!" And then he picked up a chair and threw it against the wall. It splintered into pieces. The three teenagers had never seen an adult so out of control. But Lincoln kept struggling.

"Stop," Shamira urged Lincoln. "You've really made him mad! He's not acting."

"I said go to the loft!" the Master screamed. "NOW!" he bellowed in a voice so loud the teenagers froze on the spot. "GET OUT! GET OUT OF MY SIGHT!"

Chapter 18

Several hours later, the sun was setting and the children were still in the loft of the barn. Hansum was looking out the haymow door, keeping an eye on the house to see if and when the enactors were coming to see them.

Shamira was drawing. She had taken a piece of paper from the kitchen and slipped it in her apron pocket. Using a piece of charcoal she found in the barn, she was sketching a picture of the holographic imp. Pan, though only a projection and not beholden to the laws of the universe, was making it look as if he were swinging on the top rung of the loft's ladder, occasionally doing a handstand, till Shamira chided him to pose again.

"They just lit a lamp," Hansum informed the others. "I can see them through the window now. They're sitting at the table, talking." He turned to Pan. "What do you think they're discussing?"

"How should I know? I'm a hologram, not a mind reader."

"What do you mean, I'm just a hologram?" Hansum asked. "You're the one who got them so mad at us."

"Isn't that what you wanted?"

"But the game didn't last very long," Hansum complained. "It wasn't much fun."

"Well, excuse me if I get results quickly!" Pan retorted indignantly.

Shamira giggled. "Your idea about the laxative was brilliant. Did you see the way the Podesta guy ran?" she laughed. "But he really wasn't hurt, was he?"

"No. And thank you for your compliment, Mistress. I'm glad someone appreciates me. Yes, it was a brilliant plan. May I see my picture now?"

"Just finished," Shamira said. "There."

Pan jumped off the ladder and scampered to her side.

"You are quite talented, Young Mistress," he said.

"Not really," she answered, offhandedly.

"I beg to differ."

"Are they eating supper at the house?" Lincoln asked Hansum. He was just coming up the ladder from the lower barn. He, like the enactor playing the Podesta, had some gastric problems. He found an old, cracked chamber pot in one of the stables.

"I can't see clearly, but I think the Signora is doing something by the fireplace," Hansum answered.

"Well, I hope so. After what I just did, I'm really hungry again," he whined. "And it really hurt. It was all red and gushed out like a tornado!"

"We heard," Hansum said.

"Spare us the details," Shamira said. "That's what you get for stuffing yourself with bread, oil and wine. You eat like a twelve-year-old."

"I'm thirteen!"

"Then grow up."

They sat in silence for a few moments, then Lincoln, obviously still in deep thought, finally said, "But did you hear what they said about us?" Lincoln asked. "They said, 'geniuso'. They think we're all geniuses." Everyone fell silent at this remark. Pan shook his head and rolled his eyes, literally.

"What?" Lincoln asked.

"You idiot," Hansum retorted. "They don't think we're geniuses. Saying 'geniuso' is code that they know we have a genie hidden somewhere!" Everyone laughed at Lincoln. Then Hansum became serious. "Quiet!" He cocked his head to hear something. Then they all heard it. Footsteps below in the barn. "Someone's coming," he whispered.

"Is it the Master?" Hansum asked.

"I can't see," Shamira said, peering down the loft's entrance. "It's too dark in the barn already." The ladder creaked as it took someone's weight. "They're coming up. Pan, get back in your lamp." In a blur of colors, the hologram disappeared back into Hansum's shoulder. Lincoln grimaced as he heard the sound of someone slowly taking one step at a time.

"Who's there?" Hansum called into the darkness. "Is that you, Giuseppe, I mean, Master?" The ladder groaned again.

"Yeah," Lincoln said, peering over the precipice. "I guess I'm sorry I stepped on your foot. But you hit me." The ladder creaked twice more, then silence.

"Is that you, Podesta?" Shamira asked. "I hope your stomach's better." The loft was in a gray twilight, but the square hole to the lower barn seemed a portal to a silent, black pit.

The children looked at each other.

"Signora?" Shamira queried.

Finally, a deep and melodious male voice, which was speaking in verse, echoed from the abyss.

"Not she."

"Who?" all the teens asked in unison.

"Tis one who will sweep the cobwebs from your eyes
And leave you with wondrous whys."

"It kinda sounds like that polatta fella," Lincoln guessed.

"No, not he," the voice responded.

"Who are you, then?" Shamira asked.

"Allow me ascend and share our faces.
That's what friends do, to be in each other's graces."

"We're not stopping you," Hansum retorted.

"Your beneficent invitation . . . I shall take."

A few seconds later the mysterious head of the stranger appeared.

"Greeting young students of life
From an older one of the same."

The man stepped into the loft and looked smilingly into the eyes of each teenager. He had a long aquiline nose and a pointed chin, made more severe by a dark goatee. His confident grey eyes and bushy eyebrows, long and twisted at the ends, gave him an eccentric but interesting look. Wiry salt and pepper hair fell down to his shoulders. It surrounded his chiseled face like a lion's mane. He was dressed in a simple toga, from under which finely made sandals peeked.

"Greetings, young ones."

"Who are you?" Shamira asked.

"My name is Arimus."

"My name is . . . ." Hansum began to say, but Arimus put up a hand for him to stop.

"Hansum, Shamira and Lincoln.
Your faces and cases are known to me."

"He's one weird enactor," Lincoln said. "Is he supposed to be from Verona?"
"No. I think he's a History Camp Elder," Hansum said. "Come to read us the riot act?"

"No, that is not my charge.
For the act of riot, you have already performed well.
Therefore you must have already read and studied it for yourselves."

"Are you going to send us home then?" Shamira asked.

"No, for home you're not bound.
You have much to experience and learn.
And from it you will prosper, ere you all shall burn."

"I don't understand," Hansum said.
"Yeah. And why are you talking in poetry?" Lincoln asked.

"That's the way we talk from whence I come
Some verse blank, some is rhymed,
Some's out of sync and some is timed.
But if you listen carefully, if you open an ear
What's between the lines will soon be clear."

"Do you have anything that rhymes with food?" Lincoln asked. "My stomach's queasy. I'm really hungry."

"Oh, where you're all going,
you can have the food you seek
If you work willingly and act verily meek."

"Oh, you're taking us somewhere else?" Hansum said.

"Yes, yes, you've done all the damage here
And displayed your disdain
For the help which was proffered
That was there for your gain.
So now I must take you to an old time that's real
Where all of your angers can be taken to heel."

"What the zip did he just say?" Lincoln asked.
"I think he's saying he'll take us somewhere that's going to be rougher than here," Shamira suggested.
"Another History Camp?" Hansum asked. "So, if Verona in the fourteenth century hasn't been hard enough, where next?"

"History Camp? Nay.
But Verona's the place and the era's the same,
But this time that fair setting will be not a game.
For this Arimus comes from a future long hence
To whisk you all to a Verona that's truly past tense.
Where they say to you work, or don't eat 'ere to die
This will happen for sure, whether you grumble and cry."

Hansum stepped forward and looked straight into Arimus's relaxed eyes.

"Elder Arimus, are you saying you're from the future and you're going to take us back to Verona in the real fourteenth century? And that if we don't give in and work, we can starve to death?"

"Is that what he's really saying?" Shamira asked, a bit of both fear and wonder in her voice.

"It is as Hansum suggests."

Hansum began to snicker, then outright laugh. "This is really rich. He's expecting us to believe that he can take us back in time. Look, why don't you guys just admit that you've been beaten and let us go home?"

"Yeah," Lincoln said. "I won't even tell that you guys hit me."

Arimus ignored the boys. Instead he looked over at the drawing in Shamira's hand.

"Ah, look at this image of the Pan you drew.
You have dexterous hands that belong to but few."

"It's nothing," she said and let the drawing fall into the straw.

"An eye that so senses, and a hand that can do.
Where you are going, these talents,
This asset, might just get you through."

"Didn't you hear me?" Hansum said, "We don't believe you."

"Aye. I heard you, my boy.
And if it's for proof that you're fretting
Play along more, and soon enough,
It will be proof you'll be getting."

Hansum looked deeply into Arimus's eyes, their gazes meeting in a momentary silence.

"Is it true?" Hansum asked quietly. "You're really from the future?"

"It's true."

"Wow," Lincoln said enthusiastically. "If you really are from the future, that would be . . ."

"Zippy?"

The sound of the house's wooden door latch was heard through the crisp night air. The voices of the enactors, the Master, Signora Cagliari and the Podesta could be heard in the barnyard.

"Oh Signor Podesta," the Master's voice called out, "it is so Christian of you to forgive the children their mistakes. I'm sure they'll be good now."

"Yes, but hold the lamp higher, Giuseppe," the Podesta's voice said. "I want to see where I'm going, not step in a cow pie."

"Giuseppe, take care with the jug too," the Signora's voice called out a bit shrewishly. "You're spilling the wine."

"Just you mind the new meal you cooked for the children, wife. Don't drop the plate."

Arimus laughed.

"It seem these historical actors have forgiven your fibs,
    And do bring you a repast to fill Lincoln's ribs.
We must now act in haste, to make good on my crime
But I must first change my raiment to suit our new clime.
    To change them post quick, my hand I thus flick."

Arimus flicked his wrist and his toga transmuted its shape, thickness and color. In an instant he was wearing a fourteenth-century monk's cassock. The children looked as if he had performed magic.

"How in the...." Hansum began.

"Technology is all. Just technology."

The light from the enactor's lamp was now throwing long shadows into the interior of the lower barn. It spilled upward through the ladder's opening and into the loft.

The Signora called out, "Children, we bring you food. All is forgiven."

"Quiet woman!" the Master said. "One does not have to show weakness when being kind. These children have done mean things and must know it. Now hold the lamp and I'll go up the ladder first." The sound of the Master grunting was heard as he started his climb.

"Be careful, Giuseppe," the Signora's voice said. "You're spilling the wine."

"Time is short.
We must step through yon port."

He flicked his wrist toward the open haymow and a whistling wind began. The loft filled with a bright, gold light and an outward wind sucked out loose straw from the floor. A large funnel shape appeared, composed of what looked like oversized gold-colored orbs of light the size of a man's fist. There were millions of them, a massive stream which rushed downward and converged into an opening little more than the width of a pencil lead. It looked like giant holographic sand falling through a giant hourglass. Effervescing up from the stream were larger bubbles of translucent light, shimmering globes varying in size from grapefruits to beach balls that bounced and careened all over the place.

"The bright sands and energy of time roils and falls before you.
They flow through a portal and into realities long-since lived.
Come, let us join forebears who will become mentors."

Hansum inched his way to the haymow door and looked down. The fast-descending stream of spheres inexplicably appeared at the funnel's top and disappeared into the tiny point at the bottom. It was moving so fast, it made him dizzy with vertigo.

"It's all going through that tiny hole. We'll be crushed!" Hansum said.

"From here, that's what it appears.
From there, it opens up into forever."

Several of the large globes of light bounded into the barn, flying straight at Lincoln. He tried to duck but, like large, self-determined soap bubbles, they swerved. When they reached him, though, they didn't burst. They flew right through the boy as if they both existed in different dimensions. Lincoln looked even more frightened.

"They like you."

Arimus laughed. Then he commanded:

"Come. Give me your hands.
We shall ride the sands of time
through the hourglass of the cosmos."

The frightened teenagers each took a step back. The Master was now halfway up the ladder. The light behind him cast his long shadow across the barn's thatched ceiling.

"We've no time to lose."

Arimus grabbed Lincoln's arm and forced the teen's hand to touch his monk's robe. Lincoln tried to pull away.

"Hey, my hand is stuck!" he cried. "Your cloak won't let me go! Make it let go!"

Hansum, coming to Lincoln's aid, also grabbed Arimus by the gown.

"It's got me too!" Hansum cried.

"Fear not, young friends.
It's all just technology and time."

Arimus turned to Shamira, who was now cowering by the ladder. He smiled and held out his hand.

"Come brave, adventurous Shamira. Come all of you.
Fear not the lessons of life.
Take the hand that I offer, and trust me, I pray.
This adventure you'll cherish,
For the rest of your days. Come."

Shamira took Arimus's hand. The Master's head crowned through the opening.

"We're away."

The four rushed toward the vortex and jumped out of the haymow door. For an instant, they were suspended twenty feet above the barnyard, then they tumbled down the swirling rabbit hole. The vortex collapsed and silence once again reigned in the barnyard.

Master Cagliari's head popped through to the loft, smiling and enthusiastic.

"Bambini," he shouted, "I bring you supper and a promise to start anew...." But all was quiet. "The storm's abated," he called, still in character. When he realized he had no audience, he relaxed. "Colleague, they're gone." And with that, he took a big swig from the wine jug and started down the ladder. All that was left in the loft, lying in the straw, was Shamira's lonely charcoal drawing of Pan.

Book Two
Hard-Time Reality

Chapter 1

Verona, October, 1347 C.E.

Hansum found himself face down in straw. The last thing he remembered was jumping out through the haymow door with the others. 'I don't remember hitting the ground,' he thought to himself. He wiggled his toes, then fingers. No pain. He felt straw tickling his mouth and tried to blow it out. No good. There was more than straw in there, something sticky and awful tasting. "Ppphhff!" He spit, but couldn't get it all out. He took a deep breath and the vile smell of ammonia burned his sinuses and lungs. He jumped to his feet, wheezing.

"Mmmrrraaaawwwww!" He spun his head around and saw a scrawny cow tied to a dead tree by a barn. There had been no dead tree in the Master's immaculately kept plot. And this scrawny beast was not the Master's contented animal. Nor was this his barn. In fact, where the Master's barnyard had a somewhat earthy, sweet smell, the whole area here smelled of foul puddles of urine, cow dung, carcasses and other unnamed rotting things.

Instead of a neatly partitioned lot surrounded by a stone fence, this barn was part of a long, muddy alleyway full of tumble-down sheds and out-buildings. The alley ran behind a row of unkempt houses facing a larger road. The alley and road were connected by an even muddier lane ending at the barn. The shabbiness of the area was made more extreme by the gray day. 'Day?' Hansum thought. Had he been lying outside all night? While he thought on this, he used his fingers to rid himself of whatever was still stuck at the back of his mouth. He finally gagged out the clot and was horrified to see bits of straw mashed together with what must be manure. He threw it to the ground and made a face. He saw the other two teens still on the ground. They too were slowly becoming aware of their surroundings. Hansum looked behind him to see Arimus standing calm and relaxed.

"When traveling through a vortex,
"Try landing on your feet.
It takes a bit of practice,
but will keep your clothes more neat."

As the three got up, brushing dirt from their clothes, Arimus walked over to the nervous cow and petted it. A flock of chickens ran out of the barn to see if the newly arrived humans brought food. Startled by the aggressive little creatures, Hansum took a step back and bumped into the others, who were equally frightened. Arimus laughed, earning him three petulant scowls, which he ignored. When the chickens saw there was nothing being thrown their way, they lost interest and began pecking around in the mud. One picked up the clod of filth Hansum had spat. It broke it open, found a seed within, and gobbled it down. Hansum felt himself gag again.

Arimus clapped his hands and grinned.

"We are arrived."

"Where are we?" Shamira asked.

"Verona, 1347. Just outside the old city walls."

"And you think we'll find this place more . . . interesting?" Hansum challenged. The others looked to Arimus for his answer.

"Fourteenth century Verona interesting?
Yes, a very interesting time in history.
Interesting to study. But to live? Subsist?
From your safe world you have come to a time before countries.
The time of the city-state, the family-dominated oligarchy.
The time of grand hypocrisy.

Craftsmanship, philosophy, art,
the concept of romantic love,
all are on the rise.
It is the Pre-Renaissance.
Science is soon to become the greatest weapon of war.
A time when cities compete treacherously against one another,
fighting deadly battles to gain commercial advantage.
Families assassinate family members.
Imagine, if you will, the hows and whats of this human exis-
tence, compared to your known modern comforts.
Or imagine it not. You will be living it soon, for this is your
destination.
The real, the true, the living, fourteenth-century Verona."

"You're a hell of a tour guide," Hansum said glibly.

"Oh, a guided tour you shall not get.
You're on your own, the story's set.
It will soon be you who guide yourselves along.
I only hope, you'll all be strong."

Lincoln smiled. "You're leaving us by ourselves?" he asked in
a delighted tone. "No adults to tell us what to do?"
Arimus nodded.
"And we really traveled to a different time?" Shamira asked,
seeking assurance. "It was a rough trip."

"Going back a thousand years in time means traveling trillions
of parsecs of space
Back to where the Earth was at, and to this particular place.
And now, you are alone."

"Yeah," Lincoln said with gusto.
"I think we should take what Elder Arimus says with a grain
of salt," Hansum cautioned. "We might appear to be alone, but I
know about History Camp protocol."

"You seem the most cynical of the lot,
and the cynic is ofttimes sensible.
But, then again, sensible is often what the world around you
says.
Keep an open mind."

"This place is freaky," Shamira said. "I wish I had something to sketch it with."

"How may I deny a true artist?"

Arimus reached into his monk's hassock and withdrew an old leather portfolio. Shamira stared at the cloak in wonderment. He handed her the cracked leather case and made a motion for her to inspect the contents. She brought out a dozen sheets of blank paper.

"This is really wonderful, handmade paper," Shamira said.

"Scarce resources for your talent to display.
Do not waste this paper of rag base.
For with your talent you can turn it to lace."

"Padre Aaron, Padre Aaron," a man's voice shouted. Everyone's head turned to look to the top of the lane between the alley and the road. A large man was standing there, heavily bearded and wearing dark clothes and boots.

"*Siete voi? Siete proprio voi, lo mio vecchio amico?*" he shouted excitedly. Having trained the other year as a Renaissance soldier, Hansum had learned a fair bit of Italian. He was good at languages. He thought the man was saying something like, "Father Aaron, Father Aaron, is that you? Is that you, my old friend?" But he wasn't quite sure as the accenting and phrasing were very strange.

Arimus dropped his rhyming voice and fell into the medieval Italian. He waved his hands and danced a little jig, as if he were seeing a long-lost friend.

"Agistino," he shouted in a heavy Cambrian accent. "*Agistino, fratello mio. Sono io, vostro fratello, Padre Aaron.*" Hansum was struggling to translate it in his head when he heard Pan's voice in his ear.

"He's saying, Agistino, my brother. It is I, your brother, Father Aaron."

"*Magna laude a Dio, entrambi sopravvivemmo a li nostri viaggi!*" the big man shouted back.

"Praise be to God, we have both survived our journeys!" Pan whispered in translation.

The man, who Arimus called Agistino, lumbered toward them as a bear would, on his hind legs, arms open wide. He laughed as he ran, but after they came together in a hearty embrace, he fell to his knees and began kissing Arimus's hands.

"*Calma, fratello. Calma,*" Arimus said. "*Godiamo di cotesto ritrovarsi con la grazia del Signore.*"

"*Calm, brother,*" Pan explained. "*Calm. Let us revel in this reunion with grace,*"

Agistino got up, collected himself and asked, "*Quando arrivaste nella civitate?*"

"When did you arrive in the city?" Pan continued translating.

"*Appena oggi, allo scoccar del mezzodì,*" Arimus explained.

"Just today. At mid day," Pan whispered.

"And you found us already? How?" Pan translated.

"By God's grace and a few questions."

Chapter 2

Another voice shouted from up the lane. It was a younger man, a little shorter than Hansum, but quite stout. "Padrone, Padrone!"

"*Master, Master,*" the young man called in a harsh, raspy voice. "*La signora vostra moglie sta gridando perché ella non trova il vaso da notte fra le masserizie e le casse del trasloco.*"

"*Your wife is screaming for her chamber pot. It can't be found in the moving crates.*"

"*Dio nell'alto dei cieli, dammi la pazienza! Ora mi tocca perfin di diventare bambinaia di questa donna grassa e sciatta,*" Agistino said. "*God in Heaven, give me strength. Now I am a nursemaid to a sow.*" Then Agistino turned and looked at the three teenagers, glancing at them fleetingly, like they were goats or chickens. "*Sono codesti gli orfani che tu dai a me?*"

Pan said, "*Oh, oh, Young Master. He's saying, Are these the orphans you are giving to me?*" Hansum looked at both adults with trepidation.

"Si," Arimus answered offhandedly.

"*Allora che si vengan tutti meco,*"and Pan translated, "*Then come all with me.*"

"*Datemi un poco di tempo, di grazia,*" Arimus said. "*Give me some little time,*" and after Arimus spoke some more, Pan added, "*I am reviewing their duties, both for you and the Holy Church.*"

The young man up the lane shouted again, "*Padrone, ecco il vaso da notte della vostra signora moglie.*"

"*Master, your wife's chamber pot.*"

Agistino's happy countenance turned quickly to rage. He shouted again in old Italian, to which Pan translated, "*Can't you see I'm talking with the Holy Friar?*" He made a rude gesture aimed toward the young oaf.

"*Pace, Agistino,*" Arimus said, putting a hand on Agistino's shoulder and speaking gently.

"*Peace, Agistino. An irritable bowel is a demanding God. Go find its altar of prayer for your wife.*"

Agistino's scowl turned to a smile, and he chuckled something in Italian which came to, "*That is why I love you, Father. You make me laugh with your wisdom. Come to the house when you are ready.*" Agistino then turned and ambled off.

"Does everyone here speak like that?" Shamira asked.

"Of course. It's their language."

"I know some Italian," Hansum said. "But I could hardly understand what you guys were saying. What Italian is it?"

"Italian, as it was spoken in 1347. But Italy didn't exist as you know it then."

"You're going to leave us where we don't understand what is going on?" Shamira asked.

"That would be mean and cruel.
No, dear ones, I'll give you a tool.
I take from my blouse three nibbles of food,
each eat one, and be instantly shrewd.
Consume it do, and then you'll spout,
early Italian without a doubt.
Your ears will know all ideas said,
you'll understand what your eyes have read."

Arimus took a handkerchief from his all-providing robe. Unwrapping it revealed three small biscuits. He held them out to Shamira first.

"Taste. Don't waste. I made them myself."

She took one, sniffed it, then bit off a small piece. "Pretty good," she said.
He offered one to Lincoln, who popped it in his mouth and chewed the thing whole.
"Thanks. I'm starving."
He held the last one out to Hansum.
"These will help us learn?"

"Oh more than that. They are the learning."

"There's no technology that can give us instant knowledge of a language!" Hansum retorted.

"Let's not quibble. Give it a nibble.
And if it doesn't work, withal,
I'll eat this cassock before you all!"

Hansum shrugged and ate his.
"It's not bad," he said.

"I'm happy that you are enjoying.
Now eat it all, and eat it quickly,
Your new master awaits, and he's really quite prickly.
Come you three, we'll walk while we talk, and I'll explain.
Agistino della Cappa is your new master's name.
From Florence he came, his head hung in shame.
A good man, essentially, with one weakness, the grape.
From the nectar of Bacchus, he could not escape.
Apprenticed when eight, to a maker of crystal.
His master's the man who invented the spectacle.
Agistino was at sixteen a journeyman made,
His master's daughter he married, for his talents were sage.
When his father-in-law died, the family's head he became.
In Florence he flourished and garnered true fame.
But his wife is not well, in her head she is ill.
Though in our times her malady could be fixed with one pill."

Shamira stopped walking and looked at Arimus suspiciously.
"If she's ill, why don't you use modern medicine to cure her?"
she asked.

"The past we cannot influence, with modern medical creations.
It's a time-traveler's code, of strict legislation."

Lincoln put his hand on his stomach, then burped.
"Wow. I don't know what was in that, but I don't feel queasy
anymore."

"Like I said,
It's food and something else from a day far away,

and the one time I'll feed you during your stay.
Your fates do now rest with your wills and your hands,
To succeed you will learn, dears, on how to make plans.
Back to my the story of Agistino, my friend
I care for him dearly, my love's without end.
But his life is his own and his century too
There's a limit, you'll learn, what a friend can but do.
To hide from the badgering of his wife's mental distress,
He took to the bottle and drank wine to excess.
His riches soon faded, as did his creditors' trust
All of his life now's a horrible bust.
An ubriaco he's been. A drunkard. A sot.
And finally, he stands, a miserable bankrupt.
To Verona he's fled, vowing his life to improve
I gave him the money to make that brave move."

"I thought you couldn't interfere in the past?" Hansum said sarcastically.

"In matters technological or of medicine, yes,
But people gave money in the past and were blessed."

As he said this he made the sign of the cross.

"So, Agistino and his wife, took Guilietta, their daughter.
And with no servants or maids, to Verona they brought her.
With Ugilino, their apprentice, who has little of talent,
To his master's debasement, he fits in most valiant.
And there they all live, behind that grey door,
Of their world I'll not tell you a scintilla more."

His story ended as they arrived at the main road where Agistino's rented house met the alley. Arimus swept his arm toward the door, then motioned up the road one way and then the other. The road south led to a distant red brick wall and one of the towering entrance gates into Verona. Looking north, there was a second city wall, from several centuries earlier, when the city was smaller. Above it you could see the tops of more brick tow-ers, church steeples and ancient houses. The street was busy with people, many on donkeys, horses and carts.

"All right then," he said, "now I've revealed to you all that I may. Here is the humble home where you'll live, work and pray."

"Whoa!" Lincoln grabbed at his temple.
"What's wrong?" Shamira asked, taking his arm.
"I felt something grow in my temple, under the skin. It feels like the sub-dermal. Yeah. Yeah," he said feeling around. "It is a sub-dermal," he said excitedly. "Does this mean I can talk to my home again?"
Shamira and Hansum put their hands to their right temples.
"I feel one too," Shamira said.
"Hey," Hansum said. "What's going on?"

"I told you, the food that you ate not only filled,
It gave you a tool, so say you've been pilled.
Now you can sing like a Cambrian canary,
You're brains are all full of an Italian dictionary.
And that nub on your noggin, is the switch to that talkin'."

Chapter 3

At that moment, the young man who had been calling to Master della Cappa emerged from the house carrying a steam-ing chamber pot. Close up, he was a terrible sight. One eye had a perpetual squint, the other was lazy and focused inward. His swarthy skin was pockmarked and full of blackheads. His lips were cracked and it was clear his nose had been broken more than once. His single eyebrow did not lie in any one direction, but had numerous scars dissecting it. What you could see of his matted hair was hidden by a ripped gray liripipe that was wrapped on top of his head like a beret. His voice was a rasping choir of devils.

"*Spostatevi, arriva il vaso da note pieno di escrementi!*" he shouted. Pan quickly translated it for Hansum, as, "*Get out of the way, here comes the chamber pot!*" Even though he gave a warning, it seemed like he bumped into Hansum on purpose. The brown, acrid excrement sloshed over the side of the container and barely missed him. The lout ran to the middle of the road and tossed the contents onto a big pile of horse dung. A neighbor across the road shouted from a second-story window.

"I'm still having trouble understanding what they're saying," Hansum said.

"Yeah, I don't understand a word!" Lincoln agreed.

"Me neither," Shamira added.

"Tap your temples," Arimus ordered. "Come, you know how."

As they tapped their temples, they instantly heard the neighbor shouting, "Hey, you stupid idiot! Why'd you throw that human crap and piss on those horse turds? They were beautiful horse turds. I was going to put it on my garden. Now I can't because you put that human crap on them."

Arimus then told the teens to tap again to turn it off. Hansum and the others then heard the pot-emptying oaf say, "*On, non datemi altri guai, femmina grassa e disgustosa. Getterò la merda della mia amante indove io vorrò.*" And when Arimus pointed at them to tap once more, they heard, "Oh, don't give me any trouble, you ugly, fat woman. I'll throw my mistress's merda where I want."

"Hey, who you calling a woman? I'm a man!" the fellow in the window said.

"A man? A man? I thought you were a woman with a smooth face like that."

"Are you blind as well as stupid? Can't you see the beard on my face?"

"That's a beard? My grandmother has more whiskers on her upper lip than you do on your whole stupid face."

The neighbor made a sign of disgust and left the window.

"Don't worry," the oaf laughed as he shouted, "there's more horses and merda in this world. Ha ha." Then he turned back to Arimus, smiling. His big yellow teeth, every one of them crooked or cracked, showed themselves proudly. "Father Aaron," he croaked, "thank Cristo you're here. The Master's been in an awful mood since he hasn't had wine the past month."

Arimus motioned to the boorish boy about something behind him and he stepped aside, just missing the contents of another chamber pot being tossed out the window by the man. It splattered on the street beside him. The ugly youth turned toward the thrower and bit his thumb in a gesture of insult.

"You even throw merda like a girl," he cried. "You missed."

The neighbor smiled and pointed to the lout's shoulder. He looked and saw a small piece of excrement stuck to his clothing. He flicked it off nonchalantly. The neighbor shook his head in disgust and turned away again. After a few moments, seeming satisfied that the neighbor wasn't returning with a reloaded pot, the oaf wiped his hand on his tunic, smelled his finger tips and turned back to the man he knew as Father Aaron.

Meanwhile, Hansum and the other teens had been tapping their temples, changing the dialogue in their heads back and forth from Earth Common to Italian. The oaf saw them tapping and made a face.

"I think these orphans you brought are stupido, Father. Even more than me." He tapped his own forehead and twisted his tongue. "I'm gonna be your boss!"

"Stop tapping your heads," Arimus said to the three from the future. "You look like cuckoo birds." Then he turned back to the oaf and put his hand on the lad's cleaner shoulder. "How goes it for you, Ugilino?" Ugilino smiled and grimaced at the same time. "And you say your master has been dispirited?"

"Well, let's see, Father. When you last seen him, he'd gone bankrupt. Then the money lenders and bailiffs took his house, all his animals and his equipment, except for what I could steal back or hide. He no longer has a cook, a maid, a journeyman or even an apprentice of experience. His wife talks to devils and angels. His daughter's useless in the house. We had to sneak from

Florence in the dead of night and travel to Verona like gypsies. We were robbed four times and I had to swallow the coins you gave us to hide them. I tell you, Father, if he did not have me, the devil would have him now."

"Ugilino, my son, we must give thanks to God for even these small blessings," Arimus said.

"Hey," the Master screamed as he bounded through the door. "You tell stories of your benefactor?" Agistino had a piece of firewood in his hand and swung it right at Ugilino's head. Ugilino ducked, but the lumber clipped the top of his crown. It knocked Ugilino's cap off and he collapsed onto the street. The Master continued to roar at him. "You stupido! You idiot!"

Blood spurted from a cut on Ugilino's scalp and the Master was wild-eyed and breathing like a beast. He beat Ugilino several more times on the back. Hansum and the other teens' eyes went wide with shock. Hansum had seen fake violence at History Camps, but this was real. He and the other two blanched at the sight of the blood.

"Peace, my son. Peace," Arimus said sternly, catching the big man's arm and holding it fast. "He is only answering what I asked. And you know I am familiar with your circumstances. I am your father confessor, your spiritual guide."

"I will confess my own weaknesses! I need not an imbecile to do it for me in front of the neighbors!"

Ugilino, on all fours, scrambled for his hat. He wisely crawled a few extra paces to be out of the Master's reach before getting back to his feet. The bloodied youth grinned through his pain and said, "Hey, that was a close one, Master. But is that any way to treat your future son?"

"Your blood mix with mine?" the Master boomed. "Never! I'll spill every drop of both on this avenue first!"

"Peace, peace, my son!" Arimus said again, continuing to hold Agistino back. "Ugilino, go to the town well and wash your wound. Wash it thoroughly, mind you. Then go to Urbe Market Grande. Seek out Signora Caterina Baroni, the herb merchant. Have her put some unguent on it. Tell her I sent you and will pay her when I come to the market later. Give your Master some hours to become his old, cheerful self, eh?" Ugilino held his cap in front of him, hesitating nervously. Small rivulets of blood ran down his thick brow and into his eyes. "Go, my son. Go." He turned and scurried off.

"I hate my life!" Master della Cappa said, still shaking with rage. "How have I come to this? Why is God punishing me?"

"Hush, my friend. Perhaps God, in his wisdom, is punishing you. Or perhaps not. Maybe it was just too much of the grape. What is important is to be faithful to Jesus and live each day as a staunch Christian. This is the only way out. The only way. Come, let us take my visit into your chambers. See, I have brought you three helpers for your salvation, just as I promised. I keep my promises. Now, you keep your promise to God and he will bless you. I'm sure of it."

"Maybe you're right," Agistino said. "Come, Holy Father. Let us retire to my new dung heap of a home and I'll give you the richest of my poor hospitality. Bring the orphans."

"Why do they keep calling us orphans?" Lincoln asked.

The Master stopped short, turned and glared at Lincoln.

"This one speaks when not spoken to? Does he not know that orphans must be obedient?"

"Why do you keep calling us orphans?" Lincoln asked plainly.

"I took charge of the children in Mantua," Arimus explained, "but they and their departed parents were from north of the Pyrenees originally. They do not yet know our language and customs as well as they might."

"Oh great. Now I have three more idiots to go with Ugilino." He turned and entered his hovel.

Chapter 4

Hansum had to bend his head to enter Master della Cappa's dingy, grey home. Although the dirt floor was covered in straw, like the History Camp home, this straw wasn't clean and fresh. There were old, moldy clumps of what had been straw, now turned mostly into mushy, furry clods, with bits of food and animal bones mixed in for good measure. The three large windows in the place were shuttered closed, cutting off all but a little sunlight, keeping the place in a dull twilight. Cobwebs hung low from the corners. Like at History Camp, the downstairs was one large room. There was a small area separated off in one corner by an old curtain. It was ripped and dust-covered, hanging like a ghostly shroud in the tomb of a forgotten corpse. While the History Camp ceiling was low, the ceiling here was lower and made of unmatched graying timbers and crooked logs, flattened on top to support an upper floor. Hansum could just miss hitting his head. Two large rusting grey pots lay in the similarly hued ash-filled hearth. There were steep, rickety stairs to the second level, and the banister was little more than a length of jagged limb wood. Master Agistino della Cappa turned to Arimus, his hound-dog eyes drooping. "See how the mighty master has fallen. Behold what I have brought my family to."

Arimus put his hand on Agistino's thick shoulder. "Fallen only to rise again. How can one appreciate joy if he does not know misery?"

"Then I shall be a connoisseur of joy when God deems to send me some," Agistino said, then added, "Rest yourself, Holy Father. I am glad you are here. I shall fetch my wife and daughter."

"Grazie, my son." Arimus sat at one of the benches by a table.

The Master climbed the stairs, each tread groaning under his weight.

"That was really weird," Lincoln said in a stage whisper.

"Weird? It was scary," Shamira added. "I've never seen that much blood, except for the chicken."

"Why did this Master get so mad at the ugly guy?" Hansum asked.

"Ugilino embarrassed his master in front of us," Arimus explained. "The Master was -- still is -- a prideful man. An apprentice must not do such things."

"If the Master is so mean to that ugly guy . . ." Shamira began to ask, but Arimus interrupted.

"Dear children, I know his countenance is much worn for one so young, but his name is Ugilino, not ugly."

"Well, why does this Ugilino stay around if the Master hits him?" Lincoln asked.

"Every dog needs a master. And no matter how you beat a dog, he comes back, craving attention, needing his home, his place. However, the sight of Ugilino continually reminds the Master of his own low social status. In truth, he hates himself more than he hates his mongrel."

"And Ugilino puts up with this abuse, why?" Shamira asked.

"He has had a roof over his head, for the most part, and his share of the food. And now that you three are here, the pack has grown and he senses his position elevated."

"What was that comment Ugilino made about becoming the Master's son?" Hansum asked.

"Yeah," Lincoln said. "That really turned the old guy 'rangie."

"Ah. Well, Ugilino has it in his head that one day he will marry the Master's daughter, Guilietta. He knows the story of how Agistino married his master's daughter, and dreams of history repeating itself."

"Well, for a mouth breather like Ugilino, his sights can't be set too high," Hansum snorted. "This daughter must be a real dog too."

A woman began shrieking from up the stairs, the words interspersed with howls. "Nooooooo! Noooooooooooo! How can I get oooout of bed? Aaieeeee! Leave me alooone!"

"The Holy Father is here. The one who financed our relocation. You must present yourself."

"I'm tiiirrrrrrrrrred!" the woman screeched.

"Wife, please . . ."

"Noooooooo! I caaaaaan't. Let me beeeeeeeee!" Something thumped loudly on the floor. Dust fell from the ceiling on the four below.

"Don't!" the Master shouted. "You'll break it!"

"I don't caaaaaaaaare! Leave me aloooooooone. You made me leave my home. You fired our servants. You ruined our daughter's chances. You've made me a beggar. A peasant. My clothes are a mess. I have no one to wash them! How shall we liiiiiiiiiiive? Why did I marry yooooooou?"

"I have arranged a kitchen girl for you," came the Master's voice, sounding as reasonable as possible. "She will wash your clothes. And I've new apprentices who have some grinding experience. Two years and we should be comfortable again."

"Two years! I must live in this dung heap for two years? Noooooooo!"

"Once it is cleaned it will not be so bad! We have the help now . . ."

"Noooooooooo!"

"You will do as I . . . "

"Noooooooooooooooooooooooooooooooooooooooooooooooooo!"

A larger crash. More falling dust and a sudden silence. Hansum looked over at the others. Arimus was sitting, relaxed and calm, while both Lincoln and Shamira were wide-eyed. Another female voice was heard from upstairs. This one was gentle.

"Hush mother. I beg you." And then the voice became too soft to make out. There were whispers and soothing tones. Then the creaking of a bed was heard, along with grunts and groans.

"Ohie! Ohie!" the first woman's voice complained. Then the banister shook as somebody took hold of it up top. A slipper appeared, followed by the tattered hem of a once-elegant dress. The stairs creaked as a second slipper came into view and, slowly, the mistress of the house appeared. Hansum squinted at the sight of her. Short and obese, Signora della Cappa had a jowly, pasty white face. Her mouth hung open and her eyes were dull and tired. Her dress was rumpled, slept in. Her large bosom was not so much buxom as fat. A too-tight bonnet, trimmed with sweat-yellowed lace, surrounded her face. Behind her was the Master, scowling more than ever as he was forced to wait for his ungainly wife to make her way down.

Another pair of leather slippers appeared, smaller and with a lighter touch upon the treads. No angry sounds of protest came from the stairs with these feet upon them. The dress took up much less volume as the body underneath it was slight. Both grace and balance showed in her movements. Her face, too, was surrounded by a bonnet. But this one, though not crisp and new, was unblemished, like the face it set off. Two large brown eyes sheltered under thin, crescent-shaped eyebrows, a fine nose and full lips, dark pink and natural.

Chapter 5

Hansum felt Lincoln elbow him. "Hey, who's the mouth breather now?" the younger teen teased. Hansum closed his mouth, but he didn't -- couldn't -- take his eyes off of the girl.

Arimus stood up and smiled.

"Signora della Cappa," he began, but she walked right by him and plopped down on the bench.

"My feet, they kill me," she complained. "They cause pain all the way up my legs. My back. Oh, my neck," she moaned.

"I'm glad your journey was made without harm to your family," Arimus continued.

"The journey, that's what did it. My body aches right to the bone. Because this fool of a husband. . ."

"Woman. . ." Agistino began loudly.

"Peace, my children," Arimus said. "We have all traveled far but are safe under one roof now, thanks be to God. And now, through God's good graces, all your fortunes will be made by your hands working together."

"You're right, Holy Father," Agistino said, putting his head down and crossing himself.

"And what of you, Mathtilda?" Arimus asked. "Will you honor God with your best intentions?" He waited for an answer, but it was not forthcoming. The Signora was staring at a point a few inches in front of her. "Mathtilda?" he repeated. After a moment she looked up to the ceiling.

"You're right, Michael," she said to the air. "I will tell her." She looked directly at Shamira. "Girl, bring some wine. Two cups. One for me and one for Michael."

The daughter came to her mother's side and spoke gently. "We have no wine, Mother. We've moved here only yesterday. We are not yet provisioned."

"Then watered wine only," the old lady said with a wave of her hand, like a grand Duchess.

"Who does she speak to?" Arimus enquired.

"Angels. Devils. Trees. The air." Agistino was angry, but contained himself.

"Holy Father," Guilietta said, "my mother thinks she speaks with the Archangel Michael."

"Don't be daft!" the mother exclaimed. "I do talk to him. He's right there, alighted on the ceiling. Aren't his silver wings beautiful?"

"How long has she been as this, Guilietta?" Arimus enquired.

"It got worse during our trip. Now she barely speaks but to her spirits."

"I'll send herbs to calm her," Arimus said.

"Grazie, Holy Father," thanked Guilietta.

"Si. Michael says he would like some herbs too," the Signora said. Then, looking back to the ceiling, added, "What? Si, some saffron. It's gold, like his beautiful halo."

Arimus clapped his hands loudly to break the room's gloomy spell. "So, family della Cappa, these are your new apprentices. Carmella, for the kitchen and home. And this is Romero. Romero Monticelli. And this is Maruccio."

"Those names again," Lincoln whined.

"Can't you call me Shamira?"

Hansum didn't say anything. He couldn't take his eyes off of Guilietta.

Arimus said, "No, these are your names now. Fine Christian names that the good people of Verona will recognize. Your other names, from north of the Pyrenees, will sound strange to the local ear. And this is your new home, children, where you will find shelter and sustenance. This is your new mistress, Signora della Cappa." The old woman continued staring at the ceiling, ignoring the teens. "Obey the Master and Signora as you would obey me and all will be well. This is Guilietta, their daughter."

"Hello," Guilietta said. She looked at Shamira. "You can teach me to cook and clean. I am ignorant of all these skills, but wish to learn."

"The blind leading the blind," Shamira said.

"Such a strange response, Holy Father," Guilietta said.

"I am sure you will be great friends."

The wife blurted out, "Friends with servants. Humph! Impossible."

"Hush, mother," Guilietta said. "These are orphans from far away. Their misfortune has been worse than ours. Let us be kind."

The words fell upon deaf ears. The Signora was already looking blankly at the ceiling. Arimus clapped his hands again. "The day is coming to an end. All must eat so tomorrow starts well."

"Our cupboards are almost bare," Master Agistino said, his voice quavering. "We have but the better part of a loaf of bread and an onion. And my pockets are even more empty."

Arimus reached into his robes and pulled out a bundle a bit larger than his hand. "The lord shall provide," he said. "A haunch of boiled pork."

The Master was so overcome he caught his breath. A look came upon his face that was a mixture of awe, happiness and shame. Guilietta's eyes opened wide and sparkled. The old woman's mind finally came back to the room. She quickly turned her head toward Arimus, or more correctly, toward the meat.

"Porco!" she blurted, her tongue popping out of her mouth and gesticulating around her lips.

"This and the bread should provide a meal to see you till tomorrow," Arimus said. "Then you may go to market." The smile evaporated from Master della Cappa's face and he once again looked dejected. "Not to worry, my brother," Arimus said. He put his hand in his cloak once more and brought out a little pouch. It jingled. "This should provision your home with food sufficient till your business may start bringing in coins."

The Master literally fell to his knees, took hold of Arimus's robe and sobbed. Guilietta hugged Arimus as well, thanking him over and over.

"Hush, my children. Enough," Arimus insisted. "Accept this gift, fold into your family these orphans, prosper all, and the money is well invested." He held the bag out to Agistino, but pulled it back slightly, adding, "But not for wine."

"Holy Father, the grape has not touched these lips since Florence," Agistino said crossing himself twice.

"It is true, Holy Father," Guilietta assured. "My father has been his old self since you sponsored our move. And I too have made a vow to learn the ways of the household so I can be his and my mother's support."

Arimus smiled at Guilietta, then at Agistino. "Into your hands I commend your family's and these orphans' fate. You were a prosperous tradesman before, and you shall be again." He put the pouch in the Master's large, red hand and closed his fingers around it. Agistino leaned forward, tears in his eyes. He kissed Arimus's hand and said a prayer. When he was done, Arimus helped him to his feet and added, "The day is waning. Make your meal and prepare for the evening."

Chapter 6

"Will you sup with us?" Master della Cappa asked.

"No, I shall lodge and feed with my brothers at San Zeno. But first I will to the market to get the herbs for your wife. I give you charge of the orphans, Agistino."

"Stop calling us orphans," Lincoln insisted.

The Master shot a look at Lincoln and warned, "You are now my charge. I tell you, do not speak until spoken to. This is the way to learn and this is the way of my house."

Lincoln opened his mouth wide to say something. Arimus put his hand on the youth's shoulder and said in Earth Common, "Remember, this place is not what you're used to. Take great care." Lincoln looked at Arimus belligerently but shut his mouth.

"I shall return," Arimus continued in Italian. "But until then, listen to the Master. Help each other. Say your prayers." The time-travelling History Camp counselor took a few steps toward the door. As he reached it, Master della Cappa ran to his friend and embraced him again. They kissed each other on the cheeks. Then Arimus looked once again at the assembly. "Blessings, my children. Keep well in God." Then he turned and left.

Hansum and the other two visitors from the future looked at each other unsurely. They watched the Master close the door and turn back to the room. He smiled at his daughter and jingled the little bag of coins.

"The Holy Father has once again provided us with the means for our family's revival."

"Father, I shall do what is necessary to improve our house's position. I will not be dependant."

"Daughter and helpmate, a father's dream is to dote and spoil his daughter, to make of her a useless, pretty prize to catch a rich man for her and the family. But I swear, a daughter of brains is more a boon than I would have ever thought. Almost a son."

"Thank you, Papa."

"Porco!" the Signora demanded.

The Master sighed. "Attend to your mother. Take her for a short walk while the place is cleaned and the meal prepared. It may calm her till Father Aaron returns with the precious herbs. But don't let her talk to the neighbors. Walk her in the back lane."

"Shouldn't I stay and help prepare the meal and clean?" Guilietta asked.

"No. I'll direct the new orphans . . ." He stopped when he saw Lincoln make a face at being called orphan again. "I'll direct our new . . . apprentices in their first duties. There will be cleaning and cooking enough over the next months and years."

Guilietta encouraged her ever-complaining mother to rise from the bench and follow her into the street.

"Master della Cappa," Hansum said, "perhaps I could help Guilietta with your wife. She looks a handful."

The Master glared at Hansum, waiting for Guilietta and the protesting Signora to leave the house. He raised a big finger to Hansum.

"Romero, is it? I see your moon face and eyes at the sight of my daughter. Take a care, orphan, for my daughter is my dynasty. If you ever talk to her about anything except your duties of the house, you will find yourself again looking for another position in this cold world," he said bluntly.

"I wish only to be her friend."

"A woman is a friend to a man as meat is to a meal." He continued addressing all the teenagers. "If you wish to eat and have lodgings, I have first tasks for you. Romero, go to a neighbor and borrow a flagon to start the fire. Then come back and help me scrape the pots. And we must have water. But we must boil all our water before using it. Who knows how long the rain barrel has been collecting filth and bird droppings. You, Maruccio, go to the barn where we met. There's a store of dry wood there. Bring both small and large limbs for making a fire. Then take this bucket and go to the barn and fetch water till the two pots in the fireplace are full. Carmella, clean up this place and make the table ready." He looked at all three children. "So? Is there more you need to know? Go!"

The two boys left the house and entered back into the stink and noise of the street.

"Maybe this place won't be as much fun as I thought," Lincoln began. "When Arimus comes back, I think I'll ask to go home."

"Psst. Young Masters, psst." The boys heard a tiny voice. It was Pan. He had popped a tiny version of his holographic head out from the material at Hansum's shoulder.

"Well, it's about time," Hansum said. "Have you been watching all this?"

"How could I not? This is extraordinary. Extraordinary!" A man on a donkey lumbered by. Pan disappeared back into his lamp at the top of Hansum's sleeve. When it was clear, he showed himself again and added, "Who would have thought such a turn of events would happen? Do you think this Arimus is aware I was on your person when he stole you away?"

"I'm not sure," Hansum replied, "but I'm glad you're here."

"What should we do?" Lincoln asked.

"Let us proceed as in the first History Camp. Do what you're asked and be civil for the most part. When we've amassed enough intelligence, we shall decide the best course of action. I shall continue to observe. We'll talk again when you go to bed."

"Okay," Hansum said as Pan disappeared in a puff.

"See ya, little guy," Lincoln said.

The two boys parted to do their chores. Hansum looked up and down the street to see which neighbor could be called upon for a light. He saw the man who had thrown the contents of a chamber pot at Ugilino. He was still sitting at the open second-storey window, his face all knotted, squinting as he worked intently on something in his lap. Beside him was a woman, doing the same. The man looked up and met Hansum's eyes. Hansum waved and the man looked suspiciously at him.

"Excuse me, Signor," Hansum called. "My master asked me to borrow a lit flagon to start our fire. We have just moved in."

The man and the woman exchanged wary glances. "You come from the same house as that fool who ruined my horse dung," the man said.

"Yes, I'm sorry about that. And you're right. He is a fool. My master beat him."

"We saw."

"But the rest of us are quite nice."

"Your mistress looks a bit cracked. We can hear her screams from here."

Hansum paused before he answered. "It would be wrong for me to say rude things about a lady, especially my Master's wife."

The man in the window smiled. "Come to the door. I'll a give you a coal."

He met the man and woman at the front door. "Buon giorno. My name is . . . Romero."

"Buon giorno, Romero. I am Bruno Satore and this is my wife, Nuca. Nuca said nothing and smiled an almost toothless smile.

"Buon giorno, Signora Satore. How are you today?"

Signora Satore smiled again and nodded a crooked nod. Most of her mouth was just gums. "My wife does not speak," Bruno said.

"Well, it's nice to meet you all the same," Hansum offered graciously.

"Please come in, Romero," Bruno said. "We'll get you a coal."

Hansum entered and saw that the main table in the Satores' home was covered with bolts of cloth, sharp blades, a wooden straight edge with markings and some partially completed garments. The Satores were tailors. Their home was very much like the della Cappas', but it was bright and well organized. They too had a straw-covered earth floor, but this straw was clean.

"Your home has been empty for some months," Bruno said. "A slovenly family lived there. Bad neighbors."

"It certainly still is messy," Hansum agreed. "I hope we will be better neighbors."

Nuca laughed at this comment. Her face crunched up and her laugh seemed more like the honking of a goose. Bruno smiled at her.

"My Nuca was such a beautiful girl." He cupped a hand lovingly on the side of her face. She snuggled into it. "Only a few months after we were married, many years ago, she got the fever. She survived, thanks to God, but her mind was not the same. The fever also burned her voice and almost all the power of her ears. And we could not have the blessings of children. But she's still my sweet girl." Bruno tweaked her cheek and followed it with a kiss. Nuca's lined, toothless face beamed.

"No ite. No ite," she croaked, and then she laughed.

"Si, she says that because she can't talk, we don't fight."

They all laughed. Hansum was amazed that, between the two of them, the Satores possessed less than five teeth, and the ones they had were lined with black. He turned his shoulder around so Pan could get a good view of everything.

Bruno lent Hansum a small ceramic cup to carry some embers in.

"Thank you very much. I better get back," Hansum said. "I guess we'll be seeing each other often. Nice to meet you both."

Chapter 7

When he got back home, the air in the house was dustier than ever. Shamira was using a straw broom to sweep off the table. She coughed as a cloud of dust came up at her.

Hansum tapped his temple. "This place is incredible," he said in Earth Common.

"Yeah, unbelievable," Shamira answered, blinking and rubbing her nose from the dust. "And filthy."

"Speak our language!" the Master shouted. "I want to know what you are saying at all times. No secrets in my house." Hansum tapped his temple again.

The Master was by the fireplace, kneeling over the big iron pot, scraping the insides with an old knife.

"Here is a coal, Master. I got it from the tailor across the street," Hansum said.

"Good. Maruccio has already brought some wood. He's getting water now. You can start the fire as soon as I'm finished this," the Master said, not looking up.

Hansum looked closely at what Agistino was doing. He was scraping the rust off of the surface of the iron vessel.

"Ah, iron oxide," Hansum observed quietly. "You're saving this for lens polish. Blush."

The Master stopped and looked Hansum in the eye. "The Holy Father spoke true," he said. "You do have some experience in lensmaking. Very good. By taking advantage of any resource about us, we can save the coins the Holy Father gave for things we can't provide with our own hands." The Master used a thin shim of wood as one would a dust pan and put the rust chips into a mortar bowl to be ground up for blush later.

Lincoln came in with his first pail of water. It was a wooden pail, built with staves, like a barrel, two iron rings holding them together.

"Coming through," Lincoln cried. "This thing's leakin' like there's no tomorrow!" He poured the water into the pot the Master had just finished scraping. It sloshed about and got the

Master wet. "Sorry 'bout that," Lincoln said, out of breath. "I ran but still lost almost half the water."

Master della Cappa looked like he wanted to be angry, but couldn't.

"You are a funny boy," he chuckled. "You may be entertaining to have around. When you finish, let the pail soak in the rain barrel. The wood will swell and stop leaking by tomorrow."

Lincoln's eyes widened. "Really? That's zippy." Because there was no counterpart in old Italian for the slang, it came out the same.

"Is that a curse word?" the Master scowled, raising his hand.

"No," Lincoln answered quickly.

"Good. Romero, start the fire," the Master ordered.

"Hey, I'm good at starting fires," Lincoln stated proudly.

"Sure. Go to it," Hansum said. "I'll get the water. Do you mind, Master?"

"As long as work gets done."

"Great," Lincoln said.

"Master, this curtain here is filthy. How about I use it to line the pail? It will get washed while I carry water and slow the dripping."

"Just be sure to shake as much dust as you can off first," Agistino said. "And bring more wood."

"The table and bench are swept," Shamira said, wiping her face with the back of her hand. "But this floor is filthy."

"We change the straw tomorrow," the Master said. "There is much to be done. But now that we have many hands, God willing, all will be well soon." He paused, seeming to mull over his plans out loud. "Yes, tomorrow we clean and provision the house. After that, we'll get to the business of making discs for the eyes. Yes."

Back by the barn, Hansum shook out the dusty curtain. He dunked it in the rain barrel, then wrung out the moisture and much of the dirt. He repeated the process several times and was folding the fabric to fit into the pail when Guilietta and her mother appeared. Hansum's trading jobs with Lincoln had gotten him what he wanted.

"I see you make a fine washer woman, Romero," Guilietta said.

Hansum, being the confident and good looking boy he was, had never been rattled by a woman's teasing, no matter what her age. But Guilietta was having a different effect on him. She looked him in the eye, but there was a modesty and vulnerability about her.

"Oh. I didn't see you."

"This much is obvious," she said.

The Signora stood by her daughter and looked back and forth between the two young people. Although addled, she was sharp on other levels. She tugged at her daughter's arm and began to walk.

"I want my porco!" Guilietta allowed herself to be pulled away, but smiled back at Hansum.

"The fire's only being lit," Hansum called. "It will be a while before things are ready."

The mother glared at her daughter as they walked.

"You both have looks within your eyes. Don't be a fool."

"Mother, not so loud. He'll hear."

"Who cares? He's an orphan."

"Hush!"

When Hansum returned to the house, the fire was going. Lincoln and the Master were finishing hanging the pot over the flames.

"The flue needs cleaning," the Master said. "Tomorrow I'll have you go on the roof, Maruccio. We will sweep it out."

"The roof? Clean the chimney?" Lincoln said, looking at his blackened hands. Hansum smiled as he saw a filthy Lincoln thinking deeply about something. "That could be dangerous."

The Master clapped the boy on the back and laughed.

"Life is dangerous, Maruccio," he said. Lincoln smiled weakly. His teeth shone out from his blackened face. "Such nice, white teeth," the Master added.

It took Hansum quite a few more trips to the rain barrel before the cauldron was full. His arms, although strong and muscled from sports and working out, were sore from real manual labor. He rubbed his tender biceps as he looked around the room. Shamira and Guilietta were rummaging through a trunk and bringing out wooden bowls and cups, a few cracked plates, some knifes, wooden spoons and a few ceramic jars. The Signora was sitting slumped on the bench, waiting impatiently. The Master had Lincoln skimming out the dirt from the water as it heated.

"Is this all we have to drink?" Lincoln asked.

"You eat and drink what is put on my table," the Master said with some severity.

The Master picked up the wrapped pork from where he had placed it by the fire to warm. He put it on a cracked ceramic plate. "Where's the bread?" he asked.

"I hid it in my room so the mice wouldn't get it," Guilietta said, her eyes glancing over at her mother. "I'll be right back."

"Carmella, put water from the cauldron in the cups for everyone," the Master ordered.

Shamira, not seeing a ladle, dipped each wooden cup in the boiling water, gingerly holding the edge of each and avoiding the floating scum that was left.

Chapter 8

The Master directed each person to their place at the table. He and his family on one side, the Signora in the middle; the teenagers on the other side, Shamira in the middle. When Guilietta returned and unwrapped the bread it was not like the nice, light-colored bread at History Camp. It was dark with a hard crust and spots of green mold. The Master took a blackened steel knife and cut into it. The bread fractured and bits sprayed everywhere. None of the della Cappas took notice, but each smiled broadly. After cutting the bread into uneven hunks and distributing a piece to each, the Master unwrapped the pork. Hansum couldn't believe what he was seeing, and looked at Lincoln and Shamira, who were both staring in horror. Dark veins and nerves ran throughout the white meat. It was sweaty from sitting next to the fire, and strings of yellow fat stretched, mucus-like, from the meat to the cloth as it was unwrapped. The della Cappas gave a joyful laugh.

"God bless the Holy Father," Guilietta said, crossing herself.

The Master crossed himself too. The Signora bobbed her head uncontrollably and drooled. Agistino took his iron knife and first cut the meat into thin slices and then cut them further into bite-sized pieces. He placed them into the bowls around the table. First into his wife and daughter's bowl, then his own. Then the bowl in front of Hansum, then the one in front of Shamira and Lincoln.

"We seem to be short a bowl or two," Lincoln said sarcastically.

"What? You think you are at the Podesta's palace?" the Master asked. "We share, like everybody from a poor, Christian home."

"You have your own bowl," Lincoln observed.

The Master's hand slammed down on the table.

"I am the Master. Shut your mouth."

"Romero's got his own bowl," Lincoln grumbled.

Just then the door to the house opened. A gargoyle of a head popped in. "Master, I have returned." It was Ugilino.

"The blessings just do not stop," Agistino muttered under his breath. "Your nose tell you when food is on the table?"

The fact that nothing heavier than an insult was thrown his way apparently told Ugilino the Master was his old self again. A moment later, he was sitting beside Hansum at the end of the table. He grabbed the hard bread in front of Hansum and broke it in half.

"Eh, porco! Magnifico! Grazie, Master."

"Thank the Holy Father when he returns. It was his gift."

"Oh, I saw him in the market," Ugilino said, biting off a chunk of the hard, dark bread. He continued to chew with his mouth wide open as he talked. "He gave me this satchel of herbs for the mistress." He tossed the bag toward Guilietta. "A tea to drink thrice a day," he said, looking at Guilietta with his big, decayed smile, bread now stuck between the broken teeth.

"Mama, they are the same herbs the Holy Father provided for you in Florence," she said cheerily.

"I don't like them," the Signora said. "They make me tired."

"They make you sane!" the Master shouted. "You'll take them!" He punctuated his command by banging his hand on the table again.

"I won't!" the mother whined.

"Mama," Guilietta said, touching her arm, "they didn't make you tired. They made you calm and the household was peaceful. We laughed and talked and all was well."

"For you, I'll take them. And to make the house be quiet," the mother said begrudgingly.

"When is Arimus . . . I mean, the Holy Father coming back?" Hansum asked.

"He's not," informed Ugilino, chewing on the bread. "He visits the brothers at San Zeno tonight and is off through the northern valleys in the morning. For a month, he said. Yes, he told me to tell the orphans that he would be gone for a month." Ugilino then grabbed the bowl that he and Hansum were obviously sharing. He took some of the slimy pork and, shoving it into his mouth, made ravenous eating noises.

The three teenagers stared at each other. Arimus was leaving them on their own -- in the fourteenth century -- for a month!

"But he said he was coming back," Lincoln said.

"Plans change," the Master said, chewing some pork and bread together.

"But..." Shamira started.

"Don't worry," the Master said reassuringly, "a month goes by fast."

"A month," Hansum repeated.

"We're screwed!" Lincoln meant to say, but the translator made a very obscene word come out of Lincoln's mouth. The Master's big fist crashed on the table.

"Don't you ever talk like that in my house or shop again!" he shouted. The children froze.

"Master, excuse Maruccio," Hansum said. "He didn't mean it as it sounds. And I think we shall be fine till the Father returns."

"All right then," Agistino said. He saw Ugilino hogging the food in his shared bowl. "Not so much! Romero has to eat too! And did you wash your filthy hands before you came to my table?"

Ugilino put some of the meat he had in his hand back in the bowl. With his mouth still full of food, he said, "When Signora Baroni put the salve on my head, she made me wash my hands, my arms, my face, and my head at the fountain. You did a good one on me, Master, hey, hey."

Agistino looked at Ugilino and pointed his knife at him.

"You keep what is of this house in this house. The neighbors don't need to know our business. It's bad for business."

"Yes, Master."

"Romero, eat!" the Master ordered.

Ugilino, crumbs falling from his lips, held the bowl up to Hansum and smiled. Hansum, confused at the etiquette, took the bowl, and just stared at its contents.

"Are none of you hungry?" Guilietta asked the three newcomers. She had been nibbling at both the bread and the pork, trying to share with her mother, who was ravenously shoving all the pork she could into her mouth.

"More porco!" she demanded of her husband.

"Eat your bread first, wife."

"I'll eat their pork if they don't," the Signora added.

"Now Mama, they're just being shy," Guilietta said. "They're not used to such grand meals, I'm sure. You'd better eat," she advised.

Lincoln's stomach growled again, so he knew he was getting hungry. Whatever magic might have been in that biscuit Arimus gave him was definitely wearing off. But when he looked down at the bowl he and Shamira were sharing, he thought, 'I dunno if I can eat this stuff.' He watched Shamira take a piece of the greasy pork in her fingers and bite off an edge. Then she nibbled on the hard, crunchy bread. She took a sip of the water with the bread still in her mouth, but made a face, like it scratched going down. Hansum was doing what Ugilino did, putting some of the pork on a piece of bread and popping it in his mouth. Lincoln braved the pork, nibbling a bit off the edge of one piece. He found that, being unspiced, the pork tasted neither bad nor good. But he found it hard to swallow, so he took a sip of his water. When he took the wooden cup away from his mouth, he saw the yellow fat from his lips floating at the top of his water. This repulsed him so much he gagged and spit the water in his mouth back into the cup, some of it coming through his nose. Ugilino laughed.

"Sorry," Lincoln said self-consciously, putting his cup down and snuffling. Then he put his hands in his lap, wiped them on his chausses and then his nose with his sleeve. He tried the bread. Since it was hard, he attacked it, his teeth breaking through the crust with a loud crunch. Crumbs flew and then Lincoln felt a bolt of pain sear through his upper palate.

"Owwww!" he cried, grabbing his mouth. When he looked at what had fallen into his hand, he not only saw bits of bread, but also a piece of his front tooth and a small piece of stone. He turned to Shamira and bared his teeth.

"Oh my God," she said with a look of horror on her face. "You've broken a tooth. He's broken a tooth," she repeated to the Master, shaking in her seat. "We've got to get him to a dentist."

The Master laughed. "Hey, that's a piece of stone from the miller's wheel," he said jovially. "Maybe you should take it back to him?" The della Cappas and Ugilino laughed.

Ugilino added, "Eh, now you start to look like me!" The della Cappas laughed again.

"He needs to see a dentist," Shamira repeated. "I'm serious." Since the word dentist wouldn't be invented for four hundred years, the translation program substituted the word physician.

"A doctor for a broken tooth? Ha!" the Master said, taking another bite of his bread and meat.

"When the tooth goes black," Ugilino added, "I'll pull it out with a pair of pliers for you." He stretched back the side of his mouth to show a gaping hole where a bicuspid had been. "That's what the Master did for me," he mumbled through his distorted pie-hole.

Lincoln looked into Ugilino's rotting mouth. He could see Hansum, who was sitting next to the ugly youth, cringe from its foul stench. Another streak of pain emitted from the tooth, shooting straight up through Lincoln's eye to the top of his head. He felt his face scrunch up with the pain and he pressed his hand hard over his mouth to suppress it. When he removed his hand, there was a bit of hot blood on his fingers. An unbidden sob emitted from Lincoln, followed by stinging tears.

"I want my Mama," Lincoln cried.

He looked around. Everyone had gone silent and was staring.

"I don't think this one will last very long," he heard the Master whisper to Ugilino.

"Master Lincoln, please," Pan whispered, *"please find the strength to control yourself. Your self- pity will do no good here."* Lincoln sat up and shook himself.

"You gonna be all right, man?" Hansum asked.

Lincoln didn't answer, but looked around the table again. Everyone was still staring, expressionless, except for Ugilino. He had a bit of a smile on his face. Lincoln glared at the oaf. He wanted to scream and argue, but held his tongue. He had seen the damage this Master della Cappa had done to Ugilino's scalp.

"The day, she gets dark," the Master finally said. "Everybody eat up."

Lincoln's stomach was telling him to eat, so he tried, but there was no joy in the food. He nibbled away, avoiding putting any pressure on his hurt tooth. Finally, he got his share of the food down. And while the mood of the Master's family and Ugilino appeared to lighten, Lincoln's mood, along with Shamira's and Hansum's, got heavier.

"Thank you, Holy Father," the Master said as he crossed himself at the end of the meal. "So, now we go to sleep with the angels. Ugilino, show the boys where to bed. Guilietta, show Carmella her cot in the corner. She must make sure the fire is going in the morning."

"Oh no, Papa," Guilietta said. "It is too filthy down here still. Carmella, you sleep with me tonight. This way we will be warm.

Tomorrow we all clean the house together and you will have your own nice bed after that."

"I am good at warming beds," Ugilino said.

The Master's cup flew through the air and hit Ugilino on the cheek. "You are good for warming barns!" Ugilino laughed until the Master said, "Now get out of here and take the boys with you!"

Chapter 9

"Si, Master," Ugilino said.

Hansum felt the filthy Ugilino pull at his tunic to signal him to get up and follow. Then he slapped Lincoln on the head to get him moving. When they stepped from the hovel into the dark, unlit streets of Verona, Ugilino's attitude turned as chilly as the night.

"Come on, orphans. I show you your beds," he said forcefully.

"Well, at least we have beds," Lincoln hissed.

"Idioto," Ugilino muttered.

"Where do we sleep then?" Hansum asked.

Ugilino just grunted and walked up the laneway. They came back to the barn with the tethered cow. It mooed nervously at their presence and stomped about in the mud. Ugilino pointed to the top of the barn.

"Another barn loft?" Hansum said.

"You were expecting the Podesta's palace?"

"Okay, now I'm getting pissed!" Lincoln said.

Lincoln felt Hansum clasp his arm. "Don't sweat it, man. Remember what we agreed. Be cool and play along."

"Play along? Play?" Lincoln said loudly. "This isn't play anymore. I'm hungry, I'm cold. I've got a friggin' broken tooth and now we have to sleep in a barn?"

Ugilino laughed. "Hey, he thinks he's a prince."

"And you shut up, man. I'm already sick of you!" Lincoln growled.

Lincoln barely saw it coming. Suddenly he felt the sharp crack of Ugilino's callused hand meet his cheekbone, hard. He felt himself tumble uncontrollably backwards, bouncing off the cow and then collapsing onto the muddy ground. Through blurred vision he saw the hooves of the cow almost stomp him.

"Hey!" Hansum shouted, coming to Lincoln's defense.

But Ugilino didn't look angry, he just held up his hands. "Calma, Romero. Calma. That was just to make the little one relax. He is too excited."

"You hit him on the head, Ugilino! How does that relax someone?"

"Well, look at him. He is quiet now. Hey, if I a counted how many times the Master quiets me like that, well, I couldn't count that high."

"Are you all right, man?" Hansum said, bending down to help Lincoln. "Can you stand?"

"I guess so." He stumbled to his feet with Hansum's help.

"Come on. Into the loft," Ugilino ordered. "It's almost too dark to see. Come." When the two didn't move, he repeated sternly, "Come!"

Hansum thought how in the twenty-fourth century there was always light when needed. But not here. As the boys entered the barn, their feet bumped into things on the floor. Some were hard, some were mushy. They came to the ladder and Ugilino was already half the way up it.

"One at a time," he warned. "It could break." A few seconds later, he called from the top, "Okay, come."

Hansum saw there was good reason for Ugilino's warning. The ladder's rungs were tied to the uprights with hemp twine, and most of the knots had become loose. Hansum went up, gingerly stepping on each rung, his natural physicality showing. Lincoln barely made it up. Each of his unsure steps caused the ladder to wobble more.

"Careful. Slowly," Hansum cautioned, then grabbed Lincoln's arm when he got to the top and guided him into the loft. Outside, the clouds parted and moonlight shone through the open hay-mow door. The loft was nothing more than the old thatched roof on boards over the barn. It was cramped. Piles of straw were everywhere. As Hansum's eyes accustomed themselves to the light, he thought he saw a black blur zip in the opening. There was a fluttering around his head and in his ears. Then it was gone.

"We sleep here," Ugilino announced.

"Here?" Lincoln asked incredulously. "There's no beds."

"I told you . . ."

"I know, this isn't the Podesta's palace," he said, glowering.

"Hey, he learns fast."

"Are there blankets?" Hansum asked.

"Wha?" Ugilino's face crinkled up into a questioning mass of wrinkles.

"You know, a cover to put over you when you sleep."

The ugly apprentice's face then broke out into a devilish smile. "Oh yes, Prince. I think we have one over here." He reached into the shadows and pulled out an old horse blanket. It was stiff and encrusted with the dried horse sweat, bird droppings, rain and mold. "This will keep you nice and snug. Eh, you two can share it."

"Where's the poe?" Lincoln asked. Ugilino's face wrinkled into another question mark. "The bathroom." Of course, there was no phrase for bathroom in the fourteenth century. That was about five hundred years away.

"Where do we take a, you know, a pee?" Lincoln said. Ugilino gave him a look that said he still didn't know what he meant. "Poop?" Lincoln said. More lines of confusion on Ugilino's face. Finally Lincoln did something that translated perfectly. He crouched down, screwed up his face and made a raspberry farting sound with his lips. Ugilino began to laugh.

"Oh, merda, merda! Merda and piss. Of course, my Princes. I shall get your royal commode." Ugilino went to the open hay-mow door and bent down. When he stood, he was holding an old ceramic chamber pot without a lid. He made a grand march of walking it back to the boys. "Here, your royal orphaned high-nesses, your royal bowl. Do you wish me to wipe your delicate behinds for you too?" He held it directly under their noses. It was full.

"What the . . ." Lincoln cried as the odoriferous fumes entered his nostrils.

"Oh, a thousand apologies, magnificent spawn of nobody-knows-who. The pot at this time does not have noble merda in it, only that of a peasant."

"Whose?" Lincoln asked, his eyes burning.

"Me. It is mine from last night and this morning. Oh, it was a magnificent evacuation."

"Don't you ever empty it?" Hansum asked, gagging.

"Of course." And with that, Ugilino went to the haymow door and threw the contents into the night. They heard a splash, followed by a long and miserable bovine cry.

The tension in the loft was high. Hansum could see Lincoln shaking with rage. He was about to explode. To keep the younger boy under control, Hansum took hold of his arm and squeezed tightly again.

"Ugilino," Hansum said to the ugly apprentice, "if we are to live together, it would be best we get along."

"To get along is easy. Just do what the Master and I say. And stay away from Guilietta. I saw the way you looked at her."

"It seems everyone did," Hansum said.

"Who?" Ugilino asked suspiciously. "The Master? You watch it! She's to be mine!"

"Well, that cut on your head says you're not first choice for a son-in-law either."

"The Master will come around. The Signora told me the story how her father did not like him at first. But after he saw what a good lensmaker he was and how he could be a good provider, he changed his mind."

"So you are a lensmaker?" Hansum asked.

"Not yet. But because I stole back one of the Master's lathes from the Jews who repossessed it, the Master promised he would teach me. So you see, I have a plan. And as my priest back in Florence said, a man without a plan will soon be with Satan. So I must get going."

"How's that?" Hansum enquired.

"To go out and get things."

"But it's night. The market's closed."

"Oh, my market is open all the time."

Hansum and Lincoln stared at each other, trying to think what Ugilino was referring to.

"Wait a moment," Hansum finally said incredulously. "You're going to steal things?" For twenty-fourth-century people, stealing was unknown, something only mentally ill people did. And there were very few of those.

"Of course," Ugilino laughed. "Since we only moved in I'll just roam the streets, learning what's where and whose it is. My only purchase will be if someone leaves me an easy bargain that can't be denied. Come with me, Romero. It will be fun." Ugilino smiled, his broken teeth glowing in the moonlight.

"No. No, I better stay here with Lin . . . with Maruccio. He doesn't look so good."

Ugilino's smile disappeared. "This one?" Ugilino said, jabbing his finger close to Lincoln's eye. "I agree with the Master. I don't think this one will last very long."

"I'm going to stay here," Hansum repeated.

Ugilino didn't look happy. He spit. "I will be back before morning." And with that, he was gone.

Chapter 10

Hansum and Lincoln looked around the loft. The haymow's opening used to have two working doors, but now one was lying on the floor and the other was hanging by a single leather hinge. Open to the elements, the temperature was dropping and the clouds began to cover the moon again. Another black flash passed the boys, leaving a flapping echo in their ears.

"History Camp is starting to sound pretty good," Lincoln said, shuddering.

The loft lit up from an artificial source. It was Pan, popping his head out of Hansum's shoulder. "Greetings, Young Masters," the head said. The image turned into a small whirlwind and a full-bodied, meter-high version of Pan landed, feet first, on the floor.

"So," Lincoln said, "at least we can see now."

"We better be careful," Hansum warned. "Your light could attract attention."

"Quite right, Young Master. Let's retire to yon corner where I spy a largish mound of straw. You both can ensconce yourselves within it and thus be somewhat insulated from the intemperate night air." Pan opened his eyes wide, turning them into flashlights. The boys sat in the straw and scooped it around them. Pan lounged back into the straw. "It's so nice to just kick back and relax with friends," the hologram said.

"Let's get serious here," Hansum said. "Do you really think Arimus has abandoned us here in the fourteenth century? That we're here by ourselves for a month?"

"It would appear so," Pan said.

"But why would they?" Hansum wondered. "The History Camp people, I mean."

"Impossible to really know," Pan answered. "But it's obviously a hard lesson they've planned."

"They planned to let us get beat up and broken?" Lincoln asked, feeling his broken tooth.

"I don't know, Young Master, but as you've experienced, these truly are not enactors who will restrain their actions. I think we have no choice but to continue fitting in and observing."

As if on cue, a blast of cold wind blew in through the open haymow door. Straw and straw dust blew into the boys' faces. They shivered and pulled their hats down over their ears. Then they huddled close for warmth. Pan lowered his personal light emanations and they listened in silence as rain beat down on the thatched roof.

"It's going to be a long night," Lincoln said, finally closing his eyes.

"I wonder what Charlene is doing right now..."

Chapter 11

Lincoln laughed out loud when he heard the unmistakable sound of a raspberry. He knew he was dreaming, and thought he was reliving last night's miming of going poe while crouching. Then the sound became more real. He opened his eyes and the dream disappeared. It was replaced by the sight of Ugilino relieving himself in a chamber pot about six feet from Lincoln's face.

"Buon giorno, my sleeping princes," Ugilino rasped cheerfully. "Oh, little Maruccio, such a sweet smile you had on your face." Lincoln's smile turned instantly to a frown. He tried to get up fast, but was stiff from sleeping in the cold. Hansum was in a similar state. Straw had gotten under their clothing and both scratched at themselves. Ugilino took a handful of straw and gave a perfunctory wipe at his nether regions. He then flicked it out the haymow door and pulled up his chausses. "Come on, orphans. Come eat before the Signora steals all your food."

Lincoln was trying to scratch in places he couldn't reach.

"I'm itching like there's no tomorrow!" he cried. The modern saying, translated into old Italian, sounded quite novel to Ugilino.

"You are very funny, Maruccio. I hope you don't die quick," he said going down the ladder. Hansum was ready to go, but Lincoln wasn't.

"Ugly might be able to poe in front of people, but I can't," Lincoln told Hansum. "You go ahead."

"Ah, finally my youngest apprentice arrives." Agistino della Cappa truly felt in a good mood this morning. Hope, that elusive impulse of late, seemed to be burning brightly in him. "Soon we shall have figs and olives for repast, and all will be well again," he said.

He looked at Lincoln, staring at the young man's head. Lincoln quickly pulled his liripipe off. Dust flew up and hair popped out in every direction. The table broke into gales of laughter.

"I saved this for you," Shamira giggled, putting their shared bowl in front of him. There was the same bread and pork as the night before, and a glass of warm water.

"We had wine in the morning at the last place," Lincoln said, still whistling whenever he said an *s*.

"He still thinks he is at the Podesta's palace," Ugilino joked.

"We do not have wine in this house," Guilietta whispered.

Lincoln thought for a second and looked at the Master.

"Oh, right."

"I want wine," the Signora squawked.

"Drink your tea, woman," the Master said without looking at her. "You too, Maruccio. Eat, eat." The youngest apprentice nibbled cautiously at the meat and especially the bread. Agistino smiled. "There's cleaning and preparation to get to when you're done." Then the Master said thoughtfully, "Verona may be just the place for us. We must get to know it and its people well. For nobody in this city makes discs for the eyes. They all come from Florence."

"I went for a walk last night and met people," Ugilino offered.

"You weren't out stealing again, were you?"Agistino said, glaring at the ugly apprentice. "I don't want this house to be known for that."

"Oh no, Master. In fact, I met a priest and helped him."

"What?"

"In the street. A Father Lurenzano. He was going to give the last rites to a little girl near the Arena. I went with him and helped."

"How could you help with last rites?"

"I carried the body back to his church, San Francesco al Corso. It was a long way outside the old city walls. That little girl got awful heavy. He even gave me something to eat before I came home."

It hadn't looked like the Signora was listening, but she piped up, "He's already eaten today. Give me his porco."

"Carrying the bambina was hard work," Ugilino insisted.

"Drink your tea, Mama," Guilietta urged.

"Did you see him reading his bible?" the Master asked. "Could he read easily?"

"Oh, he had a hard time, Master. Squinting and moving his head around." Ugilino held his palms out in front of him, and bobbed his head, as if he were trying to focus.

"Good, good. Maybe we can sell him some discs for the eyes."

"Oh, I get it, Master. That's very good," Ugilino said.

"We must get to know all the priests and all the merchants who can read and keep ledgers. That is how I became famous in Florence. So," the Master said, standing up and clapping his hands, "today we start our journey back to solvency. Girls, clean and put away the utensils. Ugilino, fix that shelf on the wall so the girls can put the kitchenware on it. New apprentices, gather up all the old straw and remove it from the house. Put it in a pile out front for now. Carmella, as the boys take away the straw, you sweep the floor. Then, boys, bring fresh straw from the barn. We will have a clean home today, for cleanliness is next to godliness."

Not long after that, the air was heavy with dust.

"Master, couldn't we open the shutters?" Shamira asked, coughing.

"Si, Father, it will be much cheerier that way," Guilietta said. "The sun is coming out and it looks like it will be a warm day."

The Master looked at his radiant daughter and a smile came to his lips.

"Perhaps we've been living in a dark place in our minds as well as our home. Si, let's open the shutters!"

Guilietta's mother awakened from her stupor. "No, don't let the sun in. Michael likes it dark. His halo and wings show up better."

"Quiet, woman," the Master said.

"The sun will make you feel better, Mistress," Hansum said, smiling.

The Signora seemed taken aback by this servant's audacity. She grabbed Guilietta's arm.

"Take me to my bed," she pleaded.

While Guilietta tended to her mother upstairs, work proceeded on the main floor.

"The landlord nailed the windows shut when the building became vacant," the Master said.

"I'll fix it," Ugilino said, grabbing the fireplace poker and banging the shutters with it. "This'll get the windows open quick."

"Idioto, stop!" the Master cursed. "You're breaking the frame!" He sent Ugilino upstairs to get an iron pry bar and hammer from the stash of precious tools hidden under his bed. Agistino methodically pulled the nails out one by one, extracting each carefully, and putting them in a neat pile for reuse later.

Once the floor had been cleared of the old straw, it was ready for its fresh layer. But when Master della Cappa went outside to tell Hansum and Lincoln to start bringing in the fresh straw, they were nowhere to be seen. The pile of dirty straw was no longer at the front of the house either.

"I told them to just throw that old straw all over the street," Ugilino tattled. "It's useless stuff, I said. The wind will blow it away. They've probably wasted time and took it back to the barn. Stupid orphans. Don't you worry, Master. I'll teach them good."

But when Agistino looked up the lane, he didn't see his workers by the barn. He did hear laughter and familiar voices across the street, behind the house where the tailors lived. He followed the sounds and found the teenagers standing with the tailor and his wife in a small, well tended vegetable garden. There was also a compost pile on which straw had obviously just been added.

"Look, Master," Ugilino tattled again, "those stupid orphans gave away our straw to the merda throwing tailor!"

The tailor looked up and greeted the Master. "Ah, buon giorno. You must be Master della Cappa. Welcome to Verona," he said extending his hand.

"Buon giorno," Agistino said cautiously. "Beautiful garden."

"Ah, si, si. My little garden gives me much joy. And food."

"Why are my apprentices and kitchen girl here? We're supposed to be cleaning house."

"Si, Master della Cappa, I enquired about the old straw from Romero. When they said it was to be thrown away, I offered my rot pile."

"Look, Master," Hansum said. "Master Satore and his wife, Nuca, traded us some vegetables from their garden in exchange for the hay."

"Oh no, Romero," Bruno corrected. "Not in trade. In Christian kindness and sharing. And we must bring in this crop before the frost. There's far too much to waste."

All three teens had their hands full of vegetables. There were beets, leeks, cabbage and turnips, even a few pears, cherries and pomegranates from nicely pruned trees. Agistino's mouth watered at the sight of the fresh vegetables.

"A few handfuls of vegetables for a big pile of straw? Humph!" Ugilino chided, still lobbying for favor.

"Shut up! We be nice to all our neighbors, and they be nice to us." The Master smiled courteously at the Satores.

"I think I had more future with a drunk master," Ugilino grumbled under his breath.

The Master's heavy hand met the back of Ugilino's head.

Chapter 12

Ugilino was still grumbling to himself as they crossed the road back to their house. His agitation increased as he saw the Master smiling broadly at the three orphans, their arms full of food. In the house, the Master actually laughed with joy as he said, "Children, put our neighbors' gifts on the table. Look, daughter. See the wonderful produce our neighbors shared with us."

Guilietta got up from tending the fire and smiled warmly at the sight. Lincoln and Shamira put what they had on the table. Hansum handed his bounty, several large pomegranates, to Guilietta.

"Oh, how wonderful, Father." Guilietta accepted the fruit from Hansum without meeting his gaze. But Ugilino noticed Guilietta's fingers tarry just a second more than necessary against Hansum's hand when they exchanged the red, seed-laden fruit.

He watched her hold the fruit to her face, drinking in its sweet scent. "We have not seen its like for some time."

"Girls, girls," a still enthusiastic Master said, "wash this food after you finish dusting and cleaning. Set up Carmella's sleep area and then go to the market. I will give you enough dinera to buy provisions to get us through a few days. This will give you time to learn the market and where to get the best bargains."

"Yes, father," Guilietta answered. "But perhaps Carmella and I could continue to share a bed. With winter coming it would make the nights warmer and she is teaching me to read."

The Master was amazed. "Read? Carmella, you know how to read?"

"Uh, Father Aaron taught me," Shamira answered.

Agistino crossed himself. Ugilino bit his lip and clenched his fists at this further bad luck.

"Romero and Ugilino," the Master continued, "take this canvas sheet and use it to carry fresh straw from the barn. Maruccio, as youngest, it's your job to make sure there is always firewood by the hearth. Now, go. Go, all of you."

Ugilino was silent all the way to the barn, but when they were in the barn's lower area, he spied something in the corner that could not escape his comment.

"Hey, what's the chamber pot doing down here?"

"I put it there," Lincoln answered.

"You?" Ugilino said with a scowl. He stepped toward the smaller boy, challenging him with his superior size.

"Yes!" Lincoln lisped without fear. "This way we don't have to watch each other crap. And we won't be throwing it out the window where we walk."

"Don't you tell me what to do . . ." Ugilino began, raising his hand. Ugilino felt Hansum's hand on his shoulder.

"Peace," Hansum said, smiling broadly in Ugilino's face. "It's a good idea, brother. Look at your boot. You just walked though your own merda. The Master would be some angry if you brought that into his clean house." Ugilino looked at the excrement sticking out from the sole of his ragged boot. But Ugilino felt reluctant to back away from a fight. He made an angry face, but Hansum spoke again. "Maruccio, go get the firewood as the Master asked." Lincoln quickly left, and Ugilino watched Hansum quickly climb the ladder, leaving him alone. From up in the loft, Hansum called down, "Ugilino, spread the canvas sheet on the floor. We can toss the straw on top of it."

"I . . . I was just going to say that," Ugilino said defensively.

From inside his little lamp, hidden in the shoulder of Hansum's tunic, Pan watched Hansum and Ugilino carry fresh straw to the house. After a half dozen loads, the A.I. whispered to Hansum, *"If Mistress Shamira is going to the market, it is best for me to be transferred to her. I could gather intelligence of the town."* Pan watched Hansum step up to Shamira and relay this to her. He saw Shamira nod, then speak to Hansum.

"Oh, Romero, there's a loose thread on your shoulder. Let me mend it before it opens wider." Pan saw Shamira looking straight at him as she undid the thread that held his brass lamp in Hansum's tunic. Now hidden in the dark of Shamira's closed hand, Pan heard the sound of her soft shoes on steps. The next thing the A.I. knew, he was in Guilietta's bedroom. Shamira began sewing him into the hem of her veil.

"Clever, young mistress," Pan whispered into her ear. *"Clever and cunning."* He saw Shamira smile.

When Shamira and Pan returned downstairs, Ugilino and Lincoln were bringing in a load of straw together.

"You keep telling me to stop letting hay fall, Ugilino," Lincoln complained, "but I'm not spilling it. You are."

"Don't talk back to me, orphan. I'm your boss," Ugilino said.

"And stop calling me orphan."

"That's what you are . . ."

The Master broke up the argument. "Peace! Both of you!"

"He's not listening to what I say, Master," Ugilino complained.

"He probably is," the Master answered, "but what you're saying probably doesn't make sense. You, Maruccio, don't argue with Ugilino. It gets you nowhere."

"See! The Master supports me," Ugilino said smugly.

Agistino shook his head.

"Romero, Ugilino, spread the straw and then go get one more load before we set up the workshop. Maruccio, take back this bowl to Master Satore and thank him for the coal. Then come right back. Girls, here are some coins. Off to the market with you both. We'll all be hungry in a few hours."

As they left the house, Lincoln muttered to Shamira, "I'm hungry now."

Chapter 13

Shamira liked Guilietta. She liked her sweet and earnest nature. And sleeping together in the old, creaky bed was like having a sister, something she had read of in books but never experienced. They had giggled the night away, combed each other's hair in the morning, and scrubbed themselves with hot water from the kitchen cauldron. Walking to the market, Guilietta carried a basket and a string bag, similar to what she had in the first History Camp. Shamira carried a heavy canvas bag.

"Do you know the way?" Shamira asked.

"Up this avenue to the old wall, turn right till we come to the gates, turn left through the big opening. The piazza should be right in front of us. The market's supposed to be around a big Roman arena."

Shamira remembered now. When she had visited Verona on that school trip, there was this amazing structure built over twenty-five hundred years before she was born, The Arena. She hadn't paid too much attention to the history lesson the guides had given. At the time she was a 'junior hard case in training', but even then her artistic mind couldn't help but notice the huge interlocking stones and arches of the load-bearing monument. She had sketched a bit of it on her encyclopedia slate board with a fine stylus. But when the tour guide commented positively on it, she quickly told the board to erase.

As the girls walked, they had to keep their eyes down to avoid stepping in the waste and filth that covered the street. Shamira was nervous during her first encounter with a medieval crowd. Aside from their outward grimy appearance, she also noticed the lack of teeth among them. Many looked totally defeated while others had a high energy and certain joie de vivre she had rarely experienced. And the smell. All Verona seemed to be swimming in an ocean of odor. And there were so many children, all running around like packs of marauding beasts, exuding an irresistible primal force.

As the girls reached the end of their street, the high red-brick city wall loomed above them. Looking both left and right, Shamira analyzed the perspective of the wall, its crenellated battlements and the occasional square brick tower. The structure was a mass of red that seemed to stretch out as far as the eye could see. Pan spoke into her ear.

"Walls and towers of this design do not exist anymore in modern Verona. Back in this time period, Verona was known as the city of forty-nine towers. In our time, most of them are gone, replaced in the sixteenth century with cannon-resistant fortifications."

"Freaky," Shamira commented out loud. Since, like *zippy*, the word didn't have a counterpart in ancient or modern Italian, it came out the same.

"Freaky? What does that mean?" Guilietta asked.

"Oh, just an expression from where I come from."

They turned right and walked till the sea of red brick finally ended at a large double-arched opening. This was the entrance to the old Roman part of the city. The arches were made of light-colored stone blocks. Between the two arches was a crest with the motif of a ladder carved into it. Above that, a sign, which Shamira read aloud: "Bra Public Square." She touched the sub-dermal button on her temple to see what would happen. While the scene stayed the same in her head, the writing changed to a language she didn't know. She read it phonetically. "Piazza Bra."

"It is such a blessing to be able to read and learn things quickly. You must be a geniuso."

'Was it only yesterday,' Shamira thought, 'when that word meant something different? Or was a thousand years ago? Or hence?'

"Carmella, you look deep in thought," Guilietta commented.

"Sorry," Shamira said. "I was just thinking about something."

They walked through the ornate gates and into Piazza Bra. It was a large open market with hundreds of stalls and a continual tumult of noise and movement. And in the background, looming up over everything, was the Arena.

"Freaky!" Guilietta exclaimed.

Chapter 14

The Master ran to the stairs and almost pulled his beard out when he saw what was happening. He was so exasperated, words wouldn't come out of his mouth. Lincoln and Hansum saw it too. Hansum was horrified. Lincoln began laughing uncontrollably.

"What a freak," he shouted.

"It's not funny!" Agistino said, finally finding words. Lincoln stopped laughing, but his eyes still bulged at the foolishness. Ugilino was on the stairs. He was carrying a huge heavy wooden object, all by himself. His face was obscured so he couldn't see where he was going. One foot was out in space, trying to find the next step.

"Stop Ugilino!" Agistino cried. "Wait! Wait for some help with that . . ."

CRASH!

Ugilino, along with the large object, tripped, stumbled and then tumbled down the stairs. He bounced off the railing and careened backwards, but never let go of his burden.

"My lathe!" the Master screamed.

"Aaaeee!" Ugilino cried. A moment later, he was lying on his back, the lathe on top of him.

"Are you all right?" Hansum asked, kneeling down beside the oaf.

"Idioto!" the Master shouted. "Romero, help me get this off of him. Careful."

The front of Ugilino's liripipe cap had come down over his eyes. As the Master pulled the hat away from his face, Ugilino smiled. "Hey, Master, I saved the day again! The lathe is unbroken."

"You wouldn't have to save the day if you hadn't ruined it in the first place. Imbecile! You, Maruccio, stop laughing. Help Romero move this thing. Take care. Take care with it. It is our living! Can you get up? Is your back broken? I can only hope."

"Oh, it takes more than some stairs to keep me down, eh Master? See, I'm still good as new." Ugilino moved in a way that showed he was sorer than he made out, but he didn't complain.

"Another blessing. Put it over there, boys. By the window. Okay now. Go upstairs and get the rest of the equipment. And don't drop anything."

The Master had stored the tools in a small loft and in the bedrooms for safe keeping. Inside the boxes were the tools and supplies which he and Ugilino were able to hide or steal back from creditors.

As the lathe was placed in the main room, Agistino thought how he'd prefer a separate building in which to ply his trade. Or at least a separate room. Unfortunately, this was not possible. It didn't take long to assemble all the supplies and tools. There wasn't much. Among a modest assortment of old tools and supplies, there were only fifty-seven blank discs and thirteen bone frames, two of which were broken. Not enough for a master who had six mouths to feed, plus his own. How was he going to get more supplies once they sold the first few spectacles? Who would give him credit, he wondered? Not the old suppliers in Venice or Florence. As the reality of his situation revisited him, so did an unwelcome impulse. He could feel a goblet of wine in his hand and taste the tart liquid running down his throat. Agistino quickly shook off this brief relapse, remembering the promises he made to his father confessor and friend, the gifts of money and his own hopes and dreams for the future.

The Master heard Lincoln say to Hansum, "This lathe doesn't look like the one in the other shop."

"Yes, but the principle's the same," Hansum responded. "Here's the lap, the spindle, the dop. See, that spot is where the lens has been attached."

"But it's black. Not milky, like the mastic."

The Master liked to hear the boys talking shop. It fed his thin veneer of hope.

"You know of mastic?" he asked.

"It's from a bush's tears," Lincoln answered quickly. "It only comes from one island."

"I see," the Master said, both surprised and appreciative. "Yes, you are right. At the end of my troubles in Florence, I couldn't afford mastic, so I used pitch and ash. God willing, one day soon we shall use only the best materials and make the finest discs for the eyes again."

"This machine looks different from the one we worked on," Hansum repeated.

"Yes, different shops, cities, craftsmen. We all have our little secrets and don't share them. But in the end it's all about shaping the glass. Do you think you can learn a new way? Work under a different master?"

"Sure," Hansum said. "Why couldn't we?" The Master scowled. Hansum repeated, "Why couldn't we, Master?"

"Some people can only learn to do a thing in one way. It's sometimes better to start again with someone who knows nothing."

"Like me, eh, Master?" Ugilino piped up.

"Hmmmph! You might be an exception."

"Yes, I am an exception!" Ugilino said proudly. "What's an exception, Master?"

Lincoln, Hansum and Agistino burst into laughter. Ugilino looked confused. The Master put his hand on the poor fellow's shoulder.

"Come, boys. I will create the first lens. You all watch, help a little, and then we go from there. Ugilino, heat up the pitch pot and put a lens blank on a stone, next to the coals to heat."

"Sure thing, Master. Uh, what's the pitch pot?"

"I'll get it, Master," hissed his youngest apprentice, picking up the small cauldron and steel rod to stir the coal bed.

"Hey!" Ugilino shouted.

"It's okay," the Master assured. He found Ugilino a task to keep him quiet and in one place. Sitting him on the floor, Agistino gave Ugilino three marked wooden bowls. The Master took a moment and ground three walnut-sized chunks of pumice into different grit sizes. He placed the appropriate one in each bowl to show Ugilino what he must imitate. "Okay Ugilino, now you work. Fill up each bowl to the coarseness of these samples."

Agistino then organized his tools and supplies close to the lathe before he began. This lathe looked more like a spinning wheel, though much sturdier. It consisted of a long bench with two splayed legs at one end and a third, single leg at the other. The end with the single leg was narrower, allowing the operator to straddle it. This way he faced a solid wooden flywheel mounted on two heavy wooden uprights at the wide end. The flywheel was grooved along its circumference and a loop of hemp cord ran around the wheel and onto the spindle assembly. The right hand of the operator turned a large curved-metal crank on the flywheel. The left hand did all the lens shaping.

Back in his element, and with a modicum of hope renewed in his heart, Agistino was a good and pleasant teacher. He praised Lincoln on setting the pitch pot in the coals. "Perfetto!" he commented upon seeing how Lincoln even tipped the pot forward to the front of the hearth. This way, the opening was easily accessed and not directly above the heat. Then he touched the glass blank Lincoln had set on a stone to be heated by proximity to the fire.

"Watch it, Master. It's ouchie!"

"Such a funny boy," the Master laughed. "Such odd sayings."

"These glass blanks aren't flat like at the last shop we were in," Hansum added. "They're partially shaped on one side."

Agistino smiled broadly again, and a feeling of pride and excitement came into his voice.

"Yes, this was my idea. I had a glass maker pour molten glass into a wooden mold the approximate shape of a lens. This way a lot less filing is needed." Then he put his finger to his lips and whispered, "My shop, my secrets. You don't share secrets, eh? But now that I'm gone from Florence, the glass maker probably makes them for everyone."

Agistino put on a pair of large, round spectacles, securing them to his face with two stained pieces of ribbon. Then he donned a leather cap with long tails that drooped over each ear. Thus attired, he took to his craft. He picked up a hot lens blank with a pair of tongs, scooped out a dollop of the heated pitch with a stick, spread it on the back of the blank and then carefully attached it to the dop. While it hardened, the Master inspected Ugilino's progress with the grit. "Hmmm. Not bad. Not bad at all. Look here. In the fine grit are a few large pieces. You must grind them all properly and not miss one." When the Master turned, he was surprised to find Lincoln holding all the files in his hand.

"Wonderful, Maruccio. You hold those till I need them. You are all earning your food today," he pronounced. "Now boys, watch and learn." As he took his place on the bench he said, "We make three strengths of lenses. We will make the one for old people first, the most strong. From this blank, I must file some glass first." He held out his hand to Lincoln. Without hesitation, Lincoln handed him the correct rasp. Agistino smiled and held it up to show the others. Then he began turning the wheel.

"There's no zip, zip, zip," Hansum observed to Lincoln.

"That's cause it's only movin' one way," Lincoln answered.

Master della Cappa brought the tool in contact with the blank. Glass chips flew, hitting the Master's glasses and face. He turned his head away and closed his eyes, letting the shards beat against the leather hood.

"Hey, you're workin' with your eyes closed," Lincoln commented, amazed.

"I can feel the curve," the Master said. "Now hush!" He continued with the file for the better part of a minute, until the glass was much reduced. When Agistino did venture to open his eyes, he was pleased to see his newest two apprentices staring intently at what he was doing. He took the finer file from Lincoln and repeated the process. Then he started with the bowls and grit.

Several of the bowls were wooden, not brass, but did the same thing. It took close to half an hour to complete the convex side of the lens and a similar time to finish the flat side.

"There. We have made one lens," the Master said, gently prying the lens off the dop. "Do you think you could make one, Romero?"

"Maybe not as well or as quickly as you, Master. But, yes."

"Okay then. You make the next lens."

"Hey," Ugilino shouted, "Master, that's not right! I'm the second boss. I should make the next lens!"

"Don't worry, Ugilino," Agistino said in a conciliatory fashion, "we'll teach you too. But these boys have a bit of experience. I want to see what they know."

"But I'm the older apprentice!"

"You're still the oldest, and ugliest. And I'm still the master! Do as I say!" he said testily.

"It's okay," Hansum said. "Ugilino can go first. I don't care."

Agistino became very angry, very quickly.

"Did you hear what I said? I want to see what you know." Hansum glanced at the scowling Ugilino. The Master raised his voice again. "Don't look at him. He does what he is told and so do you. I want to see what skills you have."

"Can Linc . . . I mean, can Maruccio help me?"

Chapter 15

Where Shamira found the market at the History Camp colorful and interesting, she found the real 1347 Veronian market place mind-boggling. It was filthy and unimaginably cruel in Shamira's eyes, but it was fascinating. The multitude of faces, the smells of the animals being made ready for sale, lumbering oxen and donkeys pulling carts, feces lying where it fell. There was the sound of haggling, vendors shouting about their wares and swarms of ragged children running wild, bumping into people. Guilietta pulled Shamira close.

"I must protect Papa's money," she said, patting the hidden bundle in her robes. "These children will steal it if we don't take care."

So they proceeded, arm in arm, into the heart of the market, both enthralled and intimidated by its vastness and variety. But above all the cacophony and tumult rose the still-stately ruins of the ancient Arena. It stood like a backdrop, visible from everywhere. Multi-tiered like all Roman arenas, many of its upper walls and pillars were missing.

Shamira felt many eyes fall upon her and Guilietta. Men winked or just stared. Some offered wares, others rude suggestions. They stopped at a vegetable stand and the proprietor took exception to Guilietta's comment about some beets he was trying to sell her. She looked him straight in the eye and said seriously, "Let's leave, Carmella. We'll buy our beets elsewhere." When they were back in the aisle, among the crowd, the girls began to giggle.

"*Take care, Mistress,*" Pan whispered. "*A ne'er-do-well approaches and he has his eye on you both.*"

"We are in danger," Shamira said out loud.

"Danger?" Guilietta gasped, pulling Shamira closer.

"*I see a short knife, half hidden in the sleeve of his cassock,*" Pan continued. "*I think he's a cut purse.*"

"A cut purse? A knife?" Shamira said.

"A knife?" Guilietta repeated, beginning to panic.

Shamira saw him, a walking pile of rags. His whole body was hidden beneath long robes, his face unrecognizable within the shadow of his cowl. Then she saw the hard shape of a rusted blade sticking out from one of the billowing sleeves. As the figure got close, it veered directly toward the girls. A boney hand reached out and grabbed Shamira by the arm. She looked down and saw its scaly, cracked skin, boney knuckles, filthy, long, broken nails, and the greatest oddity to Shamira's experience, a missing middle finger. Then out of the corner of her eye, in the slow motion which is panic, his other hand appeared, the one with the knife. It rose to cut the strap of the heavy canvas bag on Shamira's shoulder. She panicked and tried to turn and run, foolishly holding onto the empty sack. The robber pulled her back and the blade scraped her forearm, causing a streak of pain that her privileged flesh had never felt. She finally let go of the sack and screamed in terror. Then she no longer felt the clamp-like hold on her arm and fell to the ground. Guilietta was down by her side. Another strange man shouted after the pile of running rags.

"Run villain and let these girls be! Such preyers of young woman will be sent to where it's too late for prayers to do any good. You escape now, but the Lord shall pass judgment on you. Repent!" Shamira's savior was an old man, not much better dressed than the unsuccessful thief. He had a bulbous face and piercing eyes. His head was covered by a muslin cap, from which long, curly, salt and pepper locks escaped. He turned and smiled brightly at the two girls. "Buon giorno," he said doffing his scruffy cap. His hair sprung out. "Are you quite all right?"

"Yes, Signor," Guilietta said. "Thank . . ." and then she looked at Shamira's tearing eyes, and then down at her arm. "Carmella, you're cut!"

The man was down beside them in a flash, inspecting Shamira's wound. "The upper skin's been cut from the blow, but not through to the meat below." Then he reached inside his tunic and pulled out a miraculously clean cloth. He covered the wound with it. "You will be fine. It will only take a scance of time. Come child," he said to Guilietta, "Let us end your companion's communion with the cobblestones."

Shamira was quickly on her feet and dusted off.

"Kind Signor, you have done us a great service," Guilietta said to the man.

"Oh, a little excitement is all. Eh, I haven't seen you girls around here before."

"We're new to Verona, Signor. My name is Guilietta della Cappa. My family just moved here from Florence. This is Carmella, our kitchen girl. And you, Signor?"

"Geneto is what I'm called. So, signorinas, it's the first time in the market for you. That's why you look like two helpless chickens waiting to be plucked, hey, hey."

As the initial shock of the attack wore off, Shamira's arm began to throb. She winced. Geneto re-inspected the wound.

"The flow of the bleeding has much slowed its rate. Press the cloth and it will fully abate." A few tears dropped from Shamira's eyes.

"I need a doctor. And a dermal regenerator?"

"A physician for this? Pishaw!"

"And a what? Carmella, calm down," Guilietta said.

"Yes, calm is what is needed," Geneto said. "Come girls. I shall help you for a while and show you what's where and where's what, while Carmella nurses her little cut. So, say what needs bring you to the market and I'll direct you to your target."

Guilietta giggled. "We're looking for food to get the family and our apprentices through the day. And when we know the market, we shall provision the household properly tomorrow."

"Ah, a plan well thought out. So, where shall we start? How about the bread? There are many sellers to choose from, but let me take you to the one you can trust. It's a walk away, but it's the one for which you will always lust. Come, it's just by San Fermo."

As they began on their way through the market, Pan said in Shamira's ear, *"Young mistress, I know you are in distress, but calm yourself the best you can. There's no help to be had. It seems we really are on our own."*

Shamira sniffed, and then stood up straight, collecting herself.

They started at a bakery, which was a much busier and less friendly place than the one at History Camp, but still, it smelled wonderful. Guilietta went to buy the darker, cheaper bread, but Geneto stayed her hand.

"To be successful, sometimes one has to act successful," he said.

Shopping didn't take long with Geneto's help. Their last stop was at the herbalist stall of Signora Caterina Baroni. Caterina inspected Shamira's arm and put some herbal ointment on the wound. She laughed when she realized the girls were from the same house as Ugilino.

"How is that ugly, smelly boy?" she asked. "And how is the tea working for your mother?" Within a minute of the cream's application, Shamira's wound stopped throbbing and felt cool.

When the girls finished with Signora Baroni, they looked around and were surprised to find Geneto gone. When Guilietta asked the herb merchant where he lived, so they could thank him properly, she asked, "Who?"

Chapter 16

The Master was impressed that the first thing the boys did, before starting their own lens, was clean up the debris left from his work. Then they attached the new blank. They moved slowly, taking their time to get it properly centered. Hansum sat at the lathe nervously.

"I've not worked on a machine exactly like this before, Master. The one I worked on had a foot treadle."

"How strange," the Master said. Then he took off his leather cap and gave it to Hansum. "To protect you from the glass," he said.

Hansum started turning the wheel and, as it got up to speed, he tentatively put the file to the glass. Shards sprayed everywhere and Hansum fumbled about, the file skipping and bumping. Ugilino laughed and jeered at his mistakes.

"I'll get the knack of it, Master," Hansum said. "I'm used to having two hands to work with. Say, for this first time, can Maruccio turn the wheel so I can concentrate on grinding?" Agistino agreed. Lincoln began turning the wheel and the boys worked slowly and methodically, as a team, figuring things out step by step. The Master nodded, thinking to himself that if the boys weren't very good now, at least they seemed bright enough to learn.

He looked over at Ugilino, who had become quiet. The boy was watching his two adversaries closely, his mouth slackened and his eyes drooped. But Agistino smiled when he looked back at his new apprentices, and he sat back down and sipped contentedly on his water. He made a silent prayer in appreciation of his new helpers. When the boys got to the third bowl of grit, he saw Hansum inspect it carefully, making sure there were no large pieces hidden within the finer grit. Romero calmly asked the Master to re-inspect it with him. Together they found a few grains that should be expelled, ones that Ugilino missed. The Master looked up at Ugilino and shook his head. The ugly apprentice put his head down.

A bit later, when Agistino looked back at Ugilino, he seemed to be sitting on the floor and just staring. Not out the window, and not at anything in particular, but just down at the floor. When the front of the lens was almost finished, the Master saw Ugilino snoring quietly. He almost went over to kick him, out of habit, but then realized there was nothing he wanted the boy to do. So he just let his sleeping dog lie. Soon Hansum and Lincoln carefully removed the lens from the dop and offered it to him. He took it in his big hand and inspected the work. The boys stood expectantly, awaiting the verdict.

"Terrible!" the Master pronounced solemnly. "Two doing one job. You were slow. The lens is uneven. I could never sell it." The boys stood mute. The Master paused. "But you show promise," and he smiled. The boys laughed.

"You know," Lincoln said, "this place could be very interesting. In fact, it's . . ."

"Zippy," the Master finished. All three laughed.

Hansum thought how he found this place interesting too. And just as he thought it, the object of his interest walked into the house.

"Look who's here," Agistino said, still laughing. "Back from the market already?"

"Oh Papa, you've set your equipment up and got everybody working. How wonderful."

Just then Ugilino started to snore.

"Well, almost everyone," Lincoln said, at which all but Shamira laughed. She was holding her forearm.

"What's wrong, Sham . . . I mean, Carmella," Hansum asked.

"My arm's cut. Really bad!" she whined. "It's hurting again."

"Carmella was attacked by a man with a knife!" Guilietta told them.

"In broad daylight?" Agistino said. "In the middle of the market?"

"Stabbed?" Hansum exclaimed.

"With a knife?" Lincoln said, horrified.

"Let me look at it," Agistino demanded. Delicately, like he was working on a fine pair of spectacles, the Master's huge, dirty fingers unwrapped the bandage. He carefully separated the herbalist's poultice from the skin. The first thing the boys saw was the dark blobs of congealed blood staining the fabric. Hansum winced and Lincoln looked away. Neither boy had ever seen a wound like this. The worst injury Hansum had endured was a skinned knee or bloody nose, which were healed instantly by his A.I. Both boys had to look away.

"What is wrong with all of you?" the Master questioned. "It's only a small cut. It will be better in a week and you will hardly be able to see the scar in a year."

"A scar!" all three teens erupted at once.

"A year?" Shamira added, and she cried even harder.

"Did the thief get your goods? Or my money?" Agistino asked.

Guilietta began to tell him about Geneto's rescue and how he then took them shopping.

Meanwhile, Pan began whispering in Hansum's ear. He leaned over to Shamira, comforting her, but more importantly, to tell her Pan's message. Lincoln also leaned in to hear what was going on.

"Pan says your wound is not serious and to stop crying," Hansum said quietly. Lincoln nodded in agreement.

"That's easy for you two to say," Shamira said, pouting.

Lincoln bared his teeth at her, exposing his broken tooth.

"And Pan says we have to act happier around the della Cappas," Hansum continued, "and that we should all get together and have a meeting tonight."

Shamira pouted for a few more seconds, reflecting while Guilietta finished her story.

"And when Signora Baroni finished tending to Carmella's arm," Guilietta said, "we looked up and Signor Geneto was not there. It was most strange, Papa."

Chapter 17

"Yes, yes. Well, dinner will make everyone feel better," the Master assured. "Girls, prepare the meal. Set the food by the hearth as we're using the table. We will find another table later. Boys, finish the back of the lens." Just then Ugilino woke up, making a big fuss stretching and yawning. "So, look who wakes up when the food arrives. You, get off your ass and get the girls some firewood."

"That's Maruccio's job, Master," Ugilino complained.

"He's busy finishing a lens with Romero. Now move your ass. And what are you boys waiting for? Finish the lens. Daughter! Stop fawning over Carmella. Make dinner! Both of you!" And with that, Agistino had reestablished authority over his domain. He smiled as he sat down on the bench and surveyed his castle. Everyone was working. He especially liked the idea that he had a young man, maybe two, who seemed bright enough to learn to make lenses. He watched as Hansum had his face close to the spinning glass, rasp in hand, carefully grinding it. Then his eyes fell once again to the sorry store of blank lenses. Two knots formed, one on his forehead and one in his stomach. He pondered his options. Search Verona for a glass source? He didn't think there were any here. Order more from Florence or Murano? He still owed money in both places. Besides, his small purse of coins wouldn't stretch that far.

Agistino's deep thoughts were interrupted by a shrill "Aheeee!" this time from Hansum. Agistino looked up to see the boy spring from his bench and grab his face. "Ahhhh, my eye!" he screamed again. Agistino was to his feet instantly. He grabbed the boy's arms and pulled them away from his face.

"Do not rub your eye. DO NOT RUB YOUR EYE!" he shouted. "Daughter, the eye cup! Quickly!"

Guilietta mixed some salt and water in the small ceramic cup and rushed to her father. Agistino was forcing Hansum to bend forward. "Blink. Blink again. It's only a piece of glass in your eye."

"It hurts! It hurts," Hansum kept shouting, trying to pull away. But he could not get loose from the Master's strong hands.

"I'm going to let go of one of your arms," Agistino said. "You cannot reach for your eye with it. You could make it bleed. We must wash it out." But as soon as Agistino let the arm go, Hansum tried to reach his eye. He felt another vise-like grip on his arm.

"I've got him, Master," Ugilino said, back from getting wood.

They walked Hansum, bent over double, to the bench and lay him face down across it. Then the Master took his free hand and put his thumb and forefinger on the top and bottom of the injured eye. Pushing against the socket, he forced the eyelids open.

"Now, daughter." Guilietta was on her knees and looking under at Hansum. She held the cup of salt water tight against his eye. She nodded at her father. The Master said, "Turn him over slowly, Ugilino. Slowly, I said!"

'God, this hurts,' Hansum thought. He found himself turned over on his back, arched across the bench, still held down by the men and looking up with his one good eye. He saw Guilietta holding the cup against his face. The salty water had poured into his eye socket and surrounded the eye ball. The saline solution stung the delicate tissues.

"Try to blink again," he heard the Master say. "It will move the liquid around and loosen the glass." Hansum saw Guilietta looking intently back at him. She nodded her head slightly, to affirm what her father had said. Hansum blinked a few times. "Again,"

Agistino said. "Once more. Okay now. Turn him over again. This must be a big piece." Hansum was now back on his stomach looking down. "You must loosen the glass a little more. Blink. Blink! Take the cup away." As the cup was removed, a splash of salt water drained from his eye and onto the floor. "Romero, is it dislodged?"

"I can still feel it, but at the front of my eye."

"Daughter, see if you can clear it out. We'll hold him still."

Guilietta lay down on the straw and got her face under Hansum's. He looked down at her with his one good eye. Another drop of the salt water dripped from his face onto her lips. She smiled and the tip of her tongue came out to remove the liquid. Then she reached out slowly with both hands to try to clear the eye. He pulled back involuntarily, but was held tight from above.

"Don't worry, Romero," she said gently. "I've done this many times for Papa." She separated his eyelids again, pursed her lips and breathed slowly as she searched. "Carmella, hand me a clean bit of cloth rolled to a fine point," she said. Hansum was quiet now, watching Guilietta. "Ah, I see it," she said softly. Noticing he was watching her intently, she met his gaze and smiled. Then she slowly inserted the tiny cloth instrument. "I think that got it," she said quietly. "Let me look some more." The two stared into each other's eyes at close quarters, their four chaperones close by.

"And?" came the Master's impatient voice.

"We're done," Guilietta said, smiling. "He should rinse his eye again."

Up on his feet, the world was now moving slowly for Hansum. He could still feel his eye itching, but what he really wanted to continue looking at Guilietta. Far away in his consciousness, he heard the Master laughing and patting him on the back.

"Welcome to the lens-grinding business, my boy."

"I held him good, didn't I, Master?" Ugilino was saying.

As Guilietta walked away, Hansum saw her turn her head sideways, allowing him full view of her profile. Hansum also saw Shamira standing next to the object of his interest, staring at him, guessing what he was thinking. Shamira walked over to him, a smirk on her face.

"Romero's got a girlfriend, Romero's got a girlfriend," she teased, handing him the eye cup.

"Mistress Shamira," Pan whispered, *"let me check Master Hansum's eye. Stare into the crease where I am hiding, Master Hansum. Dear oh dear, an eye injury like this could be very dangerous. Look straight at me, yes, that's right. Now to your left, very good. Now to the right. Look to the right, Master Hansum."* But Hansum didn't look where Pan told him. He was staring at Guilietta.

"Wow," Shamira laughed. "She knows how to make you sit up and beg. She's my new hero."

Hansum gave Shamira a dirty look, then looked where Pan instructed.

"No real damage," Pan said. *"That was a close call, Master. You must be extremely careful. Lose your sight here and there's no helping you, period."*

"I've got to get back to cooking," Shamira said, and she, with Pan, walked away.

Hansum's eye started to itch again, so he closed it and lifted the glass.

"Put salt in it first," he heard a voice say. Hansum opened his eyes and Guilietta was standing right in front of him again, a pinch of salt between her slim fingers. He held out the cup and she put it in, stirring it with the end of a wooden spoon. "We must dissolve the salt well or it will hurt more than it needs to."

Chapter 18

There was a heavy banging at the door. Agistino got up and went to look out the open window. A big transport wagon, pulled by four large draft horses, had stopped in front of his house. One of the drivers was standing at the door.

"What?" the Master shouted.

"Signor Agistino della Cappa?" the driver inquired.

"Si?" the Master answered apprehensively.

"Master della Cappella? Lensmaker?"

"Si?" Agistino felt a tightness in his chest. Had his creditors followed him from Florence, he wondered? Were they about to have him arrested? "What do you want of me?" he demanded.

"Delivery from Florence."

Nervously, the Master opened the front door. The driver and his assistant took three large wooden crates from the wagon and put them at the house's threshold.

"What is all this?" Agistino asked. "I ordered nothing. I cannot pay you."

"There is no charge to you," the driver said, holding up some papers. "It was all arranged in Florence by . . . uh, let's see here . . . by a priest. Father Aaron."

"From the Holy Father? Bring them in. Bring them in," he said excitedly. "Boys, help them."

After the delivery men left, everybody stood staring at the crates. Agistino finally took the pry bar and opened one. Under the lid was a thick bed of protective bulrush stems. Under these were many small bundles of old cloth. The Master unwrapped one. A gasp escaped from his mouth.

"A lens blank!" He continued unwrapping blank lens after blank lens, each one giving him equal surprise.

"Look, Master," Hansum said. "On the paper the driver gave you, it says 'Manifest.' It is a list of what's in the crates."

"You can read it? You can read too?" he asked with astonishment, then crossed himself for the further blessing.

Hansum read out the inventory in the crates. "One thousand blank lenses . . ." The Master sucked in a huge breath and had to sit down. "Two hundred and fifty carved bone frames, one hundred and forty wire frames, seventy leather frames." A great sob came from the Master's breast and he crossed himself. "There's more," said Hansum. He read out that the delivery also contained five pounds of mastic, the same of iron oxide, three new brass finishing bowls, an assortment of rasps, files and finishing instruments. By the end of the list, the Master was on his knees, hands clasped together, his head bowed against the bench upon which he had been sitting. Gales of sobs roared from him.

"Down on your knees, children," he wailed. "Do you not see what this means? Give thanks! Oh my merciful God, oh wonderful benefactor, give thanks, give thanks, give thanks!" Agistino cried, awash in emotion. The huge man wiped his eyes with one hand and bade everyone to join him on their knees with the other. Both Ugilino and Guilietta got down immediately and buried their faces into praying hands, the others followed slowly.

"Grazie for your abundant blessings, Jesus," the Master cried to Heaven. "I know there is a place where you live for the saintly Father Aaron. Oh Jesus, he is a saint. Yes, God, that's it. Make him a saint, make him a saint," and he continued saying many Hail Marys under his breath.

"Master della Cappa..." Agistino heard Hansum say. He opened his tear-filled eyes to see his new apprentice holding a second piece of paper toward him. "There's a letter from Father Aaron." Agistino waved it away.

"I cannot read so well. Tell me what it says."

Everyone turned their expectant eyes to Hansum.

"It says, 'Dearest brother, Agistino. In faith I knew you would recover your health and vigor for life, so in faith I ordered and paid for these supplies before we left Florence. I pray you continue your good work and bring your family back to prosperity. In the love of God for man, I remain, your true friend, Father Aaron.'"

At the sound of these words, Agistino felt such a further rush of emotion that he flung himself prostrate onto the straw-covered floor. "Sweet Jesus," he cried out. "Father in Heaven, Holy Ghost, I swear to you, if I ever betray the Holy Father's faith in me, may you send an angel to strike me down and burn me alive! Grazie, Father Aaron. Grazie, Father Aaron. Grazie, grazie, grazie."

Guilietta came over to her father and helped him up. The Master sat back down on the bench and continued to sob.

"What's he blubbering on about now?" It was the Signora, awake and standing halfway down the stairs.

"The Holy Father sent us more supplies, Mama," Guilietta explained.

Another wail of emotion erupted from Agistino.

"Did he send more porco?"

Chapter 19

After his good cry and something to eat, Agistino felt a calm that he hadn't felt in a long time. In fact, as he looked over his household, he could see a similar contentment on everyone's faces, even the orphans. Since the eating table had been used for the business that morning, everyone ate where they could. All enjoyed the salty cured ham, the olives, the fruit, and of course, the white *pane*, the better quality bread that Guilietta had bought.

Lincoln took his turn on the back of the lens that he and Hansum had started. He wore the Master's spectacles to protect his eyes, so he had to stand very close to his work to see anything. Ugilino turned the flywheel, constantly asking if the speed was right, if he could have a turn with the rasp and if he should spin it the other way. Every minute or so he purposefully sped up the wheel and then howled with laughter when Lincoln complained.

"It is not a plaything," the Master bellowed several times. But inside he felt calm.

He began reviewing the list of his new supplies and making plans. Hansum sat with him, listening and offering a thought or two. Guilietta went upstairs to give the Signora a bath. She soon called downstairs and asked Shamira to add a real sponge to the next shopping list. The Master smiled, pleased that his women could now have some little luxuries. Still smiling, he sent Shamira upstairs to help his daughter.

Then Agistino stroked his chin with his forefinger and thumb, speaking half to Hansum, half to himself. "With this further gift from the Holy Father, we are at least two years advanced in building financial liquidity. Perhaps I must now rethink the approach to starting out." He smiled broadly as a thought began to take shape. "Maybe we could take some time setting up a proper shop now. Yes," he said, smiling. "Then the men and women won't be falling over under each other all day." He shot a glance upstairs, then winked at Hansum, knowing the intelligent youth knew exactly what he meant. He started explaining how they could convert the lower part of the barn to a workshop. It would take the better part of a week to put down several layers of gravel to stop it from being so muddy, remove the rotten wallboards and replace them with new wood, and add secure windows and doors. "There will be a great many other details, but if we can get the supplies and the workmen quickly, a week should suffice. You boys will work as laborers and learn much," he said with a self-satisfied smile. "Yes, a week. A week and then our new life begins."

For supper they finished the leftovers. As the sun set, Agistino told the three boys it was time to retire to the barn.

"Get to sleep right away," Agistino said. "I'll wake you when the sun comes up and we will be very busy till the Sabbath. And here," he said, reaching into the bottom of one of Father Aaron's trunks. "Take these." Relative luxury would be the boys' lot this night as Master della Cappa handed them three large wool blankets.

Chapter 20

Back in the loft, Hansum was wrapping himself in his new blanket, trying to ignore Ugilino's badgering.

"No, Ugilino, we can't go out. You heard what the Master said. We've got to get up early."

"If I say we go, we go!" Ugilino insisted. Hansum and Lincoln just ignored him and further settled into their little nests, now protected from the worst of the itchy straw by the blankets that Arimus had provided. Frustrated, Ugilino turned and slid down the ladder, leaving abruptly. As soon as Ugilino left, Pan came out, having been switched back to Hansum for the night.

"You two look rather relaxed for ones who have had teeth broken and eyes impaled," the hologram said. "And look where you're sleeping."

"Ah, it's not that bad," Hansum replied, lying dreamily in the hay.

"Yes," Lincoln added as he scratched an itch. "A sonic shower ain't everything."

"Holy Hygieia," Pan fretted. "Are the victims complying with their oppressors' desires? The fate and honor of all genies, indeed, of all Puckish pranksters and hard cases everywhere is at risk."

"Settle down, little guy, settle down," Hansum said, getting onto one elbow. "Pan, I've been thinking."

"Yes, Young Master?"

"The two lathes we've seen are very different. And this one is so awkward. Why do they make them like that?"

"It's not awkward to them. It's the latest technology. They don't know any different."

"Yes, well, can you show us a way to improve their design? To show Master della Cappa how to make a lathe that would really make him ahead of his time?"

"Hey, that's a zippy idea," Lincoln said.

"Indeed, indeed, you have been thinking, Young Master." Pan's eyes went wide with excitement. "It's ingenious, inspired . . . devious."

"Devious?"

"Yes, when History Camp officials from the future see us giving advanced technology to an ancient culture, they will come and stop us. You heard what Arimus said. Helping people from the past with advanced technology is against their time travel laws. It's ingenious. Well done, Master."

"That wasn't why I . . ."

"I shall find time over the next days to work with Shamira on this," Pan went on. "I shall instruct her to draw up plans for an advanced lathe. Not too advanced, but advanced enough to make a significant impact. Oh, I am so excited."

"But that's not . . ."

"Don't be modest, Master. You are a genius. A geniuso!"

"Pan!"

"Stop trying to argue with him," Lincoln advised. "Have you ever won an argument with an A.I.? The only way to shut them up is to go to sleep." He pulled his liripipe down over his ears and nestled down in the hay to sleep. "It's going to be an early day tomorrow. Pan, turn down your light."

When Pan heard Master della Cappa in the barnyard at dawn, he woke the boys so they would be up and ready when Agistino poked his head through the opening of the loft. They were standing there, smiling at him. He watched the Master chuckle appreciatively. They worked on the barn for a few hours before dinner, and Pan stayed with Hansum for the morning so he could observe the Master's plan.

"He seems to have a natural grasp of organizational flow," Pan whispered to Hansum. During a short break, Pan whispered again, *"Pass me over to Mistress Shamira when you can. I must go with her and Mistress Guilietta to the market, just to be safe."*

Later, at Piazza Bra, Pan saw that Shamira and Guilietta were up going to buy the same foods as they did on the previous visit.

"This will never do, mistress. People will become bored with the same diet. And besides, preparing a variety of foods can be very creative." Pan advised Shamira on what to buy, and at the house, told her how to cook varied and healthily balanced dishes which everyone would appreciate. Shamira found the ruse fun. The next morning Pan dictated a menu for the whole week.

"Carmella," Guilietta said, as she watched Shamira writing, "you are so clever and know so much. I am very happy to have you as my friend."

"I'm glad I have you as a friend too, Guil," Shamira said. "Come on. Let's get shopping. You carry the list and check it off."

"Well done, Mistress," Pan whispered. *"You are a good teacher."*

Included on the shopping list were a few extra cooking im-
plements: a new skillet, some wooden spoons and a grate with
short legs to be put over the fire. Then Shamira suggested they
buy some extra wooden bowls so everyone at the table would
have their own. Guilietta held her breath, frozen at the thought
of the extravagance.

Shamira smiled slyly as she said, "I'm sure Romero would appreciate not having to share his bowl with Ugilino." The two girls
giggled and agreed to do it. That night, Pan noticed the Master's
look when he saw the additional place settings. He said nothing,
except to meet his daughter's expectant eyes with a little nod of
approval.

"Hey, we are living like princes now," Ugilino said and he
nudged Hansum with his shoulder. "Now you can't steal my
share of the food anymore." Everyone laughed.

Chapter 21

Pan spent his time among the three teens, observing, advising and keeping an eye out for their safety. But he was also
curious.

"I find it fascinating, Young Masters," Pan said to the two
boys when nobody else was around, *"how you both seem to be so
cheery despite the odd circumstances you find yourselves in. Did
you ever work this hard physically back home?"*

"No way," Lincoln said. When Pan asked why, the answer was
"I dunno."

Hansum reflected for a few moments.

"Back home there was no real need for the individual to do
things," he said finally. "At least, it didn't appear so. But this,
this work is going to make a big difference to everybody in the
family."

"Yeah," Lincoln agreed. "And it's fun to work a bit and actually
see the results."

"Well, Young Masters, I am truly impressed," Pan whispered. *"In such a short time all the old, rotten planks have been pulled off the lower portion of the barn and you've piled it all up neatly for firewood."*

"Yeah, we can do anything!" Lincoln bragged. "We're supermen!"

"Can you imagine working like this for the rest of your lives?" Pan asked. This question caused the boys some pause.

"Hmmm. I guess you've got us there, Pan," Hansum said. "To be honest, maybe we're finding all this fun because we know it's *not* forever."

"Yeah," agreed Lincoln. "But after we go home, maybe Arimus could arrange it so we can come back and visit. It's actually kind of interesting."

Just then the Master called to the boys. He and Ugilino were coming down the lane with a big, heavy wheel barrow. It was piled with shovels and rakes with large wooden peg teeth. The Master said that now that the interior of the barn was exposed, the next task was to remove the worst of the muck and filth from the floor. It was to be replaced with layers of gravel to improve drainage. If the muck looked like decent soil or humus, they were to take it over to the Satores' garden. Pan chuckled inside his lamp as he watched Hansum and Lincoln struggle through the shoveling and how they could hardly move the wooden wheelbarrow when it was full.

"Okay, Superman," Pan whispered to Lincoln, *"make sure you keep your back straight and use your legs when you lift. If you hurt your back in this century, you could be injured for life."* And once, when Pan found Lincoln standing on a rickety box, trying to help lift a beam into place, he scolded him again. *"You don't want to break a bone in this century. An infection could kill if your inoculation implant expires."*

On the fourth and fifth days, the boys helped the carpenters the Master had hired replace the large barn door with a single entrance door and two shuttered windows on either side of it for light. It reminded the boys of the first workshop. A few stalls at the back were kept for when the Master could afford to buy some livestock.

On the sixth day, it was just finishing work. Pan stayed with Shamira to advise her on a good, nutritious meal. At dinner, he saw a very tired Lincoln drag himself into the house and lay his head on the table. He even chewed his bread with his eyes closed. Shamira and Hansum weren't much better. Ugilino laughed at them and looked very chipper.

"How can you be so happy when you work all day and are out all night?" Hansum asked.

"Good food!" Ugilino said smiling. "Grazie, Master."

"So boys," the Master continued, "we finish early today. Everyone has worked hard. Our new shop is finished, but empty. After we eat, all that's left is to put our equipment into the shop. Then tomorrow . . ." A groan elicited forth from the tired teenagers. The Master laughed. "Tomorrow is a day of rest! It is God's day! It is the Sabbath."

"Yeah!" they all cheered.

"Hooray for God!" Lincoln said weakly, his head still on the table.

"HEY!" the Master shouted.

But Lincoln could not raise his head, he was too tired. Without even opening his eyes he said, "Sorry, Master," and fell asleep.

Chapter 22

When Lincoln woke up sometime later, all was quiet. Everyone was gone from the table except for Shamira, who was sitting quietly, drawing. Also absent from the room were the spectacle-making supplies and equipment. Lincoln thought that the Master must have been in a good mood indeed to exempt him from the move and cleanup.

As Lincoln focused, he saw that Shamira kept looking up from her drawing to a small hologram suspended in the air in front of her. And standing on the table next to the drawing was Pan, reduced to about the size of a man's thumb.

"Where is everyone?" Lincoln asked quietly.

Shamira looked at him. "Oh, hi! The guys are at the shop. Guilietta and her mother are having a nap."

"What are you and the little guy doin'?"

"Drawing the design for a better lathe."

"Oh yeah," he yawned. "The one we talked about."

Pan turned to Lincoln and smiled. "Ah, like the daimon Hypnos returning from Erebos, my youngest master returns to the realm of the living."

Lincoln blinked and smiled weakly. He noticed his unfinished bowl of food had not been removed. He raised his head and leaned on his elbows, reached into the bowl and began to nibble.

"What type of lathe?" he asked.

"Observe, Master Lincoln," Pan said. He commanded the hologram to follow him across the table to Lincoln. Then, as he flicked his now-tiny wrist, his arm turned into a long, thin pointer. "You will no doubt notice how this design bears some resemblance to Master della Cappa's lathe, vis-à-vis the heavy flywheel. But we have introduced a foot pedal instead of the simple hand crank to make it move. This leaves both hands free for the shaping tools. Also, notice that instead of a birch pole, we have introduced a wooden extension rod, which is attached to both the pedal and the flywheel. At the end of the rod is U-shaped crank handle. As the pedal is depressed, the flywheel now spins in a continuous one-way motion." He moved the pointer in a circle and the three-dimensional image became animated. "This one-way motion of the flywheel produces efficiencies I am sure you can appreciate, given your experience thus far."

"Yeah, I can see that," Lincoln said. "But what I don't understand, little guy, is all this is kinda obvious. Why can't the Master figure out things like this for himself?"

"Ho ho, why not indeed, youthful lord. Obvious it is to you and me and anyone else who has lived in modernity. But remember, in the past changes happened slowly. Appreciate that every commonplace item which filled your life back home in the future was once a revolutionary idea. To wit, the example at hand: This seemingly simple foot pedal and flywheel, in combination with the articulated crank, was an invention not devised till around 1500. And it took Leonardo de Vinci, one of the greatest human thinkers ever, to conceive it. That's over one hundred and fifty years from the present time period. Seven generations of humans, in fact."

Shamira looked up from her drawing. She had just finished a detail and passed it over to Lincoln.

"This little design feature apparently doesn't get invented for five hundred years. It's a removable dop," she said. "This way one craftsman can work on multiple lenses, one after the other, without having, what did you call it, Pan? Machine down-time?"

"Yes, Mistress, exactly. An excellent drawing too, if I may say so. We shall make half a dozen removable dops for the machine. It will be known in the nineteenth and twentieth centuries as the assembly line process. All this should make the shop over two hundred percent more efficient."

"Now that I understand," Lincoln said.

"I shall have Hansum show Master della Cappa these drawings in a few days," Pan added.

"Hey, that's not fair?" Lincoln protested. "Why can't I, or Shamira?"

"This is a patriarchal society, Young Master. The older male should take the lead. You will be his trusty sidekick, and Shamira, his scribe. And me, the unseen, controlling hand, like Zeus, from high upon Mount Olympus."

"Well, I dunno . . ."

A creaking was heard from upstairs.

"Get me my pot, girl. My pot!" the Signora's voice whined. Pan pointed his wand at the hovering hologram and it disappeared. He nodded and the wand turned back into his hand.

"Mistress Shamira, put the drawings back in your portfolio. Master Lincoln, find Hansum and tell him that when we finish the plans in a few days, he must be ready to show them to the Master. Quickly! Be gone! We shall all confer tomorrow at our first opportunity." And with that, Pan disappeared in a whirling gust of holographic smoke, back into Shamira's veil.

As Lincoln exited the house, he looked up at the sun's position to see what time of day it was. He yawned, still feeling tired to his bones. As he put one wobbly foot in front of the other, making his way around puddles and animal droppings, two thoughts consumed him. One was the comfort of his straw and wool blanket, the other, the lathe design he had just seen. He was thinking about the procedures he would be responsible for, keeping the interchangeable dops loaded and turning them over.

Walking into the shop, Lincoln saw all the equipment, some new tables, the old lathe, the shaping tools, pots, all the supplies arranged neatly on hooks or shelves. Hansum was sitting on the lathe, as if he were operating it.

"Hey, you're awake. Finally," Hansum said.

"Yeah," Lincoln answered wearily. "Where's the Master and Ugly?"

"They went to some church to talk to a priest. I'm supposed to keep an eye on things. Make sure nobody breaks in before we get a proper lock. What you doin'?"

"Oh, I'm friggin' tired. I'm going up to sleep." He started up the ladder.

"How are Shamira and Pan doing?" Hansum enquired.

"Oh yeah. They're almost finished the design for the new lathe. We're going to show the Master in a few days. I was supposed to tell you."

"Was Guilietta there?"

"No. Your girlfriend was asleep with her mom."

"She's not my . . ."

"Yeah, yeah," Lincoln said, disappearing up into the loft.

Lincoln took the thick wool blanket down from where he had it airing, wrapped it around himself, and nestled into the straw pile. 'Thank God - I mean, thank goodness the Master said it's a day of rest tomorrow. I think I'll sleep all day."

Chapter 23

Brong, brong, brong. Dang, dang, dong.

Church bells from all over Verona rang out loudly in the back of Lincoln's sleeping mind. A diverse cacophony of chimes was integrated into another dream he was having. He was flying, soaring like a bird, high over Verona. But the dream ended abruptly with the Master's voice shouting.

"Everybody up. Time for church."

The bells were no longer part of his dream. They were real. Lincoln opened his eyes and saw the Master's head sticking up through the loft's opening in the floor. He was wearing a new pair of spectacles with a shiny red ribbon holding the frame on his head. His face also looked scrubbed. Lincoln blinked his eyes to try and clear up both his vision and his thinking. Was this the old master or the new one? Then Agistino smiled and a row of rotten teeth informed him of their owner.

"You boys, come to the house. Eat and then we go. If you're not there quick, no food."

Finally Lincoln got his bearings and realized he had not only slept all yesterday afternoon, but right through the night. Hansum was sleeping next to him. "I thought this was a day of rest," Lincoln said weakly.

The Master's eyes sharpened.

"We go to the church to give thanks. And rest. Now move your ass!" And he was gone.

Instead of being disobedient about getting out of bed, as in the past, the boys forced themselves up, no matter that they were sore and tired. They found Ugilino downstairs, squatting over the chamber pot in the corner of the shop.

"Do you ever sleep?" Hansum yawned.

"Yeah. Where do you go?" Lincoln asked.

"I go here and there. And sleep here, there." Ugilino said pulling up his pants without wiping.

"Don't forget to wash your hands before you sit next to me at the table," Lincoln said to Ugilino as they left the shop together.

They washed their hands and faces in the frosty water of the barn's rain barrel.

"Hey," Ugilino said devilishly. When the others looked, he pretended to wipe his hand on his rear end, then shouted, "Now I wipe my hands on both of you!" The other two screamed in mock horror and started running, Ugilino taking chase. As he touched one of them, it turned into a boisterous game of tag. When they reached the front door of the house, they stopped the horseplay, took off their hats and entered the house quietly, all smiling.

The smell in the house was wonderful. Under Pan's tutelage, Shamira and Guilietta had made rabbit pastry pie. Everyone, including the Signora, was in a good mood. Ugilino's eyes showed he was genuinely overcome with emotion.

"Master, Master, we are truly eating like princes," he said in a voice filled with awe and wonder.

After their special meal, Lincoln found himself part of a happy procession that was making its way to Church. The sun was just rising.

The Signora had been left at the house where Master della Cappa said she'd be happier and the Archangel Michael could perform a personal mass for her.

"Anyway," he said, "this first visit to church is as much for business as it is for our souls."

Lincoln saw how the townspeople stared at them. It seemed that Agistino was getting the effect he'd planned. They weren't dressed too badly, compared to many others. Guilietta was certainly pretty to look at, and it was obvious that Agistino, by his trailing entourage and bearing, was a craft-master of some success. And there were his spectacles. Most people in Verona had never seen them before. Lincoln was amused by how many onlookers went gape-mouthed or just pointed at them. The Master nodded to most and bowed to a few of the better-dressed citizens. Agistino had told Lincoln, while they were working on the shop, that the discs for the eyes had become popular, not only for their utility, but also as a status symbol. People walked around town wearing them even when they didn't need them.

Master della Cappa's strategy was to play this phenomenon to the hilt.

"What Church are we going to?" Hansum asked Ugilino.

"San Zeno," Ugilino answered. "And I think you will all see a surprise there."

"What surprise?"

"Oh, if I tell you, it won't be a surprise." And with that, Ugilino made a little pantomime of sewing up his lips and did his best to look mysterious.

Lincoln and Shamira were also receiving a guided tour of the city. With Pan's little brass lamp sewn into the hem of Shamira's veil, the imp could see where they were. He gave the two a running commentary.

"According to historical records, this is a main road called Corso del Palio. Southward it leads to one of the city's seven gates. You can see it in the distance if you look to the left. It is that larger tower with a wooden roof. If you turn your attention up the road to the right, or north, the road leads to the oldest part of Verona. You can see, not far off, the spires and flags of Castlevecchio. The older section of Verona is ringed, not only by the wall you are seeing, but also by the winding Adige River. In the early part of the fourteenth century, about thirty thousand souls lived here. That's a very large city for this period. Then again, in our twenty-fourth century, it would be among the largest cities on the planet."

They crossed Corso del Palio and continued on a narrower, unpaved sidestreet. There was a mix of row homes right on the street, and also several free-standing houses in farm fields, similar to the first History Camp. They then came to the old, inner city wall and turned left. After a while, a tower came into view. Lincoln stretched his neck up at the structure.

"Hey, I saw that tower in a dream I had last night," he said to Shamira.

"I believe that is the bell tower of San Zeno." Pan continued. *"It is seventy-two meters high and is on the spot of an old monastery. In fact, an interesting fact about the church proper is that it is actually a church built upon a church that was built, yet again, upon an original smaller church. And the original church, now*

well below ground, is the crypt of Saint Zeno, the church's patron saint and the first Bishop of Verona." A short time later, both the church and bell tower of San Zeno loomed over them.

"I remember seeing this church and tower," Shamira said, "But it was old and worn. But this is amazing. Everything is so brightly painted."

"Yeah," Hansum agreed, in Earth Common. "It's really different."

"Wow," Lincoln added. "San Zeno is zippy!"

They were also awed by the diverse population of the church-goers. The gangly workers, the tiny widows in black, the sharp-eyed, dull, hopeful, hungry, and again the children. So many children, some quietly in tow, but there were always a few breaking away from the herd and running wild in the square. Then, as they got up close to the church, they noticed the church carvings.

"One of the things San Zeno is known for, Young Master and Mistress," Pan said, *"are the carvings on the front of the church. The panels on either side of the great doors are over ten meters high. Eighteen panels depict scenes from the bible. And above the door, note the great rose window."*

"It looks like a wheel," Lincoln observed.

"Very good, Young Master. The window is called the Wheel of Fortune, with twelve spokes and window panes. And see the human figures on it. Some standing, some falling, one hanging on for dear life."

"Oh yeah. Hey, look, Sham." Lincoln giggled at the humorous carvings.

But Shamira didn't answer. Her artistic eyes seemed to be looking everywhere, letting the visual flood wash over her.

As they neared the church, they melted into the throng, a river of worshippers flowing into the cavernous building.

"Hey, there's dragons," Lincoln laughed as they approached the open doors, "and monsters. Everywhere." Gargoyles, elves, imps and dragons hovered above the crowd from on top of columns and out from keystones. More dragons were carved in the entrance stairs' banisters. As they walked up the stairs, the crowd passed between two huge carved lions, their growls frozen in red sandstone. And over it all, centered in the casing of the door, welcoming all the pilgrims to worship, was the brightly painted, eighth-century statue of Saint Zeno. And below him, the famous bronze doors of San Zeno.

"Look how these huge wooden doors are decorated with forty-eight primitive square bronze plate bas reliefs. They depict events and tales from the life Saint Zeno."

The house of della Cappa now crossed the threshold of the church. As impressed as Lincoln and the others were by the craftsmanship of San Zeno's outside, it was instantly trumped by the opulent grandeur, the overpowering gilded and tiled sumptuousness of the building's interior. The sheer internal volume and multitude of details dwarfed the group, showing how the designers were successful in their intention to say to the visitor, 'You are tiny, God and the Church are great.'

"Wow!" Lincoln said.

"What happened to zippy?" Shamira asked, equally overwhelmed at the artistic and engineering diversity.

"Zippy just don't cut it," he answered, still gawking at everything.

"The ceiling is said to imitate the construction of a ship's keel, but upside down," Pan continued. *"The complex and intersecting arches of the ceiling are covered with intricate mosaic ceramics, and every small area that isn't mosaic is covered by richly painted religious frescos. The length of the nave's roof is supported on either side by a double phalanx of massive columns carved from polished peach and tan marble. The columns support arches which, in turn, hold up the vaulted ceiling and roof. These towering walls are constructed with alternating courses of brick, limestone and more marble."*

Lincoln noticed that two thirds the way down the church's length, it was separated into upper and lower floors. "Where do those steps go?" he asked quietly.

"The stairs going down is where the original, smaller church is. The steps up are where the richer citizens and nobles sit during services. The heavy banister along the top floor is called the

ambo." The ambo ran between the two heavy ascending marble stairs at each side of the church.

"The rich people sit up there while we stand down here?" Lincoln asked. The Master looked over at the boy, scowling and putting a finger to his lips. Lincoln smiled at him.

"Yes, that is the way it is," Pan confirmed.*"Below this section is the original church, now the crypt of Saint Zeno. Marble steps, the whole width of the nave, take a visitor under one of five arches that support the ambo and floor. The under part is only about twenty feet high and its ceiling is supported by many Corinthian columns. The crypt has many parts, but the main one is the resting place of the Saint Zeno relics, protected behind an ornate wrought-iron gate."*

"Hey, Saint Zeno's bones are down those stairs," Lincoln said excitedly to Hansum.

The Master scowled, then quickly smiled and nodded toward a well-dressed person whom he caught staring at his discs for the eyes. Lincoln tried to make a funny face at Hansum, but the older boy had his gaze set on Guilietta.

'Girls!' thought Lincoln disdainfully, and went back to looking around the church. There was a constant hum of gossiping, whispering, laughing, babies and children squawking. People were lighting candles or lying prostrate on the floor in front of the stations of the cross.

"Wow!" Lincoln repeated to himself. Then his gaze went over to Hansum and Ugilino. Hansum nonchalantly moved next to Guilietta, ostensibly to get a better view of something in the church. Of course, Ugilino had to follow, bumping Hansum out of the way and pretending to squint at whatever had caught his competitor's eye. Guilietta, ignoring the boys obvious and clumsy attention, stepped away from them and took Shamira's arm.

Then something in the crowd really did catch Ugilino's eye. He began waving frantically and jumping up and down, trying to get someone's attention. It was a priest, coming down the stairs, fighting like a salmon swimming upstream against the crowd. Ugilino waved a second time, this time whistling through his teeth. Before he finished the shrill note, the Master's hand had slapped him on the top of the head. The priest saw Ugilino and waved back. Lincoln was surprised to see that this priest was wearing discs for the eyes, just like the Master. The priest elbowed his way through the crowd to the della Cappas.

"Eh, see what I told you," an excited Ugilino said to Hansum. "A surprise. It's the priest I carried the dead bambino for. I've visited his church many times since."

"You've been sleeping here at San Zeno?" Hansum asked.

"No, Father Lurenzano lives at a little church just outside the city walls. He helps the big priest here sometimes. Hey, how ya doin', Padre?" Ugilino said as the priest got to them. He was perhaps in his early thirties.

"Buon giorno, Ugilino, my son. Master della Cappa..."

Chapter 24

Hansum watched Agistino make a big show of shaking the priest's hand exuberantly.

"Father Lurenzano, this is my daughter, Guilietta." The priest looked at Guilietta and Hansum saw his eyes go wide.

"Buon giorno, Signorina," Lurenzano said. "Welcome to Verona and to church. Do you find Verona to your liking? Do you have a father confessor yet?" At this he smiled broadly, showing a black front tooth.

"Grazie for your welcome, Father Lurenzano. This is a wonderful church you have here. Yes, I am finding Verona much to my liking. And I do have a father confessor. Father Aaron has been guide to my faith since I was a little girl."

"I've not heard of Father Aaron. Is he in Florence still?"

"No, he is itinerant," Guilietta said with a little laugh.

"An itinerant priest is your father confessor?"

"Well, that's how he describes himself," Guilietta laughed again. "Actually, I believe he travels and confers with many churches in different cities. He is a scholar. I think he has even been an advisor to His Holiness, the Pope."

Hansum took a half step forward. "Father Aaron is a very interesting fellow," he interjected.

Instantly, Hansum felt Agistino's hand on his chest, pushing him back.

"Romero, what are you doing? Speak only when you are spoken to," Agistino rebuked. Then he smiled at the priest. "Yes, Father Aaron is my good friend of many years."

"A scholar to His Holiness," the young priest repeated. "Well, one cannot compete with that. However, as I have agreed to introduce your father to all the priests in the city, I shall be around your home now and again. If you are in need of a confessional, I am at your service, Signorina."

"That is most generous of you," Agistino said as Guilietta curtsied.

Suddenly the church's congregants became quiet. As one, the crowd looked to a side entrance of the church. A procession of important-looking people entered. Father Lurenzano became excited.

"It's the Podesta della Scalla. He is at church here today. I must attend. Peace be with you," he said, giving the sign of the blessing quickly as he left.

"And also with you," Guilietta, Agistino and Ugilino replied together.

The entire church watched as the Podesta and his entourage ceremoniously climbed the steps to the upper gallery. It must have been a surprise visit because priests were flocking from all sides of the church, pushing their way through the crowds. By the time the nobleman was at the top of the stairs, an older clergyman with fine silk and gold vestments was seen running to greet him too.

"Look at the Bishop!" Ugilino cried. And to the surprise and delight of Agistino, the Bishop of San Zeno was also wearing discs for the eyes.

Master della Cappa became very excited. He shook Guilietta's shoulder. "See, daughter? Our place in this city is assured."

"I did good, eh, Master?" Ugilino shouted, his face red with excitement.

"Buon, my boy, buon. Maybe you aren't useless after all."

Master della Cappa prayed harder and louder than he ever prayed before. He crossed himself with great exaggeration, kneeled with embellished humility, stood, knelt again, said "amen," all with a great fervor. And every time he looked up and saw the Bishop standing there, in front of almost a thousand worshipers wearing his spectacles, he renewed his vigor. He could hear many people whispering, questioning the object on the Bishop's face. Many were also pointing over to him. At one point in the service, Father Lurenzano stepped up to the altar to assist the Bishop, still wearing his spectacles. The Bishop whispered something to the younger priest and Father Lurenzano untied the ribbon on the Bishop's spectacles. Agistino held his breath. Perhaps he didn't like them, Agistino worried. But then the Bishop took the spectacles and read while holding them in front of the large bible. And when he looked up and began to orate, he held his hands outstretched, pointing and showing them off better than before.

"This is even better," Agistino whispered to Guilietta loudly. "He shows what they are used for."

Ugilino seemed not to be able to contain himself. "Thank Cristo!" he blurted out, and instantly found the Master's hand over his mouth. But the Master didn't look angry.

At the end of the service, Master della Cappa became the center of attention. He chatted up anyone who looked like they might have five soldi to part with, and by the time the church crowd thinned, many people had directions to the della Cappa shop. Father Lurenzano came running up to them, all smiles. He stood right next to Hansum and Shamira, completely ignoring them.

"Master della Cappa," Father Lurenzano began, "the Bishop wishes me to thank you for his discs for the eyes. To be able to read the Holy Bible again makes him feel like a young man. Many of the nobles on the upper level were impressed also."

"Bless you, Father Lurenzano. Bless you," the Master said, grabbing the priest's hands and kissing them. Then Agistino felt the something being pressed into his palm. When he looked, there was a five soldi coin staring at him. "What's this?"

"The Bishop wanted to pay you for the glasses, my son," Lurenzano said, tilting his head sideways and smiling. "That's what they cost, no?"

"Yes, but no. No! I can't take money from the Bishop!" Agistino took the coin and pressed it back in the priest's palm. He looked into the priest's seemingly-kind eyes, then grabbed his own coin pouch and took out two more coins. "And please, take these and give them to the Bishop. Thank him for me. Tell him how much I admired his service and his church." And then he took another coin. "And this coin is for your church, and for your help, Father. My household thanks you."

"It is my joy to serve," the priest said. "I will do as you ask." He closed his not-so-clean fingers around the coins. "Master della Cappa, we must let every church in Verona know of your wonderful new shop and how you can make old eyes new again."

Agistino bowed to him. The priest looked at Guilietta and she curtsied. Then Lurenzano rattled the coins in his hand and laughed. "And we see you later, eh, Ugi?"

"Si, Father, si," Ugilino answered.

Father Lurenzano laughed, turned, slapped Ugilino on the bottom, and strolled away.

On the way home, even Ugilino found it hard to keep up with Agistino's pace. The troupe of teens was like a frenetic gaggle of geese, all chasing after the gander. Ugilino caught up with Agistino and pulled at his sleeve.

"Master," Ugilino said in breathless amazement, "you gave Father Lurenzano the Bishop's five soldi back?" Then he smacked his own head. "And then all that other money."

The Master chuckled nervously, like he had just escaped the jaws of a hungry shark.

"He's not a stupid man, that Lurenzano. If he didn't offer to pay, then the glasses would have just been a gift from me. He couldn't have asked *me* for money. But him paying for them forced me to give him back even more, to look more generous than he. Oh, those priests are tricky with money."

"Trickier than Jews, Master?" Ugilino asked.

"At least Jews are straightforward. They're tough when doing business, but they don't ever do this to you," and he gave the appropriate rude Italian gesture to illustrate his meaning. Ugilino looked sheepish and took a few steps backward.

"All of you, listen," the Master said, continuing his pace. "Now is a critical time in our house's recovery. When people come to purchase discs for the eyes, we must have them. That means we must work hard over the next days to build stock. However," he said, pointing a finger in the air, "I am the only competent lens grinder, so you must all keep me supplied. We must lose no time. Girls, you keep the house in order. Keep food and drink ready. Boys, you must keep the shop clean, not fight, and do exactly what I say. Romero!"

"Yes, Master," Hansum answered, running to his side.

"I'm thinking that you might be able to learn to mount the lenses in their frames."

"I'm sure I could, Master."

"Daughter!"

"Si, Papa?" Guilietta lifted her skirts off the muddy street and hurried forward.

"Child, your mother must be kept under control. We can brook no distractions to our purpose. Do you understand?"

"Si, Papa."

"Maruccio, Ugilino!"

"Si, Master," they echoed together.

"Ugilino, you must keep the workshop clean. A clean workshop is a productive workshop. Will you do this and not run off?"

"Of course, Master. I'm your man."

"Maruccio, you must keep me supplied with whatever I need while I'm working. Learn to anticipate what tool I need. You can do this?"

"You got it, boss, I mean, Master."

"And when you have a bit of time, you help Ugilino clean and carry wood too, eh?"

"Whatever you say, Master."

Something came into Ugilino's head, like an unwelcome bird dropping. He had just become the bottom dog in the pack again. He slowed down, trying to work this out. How could the Master do this? It was he, Ugilino, who got Father Lurenzano to have the Bishop wear the discs for the eyes. It was also Ugilino who had stolen back the lathe and protected the Master when he was drunk. He should be rewarded by getting the best jobs in the shop. Then the Master would respect him and let him marry Guilietta. He fell a few steps behind as he thought all this.

Everyone looked back to see why Ugilino had slowed.

"Eh, what's a matter with you?" the Master asked impatiently, "I said we must all keep busy."

Ugilino looked Agistino in the eye. He wanted to scream, but the Master was looking back at him with such intensity, he knew it was no use. He put his head down and walked quickly again. 'What cannot be helped must be endured,' he remembered being told by another priest. 'And after all,' Ugilino thought, 'we're all eating like princes.'

The next few days were frantically busy and Ugilino did his best. He cleaned and swept the shop better than he ever did before. He picked up every grain of grit and ground glass he could find, placing it neatly in the trash box. But even as he tried to enjoy these small personal triumphs, he'd look up and see the Master patting Hansum on the back, telling him what a good job he was doing in learning to mount lenses. This rankled Ugilino so much that when he sat down to another wonderful meal, it gave him little comfort, especially when the Master trumpeted another of Hansum's successes to everyone. He was rankled even further when he saw Guilietta and the orphan boy actually exchange smiles.

Chapter 25

A few mornings later, Hansum sat next to Shamira at repast and spoke in a low voice.

"Pan wants to talk to both of us."

"Young Mistress," Pan began, *"at dinner, give the Signora an extra large portion. We need her to take a longer nap than usual. This will allow us to finish the designs for the advanced lathe. If we can finish our work today, we can display it to Master della Cappa tonight after supper."*

As expected, after the old woman stuffed herself with food, she trundled up to her bed and insisted her daughter join her. As Hansum left for the shop, given what Pan had shown him the night before, he anticipated a very interesting meeting after supper. Plus, Pan had shown him another idea he would save for a little later, plans for a hand-held telescope. This was an invention, Pan explained, that wasn't supposed to be invented for another hundred and fifty years.

When Shamira later came to the shop with a pitcher of cool water, she nodded at Hansum and said, "The plans, they're all done."

At supper, Hansum watched a very tired and obviously sore Master sitting at the table. In three days they had made twenty-one pairs of discs for the eyes; seven of each strength. Agistino's eyes were tired. Hansum watched him at the supper table, eyes closed, chewing his food.

The girls had made the same beautiful chicken dish that Shamira had learned from the first Signora. All were quietly devouring their meal when the Master asked Ugilino if he had heard from Father Lurenzano. When Ugilino said no, the Master became agitated.

"Go visit him tonight. Make sure he hasn't forgotten his promise. After all, he's been paid for this favor. But don't tell it to him like that! Don't talk about money at all." Ugilino said he was very busy and didn't know if he'd be able to go that night. The Master, so tired from his long hours of work, banged his hand on the table. "Busy? You are the least busy of all!"

"Maybe tomorrow night, Master."

"Tonight!" the Master yelled. "Why are you questioning me? I thought this priest was your friend?" Ugilino fell silent and put his head down.

Pan whispered to Hansum, *"Say, 'Master, you look tired.'"* Hansum repeated this. The Master grunted, not opening his eyes. Pan said something else and Hansum repeated it.

"Master, I have an idea to make us more productive." The Master opened his eyes into a suspicious squint. "It's an idea for an improved lathe. We can have it made by a local carpenter."

"What nonsense are you talking about? Improve? How?"

"Let me show you, Master . . ."

"Let me show you, Master," Hansum parroted. "Carmella is good with a piece of charcoal and parchment, so we worked together to make some plans."

The Master's bleary eyes opened fully. Shamira got her satchel of drawings and, after Hansum moved Agistino's bowl and swept the crumbs away, she put several pieces of paper in front of the lensmaker. He stared at the drawings, taking time to understand what he was looking at. The way in which Pan had instructed Shamira resulted in a very modern set of plans.

"See, Master," Hansum explained, "here is the front view of the lathe, a top view, and two side views, all in proportion." Parts had local measurements, all precisely worked out by Pan. "You see, Master, both hands remain free to work on the glass. The motion of the spindle is created by a foot pedal. These are removable dops. The operator can concentrate on grinding and polishing without the bother of having the lathe sitting idle when lenses are turned over or changed. An assistant can do the changing and leave the more skilled craftsperson to work only on lenses." The presentation went on for several minutes. When Hansum finished, the Master sat silently.

"These are your thoughts?" the Master finally asked. Agistino looked at Hansum, his eyes full of confusion.

"Si, Master."

"Si, Master."

"And you instructed Carmella, the kitchen girl, to put them on parchment?"

"*Si, Master.*"

"Si, Master."

Now the Master's confusion was profound. "When?"

Hansum waited for his answer from Pan, but it didn't come. Apparently, even Pan had to pause before answering this. In the past few days, Shamira and Hansum were scarcely in the same room together, let alone have time enough to consult on complicated plans. Finally, Pan whispered his response, deciding to completely ignore the question he had been asked.

"Do you think this lathe could be of benefit to us, Master?"

Another long pause by the Master.

"Where did you get these thoughts?"

"They just came to me," Hansum repeated.

The Master sat and stared. Hansum imagined what must be going through his mind. He was beginning to understand how, before modern times, things changed slowly over centuries. To see something radically advanced would be a shock.

"Put your hand on his right shoulder and say . . ."

"This design will help your shoulder from being sore, Master."

With Hansum's hand still upon the Master's shoulder, the older man looked up, and with limpid eyes said, "Tomorrow we must find the best carpenter in Verona."

"I'll run and get the ones who worked on the shop," Ugilino said, anxious to be seen making a contribution.

"No," Pan instructed Hansum to say.

"We will need a good furniture maker to construct this. The work is more fine. Especially the spindles and dops. We must employ someone with a wood lathe."

"There's a furniture maker in the market," Guilietta said. "His chairs have turned legs and backs. I've heard the Podesta even has some of his pieces."

The conversation went on long past when people usually went to bed. At one point, when it was getting dark, Agistino stretched out both hands on the table and made a pronouncement.

"Romero, I must continue making discs for the eyes. There-fore, you must work with the carpenter to make sure everything is done as it should be. So, someone else will have to learn to mount lenses."

"Master, Master," Ugilino said enthusiastically, "you could teach me to put the lenses in the frames."

The Master snorted. "Yes, and pigs will learn to sing in the church choir." Lincoln laughed till Hansum kicked him under the table. Then the Master said sternly, "Ugilino, I told you to go to Father Lurenzano's after supper."

"But Master . . ." Ugilino began. The big, red hand banged the table again. Everyone was quiet. Ugilino got up slowly, walked to the door, opened it and paused for a second. He looked at everyone, then left. As the door closed, everybody burst back into happy chatter.

The Master continued. "Carmella, tomorrow after market, you will learn to put the lenses in the frames. With your good hands, I think this will not be a problem."

"That is wonderful," Guilietta said enthusiastically. "And I will make sure everybody gets their meals, Papa."

"Just so, daughter. But after dinner, you and Romero will go back to the market. You will show him the furniture maker's." The idea of spending time alone with Guilietta hit Hansum right between the eyes. The Master added, "Romero, I trust you to assess whether this furniture maker is adequate to the job. If you think he is, bring him back to meet me. I will negotiate a price. Romero? Romero? Are you listening?" Now it was Lincoln's turn to kick Hansum under the table.

"Sorry, Master," Hansum finally said. "I heard you. I was . . . thinking."

"Our daughter in public with a servant!" the Signora objected. "Scandalous!"

"Quiet, woman. We must mobilize our house like an army. This is war! Us against the world! Us against poverty!"

Soon the plan was set. All had their instructions, except Lincoln.

"Maruccio," the Master said.

"Si, Master?" Lincoln found the Master's eyes staring right into his.

"You have been doing an excellent job, Maruccio."

"Grazie, Master."

"For one so young, even for one some years older."

This caught Lincoln off guard. He actually blushed. "Grazie, Master."

"There's not much more to say except to keep doing what you are doing."

"Well, when we get the new lathe," Lincoln said, "it will be me that prepares the dops and flips the lenses over. I've looked at the drawings and thought about it."

Lincoln and the Master were looking deep into one another's eyes. Sober, sincere, connected.

"I see you have thought about it," Agistino replied. "And thought well, Maruccio." Lincoln smiled. He actually giggled involuntarily. But he was stopped by the big finger of the Master's hand, which was held up to make a point. "But this, my young friend, you must understand. To do a job well for some days or weeks, a month even, that is one thing. But for a family to be successful, for a business to flourish, one must be prepared to work well for years. To establish a reputation and wealth, this takes a strong heart. Are you prepared for this, young Maruccio?"

Lincoln's emotions were mixed. He had been promised to be back in his home with his mother, father and A.I. nanny within a month. That time was coming soon. He swallowed hard and had to admit that whatever plan the History Camp people had put together, it must be working for him to feel so confused. He refocused and found the Master still staring at him. He answered sincerely.

"Yes, Master. I can do it."

Chapter 26

The next morning Agistino came downstairs to find the fire blazing, hot leftovers already on the table, and the girls waiting to go to the market. He took out his pouch and counted some coins for Guilietta.

"Carmella and I know exactly what we are going for, and will be back very soon, Father." She showed him a shopping list in her own beginner's hand. Aspics of meat, dried sausage, preserved carp, many loaves of bread, figs, apples, pears, chestnuts and other nutritious foods that could be eaten casually without requiring much time to prepare. Hansum and Lincoln came in and Agistino noted how even Maruccio looked like he had scrubbed and cleaned himself with extra care this morning.

"Eat, boys, eat. A full belly makes your fire strong."

When Agistino had been on his lathe for a bit over an hour, he looked around and saw that Shamira was already back from the market. Hansum was giving her a lesson on mounting the lenses. The Master got up and came to inspect her progress. He had to admit that between Hansum's quiet teaching and Shamira's dexterity, there was little he could suggest to improve her work. He crossed himself and gave thanks to both God and Father Aaron. Then the shop became suddenly noisy again.

"Master, I'm back," Ugilino shouted as he came running in the door. "The Father says he'll come tomorrow to introduce us to two more churches. I'm supposed to run to the priests today and tell them we're coming. Hey, what's Carmella doin' in the shop? That's men's work."

"She's quicker and better than me," Hansum replied. Ugilino had a look on his face that seemed to question why one person would build up another at his own expense.

Just as they were locking the shop for dinner, two parishioners of San Zeno showed up to purchase spectacles. The Master sent the others ahead, but told Ugilino to stay with him.

When the Master and Ugilino returned to the house, Agistino showed off the ten soldi already brought in before the morning meal. He said that Ugilino had conducted himself not badly with the customers. He predicted that after the next few weeks, business should be quite regular, booming even.

Just then, the Signora reached across the table to grab a few extra olives and there was a big ripping sound.

"Cavolo!" she swore, lifting her arm and exposing a large hole with dangling threads. "That was my best frock!" she whined.

"Perhaps this afternoon," Guilietta suggested, "we can visit the Satores. They can sew you a new dress."

"Yes, a whole new wardrobe!" the Signora beamed, her attitude changing instantly.

"We've no money for new clothes!" Agistino complained.

"I'm sure they would trade for discs for the eyes, Master," Hansum suggested. "They squint when they work."

"Okay, okay. But not a whole wardrobe. Just one frock. And sturdy material," Agistino emphasized. "To hold in her bulk."

After dinner, Pan watched the House of della Cappa continue its campaign. Ugilino was sent to tell the priests of their visit tomorrow. Lincoln and Shamira quickly followed the Master back to the shop to work. This left Hansum in the house with Guilietta and the Signora. Hansum stood back, watching Guilietta walk her now giggling mother up the stairs for her nap. The old lady wouldn't stop talking about how she would instruct the tailor on this or that detail of her new wardrobe.

Pan could sense how Hansum was now anxious with anticipation. He scanned the youth's respiration and heart rate and noted they had increased dramatically. They climbed even higher when Guilietta reappeared at the top of the steps. She stopped and the two young people's eyes met.

"Try to keep to the business at hand, Young Master," Pan whispered. Guilietta continued her descent. "Now your sympathetic nervous system is causing the blood vessels of your face to contract. You're blushing." But Pan could see his advice was to no avail. The boy was totally besotted. Hansum opened the door and the teens stepped out into the street. They walked side by side: Guilietta, her hands clasped in front of her, Hansum, his hands behind. Finally, Hansum said, "The weather. It looks like it may rain today."

"It was cloudy at the market when Carmella and I were there at dawn."

"But look, the light of the sun breaks through the clouds. It makes everything look soft."

"Which direction is that?"

"It is the east," Hansum said looking directly at Guilietta. "The sun comes up in the east."

Guilietta looked up at him for a moment, then quickly in the other direction. The clouds were parting everywhere. "Look, the moon is still up in that direction. You can just barely see it."

"The sunlight makes the moon pale," Hansum said. Then Pan, listening to the awkward conversation, thought to himself, 'I might as well give the kid some ammunition.' He whispered into Hansum's ear, which he repeated. "The sun is the moon's handmaiden, and yet she outshines it."

"I remember when I was younger. We had several maids," Guilietta replied.

"But none more fair than you, I'm sure."

When Hansum repeated this, Guilietta gave him a quick glance.

"Now I am my mother's maid."

"You will have maids of your own again." These were Hansum's own words. Pan raised a holographic eyebrow. It was said with a quiet conviction, implying several things. Guilietta looked at Hansum quietly and they continued walking.

In the market, Guilietta showed Hansum the furniture maker's stall. Hansum moved his head around so Pan could inspect all of the examples of chairs, tables and trunks. It wasn't fine furniture, but it was far better than most of the plank and limb stuff that most people owned.

"I understand the Podesta has some of your furniture," Hansum said to the stall attendant. He was a maimed soldier, the master furniture maker's uncle, who was now only good for sitting and talking. He was missing an eye and a foot, but spoke quite well and had a rather cheerful personality. He hobbled about with a well-carved crutch, made, he said, by his nephew.

"Yes, the Podesta owns some of our work. They are in his servants' quarters."

Despite this, Pan confirmed that the work showed skills that should make the carpenter an adequate candidate for the lathe commission. Chairs of the same design were close enough in size that he probably did know how to measure and follow a pattern, unlike many craftspersons whose work varied significantly from one similar object to another. The furniture was not made here, but in a shop outside of the southern wall, close to San Francesco al Corso. Directions given, they left the market. Many of the merchants called out to Guilietta, now a market regular. They called out their hellos and also to tell her of some foodstuffs they were getting in. Quite a few of the women raised their eyes or made hand-shaking gestures to Guilietta when they thought Hansum wasn't looking.

As they came to the Bra Gates, Hansum stopped. "What's this mean?" he asked, imitating the hand shaking movement.

"You don't know?" Guilietta looked at him mischievously.

He reached across and almost touched Guilietta, then pulled his finger back, like it had been burnt on something hot. The two teenagers giggled. Then Guilietta reached forward, put her finger on Hansum's arm, repeating the joke slowly. They stared for a second, till Guilietta lowered her eyes chastely. Then they continued on their way out through the gates and out of the market. What they did not see, though Pan did, was Ugilino. He was on his way back from San Fermo, standing, gape-mouthed, no more than fifty paces from them. He had seen this intimacy.

Chapter 27

That night at supper, Ugilino sat quietly, slowly eating his food while others told of their day's adventures. For him, the food didn't hold the magic it had a short day earlier. He listened as the Master told how seven more people came to their shop to buy discs for the eyes, how Shamira had done an excellent job with setting the lenses in the frames, how Lincoln had even worked on the lathe while the Master was taking care of a customer. Hansum and Guilietta told about having to go close to San Francesco al Corso to visit the furniture maker, Master Raphael. He had four apprentices and two journeymen and also three different-sized pole lathes for shaping wood. The carpentry master and journeymen were excited to see such detailed plans and said they looked forward to the precise work of making the interchangeable dops.

"Good, good," the Master smiled. "But remember not to tell them too much about the lathe. If they realize how different it is, they could steal the ideas and take them to Florence. I know you are too trusting, Romero."

"Don't you worry, Papa," Guilietta said. "I shall keep an eye on this one."

This was too much for Ugilino. He shot to his feet, pushing back the bench roughly and almost knocking the three other teenagers off. Lincoln's bowl spilled to the floor.

"I'm going to bed," the oaf said gruffly.

"UGILINO!" the Master shouted. "What's wrong with you? If you ever. . ."

But Ugilino didn't wait to hear the end of the Master's admonishment. He was gone.

Not long after, Ugilino could hear the orphans coming up the ladder. They moved quietly, like they didn't want to disturb him. He lay curled up in the hay, wrapped in his blanket and pretending to be asleep. Ugilino's miserable mood was made even worse when he heard how happy the orphans were.

"That new lathe is really going to be great," he heard the younger one whisper. "I'll have fun working on it with the Master." These words stung Ugilino.

"Yeah, it'll really help the family prosper." When the older orphan said family, he knew he was really referring to Guilietta.

"G'night, Hansum. Night, Pan," he heard Lincoln whispered.
"Night."
"Good night."

A happy Hansum lay in the straw, his whole consciousness
consumed by Guilietta. He replayed their walk in his mind, their
first extended eye contact, her smooth skin, the almond- shaped
eyes that became even softer when she looked at him. He was
falling into those eyes when he felt himself being roughly turned
over. The stink of a bulldog's breath filled his face.

"You think you can turn up here and take my place?"

"Ugilino, what are you talking . . ."

Ugilino's hands gripped Hansum's shoulders and held him
down fast. The brute's big knuckles pushed into Hansum's shoulder socket and pressed on a nerve. "I'm the senior apprentice! I
should sit next to the Master!"

"Calm down, Ugilino. You're hurting me. Owwww!"

"And stay away from Guilietta!" he growled, leaning down
with all his weight.

"What are you talking ab . . ." Ugilino knuckles pushed deep-
er into Hansum's rotator cuff, causing waves of pain to shoot
through his body.

"I'll tell the Master what I saw in the piazza," Ugilino growled.
"How you looked at each..." But his rage seemed to explode when
he said this. Hansum felt a knee punching into his ribs, then another into his stomach, causing him to throw up. Hansum felt his
face being rubbed into the puke. "Not such a pretty face now,"
Ugilino spit. Hansum looked up helplessly to see Ugilino's enraged visage. Then he saw a piece of heavy lumber in his hand.
"I'll change that pretty face of yours for good," he shouted at the
defenseless Hansum. A dark figure flew through the air. Lincoln
slammed into Ugilino. The larger youth flew backwards and hit
his head on the corner of the ladder. All went quiet. Hansum began to cough. Lincoln helped him to his knees. Pan popped out
of Hansum's shoulder. Actually, it was only a large, single goat
eye floating in the air, looking around and also casting light for

the boys to see. Ugilino lay unconscious. Lincoln went over to the big, motionless lump. Hansum rubbed his throat and arm. Then the eye turned into a little whirlwind. A moment later, Pan was standing by Ugilino. He bent down and looked at the prone figure.

"Is he all right?" Lincoln asked fearfully. "Is he . . ."

"He's breathing," Pan assured. "But he may have a concussion." Pan reached out, like he was going to lift Ugilino's eyelid, but his holographic hand went right through him. "Lincoln, Young Master, lift his eyelid for me. I'll do a retina and blood vessel scan to assess the damage."

"I didn't mean to hurt him," Lincoln said, scared.

"You did what was necessary, Young Master," Pan said seriously. "Don't move his head or neck, just in case. Only his eyelid. There. Uh huh. Uh huh," the imp said, looking into Ugilino's eye. It only took a few moments. "He's fine. There's a very slight concussion, but the data I get shows he's living with previous head-blow damage far more serious. This shouldn't change a thing. Master Hansum, you look pale. Shall I check you?"

Hansum waved Pan off. "No, I'm all right."

"What are we going to do about this guy?" Lincoln said. "He's nuts."

"Hmmm," Pan murmured, "I have a wee plan that might influence our friend here."

Pan had Hansum place his little brass lamp in the crevice of a beam to give him full view of the loft. While the two boys pretended to sleep, Pan expanded himself up to his full height of one meter. Then he strode over to the still-prone Ugilino, who was now snoring loudly.

"Oh, being non-corporeal can become tiresome," Pan complained. "Will one of you please wake him for me?"

Hansum threw a piece of wood at Ugilino's leg. When Ugilino stirred, Pan took on a serious look.

"Oh, oohhh. Oh, my head," Ugilino groaned.

"Rise, you worthless soul," Pan proclaimed loudly. "See what eternity has in store for you!"

"Oh shut up, you stupid orph . . ." Ugilino's curse stopped short as he opened his eyes and gazed upon the self-illuminated figure of a church fresco come to life. "I, I, I..." he stammered.

"Behold!" Pan shouted. "The dolt of death utters forth his perspicuous soliloquy. I, I, I..." and then Pan doubled over in mock laughter.

"I, I, I..." Ugilino repeated.

"Oh, disappointment is my lot. I believed I would be visiting a sinner with style. I understood you to be the Deflowerer of Florence, the Plague of Padua, the Mangler of Mantua, the Sodomiser of Syracuse, the Blight, Destroyer, Ruination, Damnation, Vexation and Virulence of Verona. And all you can muster are musty I, I, I, Is. Tsk, tsk. Such a disappointment."

"Are, are you the devil?"

"Me? The devil? Ha! The devil waste his time on a useless like you? I am but one of his minions, freed from the eternal flames for a few minutes to take you, yes, to the Satan of Sadness."

"But I am not dead."

"What? Not dead, my love? But you rot as you lie there."

Ugilino did a double take, looking quickly where his head had lain, checking to see if it was true. Then he jumped to his feet.

"No, demon spirit, I'm alive. See, I still breathe." He took several deep breaths and then looked dizzy. "And my heart," he added, "is beating like the wings of a bat."

Pan looked serious and paused for effect. He walked over to Ugilino, coming up only to his waist. Ugilino recoiled. Pan looked the youth up and down.

"Perhaps I've been sent on a fool's errand, another bedevilment by that devious emperor of demons, designed to cause me more unspeakable torment if I don't bring you back." Pan looked thoughtful. "Perhaps I should kill you to save myself more unspeakable pain?"

Ugilino gasped so loudly he wheezed. Hansum and Lincoln stifled a laugh and rustled about in their blankets, like they were dreaming.

Pan looked Ugilino solemnly in the eye.

"Yes, I can still hear your heart beating. And I can certainly perceive your breath. Phew!" He made a fanning motion in front of his nose. "Perhaps your breath is what I recognized wrongly as rotting remains."

"Si, si. That's it." Ugilino agreed. "It is the foul smell of the living, not the dead."

Lincoln snorted, and Pan could see him biting his hand to control his giggling.

"Well, no matter. If I leave you alive today, I'll come for you soon enough. To strangle you now would put suspicion on the angelic orphans that share your bed. I would not want them to suffer for your righteous reward of death."

"Si, si. That's right. They are saintly youths. I do them wrong to torment them."

"Then why do you do it?"

"The Master torments me and I them. It's my right."

"Your right? I see. Does the Master do you right or ill when he scourges you?"

"Ill, most of the time. So, sometimes I do mischief because I might as well do the crime if I am to do the punishment."

"Then both you and your Master shall share a pot of boiling oil, right next to the flayers of flesh."

This image seemed to terrify Ugilino. Falling to his knees, he looked Pan straight in the eye.

"What penance must I do to take me from the road to . . ." He seemed to be searching in his mind for the right word. ". . . perdition?" he finally said.

Pan looked surprised.

"Penance? That would bespeak a fear of Hell. I thought by your actions you longed for a place in the netherworld."

"No, no. I wish to spend eternity with the angels. Is there penance? Have I time?"

The holographic goat-man turned and walked a few paces, stroking his little goatee. "Hmmm. Penance? Penance?" Then he turned. "There might be a way."

"What? What must I do to put me in the good graces of God?" he said, walking on his knees quickly toward Pan.

"Do? Not much. But I warn you, a tally of your sins is being kept, as sure as I am a legate of Tartarus. If you are lying, confess now and accept your damnation. But if you are sincere, I may offer you salvation."

"Yes, spirit. I am sincere."

"Very well. Then mark what I command of thee and do not alter one thing that is prescribed. And then maybe, perhaps, perchance, just possibly, there is a faint hope of your ascension up, rather than ignominious descent -- down."

"Yes, yes. I shall do exactly as you say."

"Firstly, you must not do harm to these orphans again, but embrace them as brothers."

"Have I not already said as much?"

"Be not jealous or envious of their deeds and accomplishments, and covet not what either may acquire. You pause in your enthusiasm, brother. To this can you not agree?"

"I, I, I . . ." Pan raised a finger. "I agree. I agree."

"Good. You shall no longer lodge in this loft. Take yourself and your things and move into one of the stalls below. But just because one rooms in a stable, one does not have to live like an animal. At all times you must keep the place clean and aired. You must faithfully clean the chamber pot, rinsing it with water twice daily to deny the flies food. As for yourself, you must wash at the town fountain, not once a day, but twice, like the chamber pot. Thrice on Sundays. Your hair must be shorn and combed, clothes changed weekly without fail. You must clean your teeth."

"My teeth? How? Why?"

"How? With vinegar and a clean rag. Why? Because I say it."

"I've never heard of such a thing? Clean teeth to get into Heaven?"

"Then keep your foul smile and the dirt will be cleansed by Hell fire."

"I beg forgiveness. Vinegar shall be my filthy mouth's soap."

"And that is not the worst."

"More? Heaven has a high price," Ugilino said under his breath.

"The hardest of all: your duty to others in the home and out. Firstly, you must be kind, not only to these orphans, but to everyone. Above and beyond that, do whatever the Master tells you. Go to church. Go to confession. Help the priest two afternoons every week. And lastly, you must not tell the Master or anybody about my visit to you. Knowledge of visits from spirits would make Heaven and Hell a certainty, and cause trouble for faith. Anyway, none would believe if you told of one such as me."

Chapter 28

The next morning Lincoln was laughing as he splashed the cold water from the rain barrel onto his face. "I, I, I, I. . ." he repeated out loud, imitating the big oaf's first reaction at seeing Pan. He was still laughing when the door opened and in walked the Master.

"You like the cold water, Maruccio?" Agistino enquired quizzically.

"I was just thinking of something funny, Master."

"Laughter is good for the soul, my son." Just then Hansum came climbing down the ladder.

"Buon giorno," Hansum said.

"Buon giorno. Where's Ugilino?" Lincoln and Hansum looked at each other warily. The Master's smile faded. "That inconstant son of the streets!"

They worked for a time in the shop and then went to have morning dinner. They were almost finished when the door to the house opened. The Master shouted, "Ugilino, where have you . . ." then he stopped. The youth's hair was shorn to a stubble. His face, still pockmarked and blotchy, was clean. And he had a change of clothes.

"Nice duds, dude," Lincoln said. Of course, the translator simply changed it to, "Nice clothes, signor."

"Grazie, brother," Ugilino answered. "Master, please forgive my lateness. I was at morning mass and Father Lurenzano asked a favor of me."

"Where did you get those clothes? You didn't steal them, did you?" the Master asked seriously.

"No Master, no. My word on the baby Jesus," he said. "The priest gave them to me."

"You look so different, Ugilino," Guilietta said. "Very clean. Very nice."

"Grazie," Ugilino answered, clutching his hands in front of him in nervous supplication.

"What's that smell?" the Master enquired, wrinkling his nose.

"I washed my whole body," Ugilino said, touching his body in different places, trying to figure which bit of ripeness he had missed.

"No, it's not that," the Master said, sniffing the air again. "It's vinegar."

"Ah," Ugilino said. He bared his teeth. "I used vinegar to clean my mouth." His teeth were still awful, but a noticeable difference could be seen. "And Master, here." Ugilino reached into a pouch on his waist and brought out a small handful of coins. He plunked them on the table. "I took two pair of discs for the eyes and sold them at church this morning."

A shocked silence enveloped the table. Pan whispered something into Lincoln's ear and he repeated it to the table. "I think brother Ugilino has found his calling. Perhaps he can be a vendor about town for the discs for the eyes?"

"Yes, Master," Ugilino agreed enthusiastically. "Maybe I can't be a lensmaker, but I can sell our house's wares."

"Ugilino, what has caused this transformation?" Guilietta asked. "It is truly a miracle."

Ugilino put his head down. Lincoln knew Ugilino was forbidden to tell the whole reason, so he was curious what old ugly would say.

"I want to go to Heaven," Ugilino said solemnly. "I want to have a home."

Lincoln felt the tiniest bit guilty.

The Master crossed himself, then put his hand on Ugilino's arm. He picked up the pile of coins, chose the smallest and gave it to Ugilino, bidding him keep it. Then he handed him a bowl of food. The two smiled at each other.

Shortly after dinner, Father Lurenzano and Master Raphael arrived for a meeting about the lathe. Pan was whispering in Hansum's ear, making him sound quite knowledgeable. The Master negotiated a price, then said, "Romero is capable to finish the details of the lathe's manufacture. Master Raphael, I need this machine in a week. Is this possible? Good. Romero will go with you today to observe the start. He'll then visit you twice daily to see its progress. Father Lurenzano, perhaps you and Ugilino should be off to talk with your fellow priests."

"Will you not attend with us today?" Lurenzano asked.

Agistino put his hand on Ugilino's shoulder.

"I now have three trustworthy apprentices, all with different talents. I must go back to making lenses with Maruccio. But Father, thank you for your godly influence on our Ugilino. He seems to have been reborn."

Father Lurenzano looked at Ugilino, first a bit confused, and then he smiled.

"Our Ugi is special to all of us."

Chapter 29

Agistino was astounded that the new lathe was not only delivered on time, but that it worked perfectly. He was used to problems cropping up, arguments with suppliers and customers, delays and deception. It was the way of the world, his old master had told him. When Agistino shared these thoughts with Master Raphael, he agreed, but said the difference with this job had been Romero. The carpentry master praised Hansum lavishly, saying that his observations and suggestions when they had problems were as if the boy had insights and experience of a much older man, "ten older men," he added.

As for the lathe, with its multiple dops and pedal power, it more than doubled Agistino's production. They were selling the finished product almost as fast as they could make it.

When nobody was looking, Agistino took Hansum aside and clasped his hand.

"You're a good boy," he said, looking him in the eye. When he freed Hansum's hand, the teenager looked down to see five misshapen denari in his palm. "Don't tell anyone," Agistino said confidentially.

Agistino was now selling so many spectacles that he had to stay up late one night and create a hiding place for his new wealth. He carefully removed a large stone from the side of the fireplace, hollowed out the mortar and stones behind it, put his strong box in, then fit the front stone back perfectly. He piled firewood in front of it, making it impossible to see.

Pan was finally able to call a meeting of all the teens. Things had been so busy, it was almost impossible, but he had insisted, saying it was important.

"The month is over in a few days," Pan said nervously. Instead of standing in the straw of the loft, Pan's head was the only thing projecting from Hansum's shoulder. "Arimus should be back soon."

"I really do hope he'll let us come back and visit," Lincoln said.

"I'm surprised that he hasn't come sooner," Pan replied. "I thought he'd try to stop us from introducing the new lathe."

"Pan, why are you just hanging out of Hansum's arm? It looks ridiculous."

"Well, that's because something odd has happened to me."

"What?" Hansum asked.

"Promise none of you will laugh?" Pan asked.

"What is going on?" Shamira demanded.

Pan sighed, then tweaked his nose. His regular whirlwind happened, but it was purple. When he landed, the teens gasped.

"You've got a tail!" Lincoln shouted.

"And long, curly hair," Hansum said.

"And your butt is purple," Lincoln howled.

"Also, if you look closely, you'll notice the tips of my ears are twelve millimeters longer," Pan said dejectedly.

"Why did you change yourself?" Shamira asked.

"That's just it," Pan said, his eyes filled with worry. "I didn't change myself. It happened. Spontaneously."

"How?" Hansum asked.

"It was soon after we started using the new lathe."

"How could that affect anything?" Hansum asked.

"I think we somehow changed the timeline by introducing an advanced tool. Somewhere down the timeline, something has changed in history to make me different."

"But you said the History Camp people from the future would stop us before it changed things."

"That was just speculation."

"Wait a minute," Hansum said. "If we changed time, wouldn't all of our memories be changed if something like your appearance changed? Why would we remember your old form?"

"Like I said, it's all speculation. Since our society can't time travel, what happens is all speculative. Like the old science fiction of centuries past, there are different schools of thought. But this is real."

"Actually, I kind of like your new look," Shamira said.

"Truth be told," confided Pan, "so do I. But what's more important, is what should we do? I'm having my doubts that the History Camp people will play fair, so I suggest we really try to introduce something that will disrupt the historical timeline. Something to force them to show up. That's why I wanted to show you all this. Mistress?"

Shamira opened her portfolio and took out the sheets of handmade paper.

"Pan had me draw these up," Shamira said. "It looks really simple." She spread the plans out on the straw and Pan illuminated them. "We would use thick parchment to create homemade cardboard for the barrel and gaskets," she went on.

"Oh, it's the telescope," Hansum said.

"Zippy," Lincoln said excitedly. "This oughta shake those History Camp elders' tree."

"Shamira could get the needed parchment and glue from the market tomorrow," Pan explained.

"But that takes money," she said. "Master della Cappa makes Guilietta and me account for every coin."

"No problem," Hansum offered. He took out the coins Agistino had given him. "Is this enough?"

"Excellent," Pan said. "Master Hansum and Lincoln, tonight we'll stay up late and create the lenses. You shall both get to practice your craftsmanship." Pan saw Lincoln smiling at him. "What, Young Master, what?"

"You look really funny with a purple butt."

The next night, with the lenses made and the parchment and glue at hand, the teenagers gathered in the workshop. Pan stood on the workbench, supervising the making of the telescope, his new, longer tail swinging back and forth.

"No, no, no. You're putting too much glue on here," he complained, "not enough there. Don't buckle the parchment when you roll it." Putting the lenses in was the fiddly part. A cardboard gasket was put in at both ends and glued. "Let it dry first. Patience. Patience!" Pan complained, the most impatient of all. The lenses were then placed in at both ends and additional gaskets glued in front of them.

Shamira, whose deft fingers completed these final touches, held the finished telescope up. It was really quite a simple affair, but they were all pleased.

"Ladies first," Hansum said.

Shamira held it to her eye and looked across the room at Lincoln. He made a face. "It works!" she announced.

"Cool," Lincoln laughed. "Let's look at the moon!"

"Wait," Hansum said. "I'm kind of worried about giving this to the della Cappas. I know you want to provoke the History Camp time travelers, Pan, but I don't want to get the Master in trouble with them. And if improving the lathe had an effect on history, the telescope could really change things."

"How can a little thing like this cause trouble?" Lincoln asked. "What's the big deal?"

"Oh, the telescope introduced now would be a very big deal, Young Master," Pan answered. "It wasn't invented till the sixteenth century. Armies, navies, anyone could see their enemies much sooner. Events in history could be completely altered. Everyone will want one."

"That's what I've been thinking," Hansum said. "And once we show Master della Cappa this, taking it away isn't an option. He'll know how to make them. I'm worried about what the History Camp people would do about *him* then."

"Perhaps you're right," Pan said, pulling on one of his new dreadlocks as he thought. "I was sure the History Camp elders wouldn't let us get this far with the lathe. And, as I think of it, if the telescope was introduced now and it changed some battle, perhaps the timeline of the whole world could be changed. One of our ancestors might not be born or created, and we would -- phhtt -- disappear."

"Phhtt," Lincoln repeated, wide-eyed. "Freaky."

"Okay," Pan continued. "We shall give it more thought. Hide it in the straw upstairs till we've come to a conclusion about this."

"Yeah, but can we look at the moon with it first?" Lincoln asked. "After all, we made it all by ourselves," he said proudly. "Let's see how it works."

"Okay," Hansum replied, reaching for the door. Just as he touched the latch, it lifted by itself and the door swung open. Pan instantly evaporated into thin air, not even bothering to create his genie-like puff of smoke. Master della Cappa was standing in the doorway with Guilietta right beside him. Hansum stood there, telescope in hand, having no time to hide it.

Chapter 30

'Oh oh,' Pan thought from inside his lamp.

"What's that?" Agistino asked, noticing the lenses. "You made this in my shop, with my glass?" He didn't sound angry, just direct.

"I used the reject lenses from my practicing, Master. I re-ground them smaller."

"What is it?"

Pan quickly whispered in Hansum's ear.

"Just a toy I invented," Hansum repeated.

Agistino inspected the item and put the large end to his eye.

"The other way, Master," Hansum corrected.

"Point it at the moon," Lincoln said enthusiastically.

Agistino stepped back outside and pointed the telescope toward the sky. "Holy Mother of God!" he gasped, falling back into the room. "How can this be? It's magic!"

Guilietta took the telescope and stepped outside.

"No, Master," Hansum said, repeating a phrase he heard Pan use the night before. "It's not magic. It's two lenses working together. It's lenscraft."

"Romero, it's so clever," Guilietta called. "I feel I can almost touch the moon. And look, I think I can see mountains upon it."

'So, it was Guilietta,' Pan thought, 'not Galileo, who is the first person to recognize the mountains on the moon for what they are.'

"How did you know to do this?" the Master asked.

"When I was polishing a lens and comparing its surface curve against an earlier lens, I just held one up in front of the other and boom!" Hansum repeated this, then, "I noticed Maruccio looked closer to me than he was. Oh Master, it's just a toy. I'm sorry if you think I wasted your glass."

Pan watched the Master staring thoughtfully for several long moments. He could tell his mind was awhirl with all the uses for such an invention. He could tell Agistino most certainly knew this was anything but a toy.

"Romero, I'm going to take this with me," the Master said. "Tomorrow at church I'll show it around. Maybe we can sell a few of these new . . . toys, for a few soldi, eh?"

"Whatever you think, Master," Hansum said apprehensively.

"Just be careful, Master," Shamira reminded. "The glue will take most of the night to dry."

Agistino looked at Shamira and the workbench, noticing all the carefully cut bits of bonded paper, the glue pot and the glue brush in her hand.

"Yes," Hansum added. "The lenses must stay perfectly aligned to one another, at a precise distance apart."

"I helped too," Lincoln added.

"Yes," was all Agistino could think to say as he turned to leave. "Good boy." Agistino was obviously at a loss when assessing this curious group of children.

"Carmella, are you coming to bed?" Guilietta asked.

"I'll be right there. I want to clean up."

When the Master left, Pan popped back out. "So, now the telescope has been introduced several hundred years earlier than before," Pan said, a look of trepidation on his face.

"I wonder what's going to come of this," Shamira said.

"None of us has disappeared yet," Hansum said. "I guess all our same ancestors were born."

"What color is Pan's butt now?" Lincoln asked, peering around the A.I.

Book Three
Stranded

Chapter 1

Even though Hansum was tired, he found it hard to fall asleep. He tossed and turned, so more straw than usual got into his blanket. This caused more itching, which made it even more difficult to sleep. He tried to think of pleasant things, like being home again, being nicer to his parents, Charlene and his teachers. He even admitted, 'I guess I've been cured of being a hard case.' And then another thought swirled in his mind. 'What about Guilietta?' He had no answer for this. He had to agree with Lincoln and hope that the History Camp elders from the thirty-first century would allow them to visit.

"Wake up, brother Romero, wake up," Hansum heard a croaking voice say as his shoulder was shaken violently. He hadn't even realized he had finally fallen asleep.

"What? What's going on?" Hansum said, forcing his eyes open. It was still dark. He could just see Ugilino's face hovering above his, the grotesque visage even more contorted than usual. "What's wrong?" Hansum asked. Ugilino's mouth opened, but no words came out. His eyes welled and tears gushed out.

"Come!" Ugilino said pitifully before getting up and disappearing down the ladder, his sobs echoing in the dark.

"What's happening?" Lincoln said sleepily from the straw.

"I dunno," Hansum answered. "Ugi is crying like crazy and says we have to come."

As they got to the house, they heard the wails of more people. Inside, the flickering of oil lamps threw ominous shadows about the place. The first thing Hansum saw was the Master in his night shirt and cap, sitting on the bench, his arms hanging by his sides, his chest heaving with sobs. Guilietta was by him, her face buried in the fabric of his sleeve. There was a monk standing by the table, quiet and serious. 'What could have happened,'

Hansum thought. 'Has the Signora died?' Then he saw her, sitting on the other side of the table, her head slumped down and arms spread, not moving.

"The Signora?" Hansum asked. "Is she . . ."

The Signora's head popped up and she screamed toward the ceiling, "PETER, BLESSED SAINT. FOLD THE HOLY FATHER INTO YOUR ARMS!"

Hansum turned toward a confused Shamira. She was standing pale and ghost-like by the fireplace.

"What's going on?" Hansum asked. Shamira didn't answer, but stood there, shuddering.

"The Holy Father..." Agistino began, but he couldn't continue. His head fell onto his heaving chest. Ugilino sat down on the other side of Agistino and put his hand on the Master's shoulder. Amazingly, Master della Cappa didn't push it away. Finally, Agistino lifted his head. "It is a day of death!" the Master finally whispered, his voice sounding more pitiful than anyone could ever expect from him.

"My son," the monk said, turning to Hansum and Lincoln. "Terrible news has befallen us."

"What, brother?" Hansum asked.

"Grave news," the monk said, but he stopped when Agistino put up his hand.

"I shall tell," the Master said, his hand shaking so violently that Ugilino had to grab and hold onto it. "My cherished friend," the Master finally was able to get out, "and my beloved brother, my father confessor, our benefactor, the holy Father Aaron -- has been killed."

Hansum and Lincoln looked at each other, shocked. They looked at Shamira again, who was still shivering by the fire.

"That's impossible," Hansum said. "It can't be true."

"Would that was the case, my son," the monk interjected. "On his way back to Verona, just up in the northern valley, he was set upon by thieves. His remains were found by a young travelling nobleman. The Father's body was half eaten by wolves."

"Those cursed mountains and those cursed wolves!" Ugilino cried. "He was the only one that wanted nothing from me!" The

Master patted Ugilino on the shoulder, tears now gushing from both their eyes. Guilietta even reached out and put her hand on Ugilino's.

The three teenagers from the future looked on, wordless.

"But that doesn't make any sense," Lincoln said.

"His remains were just brought to San Zeno," the monk explained. "The Bishop himself is conducting services. I was sent to deliver the news. I am sorry. He was a friend to so many. You may come in the morning to the church."

Pan whispered something into Hansum's ear.

"We have to go now!" Hansum said.

"It serves no purpose, my son," the monk said. "The morning is soon enough . . ."

*"We **have** to go now!"* Pan whispered desperately.

Hansum looked at Lincoln and Shamira and tapped his language implant. "Pan says go now!"

Hansum found the cavernous church very different at night. The wonderful paintings, gargoyles, dragons and saintly statues looked ghostly as the flames from large oil lamps and torches sent portentous, dancing shadows over everything. Prayers for the fallen "Father Aaron" were being chanted by a phalanx of priests and monks. They stood around a small stone ossuary, the smoke from burning candles and incense wafting all around it. The Bishop himself walked up to Agistino, who fell to his knees and kissed the clergyman's ring.

"You're sure?" the Master asked, his whisper echoing in the great hall.

"There's not much left, my son, but we are sure," the Bishop said, motioning to the ossuary.

Pan whispered in Hansum's ear again. "We've got to see it," Hansum repeated.

"See what, my son?" the Bishop asked.

Pan whispered again. "The remains."

"My son, it is not a sight for young eyes, or old ones for that matter."

"We must," Hansum said very quietly.

Agistino, Lincoln and Hansum stepped toward the ossuary. Agistino motioned for the women to stay back. The Bishop nodded to the monks and two took hold of the small sarcophagus's lid.

"Prepare thyselves," one of them said.

When they lifted the lid, a rank smell rose that nearly made Hansum vomit. He clamped a hand over his nose and mouth, but forced himself not to turn away. Almost nothing could be seen for the thousands of wriggling maggots. A bit of skull was visible, as well as a tangle of recognizable salt and pepper hair. The three gasped and stepped back. The monks let the lid drop back into place. Another monk stepped forward.

"Master della Cappa," he murmured with quiet compassion, "there was this note and small amulet with the body."

Agistino took them, looked at the note blindly and handed it to Hansum.

"Give this necklace to the orphans living with the della Cappas in Verona," Hansum read. Then he looked up with hollow, scared eyes. Agistino held up the necklace. It was a piece of rawhide strip, tied into a long loop. On it was a small brass charm, in the familiar shape of an oil lamp. Agistino handed it to Lincoln.

As Guilietta stepped toward her father, Hansum and she exchanging pained glances. Tears fell from Guilietta's eyes and Agistino wrapped his arms around her. They sobbed in each other's arms. Ugilino lay himself down on the floor by the ossuary, spread his arms out and began to pray through a constant stream of tears. The three teens from the future huddled together and looked at the familiarly-shaped brass charm. All were lost for words.

"I am sorry for your sorrow, Signorina," the clear voice of a young man said. He had approached Agistino and Guilietta from the shadows and was now standing before them, his eyes locked on Guilietta. The Bishop stepped forward.

"Master della Cappa," he said gently, "this is Prince Feltrino Gonzaga of Mantua. He is the one who found the remains of our beloved Father Aaron."

Agistino released Guilietta and faced the young man. He was indeed wearing noble clothes, but they were faded and somewhat dirty. He wore a long saber at his side.

"Thank you, Excellency, for bringing our family back to us," Agistino said, bowing low and putting a hand to his chest. Prince Feltrino looked at him briefly, but brought his gaze back to Guilietta.

"Si, when I saw the note with the city of Verona on it, I had no choice but to bundle up what was left of the good father and come here." Feltrino looked over at the Bishop. "An obligation to the church," he smiled. Then, looking back at Guilietta, he added, "And I'm very glad I did."

Hansum saw Guilietta blush. He stepped forward, but felt the strong hand of a monk holding him back in his obvious place.

Feltrino Gonzaga looked at the assemblage and thought that, once again, he was being forced to deal with people who were well beneath him. 'All these peasant priests and monks, these crass craftsmen and horribly dressed apprentices,' he thought. 'Dreadful. And all these tears over some dead priest. It's so tiresome. But this one, this girl, this is a beautiful girl. Maybe she will make it worth the trouble of dragging that smelly carcass in a sack behind my horse.'

If he hadn't been out of money, he would never have done it. Coming to Verona, home of his Gonzaga family's sworn enemies, the della Scallas, could be very dangerous for him. He could be taken prisoner, or worse. But his plans had worked out so far. The Bishop had fed him and said he could sleep in one of the monks' cells for a few days while his horse's leg healed. Now all he needed was a way to get his hands on some money and he would be off. But this girl, wouldn't that be a lovely diversion?

Before he found the body, he had been on the verge of going home to his father and family. That would mean admitting defeat, like the Prodigal Son. He still heard his father's words before he kicked him out of their palace, "I'm sick of your gambling debts and whoring. With your sword and horse skills, I thought you'd be an asset to me. But you've been a constant disappointment. You just don't get it, do you?" Hot blood had flooded into Feltrino's face. He turned and ran out the door of their palace, his father shouting, "Don't come back till you get it!"

Feltrino had stormed from the palace not having a clue where he was headed. He got on his horse then, with only the winnings from last night's crooked dice game in his pouch, he headed out into the world.

The Bishop spoke again. "Master della Cappa is the craftsman who brought the wonderful discs for the eyes to Verona. He's going to be a rich man soon, I think."

Feltrino finally took his gaze off of Guilietta and looked at this Master della Cappa. He smiled.

"The discs for the eyes? Yes, I understand they are the talk of your city. Perhaps I shall visit your shop soon and purchase a pair, to take to my dear father as a present. I, of course, have no need of such things, being young and strong." And with this statement he looked back at Guilietta.

"My house will be at your service, Excellency," Agistino said, bowing.

It was still the dead of night when the house of della Cappa made its way home. Shamira, Lincoln and Hansum took hold of each others' arms and held on tight. Nobody, not even Pan, spoke a word. At home everyone sat around the table, mute, except for the Master's prayers, his head down on his clutched hands. Ugilino sat on the floor in the corner, knees hugged into himself, scowling. Lincoln had the leather necklace on and sat fingering the brass amulet.

"We must all speak," Pan finally whispered. *"In the loft. Immediately."* Hansum asked if they could be excused. Agistino looked up from his prayers and simply nodded.

The instant they were all in the loft, Pan popped into existence.

"What the hell is going on here?" Hansum cried at him. "If Arimus is dead, why aren't the History Camp people coming to get us? Why are they leaving us here?"

"Young Master, I am as confused about that as you," Pan said. "I have no answer."

"But why did the History Camp people let Arimus get killed?" Shamira asked anxiously. "It doesn't make any sense. They must keep track of their people."

"Youch!" Lincoln cried. He grabbed the leather necklace and frantically pulled it over his head. "It's hot!" Holographic steam poured out of the small lamp. Lincoln dropped the necklace into the hay, and the instant it landed, a blinding flash lit the loft. When the children could see again, there, lying on the hay, was an image of a man almost naked. He was face-down with his head in his arms.

"It's a hologram," Pan said.

"Who is it?" Shamira asked.

"Greetings, friend," Pan said. "Who might you be?"

"They've come for us," Lincoln announced. "We're being rescued."

The image slowly raised its head. "Oh my God," Shamira gasped.

"Arimus," Hansum announced.

There was dried blood all over the image's face. His hair was disheveled.

"Children," the image said, "this is an emergency message."

"Where are you, Arimus?" Lincoln shouted. "What's going on?" But there was no answer. Lincoln saw the smile vanish from Pan's face.

"Don't bother asking questions, Young Master," the imp said. "It's only a recorded message. It's not interactive."

"If you are seeing this message," the image started, "I am dead." The image of Arimus winced in pain. "I have not much time. Listen closely. I have traveled back and forth through time to check on you often. Then I did something foolish. I was bathing in a mountain stream and didn't have my protective A.I. cloak on. My guard was down. I was attacked. Robbed. Left for dead

-- like this." The image coughed and spat out blood. "It is imperative you all understand the truth of your situation." Arimus looked embarrassed. "I ... I am sorry. The truth is, I *am* from the future and I was a History Camp councilor, but I was disbarred. I made too many mistakes that changed the timeline. But I missed time travel so much, I stole the technology and continued doing what History Camps from my time really do. That is, take children back in time. But ..." The image coughed up more blood. Another knot of pain shot over its face. It took two deep breaths and continued. "I saw that you all ... finally began to appreciate the privileged time you come from. I was coming to return you home when this happened. Returning is now impossible. I've lost my cloak. My technology. The thieves missed this recording device. And the worst problem is ... nobody, nobody knows what I've done. Nobody knows where I am. Where you are."

The teens gasped simultaneously.

The image lay its head on the ground, panting heavily. It rallied and raised itself onto one elbow. "My young friends," it said, smiling weakly, "make the best of your new lives. Do what you must to be successful. Use the universal knowledge of your genie. I know you have one. Take every advantage. And find happiness where you can." He then winced with what must have been intolerable pain. "And remember," the image whispered, finally collecting itself, "happiness is a decision." The image smiled as best it could, then closed its eyes. A wolf's howl was heard, then a second. The image opened its eyes and looked to the side, seeing something terrifying. Then the vision turned into a puff of holographic smoke and disappeared.

Stunned silence.

"Holy Lyceius and Latona," Pan said.

"Nobody knows where we are," Shamira said.

"We really are stuck here," Hansum whispered.

Lincoln let out a long whistle from between his broken tooth. "My mom and dad. I'll never see them again and ... they're not even born yet." His eyes welled up and he began to shiver. Shamira came and put her arms around him.

They stood, saying nothing for a long time. They heard the door to the workshop creak open.

"Children," the Master's voice shouted up, "come down. We must talk."

Pan put himself back into the lamp and they all climbed down to the shop. The Signora and Guilietta were also there. The Signora was carrying a basket. She lifted the cloth covering it. It was full of food. And then she did something extraordinary. She made sense.

"You must eat, dear apprentices," she said. "Sorrow is best drowned in food, which is the stuff of life."

"God sends us these tests," offered the Master.

"And we must find happiness in sorrow," Guilietta said. "For sorrow brings those who are left behind closer together."

Lincoln began to whimper, his lower lip quivering. Tears streamed from his eyes.

"I miss my mama," he sobbed.

"Oh, my little chicken," the Signora soothed. She came over and hugged Lincoln. Lincoln sank into her fat bosom and completely broke down. The Signora cried with Lincoln and Shamira with Guilietta. The Master took a step toward Hansum, looking at him seriously. The old man's eyes were deep wells. Hansum wasn't crying though. He was angry.

Chapter 2

Hansum looked the Master up and down, studying the big man with new eyes. His clothes, with their stains, grime and body odor, his permanently stained and calloused hands, unclipped finger nails, rough face, scruffy beard and long hair became more real to the boy. Even the spaces in Agistino's mouth, where teeth had rotted and been wrenched out, cried out their humanity. It's as if they symbolized the entirety of this unyielding century's all-pervasive pain. A century that Hansum was now inextricably part of.

The Master's rough face looked at Hansum, trying to smile reassuringly. He opened his arms a little, then put his palms together.

"With God's mercy, Romero, we shall survive."

Hansum found no comfort in those words. They were just so much pap that did nothing to soothe the cruel image of what he had seen in the ossuary and all it meant. He scrunched up his mouth, getting more 'hard-case' angry than he had ever been. Agistino appeared to misinterpret this for sadness. He opened up his arms to embrace the boy he knew as Romero.

"This is all completely crazy!" Hansum shouted. Then he turned around and stomped out into the night.

"Romero!" Guilietta, her heart breaking in sympathy, called after him.

Agistino started to follow the young man, but his wife stopped him.

"Let the boy be, husband," she said. Agistino stopped and, to Guilietta's surprise, her father didn't dismiss her mother's opinion. There was something in her voice reminiscent of the person she used to be. A month of the herbs had cooled her brain. She looked over at her daughter and said, "You go."

"Mama?"

"A young girl in the streets at night?" the Master questioned.

"Then go quickly before he gets far," the Signora said.

Guilietta looked at her father to see his reaction. He said nothing, so Guilietta let go of Shamira and rushed out the door after Hansum.

Hansum hadn't gone far. He was standing out in the middle of the street, staring up at the sky when he heard her voice.

"Romero?"

Hansum turned and saw Guilietta's beautiful face looking up at him sympathetically. A full moon was coming out, lighting the darkened streets. She stepped closer and took a small handkerchief from her waistband, reached up and dabbed at the tear-stained smudges on Hansum's face.

"Where are you going?" she asked. "My father is worried."

"I don't know. I just needed to get away."

"Si, I know that feeling. Come. Let's walk. Or would you like to be alone?"

"No, no," Hansum said, feeling conflicted. "A walk would be .. . good."

Guilietta turned and slowly walked south. Hansum followed. They strolled in silence toward the Porte del Calzaro gate, the moon rising directly in front of them.

Pan had explained to Hansum that the walls of Verona then were not the structures visible in the twenty-fourth century, except for a small remnant of an old inner wall. The walls which Guilietta and Romero strolled toward were built before the advent of powerful black powder and cannons. Pan had explained how they had to be replaced with cannon-resistant walls when that technology became available. But now there were twenty-seven miles of outer wall protecting the city. Made of red brick, they were forty feet high, twelve feet thick at the bottom and eight at the top. There was a walkway at the top from which troops could both defend the city and move from one of the forty-nine towers to the next. There was also a canal that ran along the outside of most of the walls, acting as a moat. There were six gates to enter the city. Guilietta's hands were gently clasped in front of her, Hansum held his behind.

"A very sad thing happened today," Guilietta said.

"What was left of . . . Father Aaron, it was horrible."

"It is a cruel world, Romero."

"My world isn't like this," Hansum said shaking his head.

"It is everyone's world, Romero. But it can also be very beautiful. Father Aaron once told me that life is a dance. A dance where we live with one foot in Heaven and one foot in Hell. We dance back and forth between the two and are given a choice. Life is learning to always dance back into Heaven. Tell me, Romero, is it just the death of the Holy Father that makes you so sad?"

Hansum stopped and turned toward Guilietta. She stopped and looked back up at him, the moon dancing in her eyes.

"I can never go home," Hansum said. "My family doesn't even exist."

"My poor Romero." Hansum felt Guilietta's warm hand on his arm. "The death of the Holy Father has reminded you of your own family's loss."

"Something like that," he answered, looking into her brown eyes.

"Don't worry, Romero. I'm sure they are all safe in Jesus' arms."

"Everything that's happened has made me realize how much I miss my family."

Now Guilietta took his hands in hers. She looked up at him, saying earnestly, "We are your family now, Romero."

He thought what the image of the dying Arimus said, "Find happiness where you can," and "Happiness is a decision." He gently squeezed Guilietta's beautiful hands, stroking them with his thumbs.

"Will you be my family, Guilietta?" They stood in the middle of the road, hands clasped together for the first time, their eyes and lips close. Hansum couldn't tell if it was the gravity of the moon shining in the sky or that of their young hearts, but he felt them being pulled together.

"Si, I will be your family, Romero."

The clop-clop-clop of a horse-drawn wagon came out of nowhere. They both looked up, breaking the spell. The wagon wasn't going very quickly and Hansum gently pulled Guilietta to the road's edge. The driver was an old man with a beard and floppy straw hat. He smiled at them, slowing, but not stopping.

"Young lovers' kisses call forth hot wishes," he said. "Don't waste your beautiful years when life is full of tears." Then he winked, snapped the reins of the horse and continued on his way. Alone again, Guilietta and Hansum giggled, their mood lightening somewhat. Then shyly, both looked away from each other and resumed their walk. Guilietta's arms were now by her side. After a few strides, Hansum reached over and took her hand.

She did not pull away. They walked together, deep in their own thoughts, occasionally looking at one another and smiling.

As they arrived at the massive tower, the moon was now high overhead. They walked up to the closed heavy wrought-iron gate and peered through at the raised drawbridge. They could hear the fast-moving water of the canal on the other side and Hansum realized he had never been to the edge of the city before. A man's voice came out of the night.

"Buona sera." A figure appeared out of a door to the tower. It was a city guard wearing a leather tunic and chausses. He had a kettle helmet, but wore no chain mail. "Can I help you?"

"Grazie, no," Hansum said. "We're just out for a walk."

"Ah, I see. A beautiful night for such a thing." He looked at them closely. "I've not seen either of you before. Where do you live?"

"Just up the road. We've only been here a month. I'm Romero. This is Guilietta."

"My father is Master della Cappa, the lensmaker."

"Ah, si. That big shipment a while ago. So, you're out for a walk?" the guard continued. "Not advisable to go outside the gate. Besides, it's too much work to lower the bridge."

"We understand," Hansum said. "We'll just turn around and . . ."

"Say, I have an idea," the guard offered. "Have you ever walked along the top of the wall? With the moon out, it's very pleasant. You can walk over to the next gate and go home up the Corso del Palio."

"Is that permitted?" Guilietta asked.

The guard shrugged, made a face and winked.

The stairway up the tower was dark and narrow. The two teenagers followed the guard, Guilietta holding Hansum's hand. They were pointed down the length of the brick walkway and bid goodnight. Hansum found it amazing to stand on the wall. With a full moon shining, he could look over the countryside to the south for miles. Looking back over the city, he could see all the church steeples, towers, tile roofs, smoke of many chimneys wafting up into the air, and even the top courses of the ancient

Roman Arena. Guilietta leaned between two parapets and gazed up at the moon. Hansum stepped behind her and put his hands lightly on her arms.

"It's a beautiful view," she said.

"Si, and I have an especially beautiful view." He saw Guilietta smile. Then a chill breeze came up and she shuddered. "It's getting cold," Hansum added. "We should get going . . ."

Guilietta spun around in Hansum's arms and kissed him. It took Hansum a few moments to recover from his surprise, but when he did, he responded well. They kissed long and hard, and soon Hansum was oblivious to the rest of the universe, his past, present and his future. All that existed for him was an undeniable intensity between the two. Hansum finally came up from his deep well of delicious drowning and looked into Guilietta's eyes. He could now see in her that instant familiarity which each person instinctively craves.

"We'd better get going," he said, smiling. "Your father is going to wonder." They walked and skipped along the wall, hand in hand, giggling and stealing kisses.

They came to a small guard tower and looked inside the room. It was empty. Guilietta stepped in and Hansum suddenly felt himself being pulled after. Still holding his hand, she leaned against the wall and gave her beau a wicked smile. He complied by pressing his whole body against hers and they kissed deeply again and again.

Sometime later, they were walking home briskly, still giggling and laughing, stopping to kiss often, then rushing on. As they got closer, they stopped and took extra care in straightening out their clothes and expressions. They kissed one next to last time, started to walk, then needed to kiss a very last time. The last bit home, they walked as solemnly as possible, their hands by their sides, in case the Master was out front waiting.

The house was dark. Guilietta entered quietly and bid Hansum one last good night till the morrow. Never had a door taken so long to close. But finally the latch found its home. Hansum listened and heard the stairs creak as Guilietta softly walked up them. How he wished he was still with her. Finally he pulled himself away and headed for his own bed. As he walked down the alley, he skipped, he was so happy. Then he remembered. Arimus was dead. They were stuck in the fourteenth century. His bouncing walk slowed to a funeral dirge as the implications sunk in once more. He never would see his family again. His parents, who were not even born yet, would never meet Guilietta.

He was still thinking these dark thoughts when he entered the shop. He stopped short. There was the Master sitting at the lathe, literally burning the midnight oil.

"You're back," Master della Cappa said flatly.

"Si, Master."

"You okay?"

"Si, Master. Guilietta and I walked to the gates and then around a little. It cooled my head."

The Master just looked at him. Luckily he was wearing his safety glasses with the strong lenses. That and the dirt from working made it hard to see Hansum clearly. But Hansum saw Agistino more clearly now. Here sat a fourteenth-century man, hardworking, skilled, one who accepted responsibility for his family. His gruffness and his grimy outward appearance were not so terrible now that Hansum could understand them in their true context.

"Guilietta in the house?" the Master asked.

"Si, Master."

"Are you going to be able to do what is necessary tomorrow and for the next months? Forever?"

Hansum paused. This was the question that now loomed over them all.

Chapter 3

Rows of skulls peered out at Hansum from the rock ledge of the catacomb. They were the skulls of hundreds of priests who had served the church over the last hundreds of years. What was left of Arimus was joining them. He was told that, in a year or two, when all the worldly flesh had disappeared from Father Aaron, his skull would proudly be displayed with the others. Hansum, Shamira and Lincoln stared in horror at the stacks of the other bones: legs, arms, pelvises, ribs and more. They were piled up to the ceiling in deep stone cribs. The vaulted underground chamber was also crowded with living people today. The teens, the della Cappas and Ugilino were the only representatives of the deceased's family and friends. The rest were priests and monks.

In the same way that Hansum was seeing Agistino differently, he was seeing everything differently. Things seemed, looked, smelled, felt... different. The rude fabric of the monks' hassocks seemed rougher, more textured. Hansum, having now spent weeks doing manual labor, imagined the coarse wool being spun by hand and woven on simple looms. When he looked at the monks' gaunt and dirty faces, all rough with stubble, Hansum could see the plain wooden bowls of food put before the brothers each night, meager rations in each. He pictured their crude living quarters without running water to bathe or shave.

Looking into the eyes of individuals devout to their religious convictions was one of the scariest things for Hansum. No longer could he look at the faith that permeated the whole society as naive rationalization and superstition. He now saw unyielding spiritual convictions of which he must be wary. He must not misspeak. "It's all so surreal," he had confided to Pan.

As the ceremony ended, Hansum walked up to the ossuary with the others. As he tried to mumble his goodbyes, the stinging odor of the rotting, maggoty flesh in the stone box wafted into his nose and eyes. He began to weep as everything around him seemed to scream that life was a frenzied race to the grave.

Finally, the della Cappas were directed to leave the catacomb. They followed behind the procession of the Bishop and priests. As they came up into the cloud-covered cemetery beside San Zeno, Shamira began crying too. Hansum, Lincoln and Guilietta came to her aid and put their arms around her, ushering her forward. Hansum felt his hand covered by another's. It was Guilietta's. Their wet eyes met in a long, sorrowful gaze and they entwined fingers as they exited the church cemetery.

As they got to the large square in front of the church, Hansum saw Prince Feltrino standing on the steps. He let go of Guilietta's hand, lest anyone see this impropriety. He stood straight and watched Feltrino, whose eyes were locked on Guilietta. The family stopped briefly and said their goodbyes to the Bishop in public, which Hansum knew was a great honor for Master della Cappa. Many eyes were on them. It was good for business. He saw Feltrino approach and then felt Father Lurenzano's hand on his arm, quietly pulling him, then Lincoln and Shamira, away from the group. A serious looking Feltrino bowed to the Bishop, then Master della Cappa. Then he made a prolonged bow to Guilietta. He looked into her eyes, saying something Hansum couldn't hear. Hansum took an involuntary step forward, but felt Lurenzano's hand on his shoulder again. He also felt Feltrino's eyes dart toward him, and their gazes locking. The young noble moved his eyes back to Guilietta, but Hansum saw the Prince put his hand on the hilt of his sword and squeeze.

"Take care, Master Hansum," Pan whispered. *"We are now in a very new situation."*

Chapter 4

"The poor orphans," the Signora said in the dark of her bedroom.

"Who are you speaking to," the Master's voice said back to her.

"You, of course, husband. Who else?"

"I thought maybe one of your angels."

"Oh no, dear. Archangel Michael leaves when you come to bed. But he told me we must be patient with the orphans. He says they came from a home far different from ours and are feeling very lonely. But with patience and care, they will blossom."

Agistino reached over and patted his wife's side, then lay there in the dark, thinking. It had been three days since the funeral. On the day after, four people came to buy discs for the eyes. The next, six. He was almost out of stock, but couldn't get the three youths back to working as efficiently as before. The two boys were now very slow and even forgetful, almost as bad as Ugilino. The shop was becoming messy and the kitchen girl wasn't cooking. She was just putting out cold food and leftovers. And meals were always late.

"You should have gone to repast this morning, Master Hansum," Pan said. The imp was standing by the work table, his eyes at a height where he could see the lenses sitting next to the empty bone frames. "You've hardly eaten in three days. You must keep up your strength."

"Master della Cappa says I've fallen behind setting the lenses. I'm just trying to catch up."

"But you're just sitting here," Pan replied. There was a click as the latch to the shop door rose. Before the door opened, Pan was gone. Hansum looked up. The beautiful face of Guilietta peeked around the door. Hansum stood up quickly and smiled as best he could. Guilietta smiled back and came in, holding a covered plate of food. She closed the door behind her.

"You're alone?" Hansum asked.

She nodded. Hansum quickly walked over, took the plate from her with one hand and wrapped the other around her waist, pulling their bodies together. Their mouths met and a warm, comforting wave washed over Hansum from head to toe.

"Oh, I've missed your lips," Guilietta sighed while taking a breath in between kisses.

"And I, yours," Hansum replied.

"You didn't come to repast. I was worried for you. We're all worried."

"I wasn't hungry."

"I was thinking you didn't want to see me anymore."

"What?" Hansum was shocked. "No, Guilietta, no." He quickly put down the plate and took both of her hands. "It's just that . . . with all that's happened, I'm confused. Sad. I've never experienced anything like this before."

Guilietta looked up at Hansum with two clear eyes. "Then you still love me?"

Hansum realized that in all of his playing around the past few years, this was one thing he never considered, never uttered. Hansum finally found his smile again.

"Guilietta. I've loved you since I first set eyes on you." They beamed at each other and were about to embrace when the door latch clicked again. Hansum stepped over and picked up the plate. The door opened and in walked Ugilino, followed by the Master, Shamira and Lincoln. Hansum stood with the plate in his hand.

"You haven't eaten yet?" the Master said.

"It's delicious . . ." Hansum began to say, till he looked down to see the cloth still on the plate. The Master stepped over to the work table and looked at the empty frames.

"What have you been doing all this time?" Hansum flinched, but Agistino didn't shout. "Children," he said, "come stand around me. The Holy Father would not want his investment in our family to be for naught. In his good memory, we must continue with strong hearts and trust that God will help us succeed. Boys, let us to work. Girls, go to the market and provision the house again. Make meals that will nourish us well and make our hearts happy."

So, Hansum sat back down and began to work. He saw Lincoln loading the dops with glass blanks and bringing the Master what he needed. But it was not easy to keep his mind on work. He kept thinking of the maggot-filled ossuary and the skulls in the crypt. Other times he would find himself with images of his home, his parents and Charlene in his thoughts. Often he would be flying in a hover jet, high over the mountains, going to school or in space on a vacation to the moon. Then he'd hear the Master call out his name and he'd find himself, once again, staring at his hands or at something on the work table.

At night Hansum and Lincoln spoke to Pan about their fears. Were they now at the mercy of every microbe and malfeasant infesting this world? Apparently, a quarter of all newborns didn't make it to the age of one. More than another quarter didn't survive to their fifth birthday. Workers who broke bones or sustained serious injuries most often died of infections.

To allay these fears, Pan reminded the teens they still had their twenty-fourth century inoculation implants. These shielded their bodies from everything that was not symbiotic to their individual genetic sequencing. They were usually renewed every three years in youths as they grew. Implants for adults could last a lifetime, but none of the teens had those yet. And since none had ever worried about such things as inoculation dates, not one of them could accurately say when their three years were up. Hansum was pretty sure his last inoculation implant had been updated only a few months before their adventure. Shamira thought her three years were almost done, but couldn't say for sure. Lincoln didn't have a clue.

"My mom always told me it was my body so I should keep track of it," he admitted, scolding himself.

"Oh, not to worry, Master Lincoln," Pan soothed. "As soon as we are properly settled, we shall start creating and storing antibiotics and medicines that will come in handy. I'm sure I can keep us all safe." But despite all of Pan's sincere reassurances, he knew the teens had to grieve.

For Hansum, accepting his new life was the easiest. He had Guilietta, although spending time together, this was a problem. But like young lovers everywhere and at every time, ways were always found. Hansum took to getting up an hour or two before daylight and stood in the alleyway, waiting for Guilietta. They would walk to the market, strolling through the streets, hand in hand. Sometimes they would climb into the old coliseum, the Arena. Sitting high in the old stone stands, they would cuddle and kiss as the stray cats hunted for mice. They would then stand on the top tier and watch the sun rise over the city. On these clandestine mornings, Shamira would cover for them by sleeping on the cot on the main floor. If the Master came down early, the story would be she wasn't feeling well and Guilietta had gone to the market early to get this or that special item that they knew was in short supply. Hansum and Guilietta were always sure to be back before repast, except once, when Guilietta came in, laden with three bags of supplies. Her father met her at the door.

"You carried all this yourself from the market?" he asked, perplexed.

"Here's the last bag," Hansum said popping his head in the door quickly, surprised to see the Master. Hansum could see the Master scrunch up his face suspiciously.

"What were you . . ."

"Buon giorno, Master," Hansum said quickly and putting on a bright smile. "I was up early setting lenses and Guilietta came to the shop to find another carrying bag. She said Carmella wasn't feeling well, so I went with her to help." The Master stared at him warily. "Lucky I did," Hansum added, not changing his happy face one iota.

"Oh, you were able to get the fresh carp," Shamira said, adding an extra diversion. "That's your favorite, Master. Yes, it's good you went, Romero. Guil and I could never have carried all this."

Just then a tousle-haired Lincoln sleepily clomped into the house.

"Waz everyone doin' up so early?" he said wearily. He was hatless and his hair was sticking out in every direction.

"You walk in the streets and into my house like this?" the Master chastised.

"Waz wrong?" Lincoln said through sleep-filled eyes.

The Master grabbed him in a playful headlock and messed up his hair more, which of course sent the younger teen into fits.

"You want to be messy, I make you more messy," the Master teased, not letting go no matter how much Lincoln struggled. The other teenagers began to laugh. It was the first time in a week everybody laughed together. "Okay, we leave the girls to put away the provisions and make dinner," Agistino said with Lincoln's face still trapped under his armpit. "Come boys, back to the shop."

"Let me go, Master, let go," Lincoln cried, now laughing himself. "Have you ever taken a bath?" But the big man ignored him.

"Come, let's go see how many lenses Romero set before going off to do woman's work," and he strode out the door, dragging a giggling and flailing Lincoln.

The girls were still laughing when Hansum realized what the Master had said. Of course there was no sign of his work. A look of humorous panic broke out on his face as he raced after the Master, causing the girls to giggle even harder.

"What's all the laughing?" a voice from the stairs said. It was the Signora, up and moving all by herself.

"Papa was just teasing Maruccio and it was very funny, Mama."

"Oh," the Signora said excitedly. She smiled and clenched her fists, hopping up and down on the steps, which began to spring up and down precariously. "You were right, Michael," she squealed, looking back upstairs, "You were right, Holy Angel. Our house is happy again."

Chapter 5

In the shop the Master still held Lincoln in a headlock.

"You walk the streets representing my house with a head like this? Like an old dust broom?"

"Lemme go, Master," Lincoln shouted. "I'll be good, I'll be . . ."

"Yes, you'll be good," the Master laughed. "And you'll be clean." And with that, he lifted Lincoln off the ground and dunked his head in the icy water of the water barrel. The Master bobbed Lincoln up and down a few times, laughing and winking at an astonished Hansum. Then he plopped the boy back down on his feet and stood back, hands on his hips.

Lincoln danced around on the spot, gasping for air and shaking his head violently. Water sprayed everywhere. Then he stood still, frozen on the spot, a wild look in his eyes.

"*Oh, oh,*" Pan whispered to Hansum.

Hansum had to agree. Lincoln was most likely going to flip out. But nothing happened. Standing there like a wet cat, Lincoln just put his arms down by his side and took a deep breath.

"Okay, I give up," he said.

"What? What are you talking about?" Hansum asked.

"I give up," Lincoln said again. "I'm not going to fight it anymore."

"What do you mean?" Hansum asked again.

"I mean we're stuck here. We can never go back to our old life." Lincoln didn't seem to be worrying that he was talking this way in front of the Master. "I'm driving myself crazy worrying about it. But it can't be helped. And like Arimus . . . like Father Aaron said, happiness is a choice. Well, I guess I'm choosing to be happy."

"Oh my, I think he finally gets it," Pan whispered to Hansum.

"The Holy Father was wise," the Master said crossing himself. "We must take what life gives us, for we have no choice about that. And we will all make mistakes. But with work and by using the resources we can muster, we can make a good life for ourselves."

The three men, young and old, looked at each other.

"I'm in too," Hansum added.

Later at dinner, everyone seemed in a much better mood. Everyone bowed their heads and said a prayer for Father Aaron, and when they finished, they did not look sad. Shamira uncovered a bowl on the table and revealed their meal.

"Aspic of beef! Bravo, Carmella. Bravo Guilietta." the Master crowed.

"Thank you, Master."

"Thank you, Papa."

The Signora clapped her hands and bounced on the bench. Then the door opened quickly and Ugilino walked in.

"Master, Master," Ugilino called, out of breath.

"Of course, who shows up when food is served?" Agistino said. Ugilino stopped and stared at the table, looking somewhat hurt. The Master laughed. "No, come my boy. Sit in your place and tell me what makes you so out of breath." Ugilino relaxed and sat at his place by Hansum, now smiling.

"I got us another church to visit, Santa Anastasia. Next Sabbath. I already gave the priest his discs for the eyes."

"Bravo to you too, Ugilino," the Master said. "Come, let's eat. Say your prayers, Ugi."

As the meal was coming to an end, the Master dusted the crumbs off of his front, got up and went up the stairs to his bedroom. He came back holding the telescope.

"We must start showing these around," he said.

Hansum, Shamira and Lincoln looked at each other cautiously.

"I don't want to disappear," Lincoln whispered to Hansum.

"Do you really think that's a good idea, Master?" Hansum asked. "It's only a toy."

"Oh, I think we can sell quite a few of these. And it's more than just a toy. Come, we must go to the shop."

"I'm going for my nap, dears," the Signora said yawning. "No, daughter, I can get there myself."

"I'll come to the shop too, Papa," Guilietta said. "I want to learn to set the lenses, like Carmella." Ugilino made a face. "After all," Guilietta added, "if Ugilino is going to be selling so many more discs for the eyes, we must all be ready." Ugilino smiled broadly now. As they walked out the door, Guilietta asked. "May I look through the new invention again, Papa?"

Lincoln leaned close to Hansum. "Do you really think that introducing this thing to the world can change the timeline? That one of us may disappear?"

"We're gonna find out," Hansum replied.

Chapter 6

Feltrino Gonzaga was riding his horse in the direction he was told he'd find the lensmaker's. He knew he was pressing his luck staying in Verona. He could be recognized at any time by a soldier or another noble, so he moved cautiously. He would have left that morning, now that his horse wasn't lame, but he couldn't get that beautiful girl, Guilietta, out of his mind. That had been his main weakness the past few years, beautiful girls, and some not so beautiful ones. But this one was a beauty.

He was glad the Bishop of San Zeno fed him that morning because he had not been able to find much money. Only fifty denari in his pouch, part won gambling at a tavern last night, the rest robbed from a drunk at swordpoint afterward. Arriving at the street he was told the lensmaker's house was on, he pulled up on his horse's reins and looked around.

"God, look at these hovels," he muttered. "They're only good for burning. Now which one are you hiding in, my beauty? God, don't make me knock on every damned door." As if in answer to his prayers, he saw a door open and out walked the object of his adoration. Behind Guilietta was that bear of a father and that motley crew of apprentices. The girl was holding some cylinder and put it to her eye. Everyone was laughing and acting like a happy family. Feltrino found it odd that a master was so nice to his subordinates. His father wasn't this way.

"Oh look," Guilietta said, aiming the telescope across the road and down the alley beside the tailor's house. "I can see Master Satore working in his garden. It's like he's right in front of me. Look at the size of that squash." Guilietta then lifted the cardboard and lens invention, pointing it toward the city. "And look. The morning doves sit upon the roof of Castlevecchio so peacefully. There's twelve of them. And a yellow and black canary sits with them." Something walked in front of the lens. Guilietta lowered the telescope and found she was staring up at a man on a very large horse. It was the noble who was leering at her at the church, Feltrino.

"Buon giorno," Feltrino said, looking down from his mount. "Master della Cappa," he said, still keeping his eyes on Guilietta. His large stallion stepped around nervously, causing Guilietta to back up. Feltrino hit the horse hard on the neck and the animal calmed somewhat. Feltrino dismounted, straightened his sword, then held out the reins to Lincoln. "Tie my horse to that post," Feltrino said with a sneer. Lincoln, who had never been around animals, looked up at the huge beast, which chose that time to give a loud snort. "Now, you fool!" Lincoln took the reins and looked nervously about. He walked toward an old broken post by the edge of the house, but when he got to the end of the tether, the horse didn't follow. Instead, it pulled its massive head in the opposite direction. Lincoln was lurched backwards and dropped the reins. Hansum quickly took hold of them.

"He's never been with horses, Signor," Hansum said. Feltrino looked angry again.

"Romero, don't speak unless spoken to," the Master said quickly. "Not to a noble."

As the two teens tied the horse up, Lincoln looked fearful as he tried to stay away from the huge hooves.

"Fools," Feltrino chuckled. Then he looked like he smelled something bad. "This is where you make your wonderful discs for the eyes?"

"Our shop is around the back, Excellency. It's brand new. Would you like to see?" As Hansum and Lincoln rejoined the group, Agistino motioned for them to stand by Ugilino and to also take a step backwards.

"What?" Feltrino finally asked. He hadn't really heard what Agistino said. "Oh, see your shop. Yes. Perhaps the young signorina could give me a tour. I'd love to see all, especially if it's new and . . . virginal."

While Guilietta looked quickly down, all three boys became angry. Ugilino and Lincoln didn't move, but Hansum stepped toward the Prince. Agistino moved sideways, blocking Hansum's path, but keeping his eyes on Feltrino.

"I'm afraid my daughter knows nothing of lensmaking, Excellency. You wanted discs for the eyes for your father? That would be a wonderful gift from a loving son, I'm sure."

"Ah, yes. Well, perhaps another time for that," he said, trying to get Guilietta to look at him again. This seemed to be getting too much for even Agistino to put up with.

"Well, Excellency, if I can be of no service to you today, we must to the shop and work."

"I shall have a walk with your daughter then. Perhaps, even a ride," he said looking at his horse.

"She must attend to her mother!" Agistino said, grabbing Guilietta's arm and pulling her toward the house. She dropped the telescope. Feltrino picked it up with his gloved hands.

"What's this then?" he asked, looking at the two lenses.

"Oh that, it's just a toy, Excellency," Agistino said, holding out his arm to take it back.

"How is it used? I saw the beautiful girl hold it to her eye, like this." He pointed it where Guilietta had, toward Castlevecchio. His eyes went wide. "Witchcraft!" he gasped.

"Oh no," Agistino said, sounding like he really didn't want to be accused of something as serious as that. "It's lenscraft, Excellency, lenscraft. What can be used to make things that are near clear can also be used to make far things close."

Feltrino's preoccupation with Guilietta instantly evaporated. He had never seen or experienced anything like this. He put the tube back to his eye and peered into the distance. "Fantastico!" he said. "The spires of that church have come close to me." He heard a sound across the street and aimed the instrument there. He saw a man and a woman laugh as they worked in a garden. The man had picked up a long squash with a bulbous end and was holding it to his midsection. The woman was laughing with fits. Feltrino could barely hear her laughter, but he could see the glint in her eye and the black around her few teeth. They didn't know they were being spied upon. Feltrino look seriously at Agistino.

"Master. Master della Cappa," he now said with respect. "This is your creation?"

After a pause, Agistino slowly nodded his head once. "It is from my shop, Excellency."

"I would like to take this to my father, Master della Cappa. He may be interested in it." Feltrino knew at once what an important instrument of war this machine could be. And if he could bring this to his father, he would not return seemingly defeated by the world. He would be a hero.

"Well, Excellency, of course," Agistino replied. "They are to be sold. But this is the first one. I have not even put a price on it yet."

"No one else has seen these?"

"No, Excellency."

Feltrino thought deeply for a moment. "Master della Cappa, perhaps you may even consider moving your shop to Mantua. I'm sure my father will offer patronage to a craftsman such as yourself."

"Oh, Excellency, we are well settled here with a new shop."

"Perhaps you will change your mind." Feltrino went to his horse and took a piece of wrinkled parchment from a sack. "You, boy," he said to Lincoln, "turn around." Using Lincoln's back, Feltrino wrote on the paper, 'Safe passage to Mantua. – Feltrino Gonzaga'. He handed it to Agistino. "Myself or someone else will come to talk to you in the future. In the meantime, if you want to travel to Mantua, this will get you there safely." Feltrino smiled his most sincere smile for the Master. "And I'm sure we could find much better accommodations for you." He saw Master della Cappa looking at him, stone-faced, trying not to show favor or dislike for the suggestion. The girl was still standing, her hands clutched and staring at the ground, embarrassed. The ugly apprentice was not looking at him, knowing not to stare at a noble, but the other two apprentices and the kitchen girl were eyeing him very boldly, even with disdain. "Well, I must be off home," Feltrino said. "I have been too long away. I shall take your wonderful machine and show it . . ."

"Excellency, please, I must have it back," Agistino said.

"What? What did you say to me?" Feltrino said, whirling around accusingly.

"My device. It is the first and not . . . not yet perfected."

"It works perfectly well. No, I will have it and send for more."

"But Excellency . . ."

"Don't talk back to your betters, lensmaker," Feltrino said, raising his voice. "I say things once and expect obedience."

Feltrino reminded himself of his father when he spoke those words. He turned and strode to his horse.

"Hey!" Hansum shouted, stepping quickly forward.

"Romero, no!" Agistino cried. But Hansum was already next to Feltrino, reaching to grab the telescope. Without a hint of warning, Feltrino spun around, his sword now in his other hand. The metal hilt struck Hansum in the cheek, forcing him to fly backward and onto his back.

"Romero!" Guilietta screamed.

Hansum looked up and saw a sword point pushing into his tunic.

"Please, Excellency, it's yours," Agistino pleaded. "Take the . . ."

A rumble of hooves was heard up the street. Everyone, including Feltrino, looked to the noise. Half a dozen mounted soldiers were galloping into view. The officer in front had his sword drawn and his helmet's cover down. The soldiers behind him all had poleaxes at the ready. The officer's helmet turned toward where Hansum was lying and pointed his sword at Feltrino. Feltrino made to turn to his horse, but stopped, knowing there was no way he could get away. It was only moments before the group was surrounded by soldiers. Two of the soldiers quickly dismounted and pointed the very sharp spikes at the end of their poleaxes at Feltrino.

"Put down your sword, Gonzaga," the officer called. Feltrino relaxed and smiled. He clipped the sword back on his belt. "On the ground!" the officer said.

"A nice blade like this?" Feltrino said lightly. "Ah well." He dropped his sword to the cobblestones. The officer motioned for one of his men to fetch it.

"Stand away from your mount," the officer said. He lifted his visor. He had a scar running from his forehead and down to his cheek. Hansum scrambled to his feet and went to stand next to the Master. Guilietta and Shamira came to check where he had been hit, but Agistino hissed at them to back up. Another rumble was heard, this time hooves and wheels. An ornate covered

carriage came down the road and stopped. The driver dismounted and opened the passenger door.

After a pause, a thin, haughty man stepped onto the street.
He wore soft kid boots to his knees, his chausses were dark blue
velvet, his braies, gold. Around his neck was a gold and silver
chain. He looked at Feltrino and then to the officer, questioningly.

"It's him, Excellency," the officer said.

"Very good, Captain Caesar." The well dressed man, obviously a noble, walked toward the group. The soldiers parted and the
man stood next to Feltrino.

"You're Luigi's boy, eh?" he asked.

"Feltrino Gonzaga," Feltrino said, nodding almost courteously. "And you are Baron da Pontremoli." The man who, was a
baron, looked somewhat surprised. "I saw you at the peace trea-
ty when my father took Reggio from you," Feltrino explained.
"That's where this one got such a nice scar," he said pointing to
Captain Caesar. "I was ten at the time, I think."

"We received a report from someone who recognized you,"
da Pontremoli said. "Why are you skulking around a Scallari
town, Prince Feltrino?"

"Skulking? Oh no, Signor. I found the body of a priest and
brought it back to the Bishop. And now I stay because . . ." he
pointed a thumb at Guilietta.

"Who are they?" the Baron asked, looking at Master della
Cappa. "Who are you?" he asked directly.

"I am Master Agistino della Cappa, Excellency," Agistino said,
"Master lensmaker."

"You're the one making those new discs for the eyes I've seen
around town?"

"Si, Excellency."

"And your daughter?"

Agistino became very agitated. He waved his hands back and
forth in front of him. Guilietta looked doubly embarrassed now.
"No, no, no, Excellency. There has been no funny business here.
My daughter is a good Christian girl. She does not . . ."

"Si, si, si, Master. Be calm, be calm," da Pontremoli said. "Then
what is your business with this Gonzaga?"

"He just came here. He saw the new device. He was just leaving."

"What new device?" The Baron saw Feltrino put something behind his back. "What's that?"

"Nothing. It's mine," Feltrino said. "He gave it to me." He held the telescope away from the Baron. Hansum stepped forward quickly, snatched it from Feltrino's hand and held it toward the Baron. The noble took it into his long, thin palm and regarded it critically.

"It's parchment," the nobleman observed somewhat dismissively to Agistino.

"And the finest crystal lenses at either end, Signor," Agistino replied. "You put that end to your eye and look at something in the distance. The roof of the castle over there, perhaps?"

The reserved gentleman's eyebrows rose in surprise as he experienced magnified vision for the first time.

"Do you see the birds, Excellency?" Agistino asked.

"There's a yellow canary sitting with twelve doves!" Ugilino croaked enthusiastically. The Master whacked Ugilino's arm, silencing him.

"Did you create this?" the Baron asked Agistino in amazement.

The Master shrugged a little and nodded. "It comes from my shop," he repeated.

"Do you know who I am?"

"No, Signor. I just moved to town from Florence."

"I am Baron Nicademo da Pontremoli, the Podesta's secretary."

"Ahhh," Agistino said, bowing somewhat.

"And you are doing business with this Gonzaga?"

"Oh no, Excellency, I wasn't. I swear to you . . ."

"He had your device in his hand, Master della Cappa."

"That right, Excellency, but no Excellency. I wasn't . . . It's not like that . . ." Agistino was becoming quite flustered. The Baron did not look pleased.

"Excuse me for speaking out of turn, Baron da Pontremoli," Hansum said. "Signor Gonzaga picked up Master della Cappa's device when it fell and refused to give it back. Even when he asked politely." He rubbed the rising bruise on his face when he said this.

"Put him in the carriage, Captain," Baron da Pontremoli said, nodding to Feltrino. Bring his horse. He will be our . . . guest . . . at the palace." Two soldiers took Feltrino by the arms and led him away.

"Don't touch me! I protest," Feltrino argued. "You can't arrest me. I'm a noble!"

"Oh, tosh, Prince Feltrino. You are our guest," the Baron said with some sarcasm. "Our noble guest." This infuriated Feltrino.

"I am expected home by my father. Let me go. I'll get you, lensmaker. You and your whore daughter . . ." he called as he was led away. Agistino was very upset now and Guilietta fell into Shamira's arms.

"My daughter is not what he claims, Excellency. I showed him every courtesy and yet he continued his rudeness . . ."

"That is no matter, Master della Cappa. Prince Feltrino has a very bad reputation with the women. I'm sure your child is quite chaste." Hansum saw Guilietta blush a bright pink. "Now, Master della Cappa, about this device." He put the telescope to his eye again and looked down the street one way, then the other. "Magnifico! Spettacolare!" he said. Then he lowered the telescope and asked, "What do you call this amazing instrument, Master della Cappa?"

Agistino looked non-plussed. "I, I hadn't thought of that, Excellency. One just looks through it," he said. "I guess it's a looker," he finally declared.

Both Hansum and Lincoln rolled their eyes at that.

"It's a fine name," da Pontremoli said. "I'm going to take your looker to the Podesta. He may be interested in such a thing."

For the second time in a short while, Agistino involuntarily reached to retrieve the telescope, but stopped before his hands came near the person of da Pontremoli.

"It's my only one," he said.

"Can you not make more?"

"Oh yes," he said. "It's just, this is the original."

"I see," the Podesta's secretary said. He reached into his pouch and took out some coins, holding them before Agistino. Agistino looked at the coins sitting in da Pontremoli's palm.

"Oh, it's worth three times this, Signor. At least."

Da Pontremoli came nose to nose with Agistino and smiled sardonically. He took Agistino's blush-stained hand, turned it palm up and placed the coins in it. Closing the meaty fingers around the money, the Baron said, "If I am correct and you are lucky, della Cappa, my master will pay you ten times this for many, many more."

Chapter 7

As Agistino watched the Baron's carriage and soldiers rumble back down the street, he felt confused. He had in his hand silver coins which, a few moments earlier, were in a nobleman's pouch. He had been told there could be many more. This was an opportunity he could not squander. He had to think.

"To the shop," he said, lumbering away. He always thought best at his lathe.

"Those are shiny coins, Master," Ugilino said, bouncing along by him.

"Quiet, I'm thinking," Agistino barked.

The first thing Agistino did in the shop was go to his lathe, but before he sat, he realized he was still holding the note from Feltrino. He impaled it onto a nail sticking out of the wall. Then he sat down, put the coins in his pouch and barked for Lincoln to fetch the tools to make lenses for forty to forty-five-year-olds.

The first thing the girls did was to tend to Hansum's blackening eye, washing it with cool water.

After working on a lens for a while, Agistino paused and smiled. "What luck today," he said.

"Luck? What luck?" Guilietta replied, miffed. She dabbed at Hansum's forehead somewhat more forcefully than needed. "Look at Romero's eye and remember what I was called!"

"The lord works in mysterious ways," Agistino answered, still smiling. "The Podesta's own man has seen our invention and appreciates its possibilities."

"Yeah, everybody seems to be getting really excited about that thing," Lincoln observed.

"Si, and if we are to start making these, these . . . lookers," Agistino continued, "we must double our efforts at keeping up stock on the discs for the eyes." The Master's mood became serious again. "Back to work, all of us! Girls, stop fawning over Romero and let him set lenses."

While they were toiling, Pan began whispering to Hansum.

"Master Hansum, for this telescope to find wide use among the military, I believe we must modify its design slightly."

"What do you want me to do?" Hansum mumbled while setting a lens.

"Say to the Master. . ."

"Master, I have an improvement I think we should make to the looker," Hansum repeated.

"What? What do you mean?" the Master asked, looking up curiously.

"Suggest you draw them out with Shamira and that you will show him later." The Master agreed, smiling and crossing himself several times. Later, after supper, Agistino made another declaration.

"We must now work day and night for a time, to continue building stock. But right now we will leave Romero and Carmella to make some drawings of another looker. Guilietta, you wanted to learn to set lenses. Tonight I shall show you. Ugilino, you must clean up after both me and Maruccio."

"My joy is to serve, Master," Ugilino said, amazingly without complaint.

Guilietta smiled appreciatively at Ugilino and the ugly apprentice beamed. The Signora, much healthier of mind lately, announced that she was going for a walk all by herself.

When Shamira and Hansum were left in the house, Pan popped out onto the table. He cracked his tiny knuckles and whipped his new, longer tail a few times.

"Let's get to work," he said.

Sometime later, with the drawing of the improved looker finished, Pan gave them a final explanation of its attributes.

"You see, young master and mistress, the back barrel of this version moves in and out, just enough to allow the viewer to change the focal length of the lenses to accommodate his or her particular vision . . ." Pan stopped and instantly disappeared. His sensitive hearing had perceived the door to the house opening quietly. From where his lamp was, ensconced in Shamira's veil and resting on the table, he couldn't whisper a warning that someone was entering. But he could see them.

The two men were not thieves, not common ones anyway. They were well-dressed noblemen. One was Nicademo da Pontremoli, the Podesta's personal secretary. The other was Mastino della Scalla II, the Podesta himself. Pan recognized him from the images of paintings stored in his memory. 'It's true what they said about him,' he thought. 'He does look like a mastiff.' He was named after his great, great grand uncle, Mastino I. His uncle had been Podesta of Verona some fifty years earlier. Several keystones over doors and windows around Verona were still decorated with images of Mastino's dog-like image in the twenty-fourth century.

Mastino was not only the Master of Verona, but also Vicenza and their surrounding lands. The position of Podesta was a family inheritance that he had wrestled away from his two brothers. As a young and ambitious ruler, he took his city to war with the neighbouring city state of Brescia in 1332. A few years later, instead of war, he purchased Parma. Four years after that, he repeated the feat by bloodlessly conquering Lucca by the coin. After the King of France, he was the richest prince of his time.

But Mastino's exploits also gained him many enemies. A powerful league organized against him. Nobles from Venice and

Florence, the Este family, the Visconti and the Gonzagas of Mantua had raised an army against him. After three years of fighting, Mastino was left with what he had started with; Verona and Vicenza. Now, as a middle-aged man, it was his burning ambition to regain his former glories.

The Podesta looked surprised at the lowly surroundings. Pan surmised that della Scalla couldn't believe that the thing they came about was produced here. Nicademo was about to announce them, but Mastino put his hand on the secretary's arm. Shamira was actually addressing Pan, but he had vanished, so, to the Podesta, it looked like she was speaking to Hansum.

"Oh, I see," Shamira said. "If the back tube moves, it allows the viewer to adjust the looker. It makes the image more clear to each individual's eye."

"Yes," Hansum added. "These drawings should really impress the Master." Hansum looked up to speak to Pan and saw the guests. He stood quickly and put a blank parchment over the drawings. "Sorry, Signors. I didn't see you. Are you here to buy discs for the eyes?"

The Podesta took the parchment looker out from his cloak.

"Where is your master?" he asked. Hansum and Shamira saw the telescope they made the other night. Shamira reached down to the table, retrieved her veil and put it over her head.

"Master della Cappa is around back, in the workshop, Signor," Hansum said. "Shall I get him for you?"

Podesta Mastino della Scalla continued to stare silently at the two teenagers. He prided himself on being a good judge of character and believed he saw something odd in their eyes.

"No, you both stay here," he said. With a small wave, the Podesta told his secretary to fetch Agistino. There was something in the eyes of these two, a self-confidence that usually only comes with education and privilege. A kitchen girl and apprentice would usually fidget or leave a room quickly. But although they looked respectful, they did not look cowed.

He walked up to the table and put his hand on the blank parchment. He was about to lift it when Hansum interrupted him.

"Signor..." Hansum began.

"Do you know who I am?"

"I believe I saw you at San Zeno two Sundays ago, Signor. You are the Podesta."

"Podesta della Scalla," Shamira added.

"Then you must know there are no secrets from me in *my* Verona." He slid the blank parchment off of the updated telescope design. His eyesight was not good for reading, so he held the drawing first at arm's length, then close to his face. After a few adjustments, he got the focus. "Girl, you did this drawing?"

"Si, Signor. It's the best I can do with only a charcoal stick."

"Indeed. And you, boy, you conceived this?"

Pan quickly whispered something into Hansum's ear. To the Podesta it seemed like Hansum was pausing to think before he answered.

"This is Master della Cappa's shop, Excellency," Hansum parroted.

"Ah," the Podesta replied, impressed that Hansum wasn't taking credit. "Explain the difference between this prototype looker and the new design."

"Well, Signor," Hansum began, "the first example has a fixed length with two lenses. While it works well enough, the second design allows the back lens to be moved slightly. This way it can be adjusted for different people's eyes, like you did when you were trying to read the parchment. It allows the image to be crisp for each user."

Chapter 8

Just then the door banged open and the Master rushed in, followed closely by the Podesta's secretary, Guilietta, Lincoln and Ugilino. The secretary put his arm up to stop the others from getting too close to Mastino. Agistino was out of breath, red in the face, sweating profusely and still wearing his thick safety glasses and leather helmet.

"Your Excellency, I am sorry I was not here to receive you." He bowed at the waist, wincing as he went too low.

"I've come on the business of your looker," the Podesta said, holding up the telescope. "Very interesting."

"Grazie, Excellency," Agistino puffed, still catching his breath.

"Your apprentice was explaining the difference between the first example and the subsequent design. Perhaps, as the master, you could elaborate." Mastino could see his request had flustered Agistino.

"Elaborate? Subsequent? . . . What?" the Master asked confused.

"Your new and improved design, Master," Hansum prompted, pointing to the table.

"Oh, new design. Yes. Let me see. How is it coming?" Agistino said with fake familiarity. Trying to take command of the situation, he squinted at the drawing and said in a low, serious voice, "Si, si. This looks like it's coming along fine. As we discussed, eh Romero? As I instructed."

"Grazie, Master," Hansum said.

"And well drawn, Carmella."

"Grazie, Master."

"Well, there you have it, Excellency. An improved design."

"In what way?" the Podesta bated.

"You remember, Master," Hansum said quickly. "The back barrel moves to allow adjustment of the eyepiece so the viewer . . ." Mastino put up a hand for Hansum to stop. Then he stared at the Master, raising his eyebrows to bid him continue.

"Well, si. The, uh, back barrel. It slides, in and out. Here. See?"

Mastino had his answer. This young apprentice was apparently a savant and della Cappa had been lucky enough to have him fall into his life.

"Si, of course. I do see, Master della Cappa," the Podesta said. "I understand perfectly. So, della Cappa, these lookers may be of some interest to me. To give to the officers in my army and for the city lookouts. Can you supply them?"

"Si, of course," the Master agreed without hesitation.

"The new design?"

"Si, of course," he repeated. Then Agistino looked at Hansum for confirmation. Hansum nodded as minimally as possible. "How many does His Excellency require? Two, three? Half a dozen?"

"One hundred to begin," the Podesta said.

"One hundred!" the Master gasped.

"Si," the Podesta confirmed. "Is that a problem?"

"Oh no, Excellency. No. When, when do you require them?" he asked nervously.

"Oh, a few as soon as you can. The others, within a month, perhaps."

"One hundred? In a month?" he said incredulously.

"Si, Master della Cappa. But instead of paper, the cylinders must be made of something more sturdy. Perhaps brass," the Podesta suggested.

"Brass? That's expensive. How about the first ones we make from tin sheet? There's a tinsmith down the street. It would be faster. Maybe brass later. Let us make our mistakes in tin."

"Quite sensible, Master della Cappa," the Podesta said. The Master at least didn't appear a complete idiot.

"And the price, your Excellency?"

"What? Oh. Work that out with da Pontremoli. He will come in a few days to write a contract."

"As you wish, Excellency," Agistino answered.

"Before I leave. . ." the Podesta continued. He took out a leather case and opened it. There was a pair of bone spectacle frames with shards from the lenses still stuck to it. "I had an unfortunate accident the other week. I would ask for a pair of discs for the eyes. For myself."

"When do you wish them, Excellency?"

"When? Now!" He looked at Agistino as if he really were an idiot.

"I'm so sorry, Excellency. I have none to give."

Both the Podesta and his secretary looked thoroughly miffed.

"You traipse around Verona with your discs for the eyes," da Pontremoli asked aghast, "priests and butchers everywhere are wearing them, but you have none for our Podesta?"

"Had I known . . . We are so busy that I even sold my samples but an hour ago. Why, we've been grinding and polishing even on the Sabbath and through the nights. That is why I look such a wreck."

"Signori," Hansum said then paused. "Verona has blessed my Master's house with much business." He paused again. "And his discs for the eyes are so perfect and so needed that we've been . . . over blessed by requests for them." Pause. "May I suggest that the Master can make a pair of discs for the eyes this very night? Our vendor, Ugilino, will deliver them to you tomorrow." Pause. "As well, we shall have the prototype of the new looker for your approval then. In parchment, of course, but you will see how it improves the device's performance." Pause. "A week later we shall have some half dozen for you in tin, the balance of the hundred within a month."

"And, and these discs for the eyes will be a gift for His Excellency," the Master added hastily. "No charge, from me to you." He put his ham-like red hands to his bosom and extended them in a gesture of both offering and supplication.

The Podesta took a deep breath and smiled faintly.

"Very well. But do not send your vendor, send him," Mastino said, pointing at Hansum.

"Excellency?"

"And her as well," he said pointing to Shamira.

"But why . . ." Master della Cappa began, then, "As you wish, Excellency," he said, bowing.

"Let us leave, Nicademo," the Podesta said to his secretary, and he walked to the door. The Master genuflected repeatedly as he exited, and motioned for the others to do the same.

The household followed the nobles out. A noisy crowd of neighbors had assembled around the fine carriage, but fell silent when they saw the Podesta. At the carriage, the Podesta turned and faced Hansum and Shamira. He handed Hansum a card with his crest on it.

"Show this to the guard. And girl, bring your drawing." As Mastino looked at Shamira, a small light shone into his eyes from somewhere unseen. The nobleman blinked, rubbed his eyes, then turned to climb into the carriage.

"Thank you, Excellency. God bless you, Excellency," Agistino said, still genuflecting.

Hansum gave Shamira a curious look as the carriage left, seeming to say, 'That was different.' With the noble gone, the crowd became louder again, laughing and patting the Master on the back in congratulations.

"We're starting to mix with elegant company," he said aloud.

Just then the Signora came bolting down the street, her bulk heaving like a mold of aspic.

"My chamber pot, I need my chamber pot," the Signora cried as she ran into the house. Guilietta and Shamira ran in after her. The neighbors broke out into laughter.

"In the house, all of you," the Master commanded to his apprentices.

As they moved back to the house, Hansum's eyes met Ugilino's, who was giving him a very dirty look.

"Hey, it wasn't my idea for me to do the delivery," Hansum said.

Once in the house, the Master got right to it. "Before tomorrow we must produce an especially fine pair of discs for the eyes and a second looker. Romero, let me look at those plans."

While Hansum was getting them, Pan whispered into Hansum's ear. Hansum looked surprised.

"More plans?" he said out loud.

"What did you say?" the Master asked.

"Oh, uh . . . Master, I have another idea . . . for the Podesta's spectacles. Could you grind the lenses for the looker, as I've drawn on the plan here? I'll work with Carmella and draw up this other idea."

Just then Guilietta came down the stairs, holding her mother's chamber pot. Hansum looked up at her and thought how she even looked lovely even doing this chore.

"Ugilino, if you please?" Guilietta handed Ugilino the chamber pot. Without complaint he accepted it.

"My pleasure is to serve," he said, smiling at Guilietta. But when he went out the door, he gave Hansum another dirty look.

"Ugilino, come straight to the shop when you've finished," the Master ordered. "Now, Romero, what did you say? Another idea for the Podesta's discs for the eyes?"

"Yes, Master. If you don't mind, I'll stay here with Carmella and draw them up as fast as we can."

"Certainly, certainly, my boy. Come everyone. To the shop. We have two commissions for the Podesta himself. Romero, what is your idea?

"I really can't say, Master." It was true. Pan hadn't told him yet.

As soon as Shamira and Hansum were alone, Pan came out and stood, Tom Thumb size, on the kitchen table.

"What do you have in mind now?" Hansum asked.

"Another lenscraft idea," Pan said. "I thought we could introduce prescription glasses."

"What's that?" Shamira asked.

"Well, the reading spectacles are for people who are farsighted. They can see distances, but not close up. However, the Podesta can see neither far nor close well. I scanned his eyes just as he was getting into his carriage. I want to show you how to make him spectacles that do both. They're called bifocals. They were first invented in the eighteenth century by Benjamin Franklin, in what was known as the United States."

Less than an hour later, Hansum was showing the Master and everybody else in the shop the drawings for bifocals.

"These lenses allow people to see things both far and near," Hansum explained. Everybody was leaning over the table, an oil lamp on both sides of the plans. Guilietta was standing next to

Hansum and was almost as excited as her father. As she leaned in, she let her arm press against Hansum's. A shiver ran through Hansum's chest.

"Go on, go on, Romero," the Master said with excitement. "Explain it to me."

Hansum collected himself.

"By grinding slightly different curves on the inside and outside of the glass, we can create lenses to correct the wearer's far or close vision. These drawings show the exact shape of the lenses needed by the Podesta for both. After you've made both sets of lenses, Master, you then cut them in half and attach the tops and the bottoms in the same frame." Pan had projected a line image on the parchment and Shamira had carefully copied it. This way Agistino could cut out an exact template to match all the inside and outside curves against. Then she illustrated the production sequences in freehand perspective.

Agistino understood the concept instantly.

"How did you come to know of this?" he asked, an intense look in his eyes.

Pan had instructed Hansum to say, "From the Master we had a little bit of experience with before. He was working on these ideas. I improved them a little."

"I know lotsa people I can sell these to," Ugilino said, looking over the Master's shoulder. "Fifteen soldi each."

"Ugilino, that's the cost of three pair of regular discs for the eyes," the Master said.

"But it will take almost the same time to make these as three pair of discs for the eyes, Master."

Agistino's eyes went wide with amazement. He smiled at his salesman.

"You're right, Ugilino. You're right." Then he patted him paternally on the cheek. "I never would have believed it, but there just may be hope for you. Yes. Come, let us get to work."

Now that Hansum was familiar with lensmaking, he was especially impressed by the Master's skill. The Master truly proved his title by slowly, patiently and intricately filing through the brittle medieval glass, cutting the four lenses in half. Even Pan was impressed with the Master's free-hand grinding.

"This must be kept secret. This must not be shared," Agistino kept telling everyone, the sweat dripping from his brow as he labored. They all worked into the night, Shamira, Guilietta and Hansum working on the looker, the Master, Lincoln and Ugilino on the bifocals.

It was well into the night before both the Podesta's spectacles and new adjustable looker lay completed upon the workbench. Ugilino was sleeping in a corner. Hansum and the others stared at the Master's tired, but awe-inspired face. It seemed he did not know which miracle to be more amazed about, the prescription glasses for the shortsighted, the longsighted, the bifocals or the looker.

Chapter 9

"Slow down," Hansum begged. Shamira and Hansum had to walk briskly to keep up with Ugilino. With long, purposeful steps, he strode toward the Podesta's palace. The Master sent Ugilino to show the way and also protect the goods. Hansum carried a sturdy leather pouch with the precious glasses and looker slung over his shoulder.

They proceeded through the now familiar Bra Market and past the Arena. In a few blocks, the streets opened up into Urbe Square, another piazza. Pan explained as they walked that, although Piazza Urbe was not as big as the Bra Market, it was more important. It was the center for banking, wool trading, fabrics and other large commodities.

"Come on," Ugilino said, "Signori Square is this way." They turned down a narrow street lined with tall strong houses and warehouses. Ugilino seemed in an especially fine mood this morning. "Okay, we're here."

The narrow street opened up into Signori Square. There weren't any vendors, but there were soldiers. Two long, imposing buildings flanked the square, facing each other. One was white marble with a series of Corinthian columns holding up an arched walkway that ran the length of the building. The roof was topped with five statues of saints holding bibles.

"The one on your left," Pan whispered to Hansum, *"is the government administration building. The building across the square . . ."* It was made of large, gray blocks and fronted with heavy Doric columns, *"that's the treasury. And at the end of the square is the della Scalla family palace."* In the middle of the red-brick palace was a large marble doorway. Two columns held up the beautiful triangular portico with a sculpted relief of a winged lion on top. Just off the square, next to the palace, was a small, beautiful church. *"That is St. Maria Antica."* In the church courtyard was a tall, elaborate monument whose focal point was a highly decorated sarcophagus. *"That's where Mastino's predecessor is interred. The great Cangrande della Scalla."*

Ugilino puffed himself up and led the other two through the square. Two soldiers stopped them. The enlisted men wore wide-brimmed kettle helmets atop chainmail balaclavas. Both carried long-handled poleaxes with a sharp axe blade on one side and a large hammer-type weapon on the other. The ends of the staffs sported long, sharp spikes.

"What business have you here?" one of the soldiers asked.

"We're here to see the Podesta!" Ugilino announced boisterously. The soldiers laughed. Hansum took out the Podesta's calling card. Ugilino snatched it. "See. We do too have business here," he taunted, waving the card. A soldier grabbed the card from Ugilino and inspected it from all sides. Grudgingly, he sent his compatriot to the palace with it.

While they waited, the soldier looked at Hansum, who answered his stare with calm eyes and a little smile. Ugilino couldn't seem to contain himself.

"We make discs for the eyes for all the best priests and merchants in town!" he said haughtily. "Even the Podesta wants them." Then he whispered in a voice denoting secrecy, "And we have a new thing the Podesta wants. A looker."

Hansum nudged Ugilino in the ribs.

"What's a looker?" the soldier asked.

"Never mind," Ugilino said. "It's important. You're not supposed to know."

Just then they heard the clip-clopping of the other soldier scurrying back. Captain Caesar, the officer who had arrested Feltrino the day before, was with him. And at the top of the palace steps, standing by the open door, was Baron da Pontremoli. The officer motioned for the three to proceed quickly. Ugilino put his nose in the air and swaggered toward the palace. Shamira and Hansum followed. At the door, Ugilino bowed to the secretary. Nicademo ignored him and looked at Hansum and Shamira.

"What's he doing here?" he asked Hansum.

"We didn't know the way, Signor," Hansum explained.

"Come," the nobleman said sharply. Hansum and Shamira entered. When Ugilino took a step forward he found the Baron's long, thin hand on his chest. "You wait in the square." The brass and wood door closed in Ugilino's face.

Chapter 10

Hansum noted that, where Agistino's hovel had ceilings barely over six feet high, the ceilings of the Podesta's palace were over sixteen, the entrance hall, almost thirty. The Master's floors were dirt and straw, the Podesta's, intricately cut and polished marble. Windows here actually had glass in them. Where Agistino's rented premises had a crude wooden door at the entrance with a wooden latch, the Podesta's was heavily lacquered wood, inlaid with brass bolts, hinges and handle. The interior doorways of the della Cappa hovel had cloths hanging from their frames for privacy and people had to mind their heads as they walked under them. The Podesta's doorways were made of ornate oak, each eight to ten feet high and framed with heavy trim.

Nicademo led Hansum and Shamira through a reception room, a sitting room, and then a larger formal dining room. Finally he opened up a somewhat less conspicuous door to reveal the Podesta's private planning office. It was a relatively modest place, perhaps twice the size of the della Cappa house. There were several small desks with chairs for writing by the windows and a very large, heavy table in the middle of the room. The table top was covered with maps, architectural drawings, handwritten parchment letters and more. There were half a dozen large hand-lettered books in the room, each on its own pedestal.

The Podesta was standing deep in thought over his large table, studying a map. Nicademo ushered the teens in, closed the door and stood quietly.

"Si, si, I hear you Nicademo," the Podesta said without looking up. "Can't you see I'm busy?"

"The lensmaker's apprentice and girl have arrived, Excellency."

"What? Oh, thank Cristo," he said, turning around. He made a quick come-here motion with his hand. "Come, come. Come, come," he said. The secretary pushed Shamira and Hansum forward. "Give them to me. The discs for the eyes." Hansum took a small bundle out of the satchel, put it on the table and unrolled it. "Time is such a thief," the Podesta said. "My eyes are aching from looking at all these documents."

"Master della Cappa sends these with his compliments, Excellency," Hansum said as he presented the new spectacles on a scrap of red velvet scrounged from the Satores.

"The lenses, they are broken in the middle!" the Podesta said immediately.

"No, Excellency," Hansum answered. "There is a purpose to this new design. Please, allow Carmella to help you put them on. This is something new. You are the first person ever to possess such a thing." The Podesta held the glasses to his eyes and Shamira adjusted the ribbon and whale bone clasp, which Nuca had expertly attached to each side of the frame that morning. "The line should be just under the forward vision, Signor. Just so. There, Signor. What do you think?"

A look of astonishment, not once but several times, appeared on the Podesta's face.

"I . . . I can see across the room. I can see clearly. The painting on the wall. You, Nicademo. I can see you clearly."

"Look out the window, Excellency," Hansum suggested.

"The world! I can see the world! Nicademo, I have the eyes of a young man again!"

"Now, Signor, look at the papers on your table. But look through the lower lenses. Just slightly down, as if looking at something on the tip of your nose."

"Spettacolare! This is amazing!" And then he turned and looked directly at Hansum. "Romero is it?"

"Si, Signor."

"You have brought me a wonderful gift."

"Grazie, Excellency. Master della Cappa will be pleased to hear you are happy."

Mastino was close to Hansum, so he had to raise his nose in the air to look at him through the lower lenses. "Romero, Romero," he said in a very familiar and practised way. "Your master is no doubt a good man and treated you well." The Podesta put his hands on Hansum's shoulders. "But Romero, did he show you how to make these miracle lenses -- or did you show him? Eh? Eh?"

"I would not be disloyal or say anything disparaging about my house, Excellency." Pan advised Hansum to say.

"I respect what you say, young man. Very much," the Podesta soothed. "Loyalty to one's house, to one's church, to one's city, to one's patron."

"Patron, Signor?"

"Si, Romero. You are a young man of talent. Perhaps a savant. A geniuso."

"Oh no, Signor."

"Tut, boy. And young men of talent must have patrons."

"I have the Master, Signor."

"Okay, be loyal to your master. But also be honest with your Podesta. Romero, tell me truly, did your master show you how these lenses and looker work? Were these truly his inventions?" Hansum paused, looking at Shamira. "Romero? I command you to tell me. I promise that much work will come to your master's house and you will not be parted from it. So?"

After a pause and great reflection, Pan whispered into Hansum's ear. Hansum repeated, "No, Excellency. The looker and the glasses to see far and near were not conceived by my master."

"Very good," the Podesta said.

"But he ground the lenses. I do not have the skill for that yet."

"And that is why you must stay with him. Fear not, Romero. I think you have a bright future in Verona. Savants, as yourself, who conjure inventions from the air, it's like God whispers in your ear. Geniusos are rare and coveted by princes."

"Oh, geniuso, all right," Shamira said in a low voice.

"Hush, mistress," Pan whispered.

Hansum was embarrassed by the unjust praise and Shamira's reaction. He tried to make excuses.

"Excellency. I did have a bit of experience with lenses before I came to Verona. With another master, in -- in Vicenza. I just expanded on that Master's ideas."

Podesta della Scalla smiled kindly at Hansum.

"Such modesty, eh Nicademo? True modesty is a very rare thing nowadays." As he smiled, Mastino was thinking how to exploit this weakness. Still looking at Hansum, he reached his hand out to Shamira. "May I see the looker?"

Shamira reached into the satchel. While she took out the telescope, she also pulled out her art portfolio. The Podesta noticed it.

"Carmella, is it? Do you have the plans for the looker? I wish to again see the interesting way you drew them." Shamira pulled out the papers from the portfolio. There were some of her personal drawings on the top of the pile. Mastino picked them up. He was a connoisseur of art. Under his rule, many buildings, monuments and structures had been constructed. He looked intently at the drawings. The first page was a collage of quick little portraits. He was impressed. "Who taught you your drawing, Carmella?"

"No one. I guess my hand moves as my eye sees."

"And your writing?" the Podesta enquired further.

She looked over to Hansum. "In Vicenza, your Excellency. The priests," she answered.

"Ah," della Scalla said, looking back at the drawings. He saw that the images he gazed upon showed both craftsmanship and true artistic value. Besides being good likenesses, each sketch showed emotions of the subject's character, the serious, brooding Master, staring into space, next to it, the blubbery face of the Signora. Lincoln's picture, with a big smile that even showed the chip on his front tooth, had a vulnerability in his eyes that strangely evoked pity from Mastino. He looked at a second page of portraits, Ugilino, with his raggedy hat, bulbous, broken nose, one eye bigger than the other, and his crack-faced smile. And then there was a drawing of himself and one of Nicademo. Shamira had only met them for a few minutes the day before and did no drawing while they were there.

Shamira's drawing technique was far different from the drawing that was common among the artists in Mastino's circle. The arts of perspective and realistic drawing were not yet rediscovered. Painting and sculpture were stylized, stiff, and without the illusion of three dimensions. But these sketches were alive and vibrant.

"Look, Nicademo, look," he said quietly. As he passed the pictures over to his secretary, a third picture was revealed under them. A single, finished portrait, taking up the whole page. It was Guilietta, sitting at the table, preparing food. Guilietta was holding the two halves of a pomegranate in her hands. The knife that had just cleaved the fruit lay on the table, dripping with juice. She looked out from the page with a soft smile and dark, warm eyes. The picture was a story, telling the viewer exactly who she was.

Hansum had not seen this drawing.

"Wow!" he said.

"Bella," the Podesta agreed. "This is your master's daughter?"

Hansum seemed so taken by the drawing that he could not answer. He just nodded and swallowed.

"Carmella, in the following weeks, I have talks with several art masters from different churches. I will show these to them. Would you like that? And maybe one day you can meet them."

"You mean the guys that design all the sculpture and paintings in the churches?"

"And the buildings too."

"Sure. That would be . . . I mean, I would be honored, Excellency."

Nicademo had picked up the new telescope and was looking out the window.

"Excellency, this is amazing. The back chamber does allow me to make clearer the image for my eye. I can see across the square and down the street. It's like I'm right next to people and yet they don't know I'm looking at them." He looked seriously at the Podesta. "A truly strategic advantage." Then he asked Hansum, "These will be ready in tin in seven days?"

"My master is to visit the tinsmith this afternoon. A sample in tin might be ready by tomorrow."

"Tell your master that I will come in two days to draw up the contract," Nicademo said. "That should give him time to organize with the smith and determine the truth of what should be possible. Inform your master the Podesta does not want promises that are not kept. Do you understand? This is very important. Also tell him I shall bring payment for one tenth the contract."

"Practical as ever, Nicademo," the Podesta said. "Well, I am a busy man today. Thank your master for me and say your prayers."

"Grazie, Excellency," Hansum said. "May I take the looker with me?"

"Whatever for?" the Podesta asked.

"To show as an example to the tinsmith, Signor."

"Romero, Romero," the Podesta chastised. "The smith need not see what his tubes will be used for. Let him wait till there are many about the region and you are well established making them. Such foolishness. Have you ever been told you are too trusting?"

"Once or twice," he admitted.

The Podesta patted him paternally on the cheek. "It is good to have one's head in the clouds to speak with God, Romero, but one must keep one's feet on the ground too." And then he nodded at his secretary to remove them.

While Nicademo showed Hansum and Shamira out, the Podesta continued to experiment with his spectacles. He looked at document after document. He read from a large hand-painted bible on a stand. He tried writing with the spectacles on, smiling all the while. When he looked up and did not have to squint to see the paintings across the room, he laughed aloud. Still in a joyous state, he picked up the telescope and went to the window, looking out over the piazza. He saw the two young savants walk across the cobblestones toward the guards. The Romero boy smiled and nodded to Captain Caesar. They exchanged a few words. The officer smiled back and even gave the young man a small salute.

"The boy commands respect naturally," he said to himself. The looker allowed Mastino to see the detail on the guards' uniforms, even saw the filing marks on the poleax blades. He spied the officer's smile turn to a frown when the ugly apprentice came running up to the others. He could see Ugilino talking and eating a pear at the same time, even the food stuck between his teeth.

Mastino heard the latch to his office click as Nicademo returned.

"These children are a puzzle, cousin," Mastino said as he continued viewing the square.

"They certainly are, Mastino," the secretary said, both dropping the honorifics.

Mastino took the looker away from his eye.

"The town of Vicenza is ours," he began. "We have no spectacle maker there?"

"For sure, no," Nicademo answered. "Spectacles are all made in Murano and Florence, cousin, where the glass is so good." He put out his hand to try the looker again. Mastino handed it to him.

"And a peasant girl that has the knowledge of writing," Mastino continued, "besides her ability to render likenesses, all in that shambles of a house?" he laughed. "Do you believe they are truthful about learning their skills in Vicenza?"

"No, I believe them not," Nicademo answered. The two noblemen looked at each other and both shrugged. The truth didn't really matter, possessing the looker was the only important thing. "Can you imagine if the Gonzagas got their hands on this first?" Nicademo added. "We were lucky to catch Feltrino. Very lucky."

"Yes, God has favored us," Mastino agreed. "We must keep the Gonzaga for another month, say, till we have these lookers well in hand for ourselves. Too bad we can't just make him disappear."

"Yes, but the Bishop knew he was here. It could be awkward."

Mastino gave a little grunt, showing agreement, but also disappointment.

"Nicademo, make enquiries immediately to Vicenza about the children and to Florence about this della Cappa." Nicademo nodded and left. Mastino continued looking out the window with his sharp new eyes. "But these discs for the eyes are a marvel," he said aloud to himself. "Look at that. I have not seen Uncle Cangrande's sarcophagus clearly for a decade. Good day, Uncle," he said, looking at the tomb where he buried his predecessor with much ceremony. "Are you still digesting your foxglove?"

Chapter 11

Agistino said he was "over the moon, no, over the stars," when he heard that Baron da Pontremoli was coming to write up a contract. "A contract," he said to Hansum, grabbing the boy's arms and shaking him. "A contract," he repeated to everybody in the room. "They are very serious then."

"Shouldn't you practice writing your name, Agistino?" the Signora asked.

"The product is what I better practice at. The product. The sample must be ready and perfect by the time the Baron gets here."

The day after next, a note came early in the morning, announcing that Baron da Pontremoli would be there just before midday. The Master had stayed up late, working feverishly to have the looker prototype completed in tin. As soon as Shamira read the note aloud, Agistino had the girls heat up a large pot of water so he could wash. He didn't want a repeat of the first impression his family gave the nobles. So when da Pontremoli arrived, the Master was scrubbed, his hair combed, beard trimmed and he was wearing a tunic with mother of pearl buttons. He had also instructed the girls to purchase a selection of pre-made foods from quality vendors at the market. "Something to offer a noble." Guilietta looked worried when her father also told her to find a bottle of Falerno wine from the south. He assured her, with good humor, it was for the guest only. And since she would be serving them, she could make sure that he would only drink some watered-down verjuice.

When Nicademo arrived, he was invited into the house and bid sit. Master Satore had lent them red velvet to cover the table and benches. Only Guilietta was in attendance with them. The Signora had been sent to the Satores' with instructions to keep her there till the nobleman left. The Master engaged da Pontremoli in idle chit chat as Guilietta served the wine and verjuice. When Nicademo inspected the shop, he was impressed with the new lathe, the Master's organization, the amount of raw materials on hand, and the cleanliness of the workplace and its apprentices. He was most intrigued by the way Lincoln had the place organized and the way he kept track of all the lenses ground and spectacles made in a ledger.

"You read and write, my son?"

"Sure, why not . . ." Lincoln began, then said, "Si, Excellency."

Nicademo also found it curious when he saw Shamira in the shop setting lenses.

"She's good with her hands," the Master explained.

"Si, I've seen this," Nicademo commented.

They went back to the house, ate, drank some more, and wrote a contract. By the time the meeting was over, everything was deemed a great success. It was evident that Nicademo was now confident the delivery of the first six lookers could be accomplished by the next week and the rest of the hundred within a month. The contract agreed on the unbelievable price of eighty denari for each of the first tin lookers and one hundred for the brass. And he left a deposit of one tenth of the total order. Master Agistino hadn't had that amount of money in his possession in a long time.

Nicademo shook hands profusely with Agistino as he left mid-afternoon. He was well fed, impressed and had the first of the usable lookers in hand.

"Della Cappa," he said standing next to his carriage, "I must admit I had my doubts."

Guilietta was standing next to her father, smiling, her hands demurely folded in front of her. The Master laughed at the nobleman's comment.

"My house shall rise like the phoenix, with your house's patronage, Excellency."

That Saturday, Mastino della Scalla actually ran down to the front entranceway of the palace. He heard that the della Cappa apprentice was there to deliver the first part of the contract. As Hansum handed him the lookers, one at a time, Mastino tried each. They were all amazingly identical. He patted Hansum on the cheek, saying, "Good boy, good boy."

For days, the lookers were the talk of the palace. Everyone who tried one wanted to own it immediately. But Mastino gave orders that the lookers were restricted to the military for now. Part of Agistino's contract was that he could not make lookers for anyone but the Podesta until he had permission to do so, which, to Mastino, meant never.

Chapter 12

A second lathe was delivered from Master Raphael's shop during the middle of the second week of the contract. Master della Cappa put Hansum to work on it immediately. By the end of the third day, he had the lenses coming off of it perfectly and quickly. Now, with both the Master and Hansum working, it took only ten days to complete the order, almost a week ahead of plan. It had been a very busy and exhausting push of work, but everyone was high with excitement on the morning of the big delivery.

Again, Mastino was doubly pleased when he got word that the balance of the lookers were being delivered early. When he came down to the front of the palace, Captain Caesar was having his men help Hansum unload the five crates from a bloodstained push cart which Agistino had obviously borrowed from a butcher. Agistino was carrying a cylindrical case made from leather and also had on a new hat.

"Nice cap," the Podesta said.

"To go with my name, Excellency." He held out the leather case to Mastino. With my compliments, Excellency," Agistino said. "Each looker has its own home, as every important and valuable tool should."

"This was not in the contract," Mastino said, looking at the finely tooled leather.

"No, Excellency. Again, with my compliments."

Mastino nodded in reply, then looked down at the case. On its flap was embossed the design of a cap, just like the one Master della Cappa had on his head.

"Very good," the Podesta laughed. "Very clever."

"What did you called it, Romero?" the Master asked Hansum, who was carrying one end of a heavy case with a soldier.

"Marketing," Hansum answered. "Marketing, Master."

"Yes, so everyone who sees that mark knows it is of our house," Agistino explained.

"I see," Mastino said. "I see." Once again the idea was the boy's. He opened up several of the identical leather cases and found perfect replicas of the telescope. "Come della Cappa, and you too, Romero. Let my men do this work. I was just going to sit down to a meal. Join me."

As they walked through the hall, they saw a young man, his hands tied behind his back, being escorted by two armed guards. They saw him from behind, but when they turned a corner, the man jerked his head around, locking his gaze momentarily with Hansum's. It was a very dirty and unshaven Feltrino. Feltrino tried to stop, but a guard pulled him forward and out of sight.

"Excuse me, Excellency," Hansum said. "Was that Feltrino?"

"Romero!" Agistino scolded. "Speak only of what is our business."

"Yes, young Romero," agreed the Podesta lightly. "Mind your Master's wisdom."

In the dining room, Mastino watched Agistino at the long, ornate table, fidgeting in his chair. The old lensmaker was gawking at the sumptuous surroundings, unfamiliar with such grandeur. Yet the boy looked at his relative ease, not intimidated at all.

Highly decorated ceramic plates and trays were brought out and placed before them. Master della Cappa's eyes seemed to pop out of his head at the sight of the fine food. Silver chalices were put in front of each person and filled. Mastino raised his cup.

"To our continued good fortune, Master della Cappa."

Agistino crossed himself and brought the cup to his lips, but Mastino noticed he did not drink. Each ate a bowl of rabbit stew with cheese gnocchi on the side. Agistino sighed with delight as he chewed. When they were eating the eel and roe tart, the lensmaker said with his mouth full, "Eel is best in the winter."

"Just so," the nobleman agreed. "Romero, have some figs. They're very sweet."

"Thank you, Excellency. They are good."

Nicademo entered the room.

"With the ones from before, one hundred exactly, Excellency," he said verifying the count of lookers. Mastino held up the looker beside him on the table.

"One hundred and one," he said.

"My gift to you," the lensmaker said, his mouth still full.

"So many gifts," Master della Cappa. "Thank you. Nicademo, you have the Master's payment?"

"Payment? Today?" the Baron said, a surprised tone to his voice.

"Of course, today," Mastino said. "Go to the treasury and get it. I shall tell the Master of my further plans for him and his establishment."

"What further . . ." the Baron began.

"The payment, Nikki!" When the Baron left, Mastino folded his hands on the table and looked back and forth between the older and younger man. "In some weeks I am going on a tour of our northern allies, the Germans, Master della Cappa."

"How interesting," the lensmaker said, almost wiping his mouth with his sleeve.

"It is to see their new technology of cannon and powder. Do you know of cannon and powder, Master?"

"Ah, no Excellency." Mastino looked at Hansum.

"A little," Hansum said.

"Of course you do," Mastino said matter-of-factly. "But more importantly, your lookers. During my trip, I believe I may be able to secure orders for more of your wonderful devices. What do you say to that?"

"What, what could I say, Excellency?" Agistino replied. "My house would be at your service. We could maybe turn out another hundred even faster the second time."

"Oh no," Mastino said. "Not another hundred. Perhaps another five hundred. Perhaps more."

The Master nearly choked on his food.

Chapter 13

Even weeks after the meeting with the Podesta, Pan was amazed how the whole della Cappa household was still so enthusiastic about everything. For Hansum and the Master, it started right after they left the palace, weighed down with more gold than Agistino had ever had in his possession. It was hidden under the Master's ample coat.

"Such glorious food," Agistino said to Hansum as they walked through Signori Square. Then he came close to Hansum's ear and whispered, "Such glorious money!" The Baron had offered to send a soldier with him for protection, but Agistino declined, saying he didn't want to attract too much attention. He also turned down an introduction to a Jew who could hold the money securely and even pay interest.

"He is very trustworthy," Da Pontramoli had said. "Our Podesta does business with him."

"Thank you, Excellency. Perhaps later, soon, perhaps."

As they left the square and walked the narrow streets, flanked by towering strong houses, Agistino said, "Romero, we cannot wait till spring to find new apprentices. I want you to get on with your suggestion about getting apprentices from surrounding churches." Pan had suggested this to Hansum. Having the priests recommend apprentice candidates would ingratiate them to the community.

Pan stayed with Hansum during the selection process, noticing how Hansum was becoming much more independent and not needing as much of his counsel. Hansum chose two quiet, clever boys who could still live at home till the first part of their training was over. Nine-year-old Pippo was the seventh son of the miller da Barletto. There wouldn't be a place for him in his father's business and he seemed to have an aptitude for numbers. The miller was a good friend of one of the priests at San Zeno, so this was a good move. Hansum visited the mill and was amazed at the huge size and complexity of the machinery. Master da Barletto also seemed to be showing off his seventeen-year-old daughter, Serindella, to him. She was a pleasant, but amazingly homely, girl who reminded Hansum of Ugilino. The other new apprentice he chose, eight-year-old Benicio, was a foundling who lived at a monastery orphanage. He was very quiet, but did what he was told meticulously. It was rumored the boy was the illegitimate son of Father Benedict.

When Hansum presented the Master with two boys, Agistino said he thought he would have more to choose from. Since they needed two apprentices and he was only being given two to choose from, there was no choice at all. When Hansum reassured him these were the best, Agistino laughed. Everything made him happy lately.

Pan was doubly pleased with Lincoln's progress. He had appeared the most immature -- after all, he was the youngest. But when it fell to him to keep the shop organized, he rose to the occasion. When the Master or Hansum came through the door, all they had to do was grind and polish lenses. There were always many dops waiting, loaded and ready. Supplies were always where they should be and grit always plentiful. And for some odd reason, Lincoln's worst fault, his short temper and impatience, seemed to disappear when he took charge of the two younger apprentices. Within a week, he had Pippo and Benicio knowing their chores and fairly adept at assisting the Master and Hansum with the proper tools and grits. Lincoln also started making the notations in Agistino's ledger, and he learned the Master's secret hiding place for the strong box.

Pan was ensconced in Lincoln's hood, watching everyone sit down for morning dinner. The Master was laughing and joking with everyone. The only one not present was Ugilino. He was out selling discs for the eyes at the market and doing a very good job.

"Really, really, really?" Pippo, the new apprentice screeched in his high nine-year-old voice to Benicio. The two boys were bouncing up and down on their own little bench at the end of the dining table.

"What's all this foolishness?" the Master asked in mock testiness.

"Oh, Master, Master," Pippo squealed happily. "Maruccio promised if we did good till the end of the week, he would teach us to read and write!"

"Yes, and why not?" the Master replied, smiling at Lincoln.

The door opened and in walked Ugilino. He was resplendent in new clothes, including a jaunty green hat, and different strengths of spectacles hung by threads all over his red jacket.

"I sold four more discs for the eyes this morning, Master. Four," he announced even before the door was closed. And I have a special order for Patchouli, the wort merchant. Brother Romero," Ugilino called, "make a note to create middle-strength lenses in tortoiseshell frames. Tortoiseshell. Ya got that?" he asked importantly.

"Si, Signor Head Salesman," Hansum said with humor.

Pan was pleased that Ugilino and Hansum were getting along now.

"Tortoiseshell frames?" the Signora exclaimed. "I didn't know there was so much money in wort."

Ugilino also was carrying some beets and turnips by their long green and purple tops. He went over to Guilietta and handed them to her.

"Here Guilietta, Master Satore sent these. Did you hear how many more discs for the eyes I sold?"

"Thank you, Ugilino," she said smiling and looking him right in the eye. "Si, you are doing marvelously. I am very impressed. And I like your new hat." She reached up and cocked the hat at a rakish angle. Ugilino blushed vividly and took his seat. He didn't see Shamira and Guilietta smile knowingly at each other or Guilietta wink at Hansum.

The Master clapped his hands.

"Okay, everybody, let us sit and eat. Girls, bring over our wonderful bounty. Let us give thanks to God and say our prayers for Father Aaron, who sits shining at the side of Jesus in Heaven." He could now say this and not cry.

"Life is good!" the Signora said.

"My life stinks!" Feltrino said out loud. His voice echoed in the dark room under the palace. He couldn't call it a cell, because it did have a window and he even had a bed. But the window was high up on the wall and faced another wall not more than an arm's length away. His bed had only a thin blanket, but he knew that the other rooms in this prison had neither beds nor blankets. This was the room for nobles, so that at least made him feel special. But he was still in his same clothes, hadn't washed for what must be close to three weeks, and the food was always cold. Except for the time the Baron took him up to his office for questioning. He had rabbit stew that day. That's when he saw that damned apprentice.

"I understand that you left home on bad terms with your father," the Baron said to Feltrino. "Also he had no idea where you went. Word comes that he still has no idea. So sad when fathers and sons don't see eye to eye, but all too common. One day you will both have feelings of love for each other, I'm sure."

"So, you're going to let me go?" Feltrino had asked.

"Not yet, Excellency. Not yet. And since your father has no idea where you are, I think we can keep you here a bit longer."

So, Feltrino was still locked up, and all because he couldn't get that girl out of his mind. "That beautiful bitch," Feltrino said out loud. This had been the longest Feltrino had been without a woman in several years, so the thought of Guilietta made him smile even now.

"Feltrino, Feltrino, my sweet," a woman's voice said through the bars on his locked door.

"Veronica?" Feltrino said, jumping up.

"Si, it's me, with your food."

Veronica was the cook's helper who had brought Feltrino his meals since he had arrived. As she put Feltrino's plate through his slot in his cell door, he reached into the opening and grabbed her wrists. Her eyes widened in surprise, looking at him through the bars. Then she smiled.

"I've missed you," she said.

"And I you, my beautiful Veronica."

"Do you really think I'm beautiful?" she asked. Feltrino cocked his head and smiled at her.

"You are the most beautiful girl I've ever seen. Sweet Veronica. Sweet, sweet Veronica. My father would be proud to have you as a daughter-in-law."

Chapter 14

"Tell the Master we have another improved lathe design to show him after supper," Pan advised Hansum. As Hansum did so, Pan watched Agistino's curiosity become so piqued that he couldn't wait till the end of the workday.

"Yet another design? Show me now," he said getting off of his work stool. Hansum got the new drawings from Shamira and rolled them out on a table. Everyone stopped working to see Master della Cappa's reaction. It was actually Hansum's idea this time, not Pan's. He thought of it when he visited the miller da Barletto.

"I was thinking what it would be like to run many lathes off a water wheel. It would save many sore legs," he had told Pan while rubbing his own thigh.

"Ah, inspiration coming from one's own perspiration," Pan had replied.

Hansum explained to the Master how, much like a flour mill, a water wheel would turn a drive shaft that came into the work place. Along the length of the shaft, any number of lensmaking lathes could be set up, but the drawing only showed one lathe.

"Now you've gone too far, Romero," Agistino said laughing. "Running a small machine from a huge water wheel? It's ludicrous."

"No, you could run many lathes off the one drive wheel, Master. And the gears, here, would create a constant speed," he said pointing to a detail. "The leather belt around the drive shaft can be tightened or loosened to engage the spindle of the lathe. The operator uses no strength to spin the dop. He just concentrates on his shaping and polishing. And see, you can make the drive shaft as long as you want and run as many machines as you can afford off of it. Maybe six."

"Six machines? The lathe man doesn't have to power it himself? Unimaginable," the Master scoffed   .

"Maybe not even a lathe man," Hansum added brightly. "If the spindle is turned by water power, the operator doesn't have to be so strong. Perhaps we could train women too. They are much more patient and often do a better job on fine detail than men."

"Now I know you've gone crazy," the Master laughed. "A woman shaping lenses."

"Why not, Father?" Guilietta asked. "You say Carmella and I do neater and faster work than most men setting the lenses?"

"Yeah!" Shamira agreed.

"Soon you will say it's the men who should have the bambinos!" Agistino laughed. "Okay, enough. Everyone back to work." Agistino sat back at his lathe and began polishing again. But after a few minutes, Pan noticed Agistino stop grinding. "Women polishing lenses," he muttered to himself. "Ridiculous." Then he smiled broadly. "I wouldn't have to pay them as much."

Chapter 15

While everybody in the house was very happy, it could be said that Ugilino was the happiest. After all, he was the one who had gained the most. When at church or walking through the streets, people no longer scowled at him. Men nodded and smiled when he walked by, they didn't laugh or spit in his path. Some called his name or even came to shake his hand. And women no longer turned their heads away when his gaze fell on them. He noticed that some, in fact, held their gaze on him till they caught *his* eye. And lately a few men even brought their daughters up in conversation. But Ugilino didn't want any of them. Oh, he looked and fantasized about them, but he didn't want to marry them.

That's why, one Sabbath afternoon, Ugilino stopped at the city well and gave his face a thorough washing. He wet and slicked his hair, organizing the mop of tight waves with a new comb he stole. Then he put his new green cap back on at that same rakish angle Guilietta had tilted it to the other day. He even attempted to scrape the dirt from beneath his fingernails. The self-perceived dandy then strode back to the house of della Cappa. As he neared his street, a royal carriage passed him. It got to the house just before Ugilino, and he saw Baron da Pontremo-li step out of it. Shamira, who was sitting on the step drawing, got up to greet him. She was showing him her work when the Master's head popped out of the door. He bowed over and over again, and then the two men entered the house. Ugilino got to the door just as Shamira was finished putting her supplies back in the drawing satchel.

"Have you seen Guilietta?" Ugilino asked.

"She's in the workshop setting lenses," Shamira answered.

"Carmella," the Master's voice called. "Come serve wine to the Baron. Quickly."

As Shamira entered the house, Ugilino, mouth freshly vin-egared, strode off to the shop.

"Master della Cappa, I bring news," Baron da Pontremoli said seriously. He had seated himself at the bench, while the Master, Hansum and Lincoln stood at the end of the table. Shamira was getting the wine.

"What could be the matter that you come in person?" Agis-tino said with concern.

"What?" the Baron said. Then he laughed. "No, Agistino, nothing bad has happened. I bring good news. Only good news. Sit down. Please."

Agistino sighed deeply. "Carmella, pour the wine for our guest, and you-know-what for me. Grazie. Good girl."

"Master della Cappa," the Baron started, then he looked at Hansum and motioned for him to sit too. "We have wonderful news that requires some preparation on both your parts. His Excellency, Podesta della Scalla, has sent word that our lookers have received a very good welcome from the first of our German allies. What do you think about that?"

"Good news indeed, Excellency. We have been working very hard to prepare. Romero has become very proficient at polishing lenses. Maruccio, well, you know he has my shop under control. We have two new apprentices and both girls set lenses now. If we are favored with an unbelievable order of five hundred lookers, we will not fail you."

"Oh no, Master della Cappa. Not five hundred."

"Ah. Well, no matter. A hundred would be just as welcome," Agistino said, nonchalantly lifting up his verjuice to take a sip.

"You misunderstand, Master della Cappa. Not one hundred." Agistino looked confused. Baron da Pontremoli smiled again. "One thousand."

Agistino's hand began to tremble. Verjuice sprayed from the cup. Hansum lunged over to steady it, then gently took it away.

"One thousand?" the Master gasped.

"Perhaps more," da Pontremoli said. "Our master has not yet visited King Karl. We shall see what his response will be."

The Master crossed himself three times. He tried to speak, but failed. Hansum, Shamira and Lincoln smiled broadly.

"This is indeed good news, Excellency," Hansum said.

"Yes, but the reason I am here is to get your assurances that you can deliver. Truly deliver. A noble is like any other man. His word must be good. My job is to make sure that our prince can keep his word. So I ask you, quite seriously, can you deliver such quantities?"

Agistino became very still. He gulped, staring at the Baron. Then, without taking his eyes from the nobleman, said, "Romero, bring the Baron the designs for our new lathe."

Now Agistino loved the idea of a water-powered lathe. When the Baron was gone, Agistino actually did a little jig, dancing on the spot. All the teens laughed.

"We will produce lookers for all of Europe," he sang.

"Did you see the look on his face when he saw the new lathe design?" Lincoln said, continuing to laugh. "I thought his jaw was going to hit the table."

"This water-powered lathe will allow us to undersell Florence!" the Master pronounced. Then he kicked up his heels and did another little jig. He saw how this made Hansum laugh, so he made a serious face and teased, "Remember, you must not show the plans to anyone."

"Yes, Master. I think I've got that straight now."

"And the miller?" Agistino continued. "We will need to ally ourselves with him. His expertise and access to the river is essential. I shall stand by him at his church this next Sabbath. No!" he lamented. "This approach is too bold. We must act carefully. I shall give it more thought. God will present an opportunity." He sipped on his verjuice, then looked at over at Hansum, who seemed deep in thought again. "What? What are you thinking now, ruminating one?"

"Well, Master, when I visited the miller da Barletto about Pippo, besides seeing the mill, I also saw he has a seventeen-year-old daughter who is not married. Her name is Serindella."

"Yes, I know her from church," Shamira said.

"Truly?" the Master commented. "A daughter that old and yet unmarried? Is she an imbecile?"

"Hey, I'm almost that old," Shamira reminded him.

"No, Master," Hansum said. "She's not a geniuso, but quite pleasant of temperament and good about the home and business from what I've heard."

"Why, then, is she a spinster?"

"I don't wish to be unkind to a young lady, but in terms of describing her I would say Ugilino would be a good comparison." Hansum stopped short and looked at the Master, raising an eyebrow. Agistino stopped and stared back at Hansum. Then they both smiled simultaneously, as if bright oil lamps had ignited above each of their heads.

"Serindella!" the Master shouted joyously.

"And Ugilino!" Hansum added.

"Si, that would be perfect." Agistino clapped his hands together. "Finally the Lord has rewarded me for putting up with that monster of a boy!" The cogs were turning in his head.

"You're going to foist Ugi off on Serindella?" Shamira protested. She was horrified.

"It would be perfect," Agistino cried. He started talking about new clothes for Ugilino and a dinner for the two families.

Shamira, disgusted, went to the cot and picked up her drawing satchel. Lincoln just laughed at the whole thing.

"Can you imagine how ugly the babies would be?" he said, almost choking with mirth.

"It's fun to marry off children," the Master finally said, "even if they are not your own. One day, Romero, we shall have to find a wife for you!"

A pregnant pause.

"Well, Master, now that you broach the subject . . ."

There was a knock at the door. As soon as Lincoln opened it, he got down on one knee and bowed his head.

"Master," he called. "It's the Bishop."

There in the doorway was the Bishop of San Zeno, flanked by two priests. Master della Cappa hurried to the door, bowing over and over again.

"Bishop, Holy Father, welcome, welcome. Come in, Holy Father, please. How may I help you? What service may I provide?" Agistino bent to one knee before the clergyman and kissed his ring.

"Good day to you, Master della Cappa. We're thinking of discs for the eyes for most of the writing room."

"Oh, marvelous, Your Grace. Please sit down and we shall talk. Maruccio, get the cups. Make sure they're clean. Carmella, wine and victuals. Quickly."

As the priests were seated, Agistino called Hansum over to him. "Romero," he said in a euphoric manner, "go find Ugilino. I will talk to him about Serindella. Oh, my luck today keeps getting better and better. Maruccio, hurry with those cups."

Hansum went over to Shamira.

"Have you seen Ugilino?" he asked.

"In the shop, I think," she answered, "with Guilietta."

Chapter 16

"Please get off your knees," Ugilino heard Guilietta say.

The wet-haired oaf raised his head and looked up at the beauty. She sat facing him on the shop's work bench, looking him straight in the eye. He had confidently walked into the room, called her name and said he wished to talk to her. She had turned on the bench to give him her full attention. He took a few steps toward her, and recited all the wonderful things he had done the past few months. How many discs for the eyes he sold, how great a future he had. He even told how people respected him and showed their daughters to him. Then, after a long while of self aggrandizement, he knelt down on his knees and asked her the most important question of his life.

"But I don't want any of them. I want you. Will you marry me?"

Guilietta was very kind. She did not laugh and she did not look at him with disgust.

"Ugilino, you have changed into a man I thought you could never become," she said. "You are clean and pious. You go to church regularly. Yes, you have earned the respect of many merchants and priests with your sales of the discs for the eyes. But, Ugilino, you are not the man for me."

Ugilino, still on his knees, stiffened. His body trembled slightly, but inside it had been as if he had been hit harder than ever before.

"But, but . . ." he began, when he heard something by the door. He turned and saw Hansum standing there. "We're having a private conversation," Ugilino said, embarrassed and getting to his feet quickly.

"I'm sorry, Ugilino," Hansum said. "I didn't mean to eavesdrop." Ugilino shuffled his feet. Hansum added, "Odd though it may seem, brother, the Master and I were just talking about this topic a few minutes ago. He sent me to talk to you of it."

"What about?" Ugilino asked, suspiciously.

"A marriage partner for you."

"Guilietta is supposed to be mine."

"Pray tell, Romero," Guilietta said, ignoring the last statement, "what did you and Papa speak of?" Ugilino watched Guilietta stand up and take a step toward Hansum. He could tell the two were going to work in concert to some purpose against his own.

"Well, the Master is really quite excited," Hansum continued. "He has this idea that, as Ugilino is doing such a splendid job and has such a great future ahead of him, he should have a wife."

"Truly?" Guilietta extolled. "That is a happy coincidence."

"And he said it should be with another master's family," Hansum continued. "It would be good for business. And, Ugilino, he thought the miller's daughter, Serindella, would be a wonderful match for you."

"Serindella? Pippo's sister?" Guilietta said brightly. "What a wonderful idea. Why, Ugilino, she is very pleasant and I hear she even has a dowry."

"Serindella?" Ugilino gasped. "She's a cow."

"Oh, Ugilino, don't talk so," Guilietta scolded lightly.

"Why should I marry a cow?"

"If she is a cow," Hansum said smiling, "then you are a bull." Hansum chucked Ugilino on the arm in a manly fashion. "A perfect match. I will talk to her father for you, if you wish."

It took a few seconds for Hansum's little joke to sink into Ugilino's head. But when it did, he felt a rage rise up in him. He pushed back on Hansum's shoulder, much harder than Hansum's mock punch.

"A bull! A cow!" Ugilino said loudly, repeating the push harder each time he spit out a phrase. "You think you are so elevated above us because you are the Podesta's pet, that we are but barnyard animals?" The pushes almost became punches. Hansum was backed up against the wall. Ugilino put his hand on the base of Hansum's neck and held him fast.

"No brother, no," Hansum said. "We are all the same in God's eyes. But we must know who we are and what our best prospects are. Our household has done well. We are both men who have futures and will be able to afford a wife. We must choose carefully and make a proper match."

Ugilino scowled and leaned into Hansum.

"And what of Guilietta?" he asked cunningly. Ugilino saw Hansum and Guilietta look at each other in a way that could only mean one thing. "So, you marry a beauty and me a beast? Is that what you are saying is my proper match?"

Guilietta put her hand on Ugilino's shoulder.

"Hush, Ugilino. Do not talk so of Serindella. Beauty fades, but disposition stays, if it be nurtured. And she has a lovely disposition. Make a match of like and like and in time you will find it more to your liking."

"Si, Ugilino," Hansum said. "Think about it."

But Ugilino would not hear this good advice. Instead his blood boiled over.

"You are trying to take a wife from me. Before you came, Guilietta was to be mine," he shouted.

"Never was this so, Ugilino," Guilietta said. "This was a fancy of yours."

Ugilino turned and raised a hand to Guilietta. "Shut your mouth, woman!" he said, slapping her face. "I will be your . . ."

But before he could say husband, Romero was upon him with a fist to the mouth and a knee to the ribs. Ugilino fell to the ground, knocking supplies off of the table. Hansum jumped upon his adversary with the full weight of his knee, but Ugilino, a veteran of many street fights, did not submit easily. With little effort, he threw Hansum off.

"Stop!" Guilietta screamed, but neither would hear. Ugilino got hold of the pitch pot, stood up and flung it at Hansum. It would have hit him square in the face if he had not raised his arms to deflect it. Hansum dived at Ugilino, driving his shoulder into his midsection. Ugilino fell onto a workshop table, scattering more supplies. Both boys tumbled to the floor, their fists pummeling at each other. Guilietta continued screaming.

"Stop! Both of you, please!"

"I'll teach you, you orphan," Ugilino yelled.

"And I'll teach you, you stupid animal!" Hansum shouted.

This seemed to enrage Ugilino even more. He rolled over, picked up a brass shaping bowl and shot to his feet.

"I'm not an animal!" he shrieked, raising the bowl over his adversary's head. Guilietta threw herself against Ugilino to protect Hansum. Ugilino grabbed Guilietta with his free hand and shook her, the pot still in his other hand, high over his head. "I am not an animal!" he screamed.

The shop door burst open. Ugilino's eyes froze into the amazed eyes of the Master. Ugilino watched the Master's eyes move to his daughter and then to the pitch pot held high over her head. Then, without a heartbeat's hesitation, he watched Agistino's bulk fly across the shop. He felt his Master's large red paw grab the hand holding the bowl and another hand come down and chop at his wrist, forcing him to let go of Guilietta. From long conditioning, Ugilino did not attempt to fight back against his Master, but let himself be pushed into and then on top of the work table. The Master was now over his salesman. Ugilino still had hold of the pot in one hand and the Master had control of that arm. Agistino, an enraged look on his face, wrenched Ugilino's hand toward his own face. The pot cracked into the side of Ugilino's head and he let go of it. His head rang so, Ugilino was momentarily deaf.

"Peace, Father," Guilietta urged. "It was not as it appeared."

Hansum was now to his feet.

"It was not all Ugilino's fault, Master. He was upset with what you and I were talking about. I should have let you tell him," Hansum admitted.

His ears still ringing, the cowering Ugilino stared up at his Master's angry face, only inches from his own. He saw Agistino look over at Hansum, who was saying something, and also saw the makings of a good black eye starting to show on his rival. Ugilino felt the Master's fists tighten on his clothes as he was lifted several inches off the table. The Master then dropped him back down in disgust. Agistino walked a few steps away and began to yell in earnest at Ugilino. Slowly, Ugilino could make out words again.

"We give you good tidings and you give us trouble? We give you hope and you give us hell? What type of apprentice would shame a master who offers him a son's prize of a wife?"

Ugilino rolled off the table onto his knees.

"But the wife I want is . . ." he began.

"The wife you want? You? You have a wife in mind? You, you ugly bastard who I found stealing from my garbage as a child? You think you will pick your own wife?"

"But Master..."

"And you break up my workshop and fight with other apprentices? You threaten my daughter because you don't like the wife, I, your Master, have in mind for you?"

"But it's Guilietta . . ."

"Shut your mouth, bastard. Don't you mention her name with your rotten mouth." The Master swatted at Ugilino's head. The jaunty green hat flew off and landed in the straw. "Another word and I shall rip off all the clothes I put on your back and throw you back into the ditch where you came from. You have ever been my cross to carry. Look what you've done to my workshop, my place of profit. How I wish you would be in another city and haunt that place."

Ugilino cringed repeatedly as one epithet after the other was thrown at him. He saw his precious new hat lying in the straw and dirt. He grabbed it up and returned it to its perch on his head, but now it was askew with clods of dirt stuck to it.

"But Guilietta . . ."

"NOT ANOTHER WORD! GET OUT! GET OUT OF MY SIGHT!"

The Master's bellow was so loud and ferocious that it caused a cascade of images to rush through Ugilino's head. They were memories of himself as a very young boy; of his young self skulking around at night, sleeping in despicable places, subsisting on the uneatable and experiencing unimaginable humiliations. As he grew up in the streets, he knew no better. But now he knew what it was to sleep in one place with protective walls around him, without the wind or rats attacking him. He had grown used to his dry straw bed in the stall, to regular food that could be named, clothes that were not fouled rags. He felt dizzy and had the urge to puke as his head throbbed. The Master's curses became hollow echoes. Ugilino grasped at the table and pulled himself to his feet. Then, with a heart full of misplaced shame, he felt himself running out of the workshop and down the lane. He understood only one of the echoing words that followed him as his feet pounded through the wet, fetid puddles. It was his Master's voice shouting, "Fool!"

"I'm sorry, Master," Hansum said, one hand on his bruised abdomen, the other on his forehead. Guilietta had hold of his arm, steadying him.

"Life gets better and then it gets worse," Agistino moaned. He stood, swaying back and forth. "Life gives you wine and then vinegar. Sweet meats, then maggots." Agistino collapsed on the bench and looked up at the two teenagers. "And I've still got the Bishop in the house. I better get back before your mother tells of her archangel."

"I didn't mean for it to turn out this way," Hansum said.

The old man, for he looked much older than a few minutes ago, waved away Hansum's apology.

"No matter. I was a fool to believe it could be otherwise. Ugilino and Serindella? Ha. We'll have to find some other way to create an alliance with the miller. Perhaps you, Romero?"

"Perhaps Romero, what?" Guilietta asked. The Master quickly explained the plan of using a marriage of the two houses to get easy access to the knowledge and experience of setting up a water mill.

"That's how countries do it. That's how kings do it. Why not us?" he concluded. "So what do you say, Romero? You and Serindella?"

Hansum said nothing, and only glanced fleetingly at Guilietta.

"You want Romero to marry Serindella?" Guilietta asked with a certain tone in her voice. Agistino put his hands out beseechingly, and as if it was a perfectly obvious and good idea.

"If Romero marries Serindella, then we can get the miller to help us set up a mill to run many, many lathes."

"Romero marry Serindella?" Guilietta repeated, looking between her father and Hansum.

"Si!" the Master answered, now somewhat annoyed.

Guilietta gave Hansum a look which he thought could never be made by a face as sweet as hers. Hansum made a gesture for her to calm down.

"Master," he said, taking a tentative step forward.

"What?" Agistino said.

"Master, I have something to ask you."

"What?"

"Remember I was just going to ask you a question just before the Bishop knocked on the door?" He looked at Guilietta, as if to prove a point.

"Si. And?"

"It was about me marrying." He paused. The Master looked at him enquiringly, expecting him to continue. Nothing came out. Guilietta stepped next to Hansum. Without a word she reached out and took Hansum's hand. The young lovers braced for a tirade, but it didn't come. Instead Agistino became thoughtful and quiet.

"Father, are you quite all right?" Guilietta asked.

After a few more moments, he looked at the two seriously, but with measured calm.

"To this match I would have no objection," he said plainly. Both Hansum and Guilietta broke into big smiles. Guilietta, still holding Hansum's hand, became light on her feet and jumped up and down. Hansum didn't jump, but laughed happily. The Master stopped them. "Hold. This is the time for planning. Romero, you are a favorite of the Podesta. You must receive his blessing on this. The way he asks for you and talks to you, he must have plans. If this family is to prosper, it must be with his blessing. So, not a word to anyone. Who else have you told?"

"No one, Master," Hansum said.

"Ugilino," Guilietta reminded. "Ugilino knows."

"If it's only Ugilino, then there's no problem. The Podesta is away from Verona for the next while. We have time to plan. And that dog, Ugilino, he knows where his bed and food are. He will be back by tonight. If I'm lucky, he'll stay away a few days."

But Ugilino didn't come back that night, or the next, or many after that. He ran to a quiet spot by the river and threw up, then lay there with a hand in the cold water, letting it cool his body. The ringing in his head lessened and his pounding heart began to calm. Finally he sat up and just brooded. He took the hat from his head and looked at it. The new hat he was so proud of. How could the Master say he would take it away from him? Ugilino paid for it himself. He picked off the dirt and straw, staring at the hat and all it represented. It symbolized his new life, but all that was gone now. The Master thought he was going to smash Guilietta with the metal pot. He most certainly wouldn't be forgiven for that. And that bitch, no, he mustn't call her such things, but Guilietta was probably playing up what happened, putting the blame for wrecking the shop on him. And Romero, no way he would miss the chance to keep himself the golden boy. 'But we're family. Families fight but always take each other back,' he thought. Ugilino went to put the jaunty green hat back on his head. 'But we're not family. I'm a stupid, ugly bastard that can't learn to make lenses.' Ugilino wiped his face with the back of his hand, surprised to see he was wiping off tears. 'Nobody wants you, nobody needs you,' he thought. He tossed the hat into the rushing river. As the current grabbed it, the hat sped away, the green fabric turning to black in the shadows. Then it disappeared. Ugilino got up, not even bothering to dust the dirt off of his clothes, and he too disappeared into the dark.

Chapter 17

"Wow, Hansum, my man. Gettin' married at seventeen," Lincoln laughed as they lay in the hay that night. "That's freaky."

"Yes," Pan said. "To people of our time, where most people live to over one hundred and fifty, it would seem odd. There is no rush to procreate. But here . . ."

"Procreate?" Lincoln interrupted, a further realization seeming to jump into his head. He began to giggle. "That means you're going to . . . you and Guilietta . . . Hey, and they don't have preggie blocks here. You'll probably be a dad by the time you're eighteen." He giggled again. "I'll be an uncle! Shamira will be an aunt."

"And I shall be the child's teacher," Pan pronounced, "as Aristotle was to Alexander the Great!"

"But why would the Podesta have any objection if I married Guilietta?" Hansum asked, getting up on one elbow. "What is the Master so worried about? Why's he making it so complicated?"

"I can't say," Pan replied, "but the Master is correct. You must be careful. The Podesta believes you are a savant and most likely will want to keep you in his direct sphere of influence."

"But it's just because of the stuff that you've been telling me," Hansum said.

"That doesn't matter, Young Master." Pan answered. "He thinks it is you and it must stay thus."

Lincoln yawned and stretched out in the hay. "Okay, I'm tired. Let's get some shut eye. Pan, turn down your light. Man oh man. Hansum and Guilietta are gettin' married and they'll be dum dee dum dee doing."

Hansum and Guilietta's was not the only engagement with complications that day.

"But you promised to marry me after I helped you escape!" shouted poor Veronica, as Feltrino rode off at a full gallop. "You promised . . ." she trailed off. He didn't even wave or look back. The dust his horse was kicking up obscured him from view. She looked down. There was blood on her dress. It was from what had remained on Feltrino's sword when he killed the guard who came back sooner than expected. So here she was, outside the city gates, thrown off the back of Feltrino's huge horse without a word or a smile. Just thrown off. What was she to do? If she didn't go back, they would assume she was part of the killing. If she did go back, she could feign innocence, but she knew she would get flustered when the Baron questioned her. He had a kind nature, but he always got to the bottom of things. Poor Veronica stood all alone in the middle of the night, not knowing what to do.

Feltrino petted the huge neck of his horse as they galloped through the night. He found his beast plump and healthy in the Podesta`s stables behind the palace, ready and wanting to expel the incredible energy pent up in him. Feltrino knew he would be able to push the stallion all night, till he was well away from Verona. 'It's true what they say about della Scalla. He takes care of things in his possession, like he did the horse. But he's ruthless, as anyone who runs cities must be,' Feltrino thought. He would be that kind of leader when he went home to claim his place by his father. As he rode, Feltrino went over what he was going to say to his father. He wanted to save face, but he didn't have one of the lookers. What exactly should he tell him? Well, he had a long ride. He would run it through in his mind over and over again, till he got it right.

Luigi -- or Ludovico -- Gonzaga was still the thin, quiet man Feltrino had left almost two months earlier. As Feltrino burst into the dining room, he saw his father sitting at table. Feltrino strode over to him and went down onto one knee. He had determined to show his father deference, but not act cowed. He would apologize, using the wisdom he remembered Baron da Pontremoli imparting about fathers and sons, but he must quickly get to the device that brings images closer.

Luigi went to put a hand on Feltrino's head, but stopped.

"My prodigal son smells like a festering trough of hog guts," were the first words Luigi uttered.

Although Feltrino felt his ire rising -- his father could always do that to him -- he contained himself. He raised his head, grabbed his father's hand and kissed it. Then he looked his father in the eye, making sure he looked unafraid and unbroken, like he had resolved to.

"That is because I've spent the better part of the last month in a Scallari prison," Feltrino said.

Luigi looked at his son, raising his eyebrows at the news, then peered into the youth's eyes. His gaze slid to the blade hanging by Feltrino's thigh. He reached down and touched the now-dried blood. He laughed.

"Quite an adventure you've had then. Sit and tell me how you've profited from it. But first..." He looked at his butler. "Renaldo, butcher the fatted calf. My son hath returned."

By afternoon, Luigi and his military officers had been briefed on the new device that would allow Mastino to have a great and strategic advantage. They resolved to get their hands on one and discover its secret. But how?

A captain suggested a group of his men could go in and storm the lensmaker's house. Luigi's advisor suggested bribing the lensmaker to come over to them. Feltrino told how he had tried this approach and didn't think it would work. He felt his father's eyes upon him. He knew that look. It showed he understood that there was more to the story. Feltrino then spoke.

"I think it best if I go back myself. Getting into Verona with many men and out again would be tricky. Too many will cause a problem."

Over many objections to Feltrino's proposal, Luigi Gonzaga spoke.

"I now see in my son the ability to do what he says he will do. He has proved himself capable of getting out of messes. Now all he has to do is learn how to stay out of them in the first place. What is your plan, my son?"

"We need only one of the devices. I will take a wagon and horses and go into Verona as a farmer with produce. When I am in, I will find a way to get my hands on what we want."

There was a hush from the men around the table.

"That's no plan," an officer finally said.

Luigi spoke again. "Well, sometimes one has to wait patiently, like a spider, for an opportunity to come along. The wisdom is to put yourself in the situation from which to strike. I have faith in you, my son. I am very proud and glad you have come back to us."

Chapter 18

"Welcome home, Mastino," Nicademo said as his cousin dismounted the carriage. "It's good to have you home early from your trip."

"Thank you Nikki," Mastino said stretching his stiff limbs. "It's good to be home. Oh, my back and legs. Such a ride. So, all is well here?"

"Well enough. There's a meal waiting for you. Would you like to freshen up first?"

"Actually, let's walk around the square to stretch my legs."

"Good. You can fill me in about news not in your letters."

Nicademo caught Captain Caesar's eye and motioned up the square. The captain sent two men ahead. Nicademo and Mastino followed behind them.

"The demonstration of Karl's new cannon was very impressive," Mastino began. "They can throw a four hundred-pound bolder almost two hundred and fifty paces. And the roar of the cannon, it will terrify our enemies if it doesn't kill them."

"Truly?" Nicademo said. "And what was their first impression of our lookers?"

"Oh, that was the wonderful part. They fired the cannon and Karl said, 'Come, let's look at the damage,' and I replied, 'No need to soil our boots.' I pulled out a looker and spied through it. Within moments of Karl and his generals trying it, they wanted any number we could provide. And they will trade us for the cannon technology. We need not even give them money."

"So, della Cappa's brass and crystal lookers turn into gold for us."

"Romero's lookers, yes." They were halfway around the square, walking leisurely past the treasury. Some officials coming out the door stopped and bowed. Mastino just nodded as he passed. "So, how goes it at della Cappa's? Will they be able to supply?"

"They have good plans for enlarging their shop, yes, and they are very determined."

"You don't think the old man will turn to drink again? The reports from Florence you received about how he ruined his old business, it can't be repeated."

"I think not, cousin. He looks a man reformed, resolved to make his house rich. And the plan he showed me for an even more advanced lathe was most extraordinary."

"Yes, the water-driven thing you wrote about. The savant's invention again, no doubt. But one never knows about people newly wealthy. They often become more elevated in their minds than their true station." Almost back to the carriage, Mastino stopped and rubbed his neck, twisting his head one way, then the other. "People like that often cause their masters annoyances. Perhaps we should not give them this gift so easily. Maybe we should make it so they will be more appreciative of our boon."

"How so, Mastino?"

They were back to the palace's entrance. Mastino smiled at his cousin mischievously.

"Come. We'll dine and I shall tell you. It's so good when plans fall together."

"Oh, one other thing. Maybe not so good news." Mastino stopped and looked at his cousin. "Feltrino, he escaped and killed a guard."

Mastino pondered this. Then he shrugged, turned and continued into the palace.

"Ah well, we're far enough ahead now."

Four days after escaping, Feltrino was back in Verona. He kept his beard, wore commoner's clothes, a floppy, wide-brimmed, straw hat and drove a two-horse wagon full of turnips and cabbages. One of his two horses was actually a riding horse, smaller and bred for swiftness. When he somehow got a looker, he would leave the city, abandon the cart and hurry home.

After accepting whatever a market vendor offered him for his produce, Feltrino strolled toward a tavern to relieve his thirst. On the way, he bought a couple of sweet pears and munched one as he walked. He stopped as he passed a space between two buildings, spying a filthy young man rifling through a heap of garbage, looking for scraps. He'd seen countless people do this, but he recognized this wretch.

"Hey, ugly one, you work for that lensmaker, don't you?" Feltrino called.

Ugilino looked up. He was ragged and haggard again. He had found something recognizable as food and began chewing on it as he gazed at the person speaking to him.

"I know you," Ugilino said, looking hard at Feltrino. Then he made a face and spit out something even he couldn't stomach. He spit again, to clear his mouth. "I saw the way you were looking at Guilietta."

"She's a ripe piece of fruit, that one," Feltrino replied. He began to toss his second pear up and down, catching it and tossing it. "So, how goes your house?" Ugilino scowled at the young noble, then looked down. "Ah, not so good for you at home, eh?"

"I don't live there anymore," Ugilino mumbled.

"What did you say? Really?" Feltrino continued to toss the pear. He could see Ugilino eyeing the fruit. "Here," he said, tossing it to him. Ugilino grabbed the pear and chomped down greedily. Feltrino laughed. "They had good food at your old master's, I hear. Baron Pontremoli told me that while we were having lunch in his office the other week. You miss all that good food?"

"We ate like princes," Ugilino mumbled again, his eyes going soft. Suddenly he felt transported back to the della Cappa table, jostling merrily with his old family, joking and eating out of his very own bowl. He remembered happily slurping and munching on the wonderful rabbit stew before they went to church on one particular day. He was a hero that day, the day the Bishop first wore the discs for the eyes. Feltrino's voice jolted him back to the garbage-strewn alley.

"Well, I know what it is to eat like a prince. I am one. And I'm here on princely business." Ugilino looked at Feltrino with suspicion. "Come," Feltrino said. "Let's go into the tavern. I'll buy you a princely meal."

A meal and several cups of wine later, Feltrino knew all.

"What does it say, what does it say?" Agistino demanded.

Shamira had stopped serving dinner to answer the door. A soldier handed her the message and said he was to wait. The Master became very anxious. Everyone but the Signora stopped eating to listen.

"Master Agistino della Cappa," Shamira read, "Our lord, Mastino II della Scalla, has returned ahead of schedule from his business with our German allies. We have urgent business to discuss and command you to come to the palace immediately. Bring your apprentice, Romero, and any planning you may have prepared, including the new lathe. Follow the messenger to the palace. Signed by the hand of Baron Nicademo da Pontremoli, for His Excellency, Mastino II, della Scalla."

"Romero, let's go. We dine again with the Podesta!"

Feltrino and Ugilino were up the street, peering from the edge of an alley. They had been watching the house since last night. Feltrino couldn't believe how easy it had been to deceive the ugly dolt. The simpleton had gaped at him, his open mouth full of food, when Feltrino said that, after they stole a looker, Ugilino could come back to Mantua and be his squire.

"Would I have my own bed?" the fool asked.

"Why, of course."

After their night of reconnoitering, they saw Hansum and Lincoln enter the house for dinner and then watched apprehensively when the soldier rode up and handed the message to Shamira.

"That's Carmella," Ugilino said too loudly. Feltrino hit him to be quiet. A few minutes later the Master was hurrying out the door, putting on his fancy new cap. "There's the Master. There's Romero!" Ugilino cried. Feltrino swatted him again. The soldier motioned for them to follow, which they did on foot.

"What can be going on?" Feltrino said softly. Then the door burst open again and the Signora barged out. She began waving a hanky and shouting.

"Good luck with the Podesta about the looker, husband. Good luck."

Agistino turned around quickly and shushed her in an annoyed fashion, waving for her to get back in the house. The kitchen girl and Guilietta came out and grabbed the old woman by the arms and pulled her back. While several neighbors laughed, the Master turned and hurried on.

"They're going to the palace about the looker, are they?" Feltrino said. He thought for a few moments, then smiled. Ugilino looked at him curiously. Feltrino walked up the alley to his wagon and pulled something out of one of his bags. It was another piece of paper. He wrote something on it. "We'll wait awhile then have someone deliver this."

It seemed to Pan that Master della Cappa might have a heart attack by the time they got to the palace. Even though the soldier was walking his horse, it was hard for the men on foot to keep up. Hansum was sweating profusely by the time they got to their destination. They were greeted by Baron da Pontremoli at the palace door, and while he was friendly, he was also somewhat reserved. They were taken to the same dining room as before, but no sumptuous food was set before them.

"Wait here. I shall return with the Podesta as soon as possible." After all their hurrying, now they were made to cool their heels.

"Something's odd," Pan whispered to Hansum. *"It's the old hurry-up-and-wait routine."*

Feltrino flicked the boy hard on the nose then pointed at the della Cappa house.

"Do you see that house? You take this letter there, and what do you say?" Feltrino asked.

"The lensmaker told me to bring this letter to you," the boy said. He was about ten, very dirty, but he didn't look stupid. He did look peeved at having his nose beaten.

"And then what do you do?" Feltrino continued, flicking at his nose again.

"Come back and get my coin."

"Buon. Now go and be quick."

Feltrino and Ugilino watched the boy go to the house and knock. Shamira answered the door, took the note and the boy ran back.

Shamira read the note to Guilietta. "Master della Cappa requires another looker brought to the palace immediately. That's all it says."

"Things must be going well at the meeting if they need another sample," Guilietta said, smiling.

"I guess," Shamira said, staring at the note.

"There's only one left in a leather case. It's in Papa's room. We'd better hurry." Just as Guilietta ran up the stairs, Lincoln came in.

"I'm getting a snack for the boys," he said. "What's that note about?"

"They want another looker brought to the palace right away."

Lincoln took the paper. "Whose chicken scratch is this? It's not Hansum's writing."

Shamira shrugged as Guilietta came running down the stairs.

"We must go to the palace quickly," Guilietta said.

"Oh darn," Shamira said. "I've got this stew cooking. It'll burn if we don't watch it."

"You stay here then," Guilietta said, smiling brightly. "I can run fast. And on the way home I'll stop and get some wonderful fruits for dessert. Papa and Romero will most certainly bring home a huge order. We'll have a celebration."

Pan noted that when Nicademo and the Podesta finally came into the meeting room, they had tentative looks on their faces. Mastino smiled, but did not shake hands. Plus, he sat somewhat down the table from the others.

"Let me see the documents you speak of," he said to Nicademo.

Nicademo collected the plans for the new lathe as well as the lists of materials. He showed them to Mastino, who looked at them for a protracted time, nodded, then placed them even further down the table, out of reach. Then he looked up and began.

"Fifteen hundred lookers. That's how many I need for the Germans."

Master della Cappa began to breath very hard. Then he crossed himself and forced a smile.

"The lathe design we now use..." his voice broke into a squeak. He started again. "The lathe design we now use is superior to all in Europe. And it was made right here in Verona. And as you have observed, we have yet another design to make us yet more efficient. Noble gentlemen, I will not fail you and . . ." Agistino stood up and bowed as low as he could. "I thank you for your order."

Neither the Podesta nor Nicademo answered. They allowed a long silence, looking at each other and then at Master della Cappa. Agistino stood there, puzzled. The Podesta's secretary, Nicademo, took out a leather portfolio. He pulled a letter out of it and motioned for the Master to sit down. He held the letter up.

"*Oh, oh,*" Pan whispered to Hansum.

"Agistino, you are our friend," Nicademo began. "We wish you no harm. But it has come to our attention that you are indebted to several people in Florence. Men who would like to know where you are." Agistino's eyes widened and his jaw dropped. "You still owe much to some glass makers in Murano and Jews you borrowed money from in Florence." Both the secretary and Podesta kept innocent looks on their faces. The Master's head fell to his chest. He was clearly embarrassed.

"I, I had some times of trouble, Your Excellencies."

"As do we all," the Podesta answered.

"But those times are past," the Master said, doe-eyed.

"We believe you, della Cappa," the Podesta assured.

"Agistino," Nicademo said, "we have asked you here to en-quire how you will pay for the new supplies. These are very large orders and, well, you have no credit."

"Um, uh, well, I'll negotiate, I suppose," the Master said.

Continuing to do the hatchet work, Nicademo said with a lit-tle chuckle, "Oh, Agistino, our ambassador to Florence says you left a very bad taste in the mouth of the glass maker. And the Jews, they are suspicious that your ugly apprentice stole back some repossessed items."

Agistino fell to his knees and begged. "We were desperate, Signori. A sick wife and a daughter, and me ill from the grape. Before my troubles, I was great friends with the glass maker. And the Jews, they are honorable and gave me much credit in my younger days. Now that I am well, I will travel there and renew these friendships."

"Agistino, please get off your knees," Nicademo said. "There is no need. But in all honesty, I think it will be some time before your credit is honored in Florence again. Longer than we have, I'm afraid."

Agistino's machismo quickly evaporated and he looked down at the floor.

Pan whispered into Hansum's ear. *"Ask what they propose."*

"What do you propose, Signori?" Hansum asked calmly.

"Ah, very good, young man. Direct," the Podesta said. "Master della Cappa, please, off your knees. Be calm like Romero here."

Ugilino saw Guilietta run out of the house with the leather carrying case strap slung over her shoulder. He saw her wave up at the Satores' window, smile, then take off running toward the city.

"That girl has swift legs," Ugilino heard Feltrino say, smiling. Then Ugilino felt his new master pull hard on his ear. "Andiamo!" They ran and mounted Feltrino's wagon. Feltrino whipped the horses and took off quickly. "We'll get ahead of her at Piazza Bra. You'll run and snatch the looker from her."

"What? She'll recognize me." Feltrino backhanded Ugilino across the face.

"Don't question me, idiot! You won't be living in this town anymore. What's it matter?

"I guess," Ugilino said. "Hey, turn here! You missed the street."

"Now see what you made me do? Fool."

By the time they got turned around and to Piazza Bra, they could see Guilietta in the distance, striding quickly around the stalls.

"Damn!" Feltrino cursed. "We'll have to catch her at Piazza Grande Urbe. Get your ass off the wagon and go get her." Ugilino looked at Feltrino with some confusion. "Go on, damn it. Grab the looker and we'll meet somewhere around the square. Hurry! Hurry!" Ugilino looked quickly around and saw a blanket on the wagon floor. Just as he grabbed it, he felt Feltrino pushing him hard. He tumbled off the seat and landed on the ground. "Get going!"

Ugilino got to his feet and ran as fast as he could. He wove in and out of people in the aisles, bumping many. By the time they got to the Grande Urbe Square, he was only about fifty strides behind Guilietta, hidden within a dense crowd of people. Suddenly Guilietta stopped. There was a procession going through the square which nobody could pass.

"It's the Bishop with a relic of San Zeno," Ugilino heard a townsperson say. The line of people turned into a wall which Guilietta was now stuck behind. Ugilino could see Guilietta become agitated. She started pushing her way through the crowd, the leather case with the looker slung behind her. As he made his way through the crowd, he put the blanket over his back, like a cloak. Ugilino was now only feet away from Guilietta, the leather case almost in grasping distance.

Shamira finished stirring the pot of stew hanging over the nice, even bed of coals in the hearth. She put the wooden spoon to her lips, tasted it and smiled. She then looked around and saw a wooden bowl on the table. She would bring the Signora a snack. As she got to the table, she saw the note about needing another telescope. She looked at it again and something stirred in her mind. She picked it up and examined the paper. Both the paper and the writing were somehow familiar.

Shamira slammed the spoon on the table and ran out of the house. She ran down the alley and into the shop. Lincoln, caught up on work, was giving the little apprentices reading and writing lessons.

"Look at this," she said, thrusting the note in front of him.

"What about it?" he asked.

"Where's that note Feltrino gave the Master?"

Lincoln's eyes widened. He went to the nail on the wall and pulled it off. They held the notes together. It was the same paper and handwriting.

"Boys, go home. Now," Lincoln said firmly.

"But big brother Maruccio," little Pippo began.

"I said now!" Lincoln and Shamira hurried the boys out, locked up the shop and ran for the palace.

Ugilino reached forward, his fingers almost touching the leather case. Guilietta pushed herself through to the front of the line and the case moved away from Ugilino's grasp.

"No need to push," a man's voice said to Guilietta. "If you want to see the Bishop and the relic, just say per favore."

"Per favore, Signore. I need to get through on urgent business at the palace."

"You'll not get past the procession for a while," Ugilino heard the man say, "but come stand at the front here."

There was a parade of priests and soldiers walking slowly through the square. Deep lines of people were crushed together on two sides of the procession as it passed. Ugilino pulled the blanket over his head like a cowl and wormed his way the extra few feet toward Guilietta. The looker case was still slung over her back, only inches away. The Bishop was walking right in front of Guilietta, behind two priests who were carrying a small, ornate trunk between them.

"The bones of San Zeno," one of the priests cried. "The bones of San Zeno." Many in the crowd crossed themselves and cheered loudly. They were so loud and caused such a distraction that Ugilino thought to himself, 'NOW!', and he grabbed the strap of the case and pulled on it as hard as he could. "Miracles for believers!" the priest cried.

"Hooraw!" shouted the crowd.

Guilietta flew back violently as the case was yanked from her. She fell to the ground amid the crush of townspeople. Ugilino turned and pushed himself out of the crowd.

"Stop! Thief!" he heard Guilietta scream. "Stop!"

Ugilino could feel the hands of several men grabbing at him. Obviously, the sight of a beautiful young woman struggling up from the ground inspired them to be helpful. Ugilino punched one in the neck with all his might and stomped the foot of the other, tearing himself from their grasp. He broke through the back of the throng and started running in earnest.

"Stop him," he heard Guilietta cry again. He pulled the blanket tight around his neck to make sure she didn't see who it was, but heard her continuing to shout. He looked back quickly to see her running past the two men who had initially grabbed him but were now standing, nursing their bruises. Guilietta really could run, he saw. He began running down a street, and there he saw Feltrino standing and peering from around a corner. He was waving for Ugilino to duck into the alley with him. Feltrino withdrew and Ugilino careened around the corner, right into Feltrino's strong hands.

"Guilietta's chasing me," Ugilino croaked, out of breath.

"Yes, I saw her," Feltrino said, smiling. "Stand back here." Ugilino took a step behind Feltrino and watched him clench his fist and draw back his arm. Guilietta suddenly appeared around the corner and Feltrino smashed his fist into her cheek. She fell to the ground like a rag doll.

"Hey, you didn't say you would . . ." Ugilino gasped.

"Give me the looker," Feltrino said, his hand reaching toward Ugilino, still smiling as if nothing had happened. Ugilino looked at Feltrino, then down at Guilietta, lying in a heap. When he looked up again, Feltrino wasn't smiling and he had his sword in his hand. Ugilino handed the looker to Feltrino and the noble smiled again. "She shall be my toy for later," he said merrily. Feltrino tossed the looker into the back of the wagon, clipped his sword onto his belt, then bent to pick up Guilietta. "A diversion on the way home tonight." He picked up Guilietta's limp body and dumped it into the back of the wagon. He looked around and, seeing the blanket around Ugilino's shoulders, took it and covered Guilietta.

"You didn't say nothin' about hurting her," Ugilino spouted, grabbing Feltrino's shoulder and spinning him around. As Feltrino came about, Ugilino felt a sharp, excruciating pain in his arm. He backed off to find the tip of Feltrino's dagger embedded in his shoulder. "Aaaeeeiii!" he screamed, pulling away from the blade. Pain and blood gushed from the wound.

"What's the matter with you?" Feltrino shouted. "Don't ever touch me!"

"But Guilietta . . ."

"Get the hell out of here, you stupid peasant!" Feltrino screamed, bringing the dagger's tip to Ugilino's face.

"But I'm your squire. You said . . ." Ugilino then felt more searing pain as the knifepoint scraped across his cheek. Ugilino screamed and ran into the road.

"You, my squire?" Feltrino shouted in a laugh. Then he snarled. "A filthy peasant like you? And such a fool? Oh, I might as well kill you now," Feltrino said taking a step forward. Ugilino turned and ran. He heard Feltrino laughing behind him, but no footsteps following.

Ugilino ran and ran as hard as he could. By the time he got to Piazza Bra, cramping pains were shooting from his shoulder and blood streamed down his arm and face. 'I better get to Signora Baroni,' he thought. 'That dirty rotten bastard! He said I could be his . . .' Ugilino stopped dead in his tracks. He stared at two people who had suddenly stopped in front of him. They were staring at him, obviously shocked at what he must look like. Then Ugilino began to babble so quickly he was incoherent.

"Maruccio, Carmella . . . Feltrino took Guilietta. He knocked her out and put her in a wagon. He stole the looker and is going back to Mantua. I tried to save her but . . ."

"Slow down, Ugilino," Shamira said. "What are you saying?"

"You're bleedin' like a stuck pig, man!" Lincoln cried.

"It's Feltrino, he stabbed me. I tried to save her but he knocked her out and stabbed me."

"Save who?" Shamira asked again. "Speak more slowly."

"Guilietta. Feltrino has her looker, and he hit her really hard and then put her in a wagon. He's going back to Mantua with the looker. And Guilietta."

"My God!" Shamira gasped, turning pale.

"Is Guilietta hurt bad?" Lincoln asked.

"I don't know. He hit her real hard in the face and she went down. Then he put her in the wagon and covered her with a blanket and said he was going back to Mantua."

"Oh my God, oh my God!" Shamira said. "We've got to . . ." Then she stopped and looked at Ugilino hard. "How do you know he was stealing a looker and why would he tell you where he's going?"

Almost caught in his lie, Ugilino froze. "Hey, he stabbed me when I tried to save her. I hate that bastard." Ugilino saw Shamira and Lincoln's eyes widen with shock when he took his hand off of his wounded shoulder and more blood oozed out freely. He quickly clamped his hand down and winced. "Where's the Master?" he asked.

"He's at the palace with Romero."

"You better go and get them fast. The Podesta too. I'm bleedin' bad. I gotta get to Signora Baroni." Shamira continued staring at Ugilino. He could see she was trying to figure something out. "You better go, Carmella," Ugilino said to further distract her. "That bastard is probably driving out of the city gates by now. And you know what he'll do with her when he has a chance." He made a pained face, which he didn't have to exaggerate. "I've gotta go," he said, hobbling away. Lincoln stopped him.

"What did the wagon look like? Can you describe the horses?"

"Just a plain wagon, I don't know. Oh, the horses. One was a big, ugly thing. The other was a nice brown one. I gotta go." And with that he turned and limped away.

"Oh my God, my God," Shamira said.

"We gotta go. C'mon!" Lincoln grabbed Shamira's arm and pulled her forward. They ran the rest of the way to the palace. Luckily Captain Caesar was in front and recognized them.

"Captain Caesar," she panted, and then quickly explained the situation. He instantly turned and shouted to a soldier on the palace roof.

"Signal to close the city gates. All of them. Now!" he called. The soldier on the roof picked up some flags. "Come, I'll take you to the Podesta.

"What do you propose, Signori?" Hansum had asked the Podesta calmly.

"Si, Signori," Agistino said glumly as he got up and sat on the edge of his chair. "I am at your mercy. Please believe I did not intend to deceive you in any way. Circumstances . . ."

"Of course, of course, my friend," Nicademo said. "We have all been in tight places where circumstances dictate that we put ourselves in God's hands. But seriously, examine how your resources would be overstretched for such a project as fifteen hundred lookers. You have but two lathes and a small staff of youths and girls. His Excellency is dealing with kings and dukes and princes. Do you think it wise of us to make promises to kings with such a situation as yours?"

"I understand, Signor," the Master said. Hansum saw Agistino was getting himself under control. "But has my word not been good in our dealings so far? Did we not deliver early and did we not just show you a lathe design far superior to any in Christendom?"

"Yes, you have, on all accounts, been faithful, Master della Cappa. That is why we honor you with this meeting," Nicademo said.

"Thank you, Excellency," Agistino said with dignity, though his eyes were still wary. "What is it you propose? I am in both God's and your hands."

The Podesta looked at Master della Cappa and then at Nicademo, then back. He put a hand on the plans for the water-driven lathe, pushing it yet further down the table.

"Perhaps your shop and resources are too little," the Podesta said. "Perhaps we should arrange the looker's manufacture in Florence."

Horrified, Agistino lost his composure again, crying, "But they are an invention of my house!"

There was an insistent knocking at the door.

"We are busy!" the Podesta shouted angrily.

"It's Caesar. An emergency."

"Come."

The door opened and Captain Caesar walked in quickly. Hansum was surprised to see Shamira and Lincoln standing nervously in the hall. When the Master saw them, he seemed even more shocked.

"The Gonzaga, Feltrino," Caesar explained. "Apparently he stole a looker and is making his way out of Verona with it."

"Has he gotten away?" Nicademo asked.

"I've signaled the gates closed. The girl and boy just got here with the news."

"There's more," Shamira said, stepping into the room, wide-eyed. The Podesta signaled to Caesar to let her speak. "It's Guilietta. Feltrino's kidnapped her. She's with him."

In the courtyard Captain Caesar was assembling his men to chase down Feltrino. The Podesta was going too, on his big white stallion. He was so angry that yet another generation of Gonzaga was besting him, he wanted personal revenge. The Baron was trying to dissuade his cousin from going, but he would not hear of it. He also ordered extra horses, as they would be riding hard.

"I had him in my hand and I showed mercy," the Podesta complained to Nicademo. "I was only holding him, and he does this to me, stealing my lookers."

"No sign of him at the gate, Excellency," Caesar reported. "He may already be outside the walls."

The Master, Shamira, Lincoln and Hansum were standing by, looking frantic with worry.

"You must save my daughter, Excellency," Master della Cappa pleaded. "Please, save her."

"Go home, della Cappa," the Podesta said. "Your house has already done enough, letting him take a looker."

"Let me go with you, Excellency," Hansum pleaded. "I can ride well and you have extra horses. Please let me go. She is like a sister to me."

"Oh, you can ride too?" the Podesta mocked. "My savant's talents are so very diverse." Mastino saw the savant thinking. It was like he was listening to someone speak to him.

"And I can track," Hansum said. "I am an excellent tracker, if they go off road."

"It would be logical for the Gonzaga to go off road, Excellency," Captain Caesar said, "I don't know why he would be using a wagon."

"Because he's got Guilietta," Hansum said emotionally.

"Perhaps she went willingly," Mastino suggested.

"NO WAY!" Hansum shot back loudly right at the Podesta. He instantly felt Caesar's strong hand grab his shoulder roughly.

"It's okay," Mastino said, almost amused at the outburst. "After all, she's like . . . his sister."

"We are all very close," Shamira added as calmly as possible.

"That is all good," Mastino said, then he laughed. "Captain, give Romero one of the spare horses. We shall observe his skills."

Captain Caesar looked surprised.

This was a very different horse than what Hansum was used to. He looked up at the beast. Almost seventeen hands at the withers and positively massive.

"I'm used to riding Arabians," he said to the Podesta as he got up somewhat awkwardly. The horse started to test Hansum by pulling away. Hansum yanked hard with both reins and dug in his heels, bringing the animal to a dead halt. "But whatever the animal, they have to know who is in charge."

There was only one main road to take a wagon on if Feltrino was travelling to Mantua. It split several ways after a while, but until then the riders could ride at a gallop. The first fork in the road was a quiet place. Few wagons would have passed there in the last while. Hansum rode his horse to the front of the line and jumped off.

"Don't let our horses trample the recent tracks," he said. He ran from one road and then the other, letting Pan scan the impressions of both wheels and horse hooves.

"From what Master Lincoln was told by Ugilino about the wagon and horses . . ."

While Pan was informing Hansum of his observations, Captain Caesar was discussing the situation with the Podesta.

"The road to the left is the most direct route," Caesar said. "It goes through several villages, but he wouldn't care about that. The road to the right is rougher and almost a half day longer, through a valley and heavy forest. I say we go to the left."

"I think not," Hansum interrupted. "There are three recent wagon tracks under four hours old. Two go to the left and have only one horse. Our information is he was using two horses. A big wagon horse and a smaller one, shod for speed. See, notice the hoofprints. Unmatched horses. This one goes to the right."

"One of his horses was not a wagon horse?" the Podesta repeated. "And you can see that in the tracks?" Hansum nodded. "He may abandon the wagon and girl if he detects us. Captain, divide our men into three groups. The larger one on the road and send smaller ones through the forests on either side. Come, we must be quick."

Guilietta stared at Feltrino, trying not to show the hatred and fear in her heart. One side of her face felt puffy and ached. She was standing in the forest, now high on a hill, her hands tied in front of her. Feltrino was looking down into the valley with the looker.

"It's lucky I decided to get us off the road," Feltrino said. "They would have caught up with us by now. My God, I think that's Mastino himself. They're moving away from us. We should be safe here." He put down the looker and turned to Guilietta. "How does this marvel work?" he asked, referring to the telescope. "There must be many ingenious things inside to make it do such magic."

Guilietta stared at her captor blankly. She had assembled many lookers and knew it was just three lenses, one at each end of the smaller adjusting tube and a larger one at the end of the long tube. "I don't know how they work," she said. "It is learned work that only people like my father can do."

"No matter," Feltrino said. "When we get back to my city, our philosophers will take it apart and discover the magic." Then he looked at Guilietta. "I think we are safe to stay here for the night," and then he smiled sardonically.

Guilietta caught her breath.

"Please, no . . ." but Feltrino had already taken a step toward her and grasped her wrist.

"Even filthy from travelling all day and that swollen face, you are still very appealing," he said.

"No," Guilietta said again, struggling. But Feltrino's other arm was around her waist and pulling her toward him. Guilietta screamed but Feltrino laughed and put a hand over her mouth. She bit down hard.

"Bitch!" he cried and threw her to the ground. "Now I won't be so nice when I . . ." but his threat was interrupted by the sound of a branch cracking loudly somewhere close by in the trees. Feltrino drew his sword and knelt by Guilietta, the saber tip close to her throat. "Keep your mouth shut."

A large horse broke through the branches, one of Mastino's soldiers upon it. Feltrino sprang up before the man could see him, his saber extended. Guilietta watched as the man turned in the saddle at the last moment. The blade, aimed at the space between his breastplate and back plate, missed the opening and bounced off the polished steel. Guilietta didn't wait to see what would happen next. She ran into the woods.

Hansum was kneeling, allowing Pan to examine the tracks in the hard-pack road. The Podesta and Captain stood behind him, silently watching, while the other soldiers looked on from their horses. Still saying nothing, Hansum stood up at Pan's command and scoured the area ahead and then behind them. He could see the Podesta staring at him intently. Then Pan spoke to Hansum, who repeated his words.

"The tracks we're following have disappeared."

"But there are plenty of tracks on the road," Captain Caesar said.

"Those are old tracks, Signor. He must have pulled off the road at that rocky area behind us and headed into the hills. The wagon must be hidden . . ."

"A rider approaches from the trees, Master Hansum," Pan whispered. *"Two horses and one rider. About five hundred meters off the road. He'll be out of the woods in a moment."*

Hansum looked over in the direction Pan referred to.

"Someone's coming out of the forest," Hansum said.

The Podesta took out his looker and used it.

"How could you . . . he's right. It's Sanchez. He's leading a second horse. Damn, there's a man slung across it."

Sanchez could give no word whether Guilietta was still with Feltrino. After finding the riderless horse, it took the soldier time to find the body. Hansum jumped on his horse. He was chomping to dive into the woods, giving chase to Feltrino.

"Caution, Young Master," Pan whispered. *"Patience. This is war. You must keep a cool head, if you want to keep it at all."*

"I want to go to his last known site and we'll track him from there," Hansum said under his breath.

"No," replied Pan. *"It's best if two other men start there. The rest should go down the road and two should veer off every two kilometers to pick up the trail. The last group will most likely be cutting him off from the front. If we can go in as the third group, probabilities are we should be closest to him. With my enhanced sensory perception, we should be able to find him easily."*

Hansum interrupted the Podesta and Captain, who were strategizing, and repeated what Pan said, except for the last bit. Both the Captain and Podesta raised an eyebrow. So did most of the men. The Podesta chuckled.

"I concur, Captain Caesar," the Podesta said. "A sound strategy."

"Sanchez," the Captain said, "take a man and start back to where you found the body. Watch for doubling back. The rest of you, let's go."

Now with a plan and the quarry close by, everybody rode hard. After about ten minutes, the Captain pointed to two men and they splintered off into the woods. Another ten minutes later, the same. Pan cautioned Hansum to be ready. When he saw the Captain ready to point at men, Hansum swung his horse to the side and galloped off the road. The Captain scowled and brought the others to a stop.

"You may be able to ride and track, Signor," Captain Caesar called, "but if you find him, can you fight? Feltrino is a master swordsman."

"Say you won't confront him, but will come for help," Pan whispered.

The Podesta scowled when Hansum repeated this, but acquiesced.

"Da Silva, you go with him. You're our best swordsman," Mastino said. "The rest of you, let's go!"

As da Silva and Hansum clamored up the forested steep hill, their heavy horses crashing through the underbrush, Hansum whipped his horse quickly forward.

"Slow down, Master Hansum," Pan whispered. *"You don't want to get too far ahead of Lieutenant da Silva. He has a weapon, in case we catch up to Feltrino."*

"I have every intention of catching up with Feltrino," Hansum replied. "Damn. I should have taken that dead man's sword."

"You should have done no such thing," Pan whispered, speaking angrily for the first time since Hansum had known him. *"Sword training at a History Camp in our time is no preparation for here. Prince Feltrino is a trained killer. We've seen his handiwork."*

It was hard slogging going uphill in the virgin forest. Suddenly, Pan shouted in Hansum's ear.

"Stop! Here's his trail. See the broken branches? Look, two sets of hoofprints. Get off the horse and let me spectral analyze the decay of those crushed leaves to see how far we're behind." A minute later, Pan said, *"These plants were trampled twenty-five to thirty minutes ago. Have da Silva go up the hill another five minutes and move parallel to us. When Feltrino realizes we're close, he'll go uphill to hide."*

Hansum related this to da Silva, and then added, "We must be very careful that Guilietta is not harmed."

"My orders are to retrieve the device that brings images closer, Signor," the soldier said. "I was told the girl is of no great concern."

'That damned telescope!' Hansum thought. 'That's all Podesta della Scalla really cares about.' But Hansum realized that he must be pragmatic and not dwell on things he had no control over. He just stared at the man for a moment, then motioned him to move on. Hansum and Pan then continued slowly, allowing da Silva time to get into position.

"Two sets of tracks indicate Feltrino probably still has Mistress Guilietta," Pan said, as they started back on the trail. *"The twenty-fourth-century topographical map I have in my memory is still most probably valid. At the end of this ridge, the ground will still slope downward as we approach the Po River."*

After almost an hour, Pan whispered, *"Stop!"* The imp then appeared, about quarter-size, on the back of the horse's neck. Peering over its crown, Pan cocked his head and one of his now-longer ears turned into a brass hearing tube. "In the distance, about five hundred meters," he said out loud. "I hear two horses moving away from us. It must be them." Without hesitation, Hansum slapped the horse's reins and kicked him into a canter. "What are you doing?" Pan cried, his image gripping onto the horse's mane like he was holding on for dear life, his time-changed red butt bouncing up and down.

"Going after him," Hansum said through gritted teeth.

"And then what?" Pan challenged, his image continuing to bounce. "What will you do when you catch up?" Hansum pulled back on the reins. "I'm not saying don't approach him," Pan said. "Let's just agree on a plan." They talked for a minute, Hansum looking anxious.

"Fine," Hansum finally said. "I'll try to do what you say. Come on. Let's not get too far behind." Pan hid back in his lamp and Hansum continued for about five minutes, making more noise than he needed to. They wanted Feltrino to hear them coming, so he would hide and give the other soldiers time to catch up. But if Feltrino came after Hansum, he was supposed to turn and run.

"*Slow down to a walk,*" Pan whispered. "*I perceive he has stopped about three hundred meters ahead. I can scent the two horses.*" A hundred meters more and Pan told Hansum to stop. "*I sense slight motion in a thicket two hundred meters away, a bit uphill. Now is the time to do what we agreed.*"

Hansum gulped. What happened now determined whether Guilietta would remain safe. He took a deep breath and shouted, "Feltrino! I know you're hiding in the thicket with Guilietta. Feltrino . . ."

Feltrino was more than surprised to hear his name being called. And hearing the voice of that damned apprentice caused his blood to rise. He looked at Guilietta. She looked back at him, and even though she now had a gag in her mouth, he could tell from her eyes she was smiling.

"Feltrino," the apprentice's voice rang out again, "can you hear me? There are many men close by. Leave Guilietta and the looker and just go. Feltrino, answer me!"

Feltrino became agitated. "I'll kill that bastard," he swore. Then he thought hard about what to do. He rose up on his saddle and shouted. "I won't talk to a damned apprentice. I'll only talk to an officer. And if anyone comes near, I'll slit the girl's throat. Do you hear me?"

There was silence.

"Feltrino," the apprentice's voice called again. "Please, just leave Guilietta and the looker and we'll back off. Feltrino, please."

"He's by himself," Feltrino said with realization. He looked at Guilietta. Her eyes weren't smiling anymore. Then he shouted, his voice quite light, "You are by yourself, apprentice. Ha!" He quickly took the reins of the wagon horse Guilietta was on and tied them in a double knot to a tree branch. Then he flicked his own reins hard. "I'm coming to kill you." As Feltrino's horse bounded out of the thicket, he shouted again, "Did you hear me, apprentice? You're going to die!"

Feltrino's horse quickly scaled down the slope to the ridge and galloped the way he had previously come. But before Feltrino could get the animal up to speed, he heard a crashing of branches above him, then the thundering of hooves. He looked up and saw a large horse with a Scallari soldier coming at full gallop toward him, helmet closed in battle position, sword extended. Feltrino pulled hard back with his reins, but it was of no use. The two horses were going to collide.

"What's happening?" Hansum asked Pan, who once again was sitting on the neck of Hansum's horse. The noise of pounding ground and the crashing and screaming had caused him to pop out of his lamp. He was squinting, looking into the thick woods.

"Da Silva must have attacked him. Quickly, ride up and see, but don't engage in the fight. If we can extract Mistress Guilietta . . ."

But Pan didn't finish his sentence. Hansum was whipping and kicking his horse to go forward as fast as possible. Pan seemed to clench his teeth as he held on, then made himself disappear.

By the time Hansum got within a hundred paces of the fight, Feltrino and da Silva were off their horses, slashing at each other with their swords. Da Silva's charger was down on its front knees, scraping at the ground, screaming in agony. Blood was spurting from its chest. Feltrino's horse was about a hundred paces away, standing calmly. Not far beyond, Hansum could just make out the shape of another horse prancing nervously in the thicket.

Although da Silva had substantial body armor and a closed helmet, it didn't seem to be giving him any advantage. Feltrino, armed only with his saber, seemed a much superior swordsman. His sword clanked off the armor at will, coming in to test the Scallari soldier, then retiring. When Feltrino saw Hansum, he took an extra step back, looking to see if there was anyone else coming. When he saw otherwise, he renewed his attack on da Silva with a vengeance. A few thrusts, parries, feints and moves to his right, then left, gave Feltrino an opening. He thrust his sword just behind some leg armor and it broke through the quilted padding, finding flesh. Da Silva had to move to his injury and try to counterattack, but Feltrino, with amazing speed, moved away from the attack, then, two-handed, came in on da Silva's backhand, chopping his sword at the soldier's neck. A huge clang and a crack, and da Silva went down onto his face. Before he could even try to rise, Feltrino's swordpoint had found the chink in his armor again and was thrusting straight down to sever his victim's spine. A spasm and a blood spurt later, da Silva stopped moving. His horse was now on its side, whimpering pathetically. Feltrino looked up, the whites of his eyes glowing over the hundred paces between him and Hansum.

"You're next, apprentice!" Feltrino withdrew his sword from the now-lifeless body and stood, challenging Hansum.

"We must turn and run," Pan whispered.

"But Guilietta!"

"The game is to distract Feltrino. If he chases you, we are bound to meet other soldiers within ten minutes." Hansum didn`t move. He desperately wanted to go to Guilietta.

"So, you are a coward, apprentice," Feltrino called, laughing. "What? You don't have a sword? Here, I'll give you one." He picked up da Silva's sword from the ground and raised it to Hansum. Hansum looked at Feltrino and snarled. Feltrino laughed, holding his hands out and doing a pirouette, exposing himself completely. As he turned, Hansum saw the looker case and strap slung over Feltrino's shoulder and resting on his back. Hansum leaned forward in his saddle.

"MASTER HANSUM!" Pan shouted so hard it hurt Hansum's ear. Hansum pulled hard on the reins and turned his horse around. Then he kicked him as hard as he could to get him running in the direction they had come.

Feltrino's pride demanded that he chase the apprentice and kill him. He leaned toward his horse, but checked himself. There were many soldiers looking for him. He had seen them. He thought of what his father would advise. 'Suppress your pride and accomplish the mission. Pride cometh before a fall.' His father had said things like this to him often. Feltrino spit, shoved da Silva's sword blade into the ground and hurried toward his animal. He must get to the Po River and cross over to Gonzaga territory as quickly as possible.

By the time Feltrino got back to Guilietta, she had loosened her hands enough to take the gag off of her mouth and had almost loosened the knot on the pommel holding her to the saddle.

"Get off that horse and I'll run you through like I did the others!"

Guilietta's eyes went wide as she watched a hurrying Feltrino undo her horse from the tree.

"Romero?" she asked, sounding terrified to hear the answer. But Feltrino didn't answer. He was tugging on the knot, trying to force it free. "Romero? Did you kill Romero?" Feltrino, the reins free now, was pulling at the wagon horse to make it move.

Guilietta finally screamed, "Did you kill Romero?" Both horses were now trotting, Feltrino urging them on. "Did you . . ."

"Yes, I killed him. Now shut up."

It didn't take long for Hansum and Pan to realize that Feltrino wasn't pursuing.

"He didn't follow the personality profile I built of him," Pan said. "He's acting more maturely. We must turn around, but remember, no direct confrontation. Just harass and try to slow him down." Hansum drove his horse hard. When they passed by da Silva, the pool of his blood had mostly drained into the earth, leaving a dull-brown circular stain around his head. Hansum stared at him, then, not getting off his mount, he leaned over and pulled da Silva's sword from the ground.

"What are you doing, Master Hansum? What are you doing?"

Hansum let silence be his answer.

Fifteen minutes later, they were at a distance where Pan was, again, perceiving their quarry. The ground began sloping downward toward the river.

"It's about a half-hour ride to the Po. Once he crosses it, he'll be on Gonzaga territory." Hansum kicked his horse to speed up.

The land began to flatten out and glimpses of the river appeared through the trees. Finally the forest ended and there was a clear run to the water. It was a wide part of the river, smooth in some places, boiling in others.

"The way the river is running, it must be deep," Pan said. "Too dangerous for a horse."

Hansum could see Feltrino looking up and down the river, hesitating before committing to a dangerous crossing.

"Feltrino!" Hansum shouted, now only four hundred meters from him. "Please, please don't take Guilietta into the water! It's too dangerous if she's tied up!"

Feltrino looked up at Hansum for a brief moment, then turned and galloped along the shore. Throwing all care and caution away, Hansum whipped his horse into a run.

"What are you doing, Master? Stop! You cannot confront him."

"Once he's crossed the river we've lost her, or she'll drown," Hansum grunted as he rode over the uneven shore.

Pan projected himself onto the back of the horse again, a look of terror on his hairy face. "But what are you going to do when you catch up? What?" Pan shouted, his now long, time-changed tail whipping through the air. "What?"

Feltrino clenched his teeth as he rode, taking a path into a grove of trees he thought would lead him to a shallower crossing. When he came out from the woods some time later, he found himself in an open finger of land by the river, but not at a shallows. He was on a cliff's precipice, some twenty-five feet over even faster-moving water.

"Damn, I went the wrong way!"

There was no way out except the way he came. Feltrino reined his horse around, but before he could spur him, he saw that his way was blocked. It was the apprentice, and he was brandishing a sword.

"Romero!" Guilietta gasped, almost happily.

Feltrino looked behind Hansum, trying to see who else was there.

"Just let Guilietta go and you can leave," the apprentice said. "Captain Caesar and his men can't be more than five minutes away."

Feltrino sat up in his saddle. "You're still alone?" Then he smiled. "That's enough time for me to kill a lowly apprentice."

Hansum felt his heart beating in his chest. But it was beating slowly and steadily, like a war drum.

"Please, there's no need." Guilietta begged. "I'll go with you willingly."

"You'll go with me willingly or otherwise." Then he dropped the reins of Guilietta's horse and said, "I shall be back for you in a trice." He turned, withdrew his still-bloody sword and wagged it at his quarry. "My blade is getting a good washing of blood today, apprentice. Ready?" Feltrino kicked his horse and it cantered toward Hansum.

"Keep your sword centered in front of you, ready to parry," Pan whispered. *"Then get ready to back up quickly. Just play for time."*

Hansum saw Feltrino coming, his eyes cool and calm, giving nothing of his attack strategy away. His saber was in front of him, as if he were going to make a direct stab. At the last moment, Feltrino whirled his horse onto Hansum's flank and swung his blade, letting it connect in the center of his opponent's sword. Hansum deflected the blade to his right and, as Feltrino's horse passed him, he saw it come slashing back at his neck. Again, Hansum blocked. Feltrino whirled his horse around.

"You have a weak wrist, apprentice. When I kill you, I will take your sword and your horse as well as your looker. They will be fine prizes. And of course, I'll still have the girl."

"Take the horse anyway," Hansum said, quickly sliding off of it. "Please, just leave Guilietta."

"What are you doing? Get back on the horse," Pan cried into Hansum's ear. *"You're safer there."* But Hansum didn't listen.

"You're right, Feltrino," Hansum continued. "I can't beat you in a sword fight. But killing me will take too long and I don't want us swinging swords around Guilietta."

Feltrino laughed. He leaned forward in the saddle. "Such gallantry for the girl, but no manly pride. You don't want to fight?"

Hansum took several steps away from the horse, clearing the way for Feltrino to leave.

"Just take my horse and leave. And keep the looker."

"Perhaps you are right," Feltrino said. "My father would value me bringing a horse over a girl." He looked at the animal and then at Hansum, who stood, sword awkwardly half-raised. "Oh, what the hell. I'll have it all." Feltrino dropped off of his horse and rushed at Hansum, slashing his sword back and forth in a blur. Hansum's college training caused him to raise his sword to center, but he had never seen such a fierce and bold attack as this.

"Defense only," Pan cried. *"Defense only!"*

Hansum deflected the first attack, positioning his sword for the next assault. It came and he stepped back instinctively and deflected it. The blows were harder than any he had felt in competition. He realized Feltrino was just testing him and there was more to come.

"Romero!" Guilietta cried.

"Don't look at her," Pan shouted. *"Only at Feltrino's chest. Not his sword or eyes."*

Feltrino glared back at Hansum, then took a step back. He sneered and put his hands out to his side, exposing his chest, inviting an attack.

"Feltrino, please," Guilietta pleaded. "Don't kill him. I'll do anything."

Now Feltrino showed total disdain for Hansum, turning his back on him and addressing Guilietta.

"But Signorina, why would you want to spare such a coward? He comes for you, but does not fight. You need someone like me to give you manly bambinos. They would have a spine. After I kill this one, I will have you for my bed awhile before I kick you out. But you will take back with you a bambino with a proper sire."

Hansum reacted, raising his sword and running at Feltrino. The Gonzaga whirled around and deflected the blow. Hansum continued slashing, three and then four times, Feltrino blocking each attack easily. It was then that Hansum realized Feltrino was truly playing with him. He stopped and looked at his opponent, who now smiled.

"Finally he at least tries to fight like a man. Let's see if he can die like one."

Feltrino swung several long, swooping blows at Hansum. Hansum blocked them, but he could tell he was still being played with. Four, five, six blows in a row came from above, all like the play-fighting he had practiced at History Camp. Feltrino then sliced his sword sideways, stopping the blade in mid-air, posing, like someone in a play, teasing Hansum. Then his eyes narrowed and he took a deep breath. He squared off his stance and smiled.

"Goodbye, apprentice." Feltrino pulled his sword back and slashed so hard that when it connected with Hansum's blade it flew from Hansum's hand and landed fifteen feet away by the cliff edge. "No time to pray, I'm afraid," Feltrino said, and Hansum ran, diving for the sword.

"Romero!" Guilietta cried.

A rumble in the distance. Hansum saw Feltrino spin toward the noise. There were at least ten horses riding at full speed up the river toward them.

"Damn. No more playing." Hansum was now on his knees, his sword back in his hand. Feltrino came running at him, sword extended. "DIE APPRENTICE!" A hard ruby light emitted from Hansum's shoulder, straight into Feltrino's eyes. He screamed in agony.

"Fall to the side, Master Hansum!" Pan cried. Hansum did as he was told and Feltrino's sword sunk into the earth right where Hansum had been kneeling. Feltrino fell to the ground in a heap, still screaming in pain. Hansum fell upon him and punched him in the face over and over again, completely out of control. After a number of punches, Feltrino fought back. Hansum, grasping for something hard to hit Feltrino with, grabbed the case with the looker from off of Feltrino's back and started beating him with it. He felt it bend and crumple, then tore it away and threw it into the grass, continuing to pummel him with his fists.

"Get up, Hansum," Pan shouted. *"Get up! Get up! It's too dangerous to be in contact with even a blind Feltrino. Get up and get your sword!"*

Hansum rolled off and quickly got his sword, holding it out in front of him, the point about six inches from Feltrino, who was still fumbling for his prey. Hansum reached forward carefully, grabbed Feltrino's sword and threw it over the cliff and into the water. Then he backed off.

"Where are you, apprentice? Fight me, apprentice!" Feltrino shouted from his knees.

"No, Feltrino," Hansum said. "I . . . I don't want to kill you." Feltrino seemed to relax and Hansum raised the sword to his shoulder.

"Over here, Captain, they're over here," a soldier's voice shouted. Hansum looked up the path and saw the Podesta's cavalry hurtling toward them. Then he turned to Guilietta, who was still sitting, tied to her horse. Their scared eyes met. When they saw they were both alive and safe, they smiled.

Feltrino's blindness wasn't black, but red. He blinked hard, trying to make his eyes work. Finally, a little bit of the world began to seep back into his vision. He saw the ground, then the apprentice's feet not too far away. He saw the cliff, the running water, and as he turned his head, he could just make out a mass of moving muscle, horses thundering toward him. He stealthily looked up and saw the apprentice, his sword stupidly resting on his shoulder. He was even looking away. Feltrino reached down to his side and slowly took his dagger from its sheath. He leaned forward.

"ROMERO! A KNIFE!" he heard the girl scream.

Through his still-blurred vision, Feltrino saw the sword blade flash toward him. It caught his hand at the base of his thumb and then the only sound he heard was the metal of the sword hit the knife's hilt. He saw red again, but it was the red of his own blood gushing from where his thumb had been. Feltrino fell to the ground, then saw and felt the sword blade at his throat. 'So this is my death,' he thought. 'I'm sorry, Father. I have failed you.' Feltrino looked up into the eyes of his executioner, but he did not see his death there. He saw the apprentice look up quickly at the approaching horses. 'NOW!' Feltrino screamed in his mind. Without hesitation, he rolled toward the cliff. He felt himself momentarily in the air and then cold, fast-running water enveloped him. When he bobbed to the surface he was a good fifty paces from his enemies and traveling away at great speed.

Hansum turned and watched Feltrino bobbing up and down in the water, thrashing his hands to steady himself and not drown. He was soon hundreds of paces away. As many horses thundered around him, Hansum felt himself running to Guilietta and pulling at her bonds to free her. He helped her off of the horse, flung his arms around her and kissed her long on the mouth. The first words he heard were the Podesta's.

"She is like a sister to him."

Hansum heard a loud guffaw of male laughter, but he didn't care. He held onto Guilietta for dear life, and she to him. Tears were streaming from both their eyes. Things quieted as the soldiers were given orders. The Captain sent two men to try to catch Feltrino, his horse was being searched and so was the area. After a minute, Hansum felt a tap on his shoulder. It was the Podesta. He was holding the crumpled looker.

"You left none of the work for us, Romero," he said with a smile on his face. Hansum couldn't answer. He felt so full of emotion, he just stood there, shaking. The Podesta looked at him quizzically. "Why did you let him live?" he asked. "I would have sanctioned his death." Hansum couldn't get any words out, his chest now heaving in great gasps.

"Excellency," called one of the soldiers, picking something off the ground. "He didn't let all of him go. Look, a noble thumb." All the soldiers laughed. He brought it over and put it right in front of Hansum's face. Torn ligaments hung from pink flesh. The recognizable thumbnail looked ghoulishly out of place. "Do you wish to keep it as a prize, Signor?"

"Or maybe a meal," another soldier joked. Everybody laughed uproariously.

The soldier with the thumb opened his mouth and held the severed digit between his lips, smiling.

Hansum fell to his knees and retched.

Chapter 19

They didn't find Feltrino. He could have drowned or he could have made it to the other side of the river. It was getting dark when they finally came out of the hills and onto the road back to Verona. Guilietta was sitting sideways in front of Hansum. Both were exhausted.

"I'm sorry I wasn't man enough to kill him for you," Hansum said to her. "I would have if I had to."

"I'm glad you are a man who doesn't kill unnecessarily," she answered.

"My love . . . Feltrino? Did he . . . ?" Hansum began to ask, "Did he . . . ?

"No. No, my love." Guilietta replied, worry in her eyes. "Truly." Hansum smiled at her.

"Sleep, my darling," he said lovingly into her ear. "We've a long ride home."

Two soldiers were ordered to ride ahead quickly to Verona and give the news. The rest would trudge on, expecting to get back home early in the morning. The night was mild and clear and the moon was rising. Hansum had been so upset that everyone was letting him be, riding at the rear. He just rode along through the night, Guilietta sleeping in his arms. Though his body hurt in every place possible, and though he had experienced the most terrifying day of his life, he was content. Happiness flowed through him. He even dozed as his horse walked along. It was coming to the predawn when he began to feel calm again. His thoughts returned to the problem of the looker order. One of the soldiers called that the walls of the city were in sight. They would be home in an hour. Hansum perked up. He could overhear the Podesta talking to Captain Caesar about the cannons he had seen in Germany. Hansum gently sped his horse up to come abreast of them.

"War will be different with these apparatus, Marcus," the Podesta was saying. "If we can get control of these before the others in this region, we can dominate. Ah, Romero, you've recovered your composure."

"Yes, Excellency. Grazie."

"We have with us not only a young man of talent," the Podesta pronounced, "but also one of action."

"I've never experienced such a thing," Hansum admitted. "Excuse my emotions."

"But how did you overpower him, Signor," the captain asked.

"Luck," Hansum answered. The Podesta laughed. "Excellency, may I speak to you about these cannon?"

"Master Hansum, what are you doing?" Pan whispered in an exasperated tone.

Hansum saw the Podesta look over at the captain and smile.

"Leave us, Marcus," the Podesta said, still smiling. "What do you wish to speak of, Romero?"

"If Verona had superior cannon, this would be a good thing?"

"A very good thing. Princes are always wanting better tools of war. Like your lookers, it gives us advantages. Romero, are you saying you know something more of cannon than just their existence?"

"Master, please don't go here," Pan warned. *"You don't know what . . ."*

"This may sound strange, Excellency," Hansum said, ignoring Pan, "but I can't really say what I know right now."

"You know nothing and you must say nothing."

"Perhaps when we get back to Verona," Hansum continued, "I can draw up some papers on the subject and we can examine them together."

"This is a dangerous game . . ."

The Podesta stretched his arms out to the moon and laughed.

"God in his heaven is truly shining down on me and my Verona. Of course, Romero, of course. I will look at anything you want to show me."

"Thank you, Excellency. It may take some days."

"It may take forever. Or never!" Pan whispered. *"The battle has driven you insane."*

"Can I ask you about something else, Excellency?"

"Oh no. Now what?"

"Certainly," Mastino answered.

"The order for the lookers," Hansum said.

"Oh, I get it now. Clever, Master Hansum. Clever."

"Of course, of course. Why didn't I see this coming," Mastino laughed. "You are negotiating. Romero, why don't you just ask me for a boon because of your heroism, my son?"

"Perhaps I will," Hansum said. "But I sincerely believe we can deliver the lookers in good time."

"Romero, our concerns are sincere too. To judge what a man will do in the future, look to how he has acted in the past. Our fear is that if Master della Cappa becomes involved in larger projects, and with all the pressures that comes with them, he might turn to the wine again. It is his weakness."

"My Master has exchanged his weakness for the joy he gains from his family and his work. And the memory of his troubles, and the ill it brought the family, these reinforce his resolve."

"And you, Romero? Are you resolved?" Mastino questioned.

"I think I can speak for all the youth of my house when I say we have both the desire and motivations to make our lives secure. We all know what has to be done and why."

"Such wisdom for one so young," Mastino said. "Well, what must I do, Lord?" Mastino said looking up at the moon again, "Shall I change my mind for Romero's sake? He did bring me the looker."

"Excellency, I promise you," Hansum said, "the house of della Cappa has many more ideas to bring you. This I promise."

"Ah, a promise?" Mastino said. "A promise."

Guilietta stirred, waking up. She opened her eyes and looked at Hansum. She smiled. When she saw the Podesta, she looked a little frightened. Mastino smiled gently and flicked his reins, moving his horse forward to give Hansum and Guilietta privacy.

"I shall think on it, Romero," he called back. "I shall think on it."

Guilietta looked at Hansum questioningly.

Chapter 20

"Guilietta!" the Signora shrieked. "Guilietta!" She came and flung herself against the haunch of Hansum's horse, grabbing her daughter's leg and hugging it. Hansum lowered Guilietta down and the poor girl was engulfed by her mother. Hansum looked and saw the household all outside, faces beaming, jumping up and down. Tears were already streaming from Master della Cappa's face as he joined his wife in embracing their child. Lincoln and Shamira were smiling up at Hansum, and Hansum couldn't believe how sore he was as he made his way off the horse. Lincoln had to steady him as his legs almost gave way.

"Ho there, old boy," Lincoln laughed.

Shamira ran her hand over all the scratches and dirt on Hansum's face, then took one of his hands and examined the ripped calluses and cuts.

Even Nicademo's carriage was at the house. The Baron walked up and took the reins of Mastino's horse, which was at the head of all the soldiers.

"You've come back safely and successfully, my Lord. I'm so glad. Ride in the carriage from here."

"In a minute," Mastino said.

Hansum looked and saw the Podesta surveying the reunion, especially the Master. When Master della Cappa saw the nobleman watching him, he released himself from his family and clamored over to Mastino. He fell to his knees and kissed the Podesta's muddy boot.

"I don't care if we've lost the contract for the lookers, Excellency. You've brought my daughter back to me. Grazie, grazie. We can have a life making the discs for the eyes, but what is life without a child?"

"You're welcome, della Cappa. You're welcome. But you must thank Romero for your daughter's life." Agistino looked wide-eyed at Hansum. "And as for your living . . . Master della Cappa, please get up. That's better. Now Signor, listen. Romero has assured me of your sobriety and fidelity if you are given the contract for lookers. What do you say to that?" Agistino looked confused. Every eye was upon him. The air was silent. "So, what do you say?" Mastino repeated. "Will you deliver and be constant? And sober?"

"Answer our Lord," the Baron said, a huge smile on his face.

"Oh, si, your Excellency, oh si, si, si. I will be constant and faithful," he said, finally finding words. "I, I will deliver without fail. Without fail. And if wine ever touches these lips, I have already sworn that an angel of God may strike me down with fire!"

"Then listen carefully, Master della Cappa," Mastino continued. "One thousand lookers for King Karl of Luxembourg and five hundred for Ludwig of Wittelsbach. I give these orders . . . to you."

The news hit Agistino so hard that he tottered off balance and ended up sitting on the running board of the carriage. Nicademo came over and banged the Master on the back.

"It's an especially good day now, eh Agistino?" the Baron laughed.

Agistino's eyes began to well up with more tears, which he tried to stop by forcing a smile, which only turned into a comically-contorted grimace.

"It is a very good day, Excellency," Agistino said in a whimper. "I'm very glad," and then he broke down completely and cried.

"No tears, della Cappa. I thought I could trust you?" Mastino laughed. "Does everybody of this house break out in tears when they are happy?"

"It appears so," Hansum said, helping Agistino to his feet. The whole family came over and crowded together.

"Oh, I can't stand this, Nikki," the Podesta said, getting off his horse and heading toward the carriage. "Let's go home." He turned before climbing up and called, "Della Cappa." The group turned toward him. "Bring Signor Romero to the palace with you next week to work out the contract." He climbed into the carriage and then turned. "One more thing." Everybody turned to listen to what he had to say. "We will loan you the money to clear your debts in Florence."

A collective gasp came from the della Cappa household. Agistino had to be propped up again. The Signora actually fell to her knees and started praying.

"Yes, Excellency," Agistino whimpered, still swaying. "Grazie, Excellency. Without fail, Excellency, without fail," he kept repeating. "Without fail."

"Come Master," Hansum said gently."Let's go in the house."

"And Romero," Mastino continued.

"Yes, Excellency?" Hansum asked as the group stopped and turned again.

"Romero, remember your promise."

Hansum released himself from the group, looked the Podesta in the eye, smiled, and then bowed.

Chapter 21

Hansum was back home with his parents in the twenty-fourth century. He was sitting in their garden, just outside their domed house, overlooking the pristine Hudson River. It was a beautiful, sunny day. He was telling his parents all about the battle with Feltrino, how he had negotiated with Mastino della Scalla to exchange information about advanced cannon for the order of telescopes, and how he was in love with the most wonderful girl from any century, Guilietta. Hansum turned and looked at Guilietta, presenting her to his parents. Hansum's mother smiled and hugged the young woman who was to become her daughter-in-law. Hansum's father laughed happily.

"You genies," Charlene was saying to Pan. "I can't believe you gave them advanced technological information from the future. Fixing the timeline has been such a mess for the Time Commission."

"I tried to tell Master Hansum we shouldn't do it," Pan said, "but he convinced me that it was a matter of necessity. Shamira and I worked two long nights on those plans of advanced cannon and black powder. It was the only thing to convince the Podesta."

"And how did that work out for you, son?" Hansum's father asked.

"Oh, it worked out just . . ." Hansum began to say, and then he paused. He couldn't remember how it all came out in the end.

"And this whole adventure?" Hansum's mother asked. Her History Camp elder's pin gleamed in the sunlight. "How did it work out for you, son? Do you get it now?"

"So, is everybody ready for repast?" Hansum's father interrupted. "Carmella has a wonderful meal ready for us."

"Carmella?" Hansum said. "I told you, Dad, her name is Shamira."

"You are so beautiful, Guilietta," Hansum's mother said, now with tears in her eyes. She held Guilietta's face in her hands and kissed it. "My son loves you so much. I wish I could be around to see my grandchildren."

"Mother, what are you talking . . ."

"I said, a wonderful meal is ready," Father repeated. But his voice was much gruffer.

"Hey, you sound like . . ."

"Romero, wake up," the Master's voice shouted. "Romero, wake up!" Hansum opened his eyes. Master della Cappa's head was sticking out of the opening to the loft. He was scrubbed clean, beard trimmed, and not only had his new cap on, but also a wonderful jacket, vest and shirt. "Good morning, my son," he said smiling. "Everyone else is awake and dressed. We're waiting on you to eat."

"Buon giorno, Master," Hansum yawned.

"How are your wounds?" Agistino enquired.

"Oh, much better," Hansum groaned, raising himself up. He still felt incredibly sore, and his body, especially his legs and butt, continued to be badly bruised from the hard riding and fighting the week before.

"Your new clothes are down in the shop. I didn't want to bring them up in the straw. Come, my son, the Podesta's carriage will be here soon."

It all came back to Hansum in a rush. Today was the day to visit the palace and complete the contract for the lookers. As well, Shamira and Pan had secretly worked on plans for cannon and black powder. Not too advanced, but something to keep the Podesta's favor. And it wasn't only Hansum and the Master going to the palace. A letter came from the Baron, making the appointment for the meeting. In it Baron da Pontremoli had written, "During an earlier visit to your shop I was impressed with young Maruccio's talent for organization and his knowledge of letters. I would like to show him how to organize Master della Cappa's books to run what will most certainly be a larger business concern."

"Zippy," Lincoln had said, his chest puffing out.

And Shamira was also invited to view the Podesta's private art collection. She squealed, literally squealed, when she heard this.

"We must get a new dress for you," Guilietta exclaimed.

"Oh, can I, Master, can I?" Shamira begged, wide-eyed.

"Now I have two daughters to spoil and two daughters who will ruin me," Agistino laughed.

Hansum laughed even harder when he read out the end of the letter. "We shall send a carriage to bring you to the palace after first mass."

"A royal carriage?" the Signora shouted.

"Oh Papa, that's wonderful. Isn't that wonderful, Romero?" Guilietta said, looking at her secret fiancé from across the table.

Master della Cappa not only made good on his promise of a new dress for Shamira, he had the Satores make new clothes for everyone. As the family was waiting outside for the royal carriage, everybody laughed when Agistino said, "We all look pretty zippy."

The Master looked over at Hansum in his new outfit. His chausses were beige and his braies, mustard. He was also wearing a green jacket and new cap. The cap was brown felt with leather piping along the edge and a secret pouch for Pan. Guilietta and Shamira were fussing over Hansum, preening and straightening his collar. The Master frowned, a bit jealous of his little girl fussing over another man. Then he felt a fat, feminine hand at his lapels, straightening them. It was his wife. She patted him on the face.

"Never before did we supply royalty," she said. "Soon we'll have a carriage of our own."

"From your mouth to God's ears," Agistino answered. Then he did something he had not done in years. He gave his wife a kiss.

The Signora looked up at her husband and then over at Guilietta and Hansum.

"I like the orphan boy now," she said.

As the royal carriage rolled up, many neighbors ran out of their houses to take part in the excitement. The driver got out to open the passenger compartment's door and helped Agistino into the cab. Lincoln climbed up, holding a larger looker with a tripod they were bringing as a gift for the Podesta. Then Hansum climbed aboard, the cardboard tube with the secret plans under his arm.

The Signora and Guilietta waved enthusiastically as the carriage began to move. All the neighbors cheered. Both the Master and Hansum leaned out the window and blew kisses to their girls. Then they all sat back and reveled in their new situation.

"Life is good," the Master said, crossing himself.

"I had the strangest dream last night," Hansum said quietly to the two others. As the carriage trundled over the cobblestones, he whispered, "Guilietta, Pan and I were back home with my parents and Charlene. Everything was wonderful and we were all getting along. Then my mother asked me about History Camp and if I got it yet."

Hansum looked at Shamira and then Lincoln. Lincoln smiled a crooked smile, like the answer was obvious.

"Well?" Shamira asked.

"Well, what?" Hansum asked.

"Do you?"

– The end –

We hope you enjoyed
The LENS and the LOOKER.
If you would like to know what's next for
Hansum, Shamira, Lincoln and Pan,
look for Book #2 of the
Verona Trilogy,

The
BRONZE
and the
BRIMSTONE

This story shows what happens
when our three teens from the 24th-century
introduce advanced weaponry into 14th-century Italy.
Oh, Hansum and Guilietta's love story really heats up too.

Read some excerpts on the following pages,
and for more, go to:
www.lorykaufman.com

Here are a few exciting scenes from the continuation of Hansum, Shamira and Lincoln's adventure in fourteenth-century Verona, Italy.

Hansum and Guilietta's romance blossoms, but true love does not always run smoothly. Master della Cappa refuses to consent to their marriage. When he does, Guilietta runs out of the house in anger and Hansum runs after her:

"Guilietta, Guilietta, stop!" Hansum shouted as he chased his distraught lover. Guilietta slowed to a quick walk. Catching up to her and keeping pace, Hansum asked, "Why did you run away, Guilietta? Running away solves nothing."

"I could not stand it there," she said, furious. Hansum had never seen Guilietta angry.

"But where are you going, my love?"

"I don't know. Maybe I'll throw myself off the Navi Bridge."

"Guilietta, don't talk like that."

Guilietta stopped quickly and faced Hansum. Her face showed anger that shouldn't be on one so fair.

"Everything will be all right," he said. "It will all work out."

"How will it work out? You marry the Podesta's daughter and then my father gives me to some old butcher or miller?"

"I don't know. But I tell you, nothing will come out of you jumping off a bridge."

"Fat lot you care! Being offered the Podesta's Beatrice."

"Guilietta, it wasn't my idea. And I do care, my love. If anything ever happened to you, I don't know what I would do. I'd jump off that bridge right behind you."

"You would?" she squeaked, her eyes welling up with more tears.

"Guilietta, I love you." The two embraced in the street, then kissed. People passed, glancing at the two. Several little children laughed and danced around them, making kissing sounds.

Finally, Hansum said, "Come. Let's go home and talk to your father."

"No," Guilietta said. "I know my father." She took Hansum's hand and began to walk back in the direction they came. But at the first side street, Guilietta turned left, pulling Hansum with her.

"Where are we going?" Hansum asked. Guilietta didn't answer as she strode forth purposefully. "Guilietta, where are we going?"

"To see Father Lurenzano."

"Why?"

"To get married."

Married? "And who is Beatrice?" you ask? The Podesta's daughter? Yes, Podesta Mastino della Scalla believes that Hansum is a savant, a genius who has the secrets to advanced cannon and black powder, tools that will make him ruler of Europe. Of course, he doesn't know that it's Pan who, with his universal knowledge of the future, is advising Hansum. As the story goes on, Hansum is taken to a secluded estate in the country, to start producing cannons. While there, the Podesta, unaware of Hansum and Guilietta's secret marriage, introduces him to his own daughter:

Beatrice smiled at Hansum. Hansum nodded but was much more reserved. Finally Beatrice broke the silence.

"My father speaks highly of you, Signor. He says you are a great savant. I have always thought of savants as old and wizened. You are quite pleasant to look at."

"I am continually complimented by your father's attentions. I fear he exaggerates."

"She's given you a compliment, you ninny." Pan whispered. *"You must compliment her back."*

"Withal, Lady Beatrice. I think this room is more graced by your looks than mine."

"My father gave me one of your famous lookers. I have used it to spy on birds outside my window and at people in the market. It's great fun."

"The fame goes to Master della Cappa. It comes from his shop."

"Modesty again. I am not used to such as this from the young men I know."

"Perhaps they have nothing to be modest about."

"Si, but most have nothing to boast about either. And yet they do. Perhaps they should choose to boast about their modesty as you do."

Hansum couldn't help but smile. She had skewered him well with that one. He was finding it hard not to appreciate Beatrice's wit and poise. Knowing what the Podesta had on his mind, he had hoped Beatrice would be plain and boring. But she wasn't.

"I'm sorry you think my modesty a boast," Hansum said, "but how can a person take credit for their talents? One is born with them, like a man who can run fast or who can lift great weights."

"So, if you are not responsible for all the wonderful ideas you bring my father, where do they come from?"

Sparring with words was something Hansum always enjoyed, and irony was his favorite device.

"A little voice in my ear, my Lady."

"Ah, you hear voices," Lady Beatrice said, taking a step forward. Her long, sweeping skirts made a swishing sound against the floor. She was now closer to Hansum. She looked at him from out the side of her eyes. "Does your muse have physical form, or is she only a voice?"

Hansum continued the verbal jousting.

"I must admit he's not a beauty at all. What would you say if I told you he is half goat and half man?"

"I'd say he's the piper, Pan."

"Master, stop jesting. It is a dangerous game you play. You must not say anything to encourage her. And stop flirting. You are a married man, after all!"

This comment brought Hansum back to Earth very quickly. The look on Beatrice's face showed she expected him to continue the word play, but Hansum felt his face go cold.

"Your muse is Pan, Signor?"

A much sobered Hansum said, "I jest, Lady Beatrice. Forgive me."

"Not at all," the lady said. "It's fun. To extrapolate upon your theory, your supposition presumes then, that compared to man, a bird must be a genius in that it can fly and we shall never be allowed to. We are forever chained to this earth until we fly with the angels. Or do you foresee in your savant mind a way and a day when man can join the doves and the hawks in the sky?"

"I fear, if man does learn to sit between wings and soar in the clouds," Hansum said in a much sobered voice, "it would be as the hawk and not the dove."

"Do you really think it possible? What does your little voice say?"

"Don't even conjecture on the future of flight," Pan warned. *"Not in the least."*

"Alas, Lady Beatrice, my little voice says nothing about flight."

Hansum had become conservative in his tone of voice, hoping that Beatrice would conclude that he was serious in what he said.

"So, you truly do give credit to God for your talents. Then I say, let us give the credit to God, who has put whatever talents you have in your humble frame. What do you say? Shall we give all credit to God?"

"I think you are making the joke now, Lady Beatrice."

"No, truly, this coming Sabbath. Come with me and father to the local church. We shall all give thanks to God for your talents. Otherwise, if you are not humble enough in front of the Almighty, he may take your genius away."

"My lady, you are very kind, but I must not lead you on or be insincere."

"A prayer is not a promise of anything, Signor, except to God."

"But this trip to prayer is step towards a vow. And a vow is a promise." Hansum felt very confused, and couldn't stop himself from rambling. "And a vow, whispered or shouted, said in secret or on a steeple top, is still a vow. I, I must not start a thing in hopes of a promise, which I intend not, and indeed, cannot fulfill.

And I must fulfill the vows that I have thus far made to make myself worthy of that vow."

Beatrice looked perplexed. "Finally you say more than a short sentence and it is so complicated with vows that it might as well be full of ploughs and cows and sows, for all the sense it makes."

"Si, I'm sorry. Often the truth to one is a puzzle to others."

So, poor Hansum has the misfortune to not only be entangled with two interesting and beautiful women, he's also allied with one of most powerful and ruthless men in fourteenth century Europe. He's not the only one experiencing excitement, though. While he's off in the country, Shamira, Lincoln and Guilietta are having their own trials and tribulations back in Verona:

"Shoot her!"

Shamira turned and, to her continued horror, saw the guard, about a hundred paces from her, raise his bow.

Then, like a vision, two forms appeared behind the guard. It was Guilietta and Lincoln. They leaped on the soldiers back. The arrow let loose and screamed just an arm's length from Shamira's head. The man went down, with Lincoln smashing a rock onto the guard's helmet. The man threw Lincoln off and Shamira couldn't believe it when she saw Guilietta raise a knife blade high over her head. The man twisted and grabbed the knife, throwing Guilietta onto her back, and then started grabbing for the blade with both his hands. Shamira started running at full tilt toward the fray, watching as Guiletta bit into the guard's hand with all her might and Lincoln flung himself back into the guard, forcing him to roll to the stone floor. It was a twisted and writhing pile of bodies that Shamira came upon, when the guard's boot came out and kicked her in the stomach. Shamira felt herself flying sideways, toward an open parapet, and then felt her head hit hard against the stone wall. A wave of pain rang out in her brain and she staggered in a daze to the floor.

"Help me, Excellency," she heard the guard scream through her fog. She slowly turned her head to see Feltrino throwing a rope over the side of the wall and begin to climb down. Behind him, Herado Starini was staggering to his feet, trying to walk. Feltrino disappeared and Shamira had to close her eyes. She felt herself passing out, and then willed herself awake. She didn't know how long she had been unconscious. 'Seconds only,' she thought. 'Maybe a minute.'

"I'll kill you!" she heard a gruff voice scream. She opened her eyes and saw that the guard had regained his footing. He had Lincoln pushed between two parapets, the guard's hands on Lincoln's throat. Lincoln's feet were lifting off the ground and he was about to be thrown off the high wall to certain death. Shamira strained to raise herself up and saw Guilietta, dirty and bleeding, pushing herself onto all fours.

"Carmella," she heard and turned her head. Herado Starini was staggering toward her. "Carmella," he repeated, and then a look of renewed terror gripped his face. Shamira turned to look at what he saw. It was Guilietta, both hands on the handle of her knife, the blade held high. Lincoln's feet were well off the ground now and Guilietta did not hesitate. The blade came down full force and plunged into the guard's back. The startled guard let go of Lincoln and shot backwards. Guilietta retreated, pulling out the knife. The guard stood up to face his executioner, his mouth an open maw, questioning his now inescapable fate. Then he fell dead to the ground.

"Carmella," Shamira heard again, and she turned to see Herado now, almost to her. "Forgive me, Carmella," he said, leaning down to her.

"MY SISTER!" came Guilietta's scream, and Guilietta was flying over Shamira and crashing into Herado.

"No, Guilietta, no!" Shamira managed to say. She looked over, and there was Guilietta, sitting atop of Herado, the bloody knife at his throat. "He saved my life, Guilietta."

"It, it was a mistake," Herado whimpered. "I, I didn't understand. I was tricked. Please forgive me, please, please forgive me."

Guilietta, her dress bloodied and torn, stood and went to Shamira.

"Are you all right, sister?" she asked, the fierceness in her eyes still blazing.

That's right – Feltrino's back and Shamira becomes entangled with a man. Meanwhile, Lincoln ends up at the estate in the country with Hansum, helping perfect the advanced cannon and black powder. They are wildly successful. Mastino really could become ruler of Europe with their help. But powerful men have equally powerful enemies. Enemies who will stop at nothing to steal the secrets of the cannon – and Hansum:

When Hansum saw the arrow plunge through Lincoln's helmet, then saw him fall to the ground, panic and terror consumed him.

"LINCOLN!" he cried, starting to run toward him. The lieutenant grabbed Hansum's arm.

"No Signor, flee to the house. We will keep them busy while you escape."

Hansum looked up and saw the twenty mounted horses dashing out from the forest. Half went toward the cannon and the others came at a dead run toward his group. The horses were covered with armor and the men's bascinet helmets had their visors down. Some soldiers had swords, the others, poleaxes. The noise of the hooves on the ground, the men shouting, and the armor and weapon clanging filled the air with a terrifying din.

"But my friend!" Hansum screamed.

"He's fallen, Signor. Save yourself!" the lieutenant shouted. He shoved Hansum in the direction of the house and pulled down his visor. "Form around me!" he called to the five men with him. "You, go with the Signor," he said to one. "Protect him with your life." Hansum began running as fast as he could toward the woods that separated him from the manor house. Beside him ran a tall, lanky infantryman with a look in his dark eyes that Hansum had never seen before. The long scar on his face, which spoke to the fact that he had been in these terrifying battles before, had turned deep red. Looking back as he ran,

Hansum saw his protectors forming a line between him and the advancing horses. Three of the ten horses swung off to the right to go around them and were coming straight at him. The seven remaining horses barrelled towards the five standing soldiers.

"Shoulders together! On one knee! Brace!" the lieutenant shouted, pulling out his sword and stepping behind his line. "Shields!"

The men prepared themselves to take the charge. Their pole-axes were extended as far as possible in an effort to spear their opponents. "Take the horses!" the lieutenant shouted, and they lowered their weapons slightly. The cavalry fell upon them. By standing so close together, only two of the seven mounted attackers were in killing proximity of the infantry men. The horses ran into the pointed tips of the poleaxes and luck was with the Scalligers. Two spears found their way through the horses' armor. One horse reared up backwards. The other tumbled forward over the defenders. The helmet came off its heavily armored knight, causing him to become an easy target for the lieutenant's sword. Luckily, all five of the defenders survived the initial assault. They stood up, and two attacked the second downed cavalry man. As he stumbled to his feet, they began to pummel his helmeted head with the hammer side of their poleaxes. The pointed top of the helmet initially did its job and deflected most of the blows. But soon it caved, as did its inhabitant. Two of the defenders kept at killing him while the other three formed again in front of the lieutenant.

The remaining five attackers had swung their horses back around and, without hesitation, were charging again. It became a slashing, banging, cutting and spearing battle of attrition.

The fight for the cannon was not so grand. Only two men with poleaxes against eight men on horses and a bowman, not fifty paces away. Within a minute, all the cannoneers lay bleeding, dying or dead. When the attackers rode toward the cannon's horses, the animals bolted, breaking their leads. The mounted cavalry caught one horse quickly and had to chase the other.

More easily caught was Hansum. He was the most vulnerable. Feltrino rode ahead of Hansum and blocked his way. The infantryman jumped in front of Hansum and slashed at the air to make Feltrino back his horse up. The brave defender then jumped back to confront the two other attackers. He swung his poleaxe at the closest one and it hit his shield. He pulled it back again over his head to make another blow, but never delivered it. The other horseman had gotten behind him and slashed him on the back with his sword. Though the chainmail held, it threw him off balance and then the haunch of the attacker's horse ran into the poor man as he passed. He stumbled and the other rider's heavy sword came down and caught him right on the top of his head. His helmet split and the man fell to his knees right in front of Hansum.

"Perche?" was all the man could say before blood and brains spurted out of his skull. He fell to the ground dead.

Hansum screamed at the grisly sight. Feltrino got off his horse, sword in hand. Hansum looked to the infantryman's fallen poleaxe and leaned toward it. One of the prancing hooves of the horses came down on it, holding it fast. Feltrino looked at Hansum through his closed helmet. Then he sheathed his sword, lifted his visor and looked at Hansum.

"Feltrino!" Hansum gasped. Feltrino removed one of his gloves and held up the hand. It was short a thumb. But Feltrino didn't look angry or revengeful. He bowed slightly to Hansum.

"Master Monticelli," he said, respectfully. "You are my prisoner, Signor."

Just when you think things couldn't get any worse . . . Guilietta becomes very ill. Hansum, who cannot be with her, is worried sick for her. He has a dream of them communicating the way he communicated with his friends back in the twenty-fourth century – by implant telepathy. But is it a dream?

He wanted to be near her, commune with her. He began to imagine being able to touch his temple, as he had done in his previous life, so he could talk to her. He allowed himself this fantasy.

"My darling, I am ever here for you," Hansum said low, as if he were using his implant. "I am your slave, your devoted."

"Romero. My Romero. Where are you, my Romero? I hear your voice. I see you in my mind, like a window to another place. Is this a dream? Is this Heaven?" Hansum opened his eyes in surprise. It was just like the semi-telepathic experiences he'd had back home. But this was impossible. "Where have you gone, my love?" Guilietta's voice asked in his head again. "You've disappeared. Please come back to me." Dream or hallucination, it didn't matter. Hansum closed his eyes again and drew up his knees, tight to his chest.

"I'm here, my love. Don't be afraid."

"I can see you again. Oh, thanks be to God, I can see you again."

"And I you, my love. How are you, dearest?"

"I was in pain, husband, but now I am calm. And you?"

"The Podesta is not allowing me to leave the palace. I am okay, but worried for you, my darling." Tears poured from Hansum's eyes. "Oh, Guilietta, I miss you so much."

"Oh, my poor darling, to be without each other at this painful time. Be brave, my Romero, like I know you are." The image of Guilietta smiled in Hansum's mind. Hansum smiled too, thinking of the dream's irony. The dream had questioned whether he was a dream. "Father says . . . they all say, you are devils."

"No, my love. We are not. I am only a man. Just a man. A man who loves you."

"And I love you, Romero. But why do they say such things?"

"Because they see we are different. And they are right in that. But I am not a devil."

"Then what are you?"

"I am a man, Guilietta. I am a man from a different time. From the future. Why God has sent me here, I don't know. How to get back? It's a mystery. I will clear up this fear everyone has of me, and we shall be together soon, my beautiful Guilietta."

"I fear not, husband. I fear not. I am dying." Hansum didn't like this daydream anymore. He pulled his knees even closer and wept openly. "Come to me, my darling," Guilietta's voice said.

"Hold me while I go to God." Hansum heard a low male voice in the background of the dream. It sounded like the Master.

"She's talking to herself," Agistino's voice said. "What's she saying?"

"Maybe she sees St. Peter," said a voice sounding like Nuca's.

"He's right on the ceiling with Michael," the Signora's voice wept. Then Hansum saw Guillietta wince in pain. "Oh my baby," shrieked the Signora's voice, and there was the sound of someone collapsing.

"Help take the mistress to her bed," the man's voice said, frantically. "Then send Ugilino for Father Lurenzano. He's gone back to his church."

"Come to me, my darling," Guilietta's voice whispered desperately. "One last kiss before I meet Jesus. I am content that your voice is the last thing I'll hear."

"No Guilietta. You're not dying. You mustn't die!"

"I am done, my love, but I am happy."

"You mustn't die, Guilietta. I love you. I need you. I've always loved you. Before we met, I loved the idea of you. I need more of you."

"We had the time on the wall, with the moon and cool breeze showing us we were alive." Guilietta said.

"I want that time again," Hansum wept. "You cannot go. I've not had enough."

"Who's to say what's enough? Not those who say it."

And then there was silence.

Want to know more about the world of The Verona Trilogy?

Most futuristic novels don't give you the back story of their civilizations. They just plop the reader into the middle of the characters' lives and start the story rolling. The writer lets the readers infer much of how the civilization works from what happens around the characters. I do pretty much the same thing. After all, it's the characters and the story that is important, and the quality of its telling. But behind the scenes, writers of future fiction have to work out a general history for their world to rationalize why things are the way they are. I thought, why not share the back story? Some readers might find it interesting.

If you are one of these readers, you are invited to go to
www.lorykaufman.com
and click on the BACK STORY link.

This is where you will find out the answers to questions like:

• Why are only three hundred million people on Earth in Lory's 24th-century world?
• Why does the community of New York, (one of the biggest cities on the planet in 2347) have only thirty thousand people on it, and why isn't it on Manhattan Island anymore?
• Why is the planet's average size living community sixty people?
• What is a steady-state economy?
• Why does every human on the planet have a personal A.I. (artificial intelligence) from birth?
. . .and much more.

We'd also love to hear your thoughts about the story and its future. A link for contacting us is on the website too. See you there.

Cheers,
Lory Kaufman

"I write **Post-Dystopian** fiction. After society's collapse, which is imagined in so many great dystopian stories, humans will either fade into history, with the dinosaurs, or, if it learns the right lessons, society will go on to construct a civilization to last tens of thousands of years. *The Lens and the Looker*, and the rest of the Verona Trilogy, are the exciting adventures of young people doing the latter." -Lory Kaufman

On the artistic side of Lory's career, he's written, acted and directed children's theatre and musical theatre. He enjoys art, especially sculpture. He loves science fiction and historical fiction and he has been deeply involved in the green movement all across North America. All this shows through when you read his work. Lory has three grown children and works and lives in Kingston, Ontario, Canada.